MAD LOVE

MAD WORLD #3

HANNAH MCBRIDE

Copyright © 2022 by Hannah McBride

MAD LOVE

Mad World Series, Book 3

Original Publication Date: September 30, 2022

ALL RIGHTS RESERVED. This book contains material protected under International and Federal Copyright Laws and Treaties. Any unauthorized reprint or use of this material is prohibited. No part of this book may be reproduced or transmitted in any form or by any means, electronic or mechanical, including photocopying, recording, or by an information and retrieval system without express written permission from the Author/Publisher.

This is a work of fiction. Names, characters, places, and incidents either are the product of the author's imagination or are used fictitiously, and any resemblance to actual persons, living or dead, business establishments, events, or locales is entirely coincidental.

The Author acknowledges the trademark status and trademark owners of various products referenced in this work of fiction, which have been used without permission. The publication's use of these trademarks is not authorized, associated with, or sponsored by the trademark owner.

All rights reserved.

Cover Credit: Temptation Creations

Edited by: Natashya Wilson

For Sherry

AUTHOR'S NOTE

Hey, friend! If you're reading this, THANK YOU SO MUCH! This is the last book in Ryan & Maddie's story, so I'm sure you're aware of all the potential triggers and warnings.

As always, if you're related to me… just don't read this, okay? Or lie to me and say you haven't.

CHAPTER 1

RYAN

"Lawyer," I drawled, drumming my fingers on the edge of the metal table and eyeing the officer who'd just stepped into the interrogation room. He was easily in his early fifties, with thinning, greasy silver hair and a pot belly that said he was more likely used to chasing donuts with coffee instead of actual criminals. The tarnished name badge pinned haphazardly to his chest read *BURKE*.

I'd already spent forty hours in the county lockup, and I was fucking over this bullshit. I knew they were flexing their little muscles, proving that they could hold me for up to two days before officially charging me for a bullshit crime.

Okay, maybe not entirely bullshit, since I'd definitely had a hand in Adam Kindell's death, but there was no way they could actually know that. Whatever evidence they thought they had didn't exist; my team didn't make mistakes.

Officer Burke smirked, like he had all the power here, and leaned against the wall. "Thought you might want to know we're moving you to central booking."

I grinned, my shoulders bunching and my wrists inadvertently pulling on the metal cuffs that secured me to the table. My hands had started to go numb over an hour ago, but no way was I letting this asshole know I was in pain. Besides, this was better than the holding cell I'd been sharing with six other guys. "Fantastic. When does my ride get here?"

His bushy brows slammed down. "You're not going home tonight."

"Yeah, I got that when you mentioned central booking," I said, speaking slowly so the moron would understand even as my pulse started racing. *Fuck.* I needed to be finding Maddie, not trapped in a cell. "It smells like puke and fish in this room. Seriously, is Febreze out of the budget? I'm happy to buy you a few cans if you can't afford it." This room fucking *reeked*, and considering the amount of sweaty locker rooms I'd been in over the course of my life, that was saying something. Then again, it was moderately better than the stench of piss and shit and stale body odor in the cells.

His pudgy cheeks turned red. "Fucking rich prick. Think Daddy's money will fix everything."

I ticked up a finger. "No, no. I'll pay for it out of my own money." My gaze swept down his frame, taking in the well-worn uniform that ballooned around his legs and dirty shoes. "Hell, I'll even throw in extra so you can buy some clothes that fit, Officer Burke. Unless you prefer looking like a circus tent." My lips curved into a vicious smile as his face turned a mottled shade of red.

With a snarl, he rounded the table and yanked me up by the front of my shirt. The cuffs dug harder into my wrists, cutting off what little blood flow to my fingers was left. I let him, hoping he'd throw a punch. I'd take a beating if it meant I could get out of this station with a few bruises so I could look for Maddie.

Besides, no way could he hit harder than Court or Royal, and fuck knew I'd taken more than enough punches from them over the years.

I smirked at Officer Burke like this was any other day. "Tell you what, I'll spring for a bottle of mouthwash, too." I wrinkled my nose and turned away.

Officer Burke roared, pulling back a fist, and I fucking grinned.

Do it, asshole.

If he hit me, I'd be out of here before my lawyer could say *police brutality*.

The door to the interrogation room swung open. "Burke!" the man in the doorway barked. "Take a walk."

Burke sneered at me and shoved me into the chair. It rocked onto its back legs from the force, and I sighed, rolling my eyes. All I'd needed was for Officer Burke to lose his shit just for a second, and he'd have punched my ticket to freedom.

Oh, well.

I kept smirking and even managed to waggle a few fingers. "See you later, Burke."

The officer glared at me—like that would instill the fear of God in me or some shit—and stormed out of the room.

The man who had entered looked like more than an entry level beat cop, with his three-piece suit, gelled hair, and loafers that actually shined.

I met his gaze. "Fed?"

He gave me a bland smile, not bothering to tell me I was wrong. "Agent Paulson. Mind if I take a seat?"

"By all means." I looked around the barren space, with its cinder block walls, chipped floor tiles, and questionable stain in a corner near the door. "I'd offer you a cocktail, but my butler has the day off."

"Damn," he mused, and sat with a sigh. "I had my heart set on a vodka tonic."

My smirk widened. "Funny. A fed with a sense of humor."

He made a soft *tsk*ing sound. "And you're just another rich punk who thinks he can write a check to make this go away, but I'm here to give you some friendly advice."

I cocked a brow. "Oh?" This should be amusing. This guy had no fucking clue who I was.

He folded his hands and leaned forward, like this was a juicy secret. "I don't think you killed Adam Kindell."

My jaw dropped in feigned shock. "You don't? Are you here to save me, Agent Dipshit?"

He grimaced, catching the attitude I was throwing off in waves. "I think your daddy-in-law got pissed you violated his pretty little flower and set you up. Not that I blame you—I've seen her picture."

My eyes narrowed.

His head tilted to the side. "Madelaine, right? Gorgeous blonde with big blue eyes and legs for—"

"Do you have a fucking point?" I snapped. I could fake indifference and boredom with these pricks all goddamn day, but one mention of Maddie and I was a rabid dog trying to break free from his leash.

"My point is, work with me," Agent Paulson murmured, still going for the secretive angle, like we were buddies. "I've been looking into your father's business for years. The SEC—"

"The SEC doesn't have shit on my father or Cain Industries," I spat.

This wasn't news; the US Securities and Exchange Commission was always looking to take down a big fish in the financial sector, and Cain Industries would be a motherfucking whale. But they had nothing on the company, because there wasn't anything to get. CI was pretty much the only business my father hadn't corrupted, and that was because he constantly had to appease the board. It was hard to break the law when ten old white guys were counting every penny that came and went.

"Not yet," Agent Paulson conceded. "But with your help—"

"You want me to narc on my dad? On the company I just became CEO of?" I snorted and shook my head. The last thing I would do was rat out my father so he got a cushy ten-to-fifteen-year sentence in a white-collar federal prison with a personal chef and a fucking golf course.

Beckett Cain would pay in blood by the time I was done.

And then I'd incinerate whatever pieces were left before flushing his ashes down a urinal at a truck stop. Because *that* was what he deserved.

I glanced at the clock hanging over Paulson's head. "I've been here for almost two days. Where's my damn lawyer?"

The fed glanced at his imitation Rolex. "Huh. Guess he's been held up."

A slow smile started to spread across my face. "You know who I am, right? You honestly think you're going to get away with this shit?

The charges are baseless—you said so yourself. My lawyers are going to have a fucking field day when your people stop jerking them around."

He pursed his lips. "Hey, man, I work for the federal government. If you help *me* out, I might be able to do something about your state charges, but…"

"Right." I nodded. "Well, I have nothing to say without my attorney. So you, the LAPD, and every other person in this building can go back to your regularly scheduled circle jerk."

He frowned, looking annoyed and constipated. "Mr. Cain, I don't think you understand—"

"I don't think *you* understand, Agent Shit-for-brains," I sneered. "You can fuck all the way off, okay? And get me my goddamn lawyer before I slap you all with a harassment lawsuit that will have your grandchildren sucking dick on the corner for rent."

Agent Paulson regarded me coolly, and then he stood up, tugging the ends of his suit jacket back down over his wrists. "You're making a mistake."

"And yet, I still don't give a fuck." I leaned forward, my eyes flashing. "Lawyer, asshole."

He gave me a thin smile. "Sure thing, Mr. Cain. We'll get right on that."

I watched him leave, seething as my hands curled into fists. Before I could stop myself, I jerked them against the cuffs. The metal dug into my bruised wrists. But I didn't care.

Yeah, I was well versed in playing the spoiled douchebag. It was a role I'd been training for my whole life, but it was a shell, and the longer I sat here, the more it cracked.

All I could think about was Maddie.

The slow way she'd blinked her unfocused eyes in the courtroom. The way she'd been wheeled in, limp and silent.

I knew what a drugged woman looked like, and rage had filled my blood like hellfire at seeing her like that.

But it was a mere flicker compared to the impotence I felt now at not being able to do a single fucking thing to get to her. To save her.

I bowed my head, sucking in a deep breath as I tried to be patient.

Tried and fucking failed.

Not that it should've been a surprise; at this point, failure was becoming a close friend of mine.

And I hated the motherfucker.

CHAPTER 2

RYAN

It took another two hours before my lawyers were let in. Well, my grandfather's lawyer and Court. The door was barely shut before I was demanding answers from one of my oldest friends.

"Where is she?" My eyes bored into Court as he sat in one of the chairs across from me.

He grimaced. "We don't know."

Panic speared me like an ice pick to the chest. "What the fuck does that mean? It's been two fucking days, Court."

Court raked a hand through his hair. "It means Gary had everything set up. While you were being arrested, he got Maddie out a side door and into an unmarked car."

"And Ash couldn't trace it?" I stared at him. My best friend could hack almost any system; the courthouse had to have security cameras everywhere. Inside *and* out. How hard was it to see a nearly comatose woman being shoved into a car?

"The tapes were scrubbed," Court answered. "He used security cams from the bank across the street, but they put her in a black Camry. It's the most popular car in the country, man. And if that wasn't enough, there happened to be no less than twenty-six of them leaving the parking garage in the same ten-minute time frame."

"Fuck." I slammed a fist against the table, the handcuffs digging tighter into my wrists. "Track every car down. I want to know—"

"Ry," he cut me off, "we're doing that, man. But it takes time. Gary had this shit planned for who knows how long."

My gaze cut to the attorney, a man named Linus Clover whom I'd known since I was a kid. He was only a few years younger than my grandfather, and one of the best lawyers in the state.

Plus, I knew for a fact that he'd always been loyal to my grandfather and my mother. He hated my father, and I counted that as a win.

"When can you get me out?" I directed the question at him.

"The state's case is flimsy, at best," Linus replied, shaking his head. "Unfortunately, since it's an election year, they're intent on making an example that no one is above the law. I've already filed a complaint with the courts for violating your right to counsel and due process."

A low growl rumbled in my chest. "I don't care about complaints. I need to get out of here to find my wife."

Court and Linus exchanged an uneasy look.

"What?" I demanded.

Linus cleared his throat. "Gary Cabot already filed paperwork to have your marriage annulled. The psychologist who evaluated Maddie signed an affidavit stating she was likely coerced into marrying you."

I turned to Court, rage spilling into my blood and setting it on fire. "Find Gary. I want him—"

Linus held up a hand. "I'd ask you to refrain from making any... *plans* in my presence. I am, still, an officer of the court and required to report certain things."

And this was why Linus could never be bought: he was actually a good guy. He didn't give a shit about money or bribes or blackmail. He genuinely wanted to do the right thing.

It was adorable when it wasn't getting in my way of putting a bullet in my father-in-law's black heart.

"Ry, we're handling it," Court assured me, his dark eyes holding my gaze and silently communicating that my friends really were on top of shit.

Which did nothing to help the ache in my chest at knowing I'd failed her.

"I can't lose her," I whispered, my voice cracking as I let my emotions bleed through for a second before bottling them back up.

"None of us can," he replied. "Maddie's one of us. You know we'll find her."

I nodded and looked at Linus. "So, what happens now?"

He grimaced. "Now, you go to central booking. It's Friday night, and the courts are closed until Monday morning. We have your bail hearing set first thing, but you'll have to spend the weekend in a cell."

I scoffed and leaned back in my seat, tipping my head back to stare up at the stained drop-ceiling tiles. "Fucking great." I glanced back at him. "What kind of evidence do they have against me?"

Linus frowned. "There's a witness saying someone saw you tampering with Adam Kindell's car. Apparently it was seen at Pacific Cross a few hours prior to his accident."

"I didn't touch his car," I said. It was the truth; Linc had been the one to fuck with the engine, putting in a relay switch Ash had designed to override the electrical system remotely with an app on his phone.

I had been with Maddie, helping her after Kindell had fucking touched her and left her reeling and terrified.

"Kindell was a pervert," I snarled. "He was only there because he was a slimy dick who assaulted Maddie."

Linus's brows shot up. "Did she file a report?"

I gritted my teeth. "No." I hadn't even suggested she go to the cops, because I'd known I would handle it for her.

"There are old surveillance tapes," Court began slowly.

"What tapes?" Linus demanded.

I sighed and rolled my neck until it popped. "Adam Kindell had been sexually abusing Maddie—*Madelaine*—since she was thirteen. He used to go into her room at night."

Linus looked genuinely sick. "My God."

"Gary knew about it," I added. "So, if the courts think Maddie's better off with *him*..."

"You said there are tapes? Proof?" Linus looked back and forth between us.

Court's lips pressed into a thin line. "Old security tapes from when Madelaine was a kid. It shows him going into her room at night."

"Was there anything else on the tapes? Did she ever disclose what had happened? Even to another member of the household staff?" Linus pressed.

"No," I admitted. "But he's a fucking grown ass man. Why the hell would he be sneaking in and out of her room when she was thirteen?"

"I looked into Kindell when I found out about this case. For many years, he was listed as a custodian for Madelaine while Gary traveled on business," Linus began carefully.

"Meaning what?" I glared at him.

"Meaning, one could easily argue that Madelaine suffered from night terrors and he went in, as a parental figure, to comfort her," Linus replied.

"Are you fucking serious?" I jerked, ready to throttle him for even suggesting Maddie was lying.

"He's right," Court interjected. "It's what we can prove, and anything we say now will look like we're spinning a story to villainize a dead man."

"Fine," I gritted out. "But I didn't touch Kindell's fucking car. I was with Maddie. She called me as soon as he left. I was with at least ten guys at the frat when it happened, watching the game. They saw me take the call and leave, and I stayed with her the whole damn night. Her dorm's security cameras would show me a few minutes later, coming in. They'd also show Kindell leaving *before* I got there."

It was the truth.

Linc had followed him to a gas station in town, where he'd inserted the switch under the hood courtesy of Ash canceling Kindell's credit cards so he'd have to go inside to pay in cash. If anyone looked at the surveillance tapes for the gas station, all they'd see was the video loop Ash had inserted that made it look like Linc was never there.

We'd covered every single one of our bases.

Court nodded subtly at me, as if thinking the same thing.

Linus sighed. "Look, these charges won't hold up. I'm going to find out who their witness is, and we'll take it from there. Odds are it's someone who either owed Gary Cabot a favor or has it out for you. But without concrete proof, it's a moot point. The charges will get dismissed."

"The charges were never the issue," I replied. "Gary set this in motion to give himself enough time to keep me busy while he takes my wife to God-knows-where. And now he's saying I forced her into marrying me?" I let out a scoff of disbelief. Gary had some fucking balls, and I was going to enjoy cutting them off with a rusted razor before shoving them down his lying throat.

Linus shifted on his seat. "Unfortunately, *that* will take longer to sort out, Ryan. The psychologist—"

"Fuck her," I hissed. "I'd be willing to bet she owed Cabot a favor or something. No way is Maddie crazy."

"Proving it will take time," Linus warned me. "You'll need to be patient—"

"Not gonna happen," I retorted. "He took her from me. Took her, *drugged her*, and is keeping her somewhere. He's crazy on a good day, and right now he's desperate. I'm going to find her, and I'm going to get her back."

"There's a restraining order in place." Linus frowned at me.

Court chuckled and rubbed his jaw. "You honestly think a piece of paper will stop him?"

"It won't," I assured him. "I'm getting her back. I don't care who I have to go through to make it happen."

"Fine," Linus agreed, his shoulders hunched. "But first you need to prepare yourself for what happens next. You'll be taken to—"

"Central booking." I attempted to wave a dismissive hand. "Yeah, yeah."

Linus gave me a hard look. "I don't think you understand, Ryan. You'll be in with the worst sort of criminals. Murderers, drug dealers, rapists… It's not going to be easy."

I grinned, knowing full well I probably looked slightly feral. I had a lot of rage, and I had no problem unleashing it on someone who thought they could push the rich kid around.

I turned my attention to Court. "How's Bex?"

A muscle popped in his jaw. "Not great. She feels like it's all her fault."

I shook my head. "It isn't."

"Try telling *her* that," he grumbled. "She also thinks it's her fault we lost the game."

After Maddie had gone missing, Bex had managed to get my attention from the sidelines just as we'd retaken the field after halftime. We'd been ahead 21-3, ready to claim yet another victory until Bex told me she had no idea where Maddie was.

The four of us had walked off the field without hesitating, abandoning our coaches and our team. I'd heard some of the officers talking about the game, so I knew the outcome.

Without the four of us, the final score had been 23-33.

Our season was over.

But none of that mattered. Football was never going to be my endgame. I loved the sport, and yeah, I was good at it, but it was never my goal to make it to the big leagues.

For the past three years, I'd believed Phoenix was my goal. The company my friends and I had built was going to be a legacy of good in the world. A way to right all the wrongs and atrocities committed by our families.

But now I knew *that* wasn't what I wanted either.

Maddie was my future. My everything. Without her...

A shudder rolled down my spine.

There was no *without her*.

Linus heaved out a long breath. "Look, I can get these charges dropped Monday, but try not to kill anyone in lockup this weekend, okay? That'll make things significantly more complicated."

Court rolled his eyes toward the ceiling but didn't say anything. We both knew if our positions had been reversed—if Bex had been taken—he'd have needed an outlet for his frustration and aggression, too.

I shrugged, fury pumping through my veins. "I'll do my best not to kill anyone."

That was all I could offer.

CHAPTER 3

RYAN

As I was led to my cell, a guy with a tattoo of a bleeding duck on the side of his face made a kissy face at me.

I smirked back at him. He had a good fifty pounds on me, maybe a couple inches in height, but that bulk would slow him down if he came after me. And honestly, how could I take him as a threat when he had a damn mallard's bleeding ass inked on his pockmarked skin?

"Whatcha smilin' at, pretty?" the guy in the next cell drawled, his wiry arms looped around the bars as he watched me with eyes ringed in heavy liner. He grinned and licked his lips. "Yum. Nice ass, gorgeous."

I winked at him, not willing to show an ounce of fear or caring. "Thanks."

Several inmates hooted and rattled the bars, but all my response earned me was a shove from the guard at my back as he snarled "Shut the fuck up" at the others.

As quick as he'd pushed me forward, he grabbed the back of my polyester orange jacket and hauled me to a stop in front of a cell. A hulk of a man with more tattooed skin than not—even his *eyelids* were inked—glared at me.

"I ain't want no fish," he snapped, and spat on the ground. His black hair was pulled back into a low ponytail, and his scruff was well on its way to a full-fledged beard.

The guard behind me—the one who had lazily scrolled through his phone while I was strip searched—only scoffed. He turned his head and bellowed, "Open on fifty-eight!"

With a loud screech, the door unlatched and opened, and my new roommate glared at me as I strolled inside. The guard pulled the door shut, and another alarm blared, locking it.

I glanced around the tiny space. A set of bunk beds bolted to a cinder block wall, a metal toilet, and a metal sink were the only furniture. I groaned inwardly.

Taking a shit in public wasn't exactly high on the list of things I wanted to accomplish before graduating college.

"So," I started, leaning against the bars and crossing my feet at the ankles, "are you more of a top or bottom man?" I flicked a finger at the bunks.

He bared his teeth at me. "You can sleep on my nutsack, bitch."

I arched a brow. "Well, that's not very hospitable, roomie."

He punched a meaty fist into his open palm. "Fucking rich little punk. Think you're so much fuckin' better. How about I split that pretty ass open with my foot?"

"Sounds kinky," I answered, keeping my tone nonchalant as I watched him for any signs of lunging for me. Right now, this guy was all bark. "Are you even going to tell me your name before we get to it?"

He stared at me like I was crazy and not at all what he'd expected.

If he'd hoped for a sniveling bitch who would cower in the corner and suck him off for protection, he was fucking dead-ass wrong.

"They call me Grinder," he rumbled.

"Damn. Can't get 'em to stop?" I clicked my tongue against my teeth and shook my head in mock sympathy.

"Think you're cute, fuckboy?" He advanced on me with a sneer.

I straightened, bracing for him to throw a punch. "Sometimes."

He leaned into me, breath fanning my face. "How about I show everyone watching exactly what kind of bitch you are?"

Without flinching, I met his gaze. "How about I make you a better offer?"

"What? Gonna offer me some of Daddy's money?" He smirked. "Nah. I think I'll kick your bitch ass and paint the walls of my cell red. I've been meaning to redecorate." He moved for me, a little faster than I'd anticipated, actually.

Good for him, but I was guessing his home-grown version of beat downs hadn't included training from some of the top martial artists in the country. Granted, neither had mine, but Court's had, and he'd shown me more than enough moves to give me an edge.

I slammed a hand down on his wrist and yanked him into me, twisting at the last minute so his face slammed into the metal bars with a ringing *clank*. I drove a knee into his kidney, and he dropped to the floor with a gasp.

Twisting his wrist harder, I dug my thumb into the pulse point. He struggled to get to his feet, and I wrenched his arm higher until I was centimeters from dislocating his shoulder.

"Chill the fuck out," I snarled, leaning over him. "Now, are you ready to play nice, *Ben*?"

He stilled beneath me, even as the guys in the cell across from us jeered, egging me on to bend him over and show him who was boss.

"Benjamin Jones," I murmured, just for his ears. "Joined the Rippers MC out of high school after your sister was gang raped by a rival club on her way home from middle school. You got the nickname Grinder years later, after you cut off the dicks of the guys who attacked her, put them through a meat grinder, and sent them to their club's prez. How am I doing so far?"

He barely twisted his head. "You a fuckin' fed?"

"No, just a guy who does his homework," I replied.

When we'd found out I was going to the Twin Towers Correctional Facility, Ash had done his thing and managed to finagle his way into their systems and assign me a suitable cellmate. One we could help in exchange for me not waking up with a shiv to the throat or a cock on my lips. In a five-minute phone call before I was brought here, Court had filled me in. Having him as part of my legal team was really fucking helpful.

"But you missed one," I went on. "Bruno Watts."

Court had given me Ben's story. How his mom had scraped by, working three jobs after her deadbeat husband racked up thousands in credit card debt and skipped town. Ben had busted his ass in school, playing soccer and earning a scholarship to UCLA.

But that all changed the day his little sister, Carissa, was jumped by four guys from the Crenshaw Point Devils while she was walking home from school. Court hadn't gone into details, but he'd told me enough to know that having their dicks cut off was the least that could've been done to those animals.

Ben dropped out of school and joined the Rippers to protect his mom and sister. He'd made it his mission to kill the men who'd hurt Carissa. The only one he'd missed was the CPD's vice president, Bruno Watts. He'd snuck away and was hiding out in a northern chapter of the Devils.

Fuck, even if Grinder didn't cooperate with me, Watts was still a dead man. No one got away with doing shit like that to a woman, let alone a child.

Grinder hissed. "You know—"

"I know where he is," I interrupted. "And I can tell you exactly where the little weasel is hiding."

"And whatcha want for it?"

"A little breathing room," I admitted. "I'll be gone on Monday, and I'd rather not spend the next two days worried about you coming for me." I relaxed my hold on him and stepped back.

He stood and whirled on me, pale gray eyes blazing like a demon. "Where is he?"

I held up a finger. "I'll tell you when I leave. Hell, I'll even draw you a fucking map."

His chest heaved as he watched me for a beat and then spat on the ground. "You get the top bunk." He took a menacing step toward me. "If you fuck me—"

"You're not my type," I assured him. "But as a peace offering, how about if I tell you I've already handled the debt your dad left your mom in?"

He stilled, his jaw going slack. "You did what?"

"Your mom and sister are good," I assured him, keeping my tone soft. "And I *will* tell you where Watts is."

"I don't need charity," he snarled.

"Then consider it payment for watching my ass the next two days," I replied, climbing onto the top bunk and lying down.

"Why?"

I turned my head to see him standing near me, genuine curiosity in his eyes. "Because I'm not your enemy, and those fucks deserve a lot more for hurting an innocent kid."

"Whatever you say, Robin," he muttered, dropping onto the bunk under me.

"Ryan," I corrected.

He barked out a laugh. "Nah, I'm going with Robin. As in Hood. Fuck me. A rich kid with a hero complex. So, what're you in for? Illegally parked your car to help an old lady cross the street?"

I stared at the ceiling for a beat. "I killed the guy who assaulted my wife."

Grinder went quiet. "For real?"

A slow smile spread across my lips. "I mean, *allegedly*."

CHAPTER 4

RYAN

"Twenty minutes, ladies!" the guard snapped at us as we were ushered into the shower room in a group of fifty. Guards took up positions in the corners, watching with impassive expressions.

I was going on almost day four without a shower, and I needed one. But I deserved a fucking Oscar for not showing my disgust as I stepped into the space, and not just because the fifty-ish guys in here looked about as sexy as a Mrs. Claus in a G-string. The showerheads were mounted around the rectangular room, and there was zero privacy as inmates started stripping. I was pretty sure that the color green in the grout wasn't a design choice.

When I got out of here, I would never again take a clean shower stall for granted.

Most of the men didn't hesitate to strip and turn on the showerheads, creating a cacophony of water pelting moldy tiles.

With a grimace, I yanked off my clothes and went to the closest shower, wishing I could've just stayed in my cell. Unfortunately, showers were mandated by the county to help with hygiene issues.

Then again, with the smells coming from the walls, floors, and even the water, I wasn't sure how hygienic these showers could be.

Generic shampoo/body wash was located in plastic containers mounted beside the knobs, and I quickly lathered my hair as a guard shouted from the other side of the room. Turning my body slightly, I saw a small crowd gathering. Bare ass cheeks and hairy thighs parted enough for me to see the guy with the eyeliner on his knees, sucking off one man while using his hand on another. A third was kneeling behind him, impaling his ass as the guards shouted for them to knock it off. When that didn't work, they left their posts and waded into what was rapidly devolving into an orgy.

Shaking my head, I turned away from the spectacle just in time to see something flash out of the corner of my eye.

I jumped sideways, my feet slipping on the grimy floor as a searing pain lanced up my side.

Fuck me.

Water dripped into my eyes as I looked at the man beside me, a wicked piece of glass wrapped in an old t-shirt clenched in his fist. His dick flopped around as he grinned at me.

"Gonna carve you up like a fucking turkey," he gloated, looking way too happy at the prospect.

I moved away only to be blindsided by a kick that landed low on my back. A third man moved in from the right, and I had to choose if I was going to ward off the shiv or a sucker punch.

My arm shot out, and the sharp edge of the glass glanced off my forearm instead of embedding itself in my gut. The punch landed on my jaw, snapping my head to the side, and the fucker with the shiv retreated a few steps, looking for a new opening.

I glanced around, doing the mental math.

Three on one. Not the worst odds I'd ever faced, but they had me at several disadvantages. They knew this room, which became obvious as they herded me toward a corner, cutting me off from the guards' line of sight.

Not that the guards were looking at anything but the free prison porn playing out in real time.

Either I had the shittiest luck known to man, or the gangbang on the other side of the showers was a distraction to keep the guards from seeing me being attacked.

If I fought back the way I wanted, I ran the risk of the outcome being pinned on me. A new charge, one that might actually stick.

Fuck.

All I'd had to do was keep my head down for the weekend, until Court and Linus were able to have the charges dropped. But these three assholes—all of whom were inked and huge, with only a few pounds separating them—could screw up my plans royally.

I eyed the one clutching the glass. He was in the middle, and his buddy to his left shaking out his fist was probably the one who'd sucker punched me. The third man was the smallest, but he was bouncing on the balls of his feet like he was on something. The unfocused glint in his eyes made me wonder if his issues were cognitive or chemically induced.

When he sniffled hard and rubbed under his nose, like he could still taste whatever shit he'd snorted before coming in here to attack me, I had my answer.

Blood oozed down my arm, slippery and hot, and dripped to the floor before melting into the water streaming off my back. Grimacing, I squared my shoulders and waited for them to make a move. Fighting with my dick dangling seemed like a fucking horrible idea, but I didn't see these guys taking a time out so we could get dressed.

They'd caught me—literally—with my pants down.

It was annoying and a little flattering that they seemed to know they couldn't take me head-on.

A roar of jeers rose up from that side of the room as the porn spectacle continued, but I didn't move a damn muscle.

The tweaker let loose a high-pitched cackle that made my hair stand on end. "Your insides are gonna be pretty outsides, pretty."

Shiv-Man smirked.

The only one who seemed to have an ounce of brain cells was the one who'd gotten a cheap shot in. "Let's hurry this the fuck up," he snarled, his shifty gaze darting around. "We ain't gettin' paid to play with our dinner."

Tweaker licked his lips. "I'm hungry."

With a glare, I shook my head. "You're making a mistake, boys," I warned, my spine steeling as Tweaker circled to my other side. "But if you really wanna go, let's get this shit over with, shall we?"

I whirled, and my fist landed solidly on Tweaker's temple. He went down hard and didn't get up.

One down. Two to go.

"Tell me who hired you, and I'll double what he's offering," I taunted.

Brains smiled and shook his head. "We both know it don't work like that."

"Worth a try," I muttered, jumping back when the guy with the shiv lunged for me again.

I should've had a solid two feet behind me to work with, but something hard and sharp cracked against the base of my spine. Stars exploded in my vision as Brains landed a quick combination of shots to the side of my head and ribs.

A kick to the back of my legs sent me to my knees.

Shit.

I'd missed a fourth guy, who grabbed the back of my hair and wrenched my head back, exposing my throat. Shiv-Man snarled, lifting the glass higher and aiming for my jugular.

With a grimace, I jabbed my elbow back. The soft squish of flesh and a roar confirmed I'd landed a decent shot to the guy's junk. His grip on my hair slackened enough for me to jerk my head to one side.

The glass clipped the underside of my jaw, the skin burning as it was sliced open.

"Hold him!" Brains ordered, jabbing a finger behind me.

A meaty arm came around my throat and squeezed, cutting off my air.

Forget trying to get out of this situation without adding to my problems—these fuckers wanted me dead, and I was going to have to put them all down before they landed a lucky kill shot.

I tried to stand, but my feet slipped on the grimy, mildew-covered tiles. My ears were ringing, and oxygen was becoming an issue. Something sharp stabbed into my gut, and I grunted. Fire licked through my belly, and I glanced down to see a lot more red pooling under me.

Dammit.

Court was going to have my ass when he realized I'd been bested by four jailhouse punks. Of the four of us, he was the one always trying to get us into sparring and shit. He loved it all—boxing, MMA, and just beating the shit out of people. It wasn't uncommon to find him and Linc at underground cage fights, when we weren't in football season and Coach wouldn't ride their asses about injuries.

"End of the line, pretty boy," the guy with the shiv teased as he and his friend closed in on my front.

No, no, no.

No way in fuck was I being taken down by these idiots. I didn't have time to deal with shit like dying when Maddie needed me.

I managed to get to my feet, gripping the forearm of the bitch who'd attacked me from behind. With a grunt and a sharp pain zipping up my side, I dropped my shoulder and rolled him forward. His hold on me released as he twisted away to break his own fall.

My head swam and my vision blurred again. Pain eclipsed thought for a moment, and that was all it took to give the other two a chance to come for me.

I braced myself for the next hit, but it never came.

My legs went boneless beneath me, and I dropped to my knees. Slowly blinking the deluge of water from my eyes, I watched the guys in front of me go down as they were swarmed by five others. Each of the new men had the same image tattooed across his back: a demon ripping through his spine with a bloody dagger.

Rippers.

Grinder knelt in front of me, his eyes a turbulent storm as he grabbed my jaw and forced my head up. "No, you fucking don't," he growled. "You don't get to die until you tell me where that piece of shit is."

I nodded, and a shrill whistle pierced the room, the sound echoing off the tiles and making me groan. The guards had finally realized there was another issue that needed their attention.

Fucking figured.

Someone hovered behind Grinder. "Shit, they really cut him good."

Grinder's jaw tightened as he nodded. "He needs…"

I never heard what else he said, because I passed out like a bitch.

CHAPTER 5

MADDIE

I was losing track of the days.

I'd been here for... five—no, six—days.

Or was it seven?

Shit. The idea that an entire week might have passed in an endless blur was almost unfathomable.

Time had ceased to exist in this tiny room. The lights turned on and off regularly, but I'd started to get used to sleeping with the overhead lights searing through my eyelids. There wasn't much else to do.

Lights on signaled the start of a new day, but I didn't know at what time. There wasn't a clock or a window in my cell. An orderly—who it was always changed—entered and set down a tray of bland food alongside a bottle of water and a paper cup filled with pills. I'd learned after the second day that there was no point in trying not to take them. Fighting back only landed me in soft restraints while mute people ignored my pleas before shoving a needle into my arm.

Whatever drug they sank into my veins made time even more obscure. When I finally swam back to the surface of consciousness, I was never certain if hours or days had passed.

On the maybe third or fourth day, I'd tried hiding the pills under my tongue when swallowing the water. That day's orderly, a skinny woman with pinched features, damn near ripped out my tongue when she checked my mouth to make sure I was doing as I was told. When she threatened the restraints and needle, I quickly downed the unknown pills.

Then I was alone. For hours, with nothing but my thoughts for company. I tried remembering movies I'd watched, forcing my exhausted brain to play them in my mind as a distraction.

Turned out that a two-hour movie was really little more than a five-minute memory when your brain was the projector.

Inevitably, my mind always turned to Ryan. Bex. The guys. People who gave a shit about me and would be coming.

Eventually.

But now, staring down what I was ninety percent sure was day seven, I was starting to have doubts.

My head dropped against the wall as I exhaled slowly. "Where the hell are you, Ryan?" I whispered to no one in particular.

Like I'd summoned him, the lock on my door clicked in the tumbler and the door pushed open.

My heart surged into my throat, and I scrambled forward on the bed, expecting to see him storming into my cell like an avenging angel.

Disappointment crashed over me like a bucket of ice water as Dr. Browne stepped inside, a pad of paper clutched to her chest. An orderly appeared at her back with a chair that he set by the bedside before leaving.

I eyed the door. I hadn't heard it lock.

Dr. Browne sighed as she settled into the chair, looking prim and proper in a pair of cream pants and a turquoise blouse. "Please, don't, Madelaine."

My gaze snapped to hers and narrowed, my skin chafing at the name. "Maddie."

A thin smile tugged at the corners of her narrow lips. "Are we back to that?" She shook her head while scribbling something on the paper. "I had hoped that a week would be enough time for you to come to terms with the truth. But if you're still suffering from this delusion—"

"It's a nickname." My heart rate kicked up at the thought of another needle. "Just what I prefer."

Her lips flattened. "All right. Maddie, then. How are you feeling?"

"Bored," I muttered. I glanced around the room with its white walls, white tiled floor, and utilitarian sink and toilet. Other than the bed—which had no sheets because I was a suicide risk—there was nothing for me to look at. At least someone had turned up the thermostat. I'd spent the first night shivering hard enough that my teeth clacked together. It was still colder than I would've liked, though.

"The purpose of this last week was to acclimate you to your new medication regimen. How are you feeling? Any problems?" She tilted her head, waiting for my answer.

I shrugged. "I mean, I guess I feel more tired than usual." My brain felt foggy, but I was praying that it had more to do with a lack of stimulation than whatever they were pumping into my system.

"A normal side effect," she assured me. "Any thoughts of harming yourself or others?"

"I'm not suicidal," I blurted out.

Her brows lifted.

My hands balled into fists on my lap, and I forced myself to relax when her gaze lowered to them. "It's kind of cold in here at night. Can I at least get a blanket?"

"Actually," she began with a smile, "I think we can do better than that. You'll be moving to a new room shortly."

My spine stiffened. "Where am I going?"

"The level is an intake floor we use to get patients used to their new routine. You've adapted well to the medicine, and aside from your initial outburst and refusal to take your meds, I see no reason you can't be moved to a more permanent room." She smiled at me, her expression expecting a reaction.

"Thank you," I finally murmured, gritting out what I knew she wanted to hear.

Her shoulders relaxed as though I'd uttered the magic words. "We'll be moving you to the fifth floor—"

"I'm staying *here*?" I interrupted, panic settling around my heart. I'd hoped *moving* meant I'd have a shot at breaking out.

Her brow furrowed. "Of course. Highwater is an institution designed to cater to all sorts of challenged young adults. You'll start classes on Monday with some of the other students, along with individual study."

"I'm not... When can I go home?" I hated way my voice wobbled when I asked her.

"Maddie," she said slowly, "you won't be going home. Not anytime soon. Your father—"

I flinched at the mention of that motherfucker.

"—is very concerned about your mental well-being, as well as your physical recovery."

Oh, that was rich, coming from the man who had single handedly dropped the equivalent of an atom bomb on my life.

"In addition to the medication and classes, we'll have regular counseling sessions. It's my deepest hope that we'll be able to get to the root of your issues and help you go on to live a productive, healthy life."

I swallowed around a ball of silent fury. "When can I see my friends?"

Dr. Browne's forehead creased in concern. "By friends, do you mean Ryan Cain? Rebecca Whittier? Lincoln—"

"Yes," I cut her off. "My *friends*."

Sighing, she leaned back a bit in her seat and regarded me. "Madelaine—"

I sucked in a sharp breath through my teeth.

"I apologize, *Maddie*," she amended. "Your father and I believe that with time and space, you'll realize the people you viewed as friends didn't have your best interests at heart."

I glared at her. "And my marriage to Ryan? Like it or not, Gary has to accept that he's my husband."

She inclined her head slightly. "Technically, yes, you are currently married to Mr. Cain."

Everything in me went ice cold.

Currently.

As in, at this moment... but not necessarily in the future.

Dr. Browne watched me closely, like she knew exactly what she'd implied and was waiting for me to crack. To break apart or scream or fight. But all that would mean was another syringe of something that would send me spiraling into a dark abyss.

I forced my expression to be as placid as possible. "Does my father think he'll be able to undo the marriage?"

Her eyes narrowed just a bit.

I let my gaze drop, like I was embarrassed. "Ryan... He won't let me go." I shrugged helplessly, like I was a victim. "He said he'll always come after me. Always find me."

And he damn well better, or I'd find *him*, and kick his ass for taking so long.

Dr. Browne reached over and settled her hand atop mine. "You're safe here, Maddie."

My lips twisted into a sad smile. "I just want my life back."

She squeezed my hand. "And I'm going to help you get there."

I nodded eagerly.

Yes, she would help me get there.

Because I knew how to play this game now.

And Gary—and Dr. Browne—weren't going to win.

CHAPTER 6

RYAN

I jerked awake and hissed when pain lanced down my side. My head hurt like a motherfucker, and I squeezed my eyes shut as my stomach rolled. I took slow breaths, trying to figure out where the hell I was and what the fuck had happened.

"Ry?" a familiar voice asked.

I cracked an eye open to see Ash standing against the rail of my bed. I glanced around at the machines and white everything—walls, floors, bedding.

"Hospital?" I croaked, feeling like death and shit had a baby.

He nodded grimly. "How ya feeling?"

Panic flared through me, lighting up every nerve ending. "How long have I been here? Where's Mad—"

"Easy, Ry," Ash said. "You've been here for a little over a day."

Oh, fuck no. I'd been out an entire *day*? "Ash—"

He held up a hand. "Ry, they had to sedate you when you kept trying to get up."

I vaguely remembered trying to get up and maybe shoving someone when they told me to lay down.

I scowled at him. "Then why the fuck are you here, Florence Nightingale?"

He rolled his green eyes. "Because Grandpa was worried. Linc is with Bex, and Court and Linus are raising hell." He held up his cell phone. "I'm monitoring the facial recognition software while running it through every program I have access to, trying to find Gary or Maddie. And if you'd kept from getting stabbed, I'd still be at my computer."

"Fuck you," I mumbled.

"Love you, too." He scoffed and stepped back.

I glanced down. Sheets had been tugged up to my chest, and aside from when I'd jolted awake, the pain in my side had receded. "How bad?"

Ash sucked on his teeth. "Ten stitches there." He jerked his chin at the bandage wound around my right arm from wrist to elbow. Seemed like overkill for ten stitches. "Another eighteen on your ribs. Only six in your gut, but that cut went deep. You were fucking lucky it didn't hit an organ."

"That's because he can't block for shit," Court spat, striding into the room. He stopped at the foot of my bed and glared at me. "Left side, wasn't it? You never—"

"Yeah, yeah," I cut him off. "What happens now?"

His jaw clenched. "They wanted to send you back to county lockup to finish the weekend."

Ash bristled at my side. "The fuck?"

Court held up a hand. "But Linus already started paperwork for a multimillion-dollar lawsuit, since the guards failed to intervene and the charges were shaky from the jump."

My brows shot up. "Damn."

"You're lucky they stabbed your throwing arm and you're still in talks of going pro," Court remarked.

I snorted. "Yeah. Lucky me."

Court sighed, shaking his head. "As soon as a doctor mentioned potential nerve damage, I think the head of the hospital called the fucking governor to give him a heads up that he might have to reevaluate his reelection plans by the time Linus was done wringing California dry with as many liable lawsuits as he could come up with."

"So, what does that mean?" Ash snapped.

Court shrugged. "Means Ryan gets to spend a few more hours under observation and then he's being released." He looked at me. "You'll still have to show up for court in a day or so to have the charges formally dismissed, and you have to surrender your passport until then, but you're clear to come back home."

"Thank fuck," Ash grumbled, rubbing the back of his neck. "I'm going to call Grandpa and let him know." He turned and walked out the door.

Court braced his hands on the footboard of my bed. "Seriously, man, you good? You scared the shit out of us."

I nodded, rubbing a hand down my jaw and feeling the rough stubble. "Yeah, but I need you to do me a favor."

"Name it."

"Ben Jones."

Court's brow quirked. "The Ripper?"

I pressed my lips together. "Yeah. Have Linus and his team take his case. I'll cover the costs. And find out about the other Rippers who are in there, too. I want all of them taken care of. Do whatever he can to get the charges reduced or gone." My jaw clenched. "They saved my ass."

It rankled to admit that, but it was true.

He eyed me. "Ben shouldn't be a problem. Ash already looked into his charges when we made sure you were put in his cell. The others… Shit, man. Who the fuck knows what they're in for?"

"Don't know, don't care," I said, my tone cold. "Can you make it happen?"

"Consider it done." He tapped the foot of my bed. "Try and get some rest, okay?"

I huffed out an annoyed breath. "I'll relax when I know Maddie's safe."

"We'll find her, Ry."

I nodded. Of course we would.

Because not finding her wasn't an option.

CHAPTER 7

RYAN

Two days later, the judge dismissed all charges, and Linus shook my hand. I wanted to smile and celebrate the win, but we were no closer to finding Maddie than we'd been when she disappeared.

It wasn't possible that she was just *gone*. No way. There had to be a trail somewhere, and we had to find it.

Ash was running himself into the ground, barely sleeping and living off energy drinks as he exhausted every avenue he could think of. If I hadn't been more worried about my wife and what her fucked-up excuse of a father might be doing to her, I would've asked my best friend to take a break.

A grimace twisted my lips as I clasped Linus's hand. "Thanks again." I cleared my throat and glanced around the mostly empty courtroom. Apparently it wasn't nearly as exciting to watch the CEO of a top-ten Fortune 500 company be exonerated from trumped up charges as it was to see him charged.

Barely a week as the new president of Cain Industries, and I already had our PR team jumping through flaming hoops into a vat of acid.

Unfortunately, unless Maddie magically appeared on my doorstep, I had a feeling I was going to need to give them all raises for the shit they'd be dealing with in the coming weeks. I would do whatever it took to bring my wife home. I'd burn any bridge, sacrifice anyone, if it brought her back to me.

My other hand clenched at my side, a wave of helplessness threatening to drag me under once again. I shook my head and focused on Linus. "Where are we with the other charges?"

He shoved some papers into his briefcase before extracting a file for his next clients. He scowled at it. "It would be easier if their previous attorney hadn't been an absolute idiot."

"But?" I prompted.

"But it shouldn't be a problem," he finished with a thin smile, meeting my eyes. "I'll have the Rippers out by the end of the day."

"Good," I murmured, knowing I still owed them all a debt. Part of it I planned on repaying now.

The side door of the courtroom opened, and Grinder shuffled in, looking out of place in a suit that covered the majority of his ink. His eyes focused on me and narrowed, heavy with suspicion.

"The fuck is this?" he grumbled, his gaze swinging from me to Linus. His fists clenched, tugging against the metal cuffs that bound his arms in front.

"Me keeping up my end of our deal," I replied. I inclined my head toward our mutual attorney. "I asked Linus to take you on as a client. You, and your friends."

Grinder's massive shoulders straightened as he glared at me. "I don't need a lawyer. I need what you promised me."

I stepped forward and lowered my tone. "You need both." I reached into my pocket and pulled out a slip of paper, which I passed to him. "Here's the address, but you have to know your… friend is expecting you."

He took the paper, crumpling it in his hand. "Good."

The corners of my mouth tipped up in a humorless smile. "It's a long drive," I added.

"Then I'll have plenty of time to plan our reunion," he said, a familiar, dark look in his eyes.

I doubted he had much left to plan; if Grinder was anything like I expected, he'd been plotting what he would do to Watts ever since he'd found out the man had touched Grinder's sister.

"Still," I added, shoving my hands into the pockets of my pants, "I'd like to extend the use of my plane when you make your final arrangements."

His gaze sharpened. "Why?"

I shrugged. "Because it's the least I can do. I'm not your enemy, but I'd like to be your friend."

"Got plenty of friends," he replied.

"Truth be told, so do I," I admitted, liking that he wasn't a man who was easily swayed or bought. "But I can always use an ally."

He met my gaze, and whatever he found there must have been enough. He gave a slow nod. "It's not necessarily my call."

No, it wasn't. The MC had protocol and rank, but I knew Grinder was a solid guy and someone they trusted. Ash's intel was never wrong, and all signs pointed to Grinder being a key figure in their club in the coming years.

"Understood," I answered. "But the plane's yours all the same."

"Why?"

"Because I know what it's like to not be able to protect someone you love." My voice came out rough and raw. "I know how it eats at you. Rips you open inside."

His head tilted to the side, understanding in his eyes, and maybe a glimmer of grudging respect.

"Linus will handle everything here," I assured him, straightening my shoulders. "If you need anything else, including that plane, he'll give you my number. I hope you use it."

"We'll see." Grinder glanced away, done with this conversation, but not before I noted the way his frame relaxed ever so slightly.

I hid a smile and stepped back, knowing I'd see him soon enough. Nodding to Linus, I stalked out of the courtroom and left the lawyer to handle Ben and his Ripper friends.

Right now I had more important shit to deal with. I had a wife to find, a sister to protect, two companies to run...and a father-in-law to kill.

CHAPTER 8

MADDIE

Highwater was bigger than I'd anticipated. After a week in the same small room, and multiple sessions with Dr. Browne, I was finally being moved to the floor for more permanent residents.

I wasn't sure if that was a good thing or not, but I didn't have much time to focus on it since almost immediately after Dr. Browne left today's meeting, an orderly had come to escort me to my new room. He led me down a long hallway with harsh lighting, white walls, and white tile floors lined with doors that looked like the one leading to my own cell.

I wondered how many other *patients* were here against their will.

How many had been taken? Manipulated? Torn from their lives and hurled into this place?

I gritted my teeth as I walked, trying to keep my head down so the orderly—a guy named Grant, based on the white nametag clipped to his beige scrubs—wouldn't see the fire in my eyes.

We stopped in front of the elevator, and he swiped his keycard to open the doors. Once inside, he used the keycard again to select the fifth floor.

I tried not to let on that I was watching his every move, but clearly this wasn't Grant's first day.

"We get a new keycard every four hours," he said, staring at the closed doors as the elevator started to rise. "There's a chip in them that keeps them active for half a shift. That way, if one is... *lost*—" he eyed me coolly "—it can't be used by a confused patient who gets turned around."

Okay, so stealing a keycard to escape tonight was out of the question.

"Floors are in mandatory lockdown at all hours," he added. "At night, all rooms are locked from nine p.m. to six a.m. Breakfast is promptly at seven. Classes begin at eight. Your schedule will be in your room."

"With a clock?" I couldn't keep the sarcasm from my tone.

He turned and met my eyes. "I'd keep that attitude in check, if I were you."

When I saw the genuine look in his gaze, I resisted the urge to snap back. He was truly trying to give me solid advice.

Seemingly satisfied that I'd gotten the message, he turned away as the elevator doors revealed yet another hallway. This one had the same white walls and tile flooring, but the room doors were open, and I could hear people moving around. A giggle from one room, whispered conversations in another.

At least this floor wasn't utterly silent.

I followed Grant down the hall, passing four doors before he stopped at the fifth. It was half open, and I could see inside to a twin bed with a metal frame and a simple white nightstand.

"This is your room," he replied, gesturing for me to walk inside.

I stepped into the space and froze when I realized I had a roommate.

The other side of the room was identical to the side I would use—another twin bed with neutral bedding and a white nightstand. But perched on this bed was a sweet looking teenager with green eyes and shockingly red hair. The smattering of freckles on her nose scrunched as she looked at me. With her porcelain skin and soft edges, she would fit perfectly on a shelf of antique dolls.

"Guess what, Khloe?" Grant drawled, glancing at the girl. "You get your own roomie."

She scrambled off the bed into a standing position, head bowed and hands clasped in front of her, like this was a military drill.

Grant smirked a little before turning to me. "I'm sure Khloe will help you get settled, sweetheart."

"Thanks," I managed through clenched teeth, stepping aside as Grant left us, whistling on his way. The shrill sound echoed off the walls.

My gaze flicked to Khloe. "Uh, hey. I'm Maddie."

She didn't speak. Didn't move. Hell, I wasn't entirely sure she was breathing.

I shifted my weight, unease trickling through my gut. Finally I hooked a thumb at the vacant bed. "Let me guess—that one's mine?"

Khloe nodded slowly, lifting her wide eyes to meet mine.

I almost flinched. Shit, I hadn't seen eyes that haunted since I'd left the trailer park. There was zero hope left in them, just resignation and exhaustion.

"So, what're you in for?" I tried, willing some sort of life to spark in her gaze.

The tiniest frown furrowed her brow.

"Right," I muttered to myself, turning away to inspect my side of the room. In addition to the twin bed and nightstand, there was a tiny closet pre-stocked with clothes and no door and a small desk with a light bolted to the table.

There was a window between the beds, so that was something, even if it was covered by wire mesh and looked out into a bleak yard with dead grass under a gray sky. A hundred or so yards away, a concrete fence topped with barbed wire separated the enclosure from a line of trees.

As if that wasn't enough of an escape deterrent, I spotted watchtowers to the far right and left.

Highwater might be an institution, but it was also a prison.

"Do you know where we are?" I asked her.

"Highwater," she replied.

I tried not to get annoyed. "Right, but *where* is Highwater?"

She stared at me.

"I wasn't conscious when they brought me here," I explained. "So, I'm wondering where *here* is."

"Wyoming." Another soft whisper. She started wringing her hands together, her shoulders hunching as she tried to make herself smaller.

Jesus, if I breathed too hard, I might knock this girl over.

I stared out the window and noted that the mesh was bolted into place. But even if I could twist the metal to slip out, there was no way I'd survive a straight drop to the ground without breaking something.

"Guess I'm not jumping," I sighed, mostly talking to myself.

"No!" Khloe cried.

I spun to see her literally cowering away from me. She staggered back until she hit the wall and then slid down, shaking violently.

"Whoa. I was—"

"You can't *say that*," she hissed, fear dripping from her tone. "They'll hear, and then they'll come. They always come, and they always *know*."

I held up my hands innocently. "Khloe, I didn't mean to upset you."

"Promise me you won't try it," she begged, tears filling her eyes and spilling over her ashen cheeks. "I can't go back to purgatory. I *won't*."

I frowned. "What the hell is—"

An alarm chirped overhead, and I jolted, my eyes rolling toward the ceiling.

"D-dinner," Khloe stammered.

Footsteps echoed in the hallway, and girls started walking past. Most were alone, though a few walked in pairs. Only a very few spoke.

A girl with long dark hair and darker eyes hesitated in our doorway, staring at me. "New girl?" She cocked an eyebrow.

"Uh, yeah," I replied, my gaze sliding to my roommate, who still looked terrified.

The girl in the door glanced at her and sighed heavily. "Again, Khlo? You know what Underpants says."

Khloe cringed, visibly trembling. "Mrs. Underparsons hates that name."

"Yeah, well, Underpants has bigger issues than her name," the girl mumbled, running a hand through her hair. She turned back to me but waved a hand in Khloe's direction. "This is normal for Khloe, so don't worry about it."

"Right," I murmured, not sure what was going on.

"I'm Joss," she said, stepping into the room and holding out her hand.

I moved forward and shook it slowly. "Maddie."

"Well, Maddie," Joss said with a bright smile that was a little feral at the edges. "Welcome to hell."

CHAPTER 9

RYAN

I was in hell.

Exhausted, I rolled out of bed and gave up on trying to sleep. I'd barely gotten more than a couple hours a night since Maddie had gone missing, and I was going out of my fucking mind.

Scrubbing a hand over my face, I ambled to the window and stared across the Pacific Cross grounds. Light was starting to edge over the horizon, illuminating manicured lawns that glistened with droplets from the overnight sprinklers.

The frat house was situated at the top of Greek row, looming large at the top of a hill that overlooked the grounds. Alpha was a place where leaders were born and honed, trained and elevated.

Right now, I couldn't have cared less if I tried.

As the president, I should have cared. Should've been bleeding and fighting to keep myself and my brothers on top. I was halfway through my junior year, which typically meant classes and parties and being the king of the campus.

Instead, I was only here because I wasn't sure where else to go. I hadn't been to class since Maddie had gone missing a week earlier, and I didn't give a shit about the house or my *brothers*.

A loud crash in the hallway followed by a roar had me turning. But it was the familiar soft cry that had me sprinting for the door and damn near ripping it off its hinges.

Court had our fraternity brother Devon pinned against the wall as Bex hovered in an open doorway with a towel clutched around her chest.

"Fuck," Ash muttered, stepping into the fray and yanking Court off Devon, who was turning a concerning shade of purple.

Devon collapsed against the wall and slid into a useless mess on the floor as he gaped at Court. "What the *fuck*?" he cried, rubbing his throat.

Court pushed against Ash, and I moved forward to help him as more brothers stumbled up the stairs and out of their rooms to see what was going on.

"Stop," I snapped, planting a hand on Court's chest and shoving him back a step. My gaze flicked to Bex and softened. "What happened?"

Bex trembled, her hazel eyes huge. "I was taking a shower—"

"Lock the door if you don't want company, bitch," Devon hissed, glaring at her.

"Motherfucker—" Court slammed against me, rocking me back on my heels as he tried to get to Devon.

Bex ducked back into the bathroom, fear in her eyes, as Linc pushed his way through the crowd to see what was going on. His gaze landed on Court, then Bex, and finally narrowed on Devon.

"Explain," he demanded, cracking his knuckles.

Devon started to push himself up with the aid of his roommate, Brandon. "I went to take a piss and she was in there. Not my fault if the bi—"

Linc took a single menacing step forward.

"—*girl*," Devon quickly amended, "was taking a shower. I didn't fucking know."

I pinched the bridge of my nose. "Okay, show's over, people. Move it."

"He hit a brother," Devon cried, pointing a finger at Court like a fucking five-year-old. "I want—"

"You want *what?*" I growled, glaring at him. "Tell me what you fucking *want*, Dev. I'm dying to know."

Devon might not have been the smartest guy here, but he wasn't the stupidest either, and he knew the look on my face meant he needed to tread carefully. Teeth clenched, he fixed his gaze on the floor. "Nothing."

"That's what I thought," I replied and jerked my chin down the hall. "Get your ass to your room."

Pissed but compliant, Devon stalked down to his room and slammed the door as the hallway emptied out.

"You okay, Bex?" Linc asked, bending at the knees to look her in the eye.

She nodded, cheeks flushed either from the heat of the shower or embarrassment. "I'm so sorry. I could've sworn I locked the door—"

"You probably did," Ash assured her as Court moved into the bathroom doorway, blocking her from view. "One of the freshmen has a habit of locking the door to have some, uh, *alone* time. It can take a while, so Devon and some of the others don't bother waiting anymore. They have keys."

"Oh, ew," Bex whispered, her nose scrunching up with distaste.

"He could've fucking knocked," Court snapped.

"Bro, come on," Ash argued, "the guys aren't used to having a girl living here."

All of our gazes went to Bex because, yeah, she was basically living here now.

After Maddie had been taken, Court hadn't been willing to let Bex out of his sight. Linc and Ash had agreed and moved her in here while I'd been detained thanks to the district attorney buying Gary's bullshit story of me killing Adam Kindell. She was currently sleeping in Court's room, and I wasn't entirely sure what that meant for my friends.

"I'm sorry I'm complicating things," Bex murmured, shaking her head. "I should go back to my dorm."

"No," Court and Linc said as Ash and I shook our heads.

Bex was one of us. Maddie had already been taken, and I knew my girl would rip my ass to shreds if I let anything happen to her best friend.

"Why don't you get dressed?" Court suggested, starting to reach for Bex's cheek and then stopping himself. His arm fell awkwardly back to his side as he moved out of the bathroom doorway and pulled the door shut.

I sighed. "Maybe you guys should take my room," I told them. "It has its own bathroom, so..." But I hated the idea of giving it up. Maybe it made me a selfish douche, but when I was alone in there, I could almost imagine Maddie was in the bathroom on the other side of the door. I could still smell her on my sheets—peppermint and fresh air.

"Maybe it's time we all had a real talk about our living situation," Ash countered.

Linc rubbed the back of his neck. "You want to move?"

"Maddie and I talked about getting a house in town," I admitted, my voice catching for a second before I swallowed around the emotion. I met their eyes. "She wanted you guys to live with us."

The corner of Linc's mouth kicked up. "Always knew she was a kinky girl."

"Ass," I muttered, but a smile tugged at the edges of my lips. "She loved us all being together. And when she comes back—" because it was *when*, not if "—she'll need all of us."

Court glanced at the closed door. "Bex's parents won't let her. She isn't eighteen for a few more weeks."

"Who says we give them a choice?" Ash replied, folding his arms. "We have plenty of shit on Malcolm to make him sign off on it, if it comes to it."

"Blackmailing Bex's dad?" Court scoffed. "What about Betty? She *hates* us."

It was true; Bex's mom hated each of our families, and especially who she thought Maddie was. Madelaine had made Bex's life hell for years.

"I'm sure the good doctor has plenty of her own skeletons," Ash replied.

"Now we're blackmailing everyone?" Linc smirked.

Ash's green eyes flared. "Damn fucking right, if it keeps us safe and together."

"Hey, I'm not disagreeing," Linc said, holding up his hands in surrender as a wicked glint entered his dark blue eyes. "I'm down for whatever keeps *all* of us safe, and that includes Bex. Besides, Maddie might want her close."

Worry churned in my gut at what he wasn't saying.

Maddie might *need* Bex, because who knew what Gary was doing to her? He'd already beaten her up once. He'd spent several weeks controlling her diet and manipulating her through food. He'd sent Adam to fucking...

My hands balled into fists.

Yeah, the courts might have dismissed all charges against me for Adam Kindell's death, but that was only because my friends and I were fucking pros at covering our tracks. Kindell might not have died at my hands, but he'd died at my order.

And he wouldn't be the last before all was said and done.

"We need to find a house in town, but we also need a safe house." I turned to Ash. "Something private with enough room for all of us and Court's brothers. When Maddie comes home, we need a space to let her fucking breathe before we go after Gary. Maybe something in the mountains."

Ash rubbed his jaw in thought. "I've already been looking. I sent Royal a few addresses for him, Bishop, and Knight to check out. I want to make sure whatever place we find is defensible. It'd be easier if Rook was with us, too."

I exhaled hard with a nod, knowing that soon enough Rook would be with his brothers. He had a few weeks left on his contract with the Navy before he was officially discharged. A clusterfuck with his SEAL team had left one member dead, another medically discharged, and a third injured, and Rook had used that to get out of his current contract at the end of the year. He planned to work with Phoenix full time.

"What about the brothers?" Linc drawled, his gaze moving toward the stairs where sounds of the rest of the house waking up could be heard.

"As far as I'm concerned, my brothers are right here," I answered, my tone cold. "I'll hand in my resignation as president today."

Being part of Alpha had been something my father had wanted. I was a legacy, and Cain men were brothers. The same was true for my friends, but none of us gave a shit about being in a frat house.

Our lives were so far beyond parties and pussy it was a joke.

"Somewhere different might be good," Linc agreed, exchanging a look with Court.

"Why?" My spine stiffened.

"Our dads are pissed," Court answered. "Beckett and Gary left them holding the bag with the Russians. It's... not good."

"What can we do?" Ash raised a brow and waited.

Linc snorted. "Build a time machine and castrate my grandfather before the fucker could be conceived?"

"Seems a tad out of my wheelhouse," Ash deadpanned.

"Then you're pretty fucking useless," Linc retorted with a grin that quickly faded. "I can handle my dad."

"Same," Court added. "But it'd be nice for us to have a place where we don't have to worry about potential spies."

I glared at all the closed doors on this floor, knowing he was right. Their fathers could easily pay someone to spy on us here. If they weren't already.

The door opened behind Court, and Bex edged around him in dark jeans and a bulky sweater. Her dark hair was damp, and she looked way too fucking young and innocent to be standing in a hallway with us assholes.

"What's going on?" Bex asked softly, her gaze moving to each of us before staying on Court. Her body swayed toward him like he was gravity pulling her into his orbit.

"We're moving," he told her.

Her brow furrowed. "Okay. I told you I can go back—"

"We're leaving Pac Cross." He took her hand in his and held it like her fingers were made of the most fragile china in the world. "All five of us."

She gasped and turned to me, unconsciously threading her fingers with Court's. "Did you find Maddie?"

The rusty knife that had been stabbed into my chest when she'd gone missing twisted a little deeper, robbing me of my breath for a beat.

"No," Ash answered for me, "but we're preparing for when we do, and we think living off campus, away from prying eyes, will be best."

"Of course," she agreed. Bex was easily the softest and the most selfless of us all, and it didn't take a genius to see why Court was so damn protective when it came to her. "Maddie will need somewhere safe to…" She trailed off, unsure.

None of us knew what Maddie would need. To heal? Rest? Sleep? Recover?

Not knowing what was happening to my wife was like having my insides dipped in acid. It was slowly corroding my organs and shutting me down.

"You're coming, too, B," Linc informed her.

Bex let out a small squeak. "Me?"

"You," Court confirmed, wrapping an arm around her shoulders when she tried to step back. "You're one of us."

"My parents—"

"We'll handle them," Linc replied.

Her eyes rounded. "Oh, no. They're my *parents*. I get that my dad has made mistakes, but you guys can't—" her voice dropped to a frantic whisper "—*handle them*."

Linc barked out a laugh that startled us all. "Christ, Bex. We're going to talk them into letting you stay, not off them."

Her cheeks turned pink as she ducked her head. "With you guys, I never know."

"That's fair," Linc agreed with a grin.

Bex peered up at Court through a fringe of dark lashes. "So, are you asking me or telling me that I'm moving?"

Court swallowed, looking like someone had handed him a bomb. "Asking?"

She smiled up at him. "Then yes."

I exchanged an amused look with Ash, because Court might have said he was asking, but we both knew if she'd have said no, he'd have been *telling* her where her ass was sleeping tonight.

"What about school?" Bex asked, as if suddenly remembering she was still in high school and we all had a few weeks of classes left before winter break was officially upon us.

"I'll drive you back and forth," Court stated, like the answer was that simple.

"Or I can," Linc jumped in.

Bex sighed and shrugged, giving in. I'd noticed her doing that a lot since Maddie had been taken. Bex seemed determined to rock the boat as little as possible, and I had a feeling it was because she still blamed herself for Maddie's kidnapping.

Fuck knew there was more than enough blame to go around.

Ash's phone chirped with an incoming alarm, and he dug it out of his pocket. My pulse ratcheted up several notches when he met my gaze.

"Maddie?" Bex whispered, hope wavering in her voice.

Ash's lips pressed into a thin line. "Not exactly, but I finally found the doctor who Gary paid off."

Emotion wrapped around my throat like barbed wire. "Where?"

"Wyoming," he answered. "Dr. Sharon Browne is the chief of psychiatry at the Highwater Institution, a reform school for troubled rich kids."

"Guess we're going to Wyoming." Linc twisted his neck, popping the joints.

Court pulled out his phone. "I'll call Royal—"

"It's not that easy," Ash told him flatly, his eyes still on me. "Highwater is where the richest and douchiest of the world send their problem children. We're talking kids of ambassadors and foreign diplomats… Rumor even has it the prince of Belgium stashed his son there after he went on a three-week bender in Fiji."

"Meaning?" I growled.

"Meaning it's locked down tighter than a maximum-security prison," he told me. "We can't just storm in there and demand her back, Ryan. We need a plan. A good one."

I shoved down the urge to go in guns blazing. Ash was right; we had to be smart. Gary had been a step ahead of us for weeks. It wasn't a coincidence that he'd put Maddie in one of the most heavily guarded facilities in the western hemisphere.

I exhaled heavily, forcing my pulse to slow. "Fine. Let's start by paying the good doctor a visit."

CHAPTER 10

MADDIE

Staring at the lumpy mashed potatoes on my plate, I sort of missed my salads. At least they'd had color. I stabbed the plastic tines of my spork into the mound, unsure if I was willing to eat this or not. Then again, I'd eaten some pretty questionable school lunches in Michigan.

When I looked around the drab cafeteria, with its rows of plastic tables and chairs full of sullen young adults, it looked disturbingly like my old school, right down to the "Be Your Best Self" poster of a kitten hugging a tree that hung on a wall near the trash compactors.

"It's better if you don't think about it," Joss suggested from where she sat across from me. After stopping by my room, she'd offered to show me to the dining hall, which was way less fancy than it sounded.

Joss and I hadn't spoken on the way down the hall, but then again, no one really spoke as we all walked like cattle toward the promise of something to fill the ache of my empty stomach. We waited in line as we were handed trays of food, and without much else to do, I'd followed Joss to the table we sat at now.

She scooped up another bite of mashed potatoes and shoved it into her mouth before swallowing.

"Did you even chew that?" I asked, arching a brow.

She shook her head. "No. It's kind of like the meds around here—get it down as fast as you can."

"How long have you been here?" I set my spork aside, focusing on her instead of the food.

Her lips thinned as she thought of the answer. "A little over two years now, I think."

I felt my eyes get huge. "*Years?*"

Sighing, she nodded. "Yeah. Honestly, I don't think about it much now. I mean, I fought it at first. But everyone has their breaking point, you know?" She stared down at her half-eaten tray. "At some point, accepting it just made more sense. There's no getting out. No escaping. Trust me, I've tried it all, from hiding meds to seducing one of the guards." She shuddered. "I *really* don't recommend the last one."

"Jesus," I whispered. "Why are you here?"

Joss glanced around the cafeteria space. "Same reason as most people—I can't be controlled by my family, so they pay doctors and guards to do it for them."

My shock must've shown on my face, because she chuckled, the sound void of humor.

"Take a look around," she said, waving her spork at the people in the room. "I'd be willing to bet half the people in here didn't do shit to warrant this prison sentence except be born into rich-as-fuck families where image is everything."

"Sounds about right," I agreed.

Joss took a drink of her milk and eyed me. "So, what abhorrent crime landed you in here?" She snapped her fingers. "Wait, no. Let me guess. You made a sex tape with the pool boy and uploaded it to a porn site."

My brows slowly climbed up my face.

She huffed out a breath. "Okay, not that. Are you gay? Did some girl-on-girl action get you sent here to *straighten* you out?" She let out a derisive snort, her lip curling back.

I startled. "Huh?"

"There's plenty of LGBTQ-plus in here," she said, unphased by my reaction. "God forbid we not conform to the upper elite's stuffy-ass version of heteronormal." She jerked her chin toward a far table, where a girl with blonde ringlets framing a porcelain face with doll-like blue eyes sat alone. "That's Pearl. She's here because her parents sent her to one of those fucked up 'pray the gay away' camps for three years. When she fell in love with another girl, they sent her ass *here*. Last week she got her fifth round of electroshock therapy."

"I'm not gay," I admitted, watching as Pearl ate her meal with robotic movements, unaware of anything else.

"Okay, then what heinous crime got you locked up here?" She tilted her head.

"Why are *you* here?" I countered.

She didn't look bothered by the turn of topic at all. "Oh, that's easy. I'm the youngest of three. My older brother died in a car accident four years ago, but that wasn't a huge deal, since there was this whole scandal where he thought it was okay to beat the shit out of his girlfriend and land her in a coma."

My jaw dropped. "Are you serious?"

She nodded. "Yeah, but my parents were more pissed that he made our family look bad than that he hurt the woman he claimed to love and was going to marry. Then again, my dad has no problem using his fists to keep my mom in line." She smiled coldly, cruelly. She wagged a finger. "But leaving visible marks is a no-no."

I rolled my eyes. "Yeah. I have one of those, too."

Joss took a deep breath. "Then there was my older sister. She shamed the family when some prick she met got her drunk and filmed them having sex. He *did* upload that to a porn site." She looked down, jaw clenched. "My sister killed herself shortly after that."

"Oh, my God," I whispered, my hand coming up to cover my mouth.

She forced a bitter smile onto her full lips. "Anyway, I'm the last kid standing, so my parents sent me *here* to stay until they know for sure I won't bring any more shame to the family name. Eventually I'll be married off to a man of their choosing or..." She looked away for a moment before her gaze snapped back to me. "Now you know *my* life story."

Fuck it.

"Eight months ago I found out I had a twin sister," I started. "We met and decided to switch places for the summer. She died, and I took over her life. I fell in love with her fiancé, there *was* a sex tape scandal with an asshole that led to a massive misunderstanding, since the girl in the video was my sister, not me. My father—who I'm pretty sure had my sister murdered—threatened to kill my mom and best friend if I didn't do exactly what he wanted.

"Instead, my fiancé and I got married and cut both of our dads out of a family inheritance. We staged a coup with our friends, took over their company, and thought we won… Until my father had me kidnapped, declared mentally insane, and sent me here." I smiled benignly at her.

Jaw hanging open, Joss stared at me before picking up the tiny cookie on her tray and sliding it to me. "You win."

A laugh burst from my lips, surprising us both and several people sitting nearby. I quickly smothered the sound, ducking my head.

"I'm not sure this is a competition I *want* to win," I replied, pushing the cookie back at her.

She let out a long breath. "I wish I could tell you it gets easier, but this place…" She shook her head before leaning forward and lowering her voice. "Don't fight back if you can avoid it. Trust me when I say there's *nothing* you can do, and the sick fucks around here love reiterating that to people who try to push the boundaries."

"It's not in me to give up and roll over," I answered.

"It needs to be if you want to survive," she told me, deadly serious. "Maddie, these people aren't right. Who's handling your case?"

I frowned, not sure what she meant.

"Is there a doctor, or…?"

"Dr. Browne."

She visibly flinched. "Dr. Browne is the chief of psychiatry here, but it's a fucking joke, okay? She's a sadistic bitch who gets off on trial-by-fire bullshit, and she's as corrupt as they come. If she's handling your case, then I promise, your father is pulling every one of her puppet strings. Don't trust her. No matter what."

My heart slammed against my rib cage. "I have to get out of here."

"You can't." Joss's flat tone was brittle. "I've tried it all, and there's no fucking way. And your roommate? Don't trust her either. She's so far up Dr. Browne's ass, it's amazing she doesn't smell like shit. Whatever you do, you need to at least pretend to play their game."

"Joss—"

"I'm serious, Maddie." She paused. "Is that even your name?"

"Yeah," I managed to get out, a little amazed that she would bother to confirm my real name.

She gave a short, concise nod. "Okay, then just put your head down and weather whatever shitstorm they put you in. Maybe you can manipulate your father into—"

I cut her off with a snort. "He's an idiot, but I don't think he'll buy me falling in line a second time." No, Gary would probably be counting on my deceitfulness. I wasn't interested in blurring any lines between Gary Cabot and myself ever again.

We were enemies now and until one of us—hopefully him—died.

And then, because my life was always in turmoil, above the soft thrum of conversations in the cafeteria...someone called my name.

"Madelaine Cabot."

My shoulders locked up as I twisted to see Dr. Browne standing with one of the orderlies in the front of the room, both of them looking at me.

"Fuck." Joss paled a little.

"Come with us." Dr. Browne beckoned, a serene smile on her lips as she gestured for me to get up.

"Maddie..." Joss trailed off, clearly not sure what to say.

I slowly pushed back from the table and stood, flashing her a tight smile that I didn't feel. "It's okay," I lied. I abandoned my mostly untouched food and walked toward Dr. Browne, feeling the weight of almost every set of eyes tracking my every move.

"Hi, Dr. Browne," I greeted with as much enthusiasm as I could muster.

Her smile twitched at the edges. "Come with me, please." She spun on her heel and led the way out of the cafeteria.

When I stood there frozen for a moment, the orderly nudged me to start moving, his heavy brows pulled together as he frowned at me.

I hurried to catch up to Dr. Browne.

"I feel I must advise you to be careful," Dr. Browne said without preamble. "Josslyn James is one of our more difficult cases. I would hate to see her influence the progress you've been making."

I heard the thinly veiled threat for what it was and swallowed my gut instinct to lash out.

"Oh, okay. She came into my room and offered to show me around," I explained, keeping my tone neutral.

"If you have questions, Khloe can answer them." Dr. Browne paused at a set of locked doors and swiped her keycard across the black pad mounted to the wall. The light turned green, and the locking mechanism disengaged before the door slowly swung open.

"Khloe is one of our success stories," Dr. Browne boasted, but I wasn't entirely sure that the timid little mouse of a girl who'd squeaked and shook when I talked to her was something I'd call a *success*. Khloe looked ready to pass out if you looked at her wrong.

"Thanks for letting me know," I finally said. "It'll take some time to find my footing, I guess."

Dr. Browne stopped once more, this time in front of a dark brown door. I glanced around and realized this hall wasn't like the others; it was warmer. Bland paintings of fruit and landscapes hung on the tan walls, and the floors were hardwood instead of tile.

There was a sign next to the door that said *Remediation 2*.

"Where are we?" A heavy, sinking feeling opened up in my stomach.

She smiled once more. "We're on the beginning of your road to recovery, Maddie." She pushed open the door for me, but I couldn't walk through it.

Gary slowly stood up from the other side of a table, all smiles as he greeted me. "Sweetheart."

But it wasn't Gary who rendered my body immobile. Sure, seeing him was a kick to the tits, but he took a backseat as I stared at the woman at his side.

My jaw dropped open, and I tried to form words for what felt like an eternity before one actually made it out of my throat.

"Mom?"

CHAPTER 11

MADDIE

Mom smiled at me. "Maddie, honey. You look wonderful."

"Doesn't she?" Gary agreed, like they were doting Stepford parents. He even put a hand on Mom's shoulder and grinned down at her.

What.

The.

Fuck.

"Since you successfully completed your first week, I thought a reward was in order," Dr. Browne explained, pushing me into the room. "Here at Highwater, our ultimate goal is the reconnection of family. Maddie, I know you've had some issues with both your parents in the past, and the plan is to spend the next several months working through those issues."

My head swung to stare at her. "What?"

Dr. Browne's gaze narrowed slightly, an indication that I wasn't behaving like the trained pony she wanted. I could see what Joss meant now; there was a calculated coldness to everything Dr. Browne did.

"Madelaine," she prompted, arching a slender brow.

I flinched at the name. At the reminder that my sister had been murdered at our father's command. And now she wanted me to, what? Run over and hug him?

"Perhaps we should start with apologies," Dr. Browne suggested. "Maddie, it's healthy to take ownership of past misunderstandings and transgressions."

She wanted me to *apologize*? To who? My psychotic dad, or my cracked-out mom? Which one did I owe an apology to, exactly?

"Maybe I should begin," Gary said with an airy laugh. "Maddie, I should have seen how much you needed both parents in your life growing up. It wasn't fair for us to keep our family separated."

"We've all made mistakes," Mom added, lifting her hand to the table, and I saw it then. The tiniest tremor as she splayed her fingers flat against the table. She looked at me, but her gaze wasn't entirely focused and her pupils…

Fuck me. She was high. Functional, but high as a kite.

Gary's eyes narrowed. "Dr. Browne, would you give us a moment with our daughter?"

Dr. Browne bristled but didn't argue. It was pretty obvious from Gary's tone that he expected her to comply with his request, not argue.

Joss was right; Gary was controlling Dr. Browne.

"Of course," she said brightly, touching my shoulder as she left. She pulled the door shut, and all I could do was stand there and gape at the creatures who'd birthed me.

"Sit down." Gary's cold voice lost any pretenses of warmth and reconciliation.

I didn't move. It was a small act of defiance, but it was all I had. I folded my arms and leaned against the door like I didn't care, even as my heart thundered in my chest.

"Fucking cunt," he spat, dropping heavily into his chair and causing Mom to flinch away from his side.

"Gary," she whispered, reaching for him with a more noticeable tremble. "I need—"

"You need to shut the fuck up," he snapped, glaring at her until she withdrew her hand and cradled it to her body like a scolded child.

"Useless bitch. You'll get what I give you, which is nothing unless your daughter sits her ass down."

Mom turned her pleading eyes to me. "Maddie, baby, please... Your daddy—"

A hollow laugh burst from my chest. "He isn't my anything, and you're out of your mind if you think he's helping you. Jesus, Mom, wake *up*."

Mom let out a soft, keening sound and buried her face in her hands.

I glanced around the room, wondering if there was some secret two-way mirror set up in here for the doctor to watch and see what sort of shitshow she'd signed on to. But there wasn't a mirror of any kind or even a camera tucked into a corner to record what was going on.

"Sit. Down." Gary's voice shook with barely contained rage. A second later, Mom cried out in pain, and I realized he'd grabbed her under the table and was hurting her.

Hurting her because I wasn't complying.

My heart twisted, and even though I'd lost count of all the ways my mom had failed me, I couldn't watch her suffer when I could stop it.

Reluctantly, I pulled out a chair and sat down across from them.

With a loud gasp, Mom twisted away from Gary as he released her.

"Where is it?" Gary demanded, placing his hands flat on the table.

I cocked a brow. "Where's what? Your sanity? I'm starting to think it never existed."

"You know exactly what I'm talking about," he hissed.

I snapped my finger. "Oh, you mean your *real* daughter? Pretty sure you had her killed."

Gary didn't even blink. Zero reaction at my accusation. "The money, Maddie. Where the fuck is my money?"

"*My* money is currently safe and only accessible by myself or my husband," I replied, unable to keep the smirk off my lips.

With a snarl, he reached down and unclipped something. A second later, he shoved a stack of papers at me across the table along with a fountain pen.

I barely glanced down. "What's this?"

"A statement I've had my attorneys draw up for you," he replied with a smug look. "Sign it."

"No," I replied, leaning back in my seat and glaring at him. "I'm not signing something when I don't even know what it's for."

"It's a statement saying that you agree Ryan Cain manipulated you into signing over your trust funds," he ground out. "I've already filed the paperwork to have your marriage annulled, and since I now have complete guardianship of you, this will help divert the funds you two stole back to the family where the money belongs without having to go through other, more costly channels."

"You mean back to *you*," I snapped. "No way am I saying Ryan manipulated me when the person who really did is *you*." I waved a hand around the room. "You want to lock me up here? Fine. Want to pump me full of drugs until I'm as strung out as my mom? Go for it. I'm done pretending to give a shit about you, your money, or your family."

He slammed a fist onto the table. "You will obey me, Madelaine."

I laughed. "Hard for a dead girl to obey anyone, *Dad*." I braced my hands on the table and leaned forward. "You're a monster and a murderer. I'd rather die than help you get a single cent of that money."

"Oh, but what good would killing you be?" The cruel look in his eyes, the blue color of them identical to my own, sent a shudder rippling down my spine. "There are so many other people I can hurt to prove my point." His gaze moved to my mom, who had pulled her knees up to her chest, clearly not caring that we were in an office and she was wearing a skirt.

I faced the ugly truth Ryan had been saying for weeks, even though it hurt.

That wasn't my mom.

She was a husk of a woman now, a shell of who she used to be. Or could have been. Nothing more than a phantom. And while I didn't want her to hurt, I had to stop prioritizing her life over my own survival. Especially when she was proving by the freaking second that she would always choose a needle over me.

The only other person he could threaten was Bex, and I knew that, because I'd been taken, the guys would have her locked down tight. In fact, it wouldn't surprise me if Court had handcuffed her to his side or put a tracking device under her skin.

"You know, I am a little curious," I said, going on the offensive for a change as I stared at Gary with as much hatred as I could. "How'd you do it?"

"Do what?"

"I'm assuming the people around here don't work on credit," I replied. "How are you paying them off?"

"The same way I paid off the district attorney to have your husband charged with Adam Kindell's murder." He grinned at me.

My world stopped. Totally freaking stopped.

"You did what?" Icy slush filled my veins, freezing me from the inside out.

Gary tilted his head, still smiling as he watched me start to crack. "Oh, honey. Didn't you wonder why your dear husband hasn't been around to save you?"

Fear prickled under my skin like thousands of ants crawling across my nerves.

"I suppose you were too out of it in the courtroom to notice him being hauled away in cuffs." Gary reached down and pulled out a newspaper. He tossed it at me, and my heart quit beating when I saw the headline.

CAIN INDUSTRIES CEO ARRESTED FOR MURDER

The picture of Ryan being led out of the courthouse in cuffs, a stony expression on his perfect face, rocked me to the core.

No.

No, no, no.

"He's out now," Gary added, but whatever sort of reprieve that should have been never came, because Gary still looked way too happy. "He's recovering."

"Recovering?" I echoed with a weak breath.

He made a soft *tsk*ing sound and nodded. "Prison is a violent place. I heard he was stabbed and beaten. Pity."

Oh, God.

I could actually feel my heart splintering into pieces. Ryan had been hurt. He'd been in freaking *prison*.

"But he's out now?" I gasped, my brain latching onto that fact.

"For now."

"You did this," I hissed, fiery rage melting the ice in my blood and turning it molten.

Gary glared at me, his jaw tight. "And I'll do more until you give me what you stole, you little bitch."

"Fuck you," I retorted, my last bit of patience snapping as I stood up, hands balled into fists. "Go to hell, asshole."

Gary got to his feet across from me, his chest heaving as Mom curled herself into a tighter ball on the chair.

"I'm going to make you pay for this, *both* of you," Gary vowed, spittle flying from his lips.

I spread my arms wide. "You know what? Go for it. If you kill me, Ryan gets everything. And thanks for letting me know that my husband is recovering—that means you tried and *failed* to hurt him. Good luck getting a second shot."

I knew Ryan, and no way would he—or the guys—let something like that happen again. If Gary had managed to hurt Ryan, it had been his only chance at it. I trusted my husband and our friends completely.

That meant I needed to keep treading water until they came for me—and they *would* come for me. It was just a matter of time.

Gary rounded the table and grabbed me by the shoulders. I jerked back, my hand coming up and cracking across his face hard enough to split his lip.

He raised a hand to his mouth and then eyed the blood on his fingers. "Oh, Maddie. That's going to cost you." He turned his head and shouted, "Doctor!"

A second later, the door opened and Dr. Browne strode in. Her wide eyes took in the scene and immediately turned toward Gary for answers.

Bitch.

Gary held up his bloody hand, his expression morphing from unbridled rage to worry. "I think my daughter might need more time."

Dr. Browne's eyes narrowed into slits as she focused on me. "I'd truly hoped we were past this."

"Come on, Angie," Gary called to my mom, holding out a hand for her. His eyes met mine. "I'll see you later, sweetheart. Try to be good."

"Go to hell," I snapped before I could stop myself.

Dr. Browne sighed and snapped her fingers like she was calling a dog. A second later, two male orderlies came into the room and flanked me.

Oh, God, not again.

She raised a hand, and I tried to sidestep the guys, but there was nowhere to go. One grabbed me by the arm, and I tried to pull away only to feel the sharp sting of a needle sinking into my shoulder.

"No..." My protests faded as the world bled away into nothing.

CHAPTER 12

RYAN

Dr. Browne had done well for herself, if the sprawling two-story cabin was anything to go by. The circular driveway was protected by an eight-foot-tall wrought iron gate that required a code to gain access. Beyond it, the drive was lined in evergreen trees that opened up to expose a house of dark wood beams and massive glass windows. It looked like an architectural dream, and I glanced down at the file Ash had amassed on the doctor.

She was divorced with two grown children, and, judging by what he'd unearthed on social media, neither child had shit to do with their mom. Her ex-husband had traded her in for a newer model who'd been in the same sorority as their oldest daughter.

Sharon Browne was a divorcee who lived alone in a big house with two cats and a security system that Ash had hacked in less than five minutes. Everything about her looked like she was trying to project an image of a woman in control and above the rest of her peers.

The telephoto lens I was using gave me a view into her home office. Pictures adorned almost every available surface. Images of Dr. Browne with senators and congressmen, CEOs and ambassadors. There was even a picture of her with a past president and a former sheik.

She was a woman obsessed with herself and her own career. A career she'd made at the expense of victims and people who genuinely needed help. The more I'd looked into the Highwater Institution, the more my gut had roiled with worry. The institution was nearly a hundred years old and had originally been set up as an asylum for people who wanted to put away relatives. In the past twenty-five years, it had made the jump to elite psychiatric facility for the rich and depraved.

I lowered the lens and glanced at the man sitting behind the wheel. "Ready?"

Royal looked at me with a ghost of a smirk. "Are *you*? You don't usually get your hands dirty."

I glared at him, not bothering to respond, because he was right. I was usually the guy calling the shots behind the scenes with Ash while Linc and Court—along with Court's brothers—handled anything that might need the subtlety of a sledgehammer.

But this was Maddie, my fucking wife. I wasn't willing to leave her fate in anyone else's hands. If I had to rip the answers I needed from Dr. Browne, then I would. Piece by bloody piece.

Royal gave a short nod. "Okay, then. Let's go." He opened his door and got out silently. The guy was fucking huge, several inches over six feet and with a physique that was textbook Navy SEAL. It was unreal how quietly he could move. And not just Royal, but all of his brothers.

I got out, my door brushing the heavy undergrowth of the copse of trees we'd parked behind. Ash had already hacked and disabled the security cameras around the property earlier in the day.

The light in Dr. Browne's study turned off, and then another light dimmed as she headed down the hallway, presumably to her bedroom.

"Go," Royal ordered, his tone hard and cold as he jerked his chin toward the eight-foot fence that wrapped around the property.

I broke into a sprint and jumped up, reaching the top of the fence without a problem. The damn thing was decorative more than anything else, and it shuddered as Royal scaled it alongside me.

We dropped onto the other side and exchanged glances before

moving as one to the side of the house where a door led to the kitchen.

Part of me wanted to kick in the front door and make as much noise as possible. I wanted Dr. Browne to feel terrified, to feel an ounce of the fear I knew Maddie had felt. But Ash's recon had shown that her house came complete with a panic room on the other side of her closet. We couldn't risk her getting in there first, or this would all be for nothing.

Royal knelt in front of the door and had it unlocked in seconds. We stepped inside and glanced around a large space that looked utterly untouched. Walking through the cavernous kitchen, I spotted a few takeout containers scattered on the counter.

I knew Royal had spent the trip to Wyoming studying every inch of the floorplan, so I followed him down a hallway and up some stairs without hesitation. I counted each of the doors we walked past, my hands reflexively balling into fists with each step as I pictured squeezing the life out of Dr. Browne.

Royal spun and arched a brow at me, looking pointedly at my hands. He was trying to tell me to chill out, and I knew it. I needed to bottle up my emotions and handle this without letting my heart weigh in. And once upon a time, I would have. I *could* have. But not now. Not when the thing at risk was my heart itself.

God, I'd turned into such a fucking pussy, but Maddie was everything. It made me irrational and volatile, but I couldn't change it.

Rolling his eyes, Royal eased open the door we'd stopped in front of.

The bed was empty, but there was a light on in the bathroom. The door was almost completely closed, and the shadow of the person inside walked back and forth before the light turned out and the door opened.

The look of surprise on Dr. Browne's face was almost comical. Illuminated in the moonlight, her jaw dropped open, and then true terror filled her eyes and she let out a wailing screech that probably could set off car alarms before diving toward her closet.

I took two steps and intercepted her, wrapping an arm around her waist and tossing her backward so she landed on her bed with a yelp.

"Stay still or we'll tie you to the fucking bed," Royal growled.

Clutching the front of her top to her throat, she started sobbing. "Don't rape me."

I couldn't help it; I laughed. The idea that I'd want my dick anywhere near this bitch was a fucking riot. Even Royal cracked a grin, but somehow it made him look even more unhinged.

"No one's going to touch your shriveled up cunt," I assured her, my tone biting. "But you're going to give me answers."

She sniffled and had the nerve to look affronted for a second before her gaze focused on me and she gasped. "You."

I smiled. "Me." I went to the side of the room with a small writing desk and chair and dragged the chair back on two legs to sit across from her. "Where's my wife?"

She lifted her chin. "I'm not going to risk my patient—"

"Oh, lady, cut the bullshit," I snapped, the last threads of my patience dangerously close to snapping. "We both know the real risk to Maddie is her fucking father."

Her cheeks flushed as her gaze darted away.

"I want her back," I went on, leaning forward and lowering my voice. "And you're going to help me."

"I can't." Dr. Browne sucked in a deep breath and met my eyes.

"Then you're of no use to me," I replied, nodding to Royal who stepped forward with a gun drawn. He didn't hesitate to press it to her temple.

"Wait!" Dr. Browne shrieked, trying to scramble away from the weapon. Royal simply used his other hand to grab the nape of her neck and hold her still. "Please! Wait! I can help you!"

Royal yawned loudly, like this was the most boring part of his day.

"Then let's go get her," I growled, getting up.

"You can't. *We* can't," she amended, holding up her hands. "You'll have to wait until next week."

"Not a fucking chance." My chest heaved as I stared down at her, wishing I could wrap my hands around her thin neck and squeeze. "We're going now."

"You *can't*." Dr. Browne all but wailed as Royal dragged her to her feet. "You don't understand—she's in our lockdown ward. It's a separate facility. She'll be there for another ten days."

I clicked my tongue against my teeth and reminded myself we still needed this woman alive. "You run the fucking facility. I'm sure you'll think of something, doc."

"But—"

I stepped forward, crowding her space and grinning when she swallowed, her wide eyes fixed on me. "We're going to get my wife. *Now*."

Royal shifted on his feet, the only sign he wasn't okay with my announcement. The plan was to get Dr. Browne to agree to help us get Maddie, but not necessarily this very second. Royal was a planner and would want to make sure every possible outcome was accounted for. We'd run through scenarios where Maddie was in a room on the fifth floor, a space that seemed more like juvie than anything else.

We hadn't planned on her being in a lockdown ward. There was no telling what kind of problems we might run into there. I was switching up the plan by insisting we go tonight, but Royal would just have to fucking adapt, because I wasn't letting my girl sit in a cell for another night. If I had to go alone and leave his surly ass here, I would.

After a long pause, Royal gave me a curt nod, accepting the situation for what it was. Satisfaction unfurled in my gut, and I turned to the doc with another vicious smirk. "Let's go."

For all the security guards and protocols in place to keep people in Highwater, there was barely a pause at the front gate when Dr. Browne drove up with Royal and I in the car to get access shortly after midnight.

The guards nodded at her, clearly unwilling to question their boss's motives even with two strangers in the car.

Dr. Browne parked in her assigned spot near the front entrance and cut the engine. She braced her hands on the steering wheel. "You both should reconsider—"

I scoffed and rolled my eyes. "You should really shut the fuck up before you piss me off even more." I turned to face her in the passenger seat. "But I've gotta know—why?"

Her brow furrowed.

"Why are you doing this? Is Gary paying you? Blackmailing you?" I watched her closely and felt Royal doing the same from where he sat in the middle of the back seat.

"No," she replied, blanching a bit before her gaze darted away.

Royal laughed, the sound chilling. "Fucking hell. You love him."

My eyes narrowed, because no way... but sure enough, Dr. Browne's cheeks turned red. "Seriously?"

Her jaw clenched as she stayed silent.

"That's kind of pathetic," I mused, rubbing my jaw. "Weren't you trained to spot a sociopath in psych school, doc?"

Her head whipped around and she glared at me. "You don't know what you're talking about."

"And you don't know who you're dealing with," I shot back. "That man is a murderer, amongst other things. You think it's *normal* to lock up your own daughter?"

"It is when she makes decisions to associate with dangerous people." Dr. Browne's haughty look was almost amusing. This woman was insane if she thought Gary Cabot was anything other than a sadistic asshole who was using her.

"You're never gonna get through to her," Royal commented from the back, shaking his head. "She's a fucking nutcase."

He was right, and I was done waiting. I shoved open my door and nodded my head for her to do the same as Royal got out on her side in case she decided to do something stupid like run or scream.

Dr. Browne flinched as we flanked her, and as we approached the glass doors leading into the main lobby, I could see her eyeing the front desk guards.

"Don't," Royal growled. "We're trying to do this the easy way. The hard way is we come in here, gun blazing, and burn this place to the ground."

She stopped in her tracks and gaped at him. "There are innocent children in here."

He tilted his head, looking every inch the mercenary killer that made him a vital part of Phoenix. "My mission is to get Maddie out. I don't give a fuck about collateral damage. If you scream or call for help, I'll put a bullet in your head, and I won't stop until we get to her."

That was a fucking lie, but she didn't know that.

"You're a monster," she whispered, horrified.

He leaned forward with a smile. "Takes one to know one, *doc*."

Clearly rattled, Dr. Browne moved forward and opened the door. She paused at the front desk, where one of the guards looked up, surprise on his face.

"Dr. Browne." His gaze flashed to us. "Is everything all right?"

She squared her shoulders and nodded. "I received an alert that one of my patients needed me."

He nodded but seemed confused as to why Royal and I were there.

Royal stepped closer to her, his shoulder brushing hers. "We're here to protect Dr. Browne. There have been some recent threats, and we need to ensure her safety." With our black shirts and tactical pants, it wasn't a stretch to imagine us being her bodyguards.

The guard's eyes widened. "Oh. Is there something we should be on the lookout for?"

"We've already got a meeting planned with the head of security in the morning," Royal explained without hesitation. "Tonight we couldn't convince the doc to stay home. You know how she can be."

The guard laughed. "Committed to her work, right?"

"Exactly," I chimed in with a chuckle. "We'll be in and out." I turned my gaze to Dr. Browne. "Let's go see that patient, shall we?"

She nodded stiffly and walked ahead of us to the bank of elevators. She didn't speak until the doors slid shut behind us. "You won't get away with this. There are cameras everywhere."

"Let us worry about that," I replied. I'd already called Ash, and he was working on scrubbing their security system. There would be no trace of us ever having walked in here on their security feeds.

The elevator opened in front of a set of imposing steel doors that needed a retinal scan in addition to a keycard to access whatever lay on the other side.

Royal and I exchanged a look, and my pulse thumped at knowing Maddie was close.

Hang on, baby. I'm coming.

"Open it," I snarled when Dr. Browne hesitated.

With a sigh, she used her credentials to unlock the doors and push them open. Another guard desk awaited inside, but it was empty.

Royal's brow quirked up. "Wow. Security around here is impressive."

Dr. Browne frowned. "They should be here, but it doesn't matter. She's down here." Leading the way down a long corridor of windowless doors, she paused at the second to last on the right.

There was a small sign with the number 1104 and a chart hanging from a clipboard beneath it. I snatched it off the wall and skimmed it, rage filling my chest. "What the fuck is this?"

Dr. Browne didn't meet my eyes. "Instructions for her care specific to her case."

Disgusted, I didn't flinch when Royal grabbed it from me and started reading aloud. "Medications…" He looked at me. "Is Maddie taking anything?"

I shook my head slowly. "No, never."

His brows shot up. "There are some heavy sedatives and antipsychotics."

Dr. Browne stared at the floor.

Royal's breath hitched, and his blue eyes went arctic. "No-touch protocol? Are you fucking kidding me?"

I frowned. "What—"

"It's a motherfucking torture technique," he explained, still glaring at the doctor as he spat out the words. "It's all psychological shit. Keeping rooms at freezing or blazing temps, playing nonstop sounds so you can't think or sleep… It's designed to break a person mentally.

What the fuck could an eighteen-year-old girl do to warrant the kind of shit they use to break CIA spies and terrorists?"

My hands clenched into fists, and I physically forced myself back a step so I wouldn't kill the woman in front of me. "Open the motherfucking door." When she didn't move, I punched the wall hard enough to make her jump. *"Now."*

She fumbled with her keycard before swiping it over the lock. A green light flashed, and I pushed past her to open the door, bracing myself for whatever sight greeted me next.

CHAPTER 13

RYAN

It took a second for my eyes to adjust to the glaringly bright light that seemed to come from everywhere. Overhead, the walls, even the fucking floor. It was blinding, and I couldn't escape it even when I blinked.

I scanned every single inch of the space. Twice.

There was a twin bed with a metal frame bolted to the floor, and a metal toilet and sink. That was everything in the room, which felt like it was only a few degrees above freezing.

Maddie wasn't there.

I turned, and as if he sensed I wasn't completely under control, Royal shifted his body between me and Dr. Browne. Like he knew I was seconds away from throttling her bony ass.

"*Where is she?*" I demanded, sick of her games and ready to make good on Royal's earlier threat of burning this all to the ground.

Dr. Browne looked genuinely confused. "She isn't in there?" She tried moving around Royal to see inside. "But that's—"

I stepped forward, and Royal planted a hand on my chest. "Easy, man," he admonished softly. "Keep your head in the game until we know what's going on."

I lifted a brow, wondering if he'd be so calm if it was one of his brothers who was missing.

The doc's gaze shifted down the hall, and I could see her working out in her head if she could get to the door and on the other side before Royal or I caught her.

"You won't make it," Royal told her, his tone mild as he watched her like a damn pit bull.

"Dr. Browne!" someone called from down the hall.

We all turned, and Royal brushed closer to her back, leaning to whisper in her ear. "You better watch what you say, doc, or we'll shoot our way out of here. Starting with *you*."

Her breath caught as she trembled. "J-Jared," Dr. Browne stammered, stepping away from Royal. "Where is my patient?"

Jared, a young guy in gray scrubs, stopped several feet away and frowned at her. "What?"

Dr. Browne snapped her fingers and pointed at the room. "Madelaine Cabot—"

"We moved her," Jared said slowly, "just like you ordered."

Again, Royal pushed me back.

"Moved her where?" Dr. Browne demanded, eyes wide.

Jared's expression turned uneasy as he looked at us and back at her. "Is everything okay, Dr. Browne? You sent us a message over an hour ago that she was transferring facilities. I just finished putting everything on your desk."

Dr. Browne looked at me, and there was no denying she was as confused as we were.

"Dr. Browne?" Jared posed her name as an uncertain question, his gaze once more flickering to Royal and me.

"Thank you, Jared," she finally replied with a tight smile. She glanced at me. "Let's discuss this in my office."

"Actually, while you're here," Jared began, "the patient in room eleven-oh-nine had another seizure. We're thinking it might be the strobe lighting—"

"I'll look at the file in the morning." She cut him off sharply. "Thank you."

Dismissed, Jared kept going down the hallway but glanced over his shoulder at us, as if he still wasn't sure everything was okay.

Royal huffed a low laugh. "Strobe lighting? You're a fucking piece of work, lady."

She squared her shoulders. "Sometimes unorthodox procedures are necessary for—"

"Oh, save it," Royal snapped, rounding on her. She stepped back, his sheer size intimidating enough without the look of blazing hatred in his eyes. "I've known people like you my whole life. Entitled assholes who get off on seeing just how many ways they can hurt a person. You're not helping people here—you're using what little power you have in your pathetic life to bully others weaker than yourself."

Fire ignited in the doctor's eyes as she stared up at him. "You're just another useless grunt, and I may not know where the girl is, but I'm thankful it's far away from you." She turned to me. "*Both* of you."

"If you don't know where Maddie is, then you're no longer useful to us," I answered, ice water filling my veins. "Now you're just the bitch who hurt the woman I love."

A low chuckle rumbled out of Royal. "You're fucked, lady."

I glanced at Royal. "Get rid of her."

"Wait!" She threw up her hands, her face pale as Royal reached behind his shirt for the gun he'd stashed there. She stumbled back a step. "If there's a transfer order in place, Jared left the paperwork on my desk. I'll take you there."

"Good fucking idea," I replied, folding my arms across my chest and waiting for her to move.

Shoulders slumped, Dr. Browne turned and led us down several hallways before stopping in front of a set of doors with frosted glass inserts, her name written in block letters in the middle of the glass.

With a barely audible sigh, she pushed open one of the doors and turned on the lights.

I was mildly surprised her office wasn't locked until I saw a locked room beyond, likely where she kept her patient files. This room was nothing more than an office with a desk, a seating area, a few fake plants, and a wall full of framed accolades.

In the middle of the glossy top of her cherrywood desk was an envelope. Dr. Browne grabbed it and opened it. She barely had the papers out before her gaze snapped to me. Her hand shook as she wordlessly passed them to me.

I snatched them from her grasp. The sticky note on the top page caught my attention first.

You lose.
—G.C.

Fucking Gary.

The paper under that made my breath catch and pain sear through my chest. A signed annulment document invalidating my marriage to Maddie.

He'd done it. He'd managed to take her away when I'd finally made her mine.

I swallowed down a roar of pure fury and looked at the next page. A restraining order barring me from coming within five hundred yards of Madelaine Cabot.

But beneath that was a newspaper notice. Who the fuck actually read newspapers anymore?

Apparently I did not, because I could only gape in horror as my eyes focused on a picture of Madison—or Madelaine, I wasn't entirely sure—and motherfucking Charles Winthrope. The douche who had constantly been sniffing around Maddie.

It was a goddamn wedding announcement.

My heart thundered in my chest, and for a second, I wondered if it was true. If Maddie could be manipulated into marrying someone else the way she'd almost been forced to marry me before…

I slammed closed that line of thinking.

No. I trusted Maddie. Hell, the pictures they'd used in the paper looked like professional headshots, not a staged engagement photo. It could all be a bullshit bluff on Gary's part to fuck with me.

I snorted and handed the papers to Royal. Like a fucking piece of paper could keep me from going after her. Besides, the paper said I couldn't go near *Madelaine Cabot*.

Madison Porter was all fucking mine, now and forever.

And fuck that engagement. It was bullshit.

"I didn't know," Dr. Browne breathed, shaking her head and backing away from us.

Royal barely spared her a glance. "Looks like Gary left you holding the bag, doc." He gave her a pitying look. "Sucks for you. Guess you really aren't needed anymore." He pulled out the gun, letting it dangle in his fingers like an extension of his arm.

"Please," she begged. "I didn't... I never..."

"Shut up," I ordered, watching with detached coldness as she scrambled into the chair behind her desk. "Where's the key for the files?"

"In my desk," she replied. She reached for the top drawer.

Royal cocked the gun and leveled it at her head. "Slowly," he advised.

A tear rolled down her cheek as she opened the drawer and lifted out a silver key.

Royal scoffed. "Wow. Really fucking secure."

She flushed. "We're on a locked level with the highest security clearance."

He looked around. "It shows." Disdain dripped from his tone, and all I could do was laugh. The sound came out hollow and cruel, swearing pain if she even tried fucking with me.

"I want Maddie's file," I told her. "Now."

She got up and hurried to open the door. Inside were more locked cabinets, each with a number pad. She didn't pause, punching in an access code and opening the cabinet closest to the door. A moment later, she had Maddie's file and handed it to me.

"Thanks," I said, like she'd done me a solid instead of acting under the threat of Royal's gun. I looked at my friend. "We're done here."

Royal's smile was the thing nightmares were made of. Like he'd closed off every single thing that made him human and slipped into the Iceman call sign his team had given him when he'd been a SEAL. His finger brushed the trigger, and the doctor literally dropped to her knees.

I couldn't help the mirthless chuckle that escaped me as I reached down and plucked the key from her fingers. "Keycard." I held out my palm and waited for her to give it to me. "Have a nice night, doc."

We left the room, locking her inside as we went.

"What now?" Royal asked as we stepped into the hallway.

I paused and let out a heavy breath, feeling the anxiety I'd been fighting since seeing Maddie's empty room. The fear flooding my veins was almost enough to drive me to my knees. "I don't know. I just don't fucking *know*."

Royal clamped a hand on my shoulder and squeezed to the point of pain. "Keep it together, Cain. Your girl needs you."

"We're back at square one." I scrubbed a hand down my face, exhaustion pulling at my bones. "We need to find Gary. We find him, and we'll find Maddie."

"Then that's what we do," Royal agreed.

"But if he hurts her…" Fuck. I wanted to slam my fists against the wall until they bled.

Royal shook his head. "Don't think like that. Your girl's a fighter. She doesn't break easy."

"I told her I'd protect her." Hell, I'd *vowed* to protect her, and I'd fucking failed.

"Then don't give up on her."

I met his gaze. "That'll never fucking happen."

CHAPTER 14

MADDIE

I started to wake up, plagued by dreams of bright lights and skull-fracturing heavy metal screams. Had it all been a nightmare?

Please, God, let it have been a nightmare.

My head was freaking killing me. I cracked an eye open and gasped, because this room wasn't another room at Highwater. It was clean and decorated in soft blushing pinks and whites. The sheets under me were soft and luxurious.

My joints ached, my body protesting every tiny movement, but I needed to know where I was. Pushing myself into a sitting position, I looked down at the duvet wrapped around me, my pale hands looking out of place on the white covers.

This wasn't Highwater, and it sure as hell wasn't the cabin where Gary had held me hostage before. It wasn't my room at Pacific Cross, or the room I shared with Ryan at his beach house.

I swung my legs over the edge of the bed and winced as pain throbbed between them and radiated across my belly. Bruises dotted my thighs and calves, and I honestly wasn't sure where a lot of them had come from.

Panic spiraled in my chest, my breaths coming in short, ragged pants as I did a quick mental inventory about why I'd be hurting *there*.

I looked down, seeing that I was fully clothed, but unease coiled in my stomach until I felt sick.

I definitely hadn't been wearing shorts the last time I'd checked. I'd been in the itchy pants and thin cotton shirt from Highwater.

Slamming my eyes shut, I took deep breaths and tried to compartmentalize how I was feeling, tucking my emotions and fears into boxes I could unpack later. Right now I had bigger issues to worry about. Like where the hell I was.

My feet settled on the warm wooden planks of a heated floor, and I slowly padded to the window on the other side of the room. Looking out, I saw a world of white. Snowy mountains loomed in the distance, and even more snow was falling. It was hard to make out much due to the thick blanket of white covering the world.

It looked picturesque and perfect.

And like I was nowhere near civilization.

I tried pulling up the window, but a closer look showed it was nailed shut. With a hiss, I slapped my palm against the frame. *Of course.*

I spun away and looked around to see if there was a bathroom. Luckily that door *wasn't* nailed shut, and I quickly locked myself inside to do what I needed to. When I looked at myself in the mirror above the sink, I flinched.

I looked like shit. My hair was a mess. I was pale, and there were more bruises on my throat and arms from the needles that had been shoved into me over the past week or so.

After drying my hands, I ran my fingers through my hair, flinching when I hit a massive tangle. I dropped my hands to the edge of the counter and looked myself in the eye, steeling myself for whatever was going to happen next.

I turned and exited the bathroom, ready to kick down the door to wherever the hell I was.

Except I stopped, because I definitely wasn't prepared to see my mother standing in the middle of the room.

So much for preparing myself.

She looked like she had when I last saw her in the remediation room, dressed in a pale yellow skirt with a flowery blouse and kitten heels. Unlike before, her eyes were clear and sharp, and her hands were clasped in front of her.

"Maddie," she greeted with a warm smile that almost bordered on motherly.

"What the hell is this?" I demanded, looking around. The room's door was behind her, and I had a feeling I could shove through her, but there was no way of knowing what was on the other side.

A small smile turned up the corners of her mouth. "Why don't we sit down?" She waved a hand at a sitting area, two upholstered chairs and a table between them with a covered tray. "Please, sweetheart."

I flinched. "Don't call me that."

Her mouth flattened. "Your father will be upset if you can't be civil, and we both know he's not at his best when he's angry." A soft, forced laugh made its way past her lips. She walked to the chairs and sat in one, crossing her legs at the ankle like a debutante.

"Where am I?" My hands balled into fists at my sides, my wrists aching from where the restraints had held me down for hours.

"Sit down, honey. I brought you something to eat." She ignored my question and lifted the lid of the tray.

Yeah. Yogurt and granola were the way to win my trust.

"Where. Am. I?" I enunciated each word even as my stomach clenched and longed for something to eat.

She huffed and straightened her spine before snapping her fingers like I was an errant puppy. "Sit down, Madison."

I couldn't stop the laugh that bubbled out of me. "Madison? Don't you mean *Madelaine*?"

Irritation flickered in her eyes. "Can't you just do what you're told for once? Your father is being very generous and offering to take care of us!"

"Generous?" My jaw dropped open. "Are you fucking kidding me?"

She winced. "Don't be crass."

I stepped back. "Seriously? I learned that word from you when I was *two*, Mom." I waved a hand at her. "Jesus, *look* at you."

"Yes," she snapped, leaning forward. "*Look* at me. I'm not passed out in a rusty trailer, wondering what orifice I'll have to sell for my next fix."

I stared at her for a beat, wondering if it was even worth trying to get through to her. Eventually, I felt that same old sense of guilt and loyalty that was like an anchor around my neck.

Instead of sitting on the vacant chair, I walked to her and dropped into a crouch. I took her hands in mine. "Mom, let's get out of here. We can go now—"

She ripped her hands away. "No, Maddie."

I clenched my teeth. "He's not a good guy, Mom. Gary is—"

"Willing to give us everything we want," she insisted, reaching out to grab *my* hands. Her nails dug into my skin, desperate and crushing. "Why won't you just do as you're told?"

"Because he's a *monster*," I answered, my eyes searching hers for *something*. Anything that would let me know she wasn't buying his lies. "He killed Madelaine."

She sighed. "Oh, Maddie. Your sister died in a fire. Gary told me all about it. It was a tragic accident."

My brittle laugh echoed between us. "Are you really that far gone? He *killed* her."

For one second, Mom looked completely in control, and then my cheek was throbbing where she'd suddenly slapped me. Caught off guard, I fell on my ass as she glared at me. The look of contempt in her eyes was one I knew all too well.

"Listen to me, you little bitch," she seethed, leaning forward to grab my chin in her bony fingers. "I've *finally* got the life I was always meant to have. You're not going to fuck it up for me. Now, do what your father says."

In that moment, something in my heart broke. Whatever tiny sliver of hope I'd been clinging to that my mom might help me dissolved like cotton in acid. I was on my own, and my mother didn't give a damn.

"No," I replied softly before jerking free of her hold and getting to my feet. I ran for the door and wrenched it open as she shouted after me.

My room was near a staircase, and I didn't hesitate to hurry down it, not sure where I'd go but knowing I had to at least try to get away.

I tripped on the last step and caught myself on the railing, my gaze landing on the exit less than twenty feet away. The glass panes on either side of the heavy oak double doors showed glimpses of the outside. Of my salvation.

Without pausing, I lunged for them and screamed when an arm clamped around my hair and yanked me back. I felt the skin on the crown of my head *pop* at the force of being stopped so viciously, and tears sprang to my eyes, but I wasn't sure if it was from pain or frustration at being so close and being pulled away.

"No you don't," a familiar voice growled, the pressure on my hair tightening.

I still pulled back, not caring if I went bald in the process. My heart thundered in my chest, the sound of roaring blood filling my ears as I cried out again, frantic to be free.

"Fucking *stop*." A hand clamped around my arm, and I lost whatever small leverage I'd had. I was spun and pushed face-first into a wall. My nose hit it hard enough that stars burst behind my eyes, and I vaguely wondered if it was broken. One arm was twisted behind my back, and I braced my free hand to try and push off the wall, but it was useless when the person holding me leaned his weight against my back.

"Stop it," Evan snarled, his mouth close to my ear.

I struggled more, and he wrenched my arm tighter, higher, threatening to dislocate my shoulder.

"Bring her here," Gary snapped from my right, and I turned my head to see him standing several feet away with a look of annoyance on his face. Without waiting for Evan's response, he turned and walked down the hall and around a corner, the click of his dress shoes echoing on the hardwood floors.

Evan's breath fanned across my face. "Can you walk on your own? Or do you want me to drag you down there?" His fingers tightened in my hair as if to make a point.

A whimper slipped past my lips unbidden. "Fine," I managed.

Evan's hold relaxed, and he stepped away from me. My arm throbbed at the shoulder joint as I straightened it slowly and turned to face him.

"Don't look at me like that," he muttered, glancing away with a tight jaw.

"Like what?"

His eyes snapped back to me. "Like either of us has a choice." Before I could start to figure out what that meant, he nudged me down the hall. "Let's go, Maddie."

I didn't bother hurrying to where I was certain Gary was waiting for me. I took my time walking down the hall, memorizing as many details as I could in case I got the chance to run again. This house didn't seem as big as Gary's house in Los Angeles. That monstrosity on top of a hill, overlooking the valley and homes below with its manicured lawn and blindingly white outside.

This house seemed like…well, a house. Turning the corner Gary had, I found a small alcove outside a pair of open doors that led to an office. When I hesitated, Evan gave me a gentle push to enter. Once I cleared the threshold, he followed me in and closed the doors.

Gary waited for me, the same constipated look of annoyance on his face. He sat behind a large mahogany desk that matched the wall of built-in bookshelves to his right. Two chairs sat in front of his desk, the legs and arms the same dark wood color, the seats dark green.

"Sit," he ordered, jerking his chin at the chairs.

My spine stiffened, and I prepared myself to fight him on everything, including whether or not I would sit anywhere, let alone where he demanded.

With a sigh, Gary glanced past me to Evan. "Get Angela."

Alarm bells went off in my head as Evan slipped out of the room. "What? Why?"

"Sit. Down." He glared at me, the cold look in his eyes sending a chill through my bones.

Seething inside, I did what he said, but sat in the chair opposite the one he'd indicated.

I would take any win, no matter how trivial or small, against this monster.

"Where am I?" I asked.

"Where you belong," he replied, then added, "for now." He leaned back in his chair, his lip curling with disdain when he finished his assessment of me. "You look awful."

"Sorry," I muttered. "Next time I'm kidnapped, held captive, and drugged, I'll ask them to make sure to include a mani-pedi."

He shook his head. "I'll admit that you've surprised me. I thought you'd be much easier to break than your sister."

"Well you could always set me on fire, but that seems a little redundant," I deadpanned, glaring at him and daring him to deny he'd killed Madelaine.

A smile ghosted across his mouth. "The fire was Evan's idea. I wanted her sold to a brothel in Thailand and worked until there was nothing left of her for fat old men to use. That cunt cost me a lot, and she deserved to pay. But Evan was right; she needed to be put down for good."

"Wow," I muttered, shaking my head. "I guess we're done with pretending you're anything resembling a human being, aren't we?"

"Well, I'm done pretending you're worth anything more than a poker chip," he agreed. "But you do still have some value, and I'm ready to cash it in."

I was stopped from asking what he meant by that when Evan and my mother came in. Evan closed the doors and stayed by them while my mother went to stand next to Gary's desk.

"But before that, I think it's time I reiterate your place," Gary finished, standing up and pulling off his suit jacket. He laid it over the back of his chair before turning and backhanding my mom across the face. She cried out and fell into the wall.

"Jesus," I hissed, starting to get up. Hands clamped down on my shoulders and kept me in the chair as Gary punched her in the stomach.

Mom coughed and dropped to her knees in time for Gary to kick her ribs.

"Stop!" I screamed, struggling against Evan.

Gary grabbed a handful of Mom's hair and wrenched her neck back while looking at me. "I told your mother to help you get ready, and yet here you are, looking like *that*."

"That wasn't... I..." Shit. I tried to formulate a response.

"I'm sorry," Mom gasped. "Please—"

He reared back and slammed his fist into the side of her head with a sickening *thunk*. My stomach twisted, and I thought I'd throw up.

"*Stop*," I begged, tears spilling over as I watched my mother curl into a ball. "Please, just stop. I'm sorry, okay?"

"I don't give a fuck if you're sorry," Gary retorted, stepping back from Mom and dropping into his chair. "She disobeyed me, Madison. It's time you learned there are consequences for your actions."

I stared at Mom, feeling helpless and beyond frustrated as pressure swelled in my chest while she sobbed into the floor, hands around her ears.

"Have you learned your lesson yet?"

I turned my attention to Gary, who nodded at Evan. A second later, Evan let me go and moved away.

"Just... don't hurt her," I whispered, rubbing my forehead with shaking fingers.

"Now," Gary started, his tone way too calm for someone who'd just beaten the shit out of a woman, "let's discuss our next steps. You and Ryan fucked up a lot of things for me, but I've figured a way out of it."

Here it came. I wrapped my fingers around the arms of the chair, steeling myself.

Gary glanced at a paper on his desk. "The money issue is being sorted out, but it's going to cost both of us, I'm afraid."

I tried to pick my words carefully, my attention divided between Gary and my mother, who was slowly starting to get up. "I don't know where the money is. Ash buried it in offshore accounts. It's not like I memorized the account numbers."

"It doesn't matter. I have someone else working on locating them now, and as soon as they do, you'll sign them over to me." Gary flashed me an almost pleasant smile. He turned to my mom, who was now on her feet. "Why don't you go get some ice for your face, Ang?"

Mom gave him a small smile and a weak nod. "I will. I'm sorry, Gary."

His expression chilled. "Don't let me down again, sweetheart."

My mouth fell open as I watched them, wondering what kind of sick *Twilight Zone* episode I'd stumbled into.

"I won't," she promised. She spared me a glare, full of contempt, as she left the room.

"Where were we?" Gary murmured, rubbing his jaw. "Oh, right. What *you're* going to do to fix the mess you've created."

I wouldn't bother touching that comment. Instead, I sighed and asked, "And what am I going to do?"

"What we originally planned," he replied. "Get married."

I couldn't help glancing at my bare left hand. "Already did that."

"You did," he agreed, "and I *un*did it for you."

I frowned until he pushed a paper across the desk at me. I took it slowly, like it was a viper waiting to strike. As I read the Dissolution of Marriage line, I kinda wished it *had* been a viper.

But I still didn't get it as I looked up at him. "So, you want me to, what? Remarry Ryan like you originally planned? Sorry if us eloping messed up your grand wedding plans."

He laughed like I was an idiot for suggesting such a silly thing, and worry started eating at my insides.

"God, no." He actually smiled at me. "If I could get away with it, I'd finish what those idiots in prison couldn't and put Ryan Cain on a slab in the morgue."

My heart squeezed so sharply, so violently, that my vision went blurry. "No. You can't—"

"I think we're past you telling me what I can't do," he interrupted, arching a brow. "So, let me tell you what *you're* going to do unless you want me to commission one of Jasper Woods's old sniper buddies to test their skills with the back of Cain's head."

Air rushed out of my lungs and wouldn't come back in.

"I've arranged a new marriage for you. One that will happen

before the end of the month." Gary smiled benignly, shrugging. "I get my money, minus a fee I have to pay your new fiancé for taking you off my hands, and he gets a pretty, *compliant* wife."

I stared down at the floor, wondering if I could let him think for even a second that I was considering it.

The obvious answer was yes. I should tell Gary what he wanted to hear and bide my time until I could break free. But something in me wouldn't yield, wouldn't even joke about giving to someone else what I'd already vowed to Ryan.

Ryan wouldn't want me to give in to this. He'd tell me he could take care of himself, and he could. Especially with the guys behind him. No, Gary wouldn't get a chance at Ryan again, and I just needed to hang on until Ryan got me out of this mess or I figured it out for myself.

Either way? Fuck Gary Cabot and his demands.

"No."

Gary's eyes narrowed. "What did you say?"

I took in a deep breath and met his eyes. "I said no. I won't do it. I love Ryan, and I won't marry someone else."

His head tilted to the side. "Did you not see what I just did to your mother?"

"I saw it, and I also saw her accept it. If this is the life my mother chooses, then fine. I'm done trying to help her if she doesn't want it." I leaned forward, fire in my belly and hate in my eyes for this asshole. "But I'm done playing your games."

"Care to make a wager on that?" The teasing lilt in Gary's tone sent alarms blaring through my brain, but I ignored them.

I was so sick of being his puppet. Of him thinking he could control and manipulate me.

I was done.

"Lock me up." I shrugged like it didn't bother me. "Do whatever you want, but I'm not playing along, and I won't betray Ryan."

Gary chuckled and glanced over my shoulder at Evan. "She still thinks she has a say. It's almost adorable if it wasn't so troublesome."

He turned his attention to me. "I'm amazed at how selfish you can be, Madison."

I snorted. "Seriously? *You're* going to lecture me on—"

He held up a hand. "Let me show you what happens when selfish little girls don't learn their lessons. Someone pays the price." His smile went glacial as he reached for the laptop on the corner of his desk. Looking away from me, he opened it and tapped a few buttons before spinning it around so I could see the screen.

It was a website. Frowning, I narrowed my eyes and focused more. It was a Detroit news site talking about yet another murder. Not surprising, but apparently this one was getting extra attention because the murdered person was a little old woman who had been mugged and stabbed to death outside the library where she…

My entire world tilted on its axis as the blood rushed to my toes.

"No. No, no, no." I covered my mouth in horror as Gary angled the laptop so he could scroll down to the attached photo. Flowers were placed at the entrance to the library where I'd worked with Marge.

Marge, the only adult in my life who'd given a shit about me. Who had let me spend hours at a small table in the library when I was a kid and needed a safe place when Mom was on a bender. Marge, the woman who had driven me home and looked out for me as best she could.

She was dead.

Murdered.

And Gary had killed her…

… because of me.

I lifted my eyes to him, unable to see him through the blurry mess of tears.

He snapped the laptop shut and smiled at me. "I think I've made my point, haven't I? Evan, take her back to her room. She needs to get ready. Her new fiancé will be here soon."

CHAPTER 15

MADDIE

I was numb as Evan led me from Gary's office and herded me up the stairs. I stumbled twice, not feeling my feet as I moved forward. All I could see was Marge.

She'd cared about me when no one else had, and I'd *left* her. I'd assumed Madelaine's life and, aside from a few calls at the start of summer that she never returned, I hadn't looked back. I'd walked away, found love, and fucking left her behind.

I pushed open the door to my new room and looked around helplessly. I wanted Ryan and my friends. I wanted to go back to us all being together at Brookfield with Cori and their grandpa and Court's brothers.

Dammit.

The sense of being completely alone was crushing me. I couldn't do this. It was too much.

I could feel Evan watching me, maybe waiting to see if I'd really fall apart or to report back to his boss that I wasn't behaving.

What would Ryan do?

"Stop it," I whispered to myself, squeezing my eyes shut and balling my hands into fists. I swallowed down the rising tide of panic and forced myself to clear my mind.

I couldn't control what had happened to Marge. Or what my mother did. I couldn't control Gary or Evan.

But I could control *me*. How I handled things in this moment and going forward was all on me. I could sit down and fall apart, or I could collect all the broken pieces and forge them into something stronger. Something no one could take away.

"It's easier if you do what he says," Evan said. "I tried to tell you. *Both* of you."

I turned slowly to face him. "You killed Madelaine."

He didn't flinch. "Yes."

"You set the fire."

He nodded. "Yes. After I killed her."

A gasp ripped from my chest. "The fire didn't…"

Evan's jaw clenched. "Have you ever seen someone burn to death? It isn't pretty. The fire isn't what gets them. Choking on smoke, your lungs seizing up and your airway collapsing… It's a brutal way to die. So, yeah. I killed her before that, because I'm not a total monster."

"Yeah. You're a real saint," I snapped.

"Your father had a few other ways he wanted her to die. My way was by far the most humane, so take comfort in that."

"You murdered my sister, and you're standing here telling me about it like we're talking about the weather." I folded my arms protectively over myself and stepped away from him.

The corner of his mouth twitched. "Relax. If Gary wanted you dead, you'd be dead. I'm not the one you have to worry about, unless you keep pushing back."

"Did you even care about my sister?" I remembered the way she'd introduced him as her boyfriend months ago. God, it felt like a different lifetime.

He shrugged. "She was a job, but I guess I cared a little since the idea of her suffering didn't bring me any joy."

"Well, aren't you a prince?" I drawled.

"What do you want me to say? Gary knew she was out of control and trying to find you, so he had me handle her."

My eye twitched. "*Handle* her?"

"Seduce her." He didn't seem even remotely sorry about it.

"Great, so you're Gary's whore. Good for you, Evan." I slow-clapped for him, amazed at the sheer fucking audacity.

His eyes narrowed. "I would've thought that if anyone would understand, it was you."

"Me?" I gaped at him.

Evan's head tilted, like I was a puzzle he couldn't quite work out. "You know what it's like to struggle every day. To be abandoned and hurt by the people who were supposed to protect you. To grow up living in fear, starving and cold. I swore I'd break the cycle."

"So did I, but somehow *serial killer* wasn't the way my pendulum swung. I wanted to be better. *Do* better." I shook my head and waved a hand at him. "You became a worse version."

He inclined his head. "Perhaps."

"How long did you work for Gary before he asked you to kill my sister?" As twisted as it was, I was learning more now from Evan and his sociopathic nonchalant answers than I had in the last eight months.

He eyed me with suspicion. "Why?"

"I'm wondering if you were there the whole time Madelaine was being abused," I replied. "I'm wondering if you knew Adam was hurting her."

"Yes," Evan replied. "Madelaine told me about him. About what he used to do to her and when she decided it was easier to give into his advances. That was when she learned to use sex to manipulate men. The only one she couldn't influence was her father. That was a line not even he would cross."

"Thank God for small mercies," I spat. "You're an asshole."

"Why? Because I didn't care? Because I accepted long ago that I could be the hunter or the prey and chose the one that ensured I wasn't a victim?" His gaze hardened. "Don't be deliberately obtuse. Do what Gary wants and stay out of his way."

"Or what? He'll have you seduce and kill me, too?" I scoffed and rolled my eyes.

"No," he answered. "You're it, Madison. There is no fallback plan.

Madelaine is dead, and that means Gary has no one else to use except *you*. He won't kill you, but he'll make you beg for death every day for the rest of your life if you test him. That little old lady was a warning. He'll kill everyone you love, brutalize and violate them. He'll take them apart and make you watch every second."

I swallowed and edged back from him, from the promise of violence and pain in his eyes.

His gaze slid past me. "You have less than two hours to get ready. Don't be late." He turned and left, sliding past my mom as she came into my room.

She faced me, one of her eyes puffy and swollen, her cheek still red and starting to bruise. She offered a brittle smile. "Let's get you ready for tonight."

"I can get ready by myself," I snapped.

Her eyes narrowed and she closed the door before coming to stand in front of me, her toes brushing mine. "You're not going to ruin this for me, Madison. Now, get yourself into that shower while I get your outfit ready. Your father selected it special for this evening."

Of course he had. Probably picked the underwear, too.

Part of me wanted to argue. To fight her and dig in. But I was tired, and this wasn't necessarily a battle I needed to worry about. If Gary and Mom wanted to dress me up like a doll and parade me in front of a guy they thought could tame me, good for them.

And good luck.

The pale blue dress wasn't the worst thing I'd ever worn. Honestly, part of me wondered if Gary would dress me up in something short and tight so that the guy he was selling me to could see all the goods on display.

With its corseted bodice and skirt that flared into soft layers around my knees, the silk dress was actually something I might've picked for myself. It was the kind of dress a little girl would twirl in until she fell over from dizziness. The thin straps were beaded with pearls that matched the choker on my neck and the pearl studs in my ears.

Mom had tried doing something with my hair, but she'd never been good at more than a sloppy ponytail, so I finished the task myself, pulling it back into a long French braid with a few pieces framing my face. Once that was done, I applied my own makeup while Mom watched and made comments.

No black eyeliner. Neutral eyeshadow colors. Soft pink lip gloss.

As I finished slicking a third coat of gloss onto my lips—because the extra shine was needed, apparently—Mom pulled out a pair of white ballet flats and dropped them at my feet.

After I put them on, I got up and looked at myself in the mirror. A second later, Mom appeared at my back and beamed. "Beautiful."

I resisted the urge to snort. Sure, I looked great if the guy was into the Lifetime-movie battered fiancée look.

Bruises dotted my body. My arms, wrists, legs... The choker hid the majority of the one on my throat, but there was no denying I'd been through some shit. I briefly wondered if whoever Gary was pushing me onto would be horrified or turned on by all the marks.

"Now," Mom continued, brushing an imaginary blemish from my shoulder, "let's go make sure your father approves."

"Of course." I couldn't keep the sarcasm out of my tone. Honestly, I didn't bother trying.

I followed Mom back through the house to Gary's office so she could present me to him. Again, I swallowed the urge to scream at the top of my lungs. Evan was standing in front of Gary's desk, and we'd clearly interrupted them.

Gary's annoyed gaze flickered to us. "Knocking is the proper way to enter a room, Angela."

"The doors were open," I pointed out.

Mom sucked in a sharp breath. "I'm sorry, of course you're right. I just wanted you to see how pretty our girl looks." She stepped back and wrapped an arm around my waist.

I flinched but managed not to pull away as Gary's gaze crawled over me.

"Not bad," he finally muttered. "Make sure everything is ready for our guest. I want dinner served promptly at seven."

"Of course," Mom agreed, practically purring at him. She squeezed my waist like this was normal. "You look stunning, Maddie." She gave me a wide smile as she left the room, her hips swaying with exaggeration that I cringed at because it was solely for Gary's benefit.

Gross.

My nails cut into my palms until I was sure they were bleeding.

"We'll finish up later, Evan," Gary said. "Maddie and I need to make sure we're on the same page for this evening so things go well."

Evan gave him a curt nod and walked out, closing the doors and leaving me alone with Gary.

"Why don't you have a seat?"

"I'm good standing," I replied.

He smirked. "It wasn't a question. Sit down, Maddie."

Hands still clenched, I complied and sat on the edge of the seat.

"You look lovely," he complimented. When I didn't answer, his face contorted into a scowl. "The polite thing to do is say 'thank you.'"

"Thank you," I ground out.

His glare intensified. "Try sounding like you mean it."

"Why? We both know I don't," I snapped.

He slammed a fist on the desk. "I won't have you be disrespectful to your new husband."

"Do you want to tell me how to suck his dick, too?" I snarled before I could censor my own thoughts.

Gary's face went a disturbing shade of purple and he stood up fast enough to send his chair toppling over backwards. He rounded the desk and shouted for Evan at the same time.

A chill slid down my spine at the unhinged look in his eye.

"It was a—" My words were silenced when he grabbed my throat. The pearls dug into my skin, pressing against my windpipe.

"Sir," Evan said from behind me as I clawed at Gary's hands. "You know marking her might be an issue. He'll want to announce the engagement immediately, and we'll be taking photos."

Instantly Gary's hands relaxed, and he stepped back. His whole body was trembling as he glared at me before his gaze moved to Evan. "Hold her shoulders down. Don't let her up."

Evan's hands pinned me to the chair for the second time that day. His hold was unbreakable, but not as tight as it could've been. Not enough to bruise or *mark* me.

"It's a pity that you're such a clumsy girl," Gary said, towering over me. He reached for my wrist with one hand and my pinkie finger with the other. Slowly, he started to bend it backward.

I cried out and tried to twist away, but there was nowhere to go. Gasping breaths clawed from my chest as the pain splintered from my finger up my arm. I bit the insides of my cheeks until I tasted blood, waiting for the digit to crack and the pain to amplify.

"What the fuck is going on here?" a voice boomed from behind us.

Gary looked up with a sneer but stopped where he'd been about to break my finger. "You're early."

"And you're touching what belongs to me," the voice replied in a dangerously familiar accent. "Let her go. Now. I'm not buying damaged goods." A pause. "Well, further damaged goods. I see she's got a few marks already."

Gary chuckled, the sound ominous as he let me go. "I'm sure you understand what it takes to discipline someone as willful as she is."

A barely muffled scoff. "Indeed, but I've never needed an extra set of hands to help me control a woman."

Gary's cheeks turned crimson. "Until she's yours, I'll handle her as I see fit."

"We'll see about that."

Gary looked at Evan and jerked his head. A second later, Evan released me, and I turned to see the newcomer, not entirely sure why I knew that voice or why hope fluttered in my chest as he spoke.

That quickly, hope fled as I looked into cold, emotionless eyes. This wasn't the guy I knew. The guy who'd sort of been my friend.

Charles smiled down at me, no warmth or caring in his expression. "Hello, Maddie. Or should I say, hello, my darling future wife?"

CHAPTER 16

MADDIE

"I'm not marrying you," I blurted out, recoiling in my chair even as Charles stared at me with those mossy green eyes. In a formal charcoal-gray suit and white shirt, he looked like he was going to a board meeting.

His head tilted. "Not today. But soon enough."

"Why?" I whispered, ignoring the fact that Gary and Evan were still in the room and watching.

He chuckled, the sound familiar and foreign at the same time. "Business, of course, sweetheart."

I flinched. "Don't call me that."

His eyes hardened, his jaw going tight. "I'll call you whatever I bloody well please."

I bristled, forgetting where I was and seeing him only as the guy who had been nice to me. "Like hell—"

"Enough," he snapped, then turned to Gary. "I see what you mean."

Gary crossed his arms and leaned on the edge of his desk. "She needs a firm hand."

"Obviously," Charles agreed, shaking his head and glancing at me. "But she's pretty enough and will be able to give me heirs. That's all that matters."

I clenched my jaw to keep from saying something that would get me slapped or worse. It was disgusting to hear them talk about me like I was nothing more than a broodmare to be traded and bought.

Freaking awesome.

All I could do was glare at the floor until Gary started laughing.

"See? Apparently she *can* be taught," he commented. "But she isn't yours until I get what I'm owed."

"I have my associate working on locating the funds. It shouldn't take more than a day or two." Charles straightened and shoved his hands into his pockets. "Ash Newhouse is good, but Tyler is better."

I perked up at the mention of Ash. My gaze flickered back and forth between them.

Gary smirked. "Even better, but that doesn't help me at this present moment. And until the money is in my account, I'm afraid I can't let my precious daughter go."

"Of course." Charles reached into his inner suit pocket, and Evan stiffened, going on alert.

Not that I would be lucky enough for Charles to pull out a gun and shoot Gary.

"Easy, mate," Charles said with a laugh. He extracted an envelope and passed it to Gary. "Consider this a show of good will."

Gary took the envelope and opened it, his brows pulled together. A slow smile spread across his face. His gaze moved to me and then Charles. "Not a bad down payment."

Charles's hand settled possessively on my shoulder, his thumb stroking my bare skin. "I wanted to prove I was serious."

His touch felt wrong, and I endured it for only a second before I jerked away. Or tried to. His hand tightened and he glared at me. "Sit still."

"Get *off* me," I hissed, not bothering to mask the contempt in my tone.

Gary laughed again, the sound caustic. "I tried to warn you."

"Leave us," Charles demanded, not breaking eye contact with me.

"Why?" Gary pressed. "I think I'd rather see for myself that you can handle her."

Fucking asshole, I seethed.

"As tacky as that sounds," Charles drawled, "I won't have an audience while I discipline my property."

Gary *tsk*ed under his breath. "Not yours yet, son."

"I can cancel that check and walk away from this deal right this second," Charles reminded him. "You need me more than I need you."

Gary glowered for a moment before dipping his head with a grimace. "Fine. But first, we need the photo for the announcement."

"Get up," Charles demanded and literally snapped his fingers like I was a dog.

I stared at him and didn't move fast enough, because a hard hand clamped onto the back of my neck and wrenched me up.

Charles smirked as he went to stand in front of Gary's bookcase. He caught me when Evan shoved me forward. His hands landed on my hips and pulled me close.

"Smile, love," he whispered in my ear as he wrapped his arms around me from behind.

I started to struggle, and he held tighter while Gary glared at me from the other side of his phone.

"Fucking behave," he hissed at me.

"Go to *hell*," I shot back, still fighting.

He paused, eyes narrowing with scorn. "That library you used to help at had a children's program, didn't it? Met on certain days. It would be a shame if something were to happen to all those innocent lives."

I stilled, remembering Marge's death.

"Now smile," Gary commanded.

I forced myself to smile even as I died inside.

"Let's get something a bit more... intimate," Gary suggested. "Charles, why don't you kiss her?"

Charles shifted me around in his arms and I barely felt it.

"Make it look good, honey," Gary called.

Charles's lips touched mine, and everything in me wanted to step back and run as far and as fast as possible to get away. Instead, I stayed still and didn't move as Charles tried to coax my mouth open.

He tasted like licorice and brandy, and all wrong. His lips slanted over mine, trying to coax me into the kiss, but I was about as turned on as an onion. His lips weren't the ones I was used to moving against mine. The ones I loved and that could drive me crazy.

"For fuck's sake," Gary hissed. "Do better, or I'll have Evan come help you."

Flinching, I raised my hands and let them rest on Charles's chest. I tilted my head and let my lips part enough for him to kiss me in earnest, his tongue touching my bottom lip.

Something in my heart cracked.

"Perfect," Gary murmured, and I was turning away before he'd even finished speaking.

Charles let me go and stepped back with an unreadable expression while I forced myself to look anywhere but at the guy I'd thought was my friend.

"Send the photo and announcement to all the major publication outlets," Gary ordered Evan. "I want the entire world to know my daughter will be marrying a future duke."

"On it," Evan replied and stalked away.

"Leave us," Charles demanded, jerking his chin at Gary. "My bride and I need to have a chat."

Gary smirked knowingly. "Very well. I'm going to make sure everything is prepared for dinner." He turned and left, and as soon as the doors were closed, I yanked myself away from Charles.

"What the fuck is wrong with you?" I demanded, rounding the desk and making sure to keep it between us. I wiped my lips, needing to rid myself of his taste and feel.

Charles watched me. "You don't seem happy to see me."

My brows shot up. "You're kidding, right?"

His eyes narrowed and he reached into his pocket to pull out his cell phone.

My muscles tightened. "What—"

He held up a finger as he tapped a few buttons, then he pocketed his phone with a smile. "Okay, we can talk now."

"Talk?" I scoffed, looking at him like he was out of his damn mind.

His gaze darted to the closed door before he stepped toward me. I instantly moved back, and his brows slammed down. "I'm not going to hurt you, Maddie."

"Bullshit," I spat, readying myself to claw his pretty face off if he touched me again. "What the fuck do you think you just did? I didn't want you to kiss me!"

He actually looked ashamed. "Maddie, *please*. I don't know how much time we have until they come back." His gaze searched mine, softening enough that I could see the guy I'd met in the quad my first day at Pacific Cross. The guy who had been willing to be my friend when the school turned against me. He'd stood up to Ryan and tried to protect me even when I didn't need it.

"I don't understand," I uttered, more confused than ever. Everything was changing so fast that I couldn't keep up anymore.

He held up his hands and moved around the desk to stand before me. "Listen, it's not what you think, all right? I'm playing his game for now—we *both* have to so we can get you out of here."

"Why are you even here?" I asked, still not understanding but wanting to so badly that my chest ached.

"Your father and mine used to do business together. Things soured a few years back, but unfortunately there are still some accounts that overlap with Cabot Global." He paused as if to make sure I was keeping up. When I nodded, he went on, "Gary reached out and offered me a deal—if I could help him access some money that had been stolen from him by his competitors, then he would give *you* to me." He blushed and looked down.

"Why would you even entertain that idea?" I demanded.

"Because I knew something had to be wrong," he admitted, "and I was curious. If it wasn't me, then it would be someone else. I wasn't the only person he offered you to. I was just the one who had someone employed who could help him recover his money."

I buried my face in my hands, a slow throb building in the base of my skull. "I still don't get it."

He took my hands in his, gently pulling them down. "Maddie, I'm not here to hurt you, but I had a feeling you were in trouble. And when news hit that Ryan had been arrested, I assumed the worst."

"That was a safe assumption," I admitted. "But—"

"My motives aren't entirely altruistic," he confessed, looking down. "Gary took something very valuable to me, and I intend to make him pay for it. Helping you is my way into his orbit, but Maddie, I need you to play along. At least for now. I swear I'll get you out of here."

"Call Ryan," I whispered, hope fluttering in my soul for the first time in forever. "He can get me—"

"Please forgive me, but I can't." He looked truly apologetic. "You're the connection I need to Gary. I promise I'll protect you, but I have to see this through. At least for now."

I began to shake my head.

His hands squeezed mine, the touch bordering on desperation. "Please, Maddie. I'm begging you to help me. If it's too much, then I swear I'll get you out and back to Ryan. Just give me a few days."

I dropped my head back to stare up at the ceiling. "Charles, I just want to go home."

"So do I." His voice broke at the end, and he cleared his throat. "But I have to see this through. Not just for me but for… for her, too."

"Her?"

His lips pressed together, and he looked back at the door again, like he was waiting for someone to bust through. "I can't explain right now."

As if he'd summoned them into existence, I heard footsteps coming down the hallway.

"Please," he begged, meeting my eyes again. "Trust me."

My eyes slid shut, the weight of the world pressing on my shoulders as time slipped through my fingers. "Okay. I'll trust you." My eyes cut to the door as the footsteps drew closer. Squaring my shoulders, I turned to Charles. "Hit me."

His eyes snapped open wide. "What? No fucking way."

"Do it," I ground out, knowing if Gary walked through that door and I looked just the same way as he'd left that he would get suspicious. "Dammit, Charles, fucking *do it*."

"Look, Maddie, it's *fine*. My phone is blocking anything he might be using to record our conversation right now."

Damn, I should've thought of that because Gary was sneaky as a weasel. "Okay, but isn't that *more* suspicious? He's sick, and I'm sure he'll want proof that you taught me a lesson or something, so we need to make it look real."

He met my gaze and shook his head. "No—"

"If you don't, *he* will," I hissed back. I sighed quietly. "I'd rather it be you."

"Dammit, Maddie." He looked absolutely sickened at the idea, and I felt better about making the decision to trust him.

For now at least.

"Charles—"

The doorknob started to twist, and I saw the moment Charles realized I was right. It was a split second before his open palm cracked across my face with enough force to make me fall into the desk.

Ow, ow, fucking ow!

My cheek throbbed, and even still, I knew he'd reined in his strength. He wasn't as big or muscular as Ryan, but he was on the soccer team at school and in great shape.

Gary chuckled from the doorway. "Dinner's ready, unless you need a few more minutes to finish up?" No one should sound that happy about seeing their daughter in pain, and his happiness only strengthened my resolve to beat this man at his own game.

Charles kept his back to the door and Gary, facing me. He'd gone a little pale, and I could see the slight tremble in his hand as he watched me. "No. I think Maddie and I are on the same page now, aren't we, darling?"

I nodded slowly, holding his gaze and hoping he could see that I was okay. I slowly straightened, and he reached out to grab my elbow. As he guided me toward the door, his hand was still shaking. I pretended to trip, giving myself an excuse to cover his hand with mine under the guise of catching my footing. I gave what I hoped was a reassuring squeeze.

After a beat, his touch on my elbow tightened for a split second. Then his mask slipped back into place, and he turned to Gary. "What's for dinner? I'm famished."

CHAPTER 17

MADDIE

The way my mother fawned all over Charles was more than a little disturbing. The second we walked into the room, she wrapped her arms around him in a hug that smashed her chest against his, and she stayed there until Charles actually had to push her away. She had changed into a green dress that accentuated the sharp angles of her skinny frame, and when she smiled, I realized she'd had some dental work done recently, too.

But not even the heavy makeup could hide the bruises on her face from earlier, and I could only look away as Charles's inquisitive gaze landed on me over her shoulder during their never-ending hug.

Evan didn't join us for dinner. I sat between Gary and Charles with my mother across from me. Acute tension filled the room as my mother chattered manically about the floral arrangement in the center of the table. She waved her hands and downed two glasses of wine before the first course was even brought out.

This was off to a stellar start.

I kept my head down and picked at the food. I was too anxious to eat even though my stomach felt hollow. My insides had been carved open and scooped out like a jack-o-lantern, leaving me with just a thin shell holding what was left together.

All it took was one small blow and everything would implode, and the more my mother tried to flirt with my... whatever Charles was, the more my anxiety coiled in my gut as I waited for Gary to lose his shit.

Finally, after Mom not so teasingly asked Charles if he had any handsome older brothers, Gary shut her down.

"Enough, Angela," he snapped, glaring at her as he sipped his glass of bourbon.

Mom ducked her head. "I'm sorry." She trembled, and I wasn't sure if it was because she expected Gary to hit her or because she was starting to come down from her high and needed something to level her out before she crashed.

Either way? This entire situation was beyond messed up.

"So, Charles," Gary began as the starter plates were cleared away, "tell me how you've been. It's been, what? Five years since I last saw you at your mother's funeral?"

If I hadn't had my eyes laser focused on my now-empty place setting, I might've missed the way Charles's fingers tightened around the stem of his wine glass for just a second.

"Yes," he answered in a smooth tone, sounding completely unaffected.

"What made you decide to switch to PC from Oxford? Finally tired of the abysmal weather in the U.K.?" It sounded like Gary was... mocking him. "I remember your mother absolutely hated it."

That caught my attention. Gary had known Charles's mother? I lifted my gaze to Charles.

He didn't bat an eye. "I wanted a change of scenery before I locked myself into my role and titles. I figured, why not spend my last two years on the other side of the pond? PC does have an excellent pre-law program."

"And your father?" There was a calculating gleam in Gary's icy eyes. He knew something, was prodding at something, that he was hoping would upset Charles.

Why?

Charles's lips quirked into a thin smile that showed a hint of his dimples. "He sends his regards and looks forward to us being united once and for all."

The smile disappeared and Gary's face twisted into disgust. "I'm sure he does."

I leaned back as silent servers brought out the next dish and caught Charles's attention. He flashed me a quick wink that helped settle my stomach enough for me to pick up my fork and eat. I skipped my glass of red wine and sipped my water as I chewed on autopilot, not really tasting the food as I tried to pay attention to what Gary and Charles were talking about.

A few business deals both companies were involved in. Something about stock prices rising—that made Gary happy—and a deal that fell through in Bangladesh—that made Charles *un*happy. Mom was on another planet, fixated on the centerpiece as her lips twisted to one side. She ignored her food and finished her third and fourth glasses of wine.

"Blue and yellow!" Mom exclaimed with a bright smile when there was a lull in conversation. I jumped and looked at her before my gaze shot to Gary.

He clenched his jaw. "Blue and yellow *what?*"

"For the wedding," Mom babbled, waving a hand and sloshing the contents of her water goblet, since Gary had cut off her alcohol. Her eyes tried to focus on me. "They'd be perfect colors, Madis—"

"Angela!" Gary barked, glaring at her.

Mom's face crumpled, and she started to sob.

Loudly.

Charles shot me a worried look, but I battened down the hatches and prepared myself to ride out whatever chaos Hurricane Angela threw at us next.

"My poor girl," she wailed, grabbing her napkin from where it still sat beside her plate instead of across her lap. She knocked all the silverware to the floor with a clatter as she lifted the white linen to her face. "I miss my daughter."

Charles leaned forward. "Madam, your daughter is right here."

Another gut-wrenching cry. "Not the one I want!"

"For fuck's sake," Gary seethed, shoving out of his seat and grabbing her arm. Even from across the table, I could see his knuckles turn white. "It's time for your medicine, Angela."

"Is she unwell?" Charles asked, arching his brows.

Gary yanked her to her feet so fast that she pitched forward, her forehead hitting his chest and smearing a layer of makeup onto his white shirt. Sneering, he pushed her away, and Mom toppled over her chair.

"Jesus," I hissed, getting up. I started around the table to check on her, because she was still sobbing and had her legs in the air, but Gary grabbed my arm and threw me back into my chair hard enough for it to rock back on two legs. Charles caught it with his hand and helped me balance.

"I told you not to touch my fiancée," he reminded Gary, the picture of apathy as he watched the scene unfold.

Gary jabbed a finger in my face. "I'll do as I fucking want until all the money is in my account." He turned and shouted for Evan, ordering his lackey to collect Mom and take her upstairs.

The side door opened, and a server stepped out with the dessert. She made it two steps into the room before Gary knocked the tray from her hands and screamed for her to get out.

If this had been anything but my own life, I probably would've cracked up at the theatrical farce this night had turned into. As it was, exhaustion pulled at my mind and settled into my bones. Between the drugs still circulating through my system and the events of the day, cracks were forming in my head.

Maybe that was why a soft giggle managed to slip past my lips before I pressed them together.

I knew I'd messed up the second Charles stiffened and Gary turned to me, his eyes full of that crazy darkness that went soul deep.

"Something funny?" he demanded in a clipped tone.

"Easy," Charles admonished, pushing back from the table and ready to intervene if Gary went after me.

Again.

Gary's eyes cut to Charles, and there was no denying the mocking glint. "I suppose you're all right with her being an insipid bitch?" He scoffed. "Maybe I was wrong. Maybe I should find someone else to handle her."

"Maybe you should stop making the same insolent threats," Charles countered, tossing his napkin onto the table and standing up. "I'm growing tired of them, and we both know it all circles back to the same thing—you need my help."

Charles stepped between Gary and me. "Let's conclude our business in private, shall we? I tire of interruptions from our lessers, and I need a bit more information so Tyler can transfer the funds without delay."

Gary breathed in deeply, his chest swelling. "Fine."

"Go to bed, Madelaine," Charles ordered me, that chilly tone back. "I'll see you tomorrow."

I meekly scooted my chair back and murmured my excuses, grateful to have a buffer between myself and Gary. Then I rushed up to my room and almost screamed at the missing lock on the door. I craved a moment of feeling safe, even if it was a lie.

I'd survived another day, but I wasn't sure how many I had left.

Sliding down the door, I pulled my knees to my chest and dropped my head. Tears burned the backs of my eyes, but I willed them away.

"I can do this," I whispered, needing those words to brand themselves into every part of my heart and mind. "I can do this."

Maybe if I said it enough, it would be true.

CHAPTER 18

RYAN

After the shitshow at Highwater, we'd needed a safe place to think and regroup. A place where, once we found Maddie, we could figure out our next moves.

The house Ash had found in the mountains of Wyoming was perfect. Purchased under a bogus company name as a corporate retreat, the three-story cabin had nine bedrooms and twelve bathrooms, and was accessible only via a single road that wound up the mountain for over a mile. Even so, Bishop and Knight locked the place down tighter than the Pentagon with cameras and security feeds—which Ash made sure were unhackable—and a myriad of sensors that let us know if so much as a rabbit's tail passed a little too close to the perimeter.

The first day of December dumped nine inches of snow on the area, but no one seemed to care. It marked ten days since I'd seen my wife.

Pain lanced through my chest.

Ex-wife, thanks to Gary's bullshit.

"Stop tensing up," Knight snapped as he prodded the stitches on my side and checked how I was healing. All the other bruises and cuts had healed except this one. Fucker had stuck that knife in pretty deep.

I glared at him and didn't bother relaxing.

He sighed and lowered my shirt. "You're healing fine, but you should—"

"If you say rest, I'll hide your leg," I threatened, my gaze dropping to where the prosthetic was hidden by his jeans.

"Fucker," he griped, shaking his head and stepping away. He closed up the medical kit before turning back to me. "We should be able to take the stitches out by the end of the week."

"Yay," I deadpanned, not giving a shit about the pieces of material holding my side together. It itched like a bitch, to the point that the healing process was becoming almost worse than actually being stabbed.

Rolling his eyes, Knight turned away and washed his hands in the sink of the bathroom that connected his and Bishop's rooms. Knight had gotten a lot of field experience during his time with the Army, and after he'd lost part of his leg in an IED explosion in Iraq and been discharged, he'd taken medic training. Having someone with medical experience helped when things went sideways on a Phoenix mission, and we'd been wondering if it was time to seriously consider expanding the team and adding a fulltime medic.

"Hey," I said, catching his attention. "Have you ever wanted to go back to med school?"

Knight's dark brows slammed down over his equally dark eyes. "What?"

I shrugged, trying to play it off. "You're good at this shit." I waved a hand at the kit he was stashing under the sink. "We've talked about expanding the team, and we thought having someone around with medical experience would be an asset."

He leaned a hip on the sink. "Would I like to? Sure. But we're a three-man team, Ry. Even when Rook joins us next year after his contract is up, we're still not ready to lose a member. You'd be better off hiring a doctor."

"Maybe. But if it's something you want—"

"Fuck," he huffed with a smirk. "Maddie really has you by the dick, doesn't she? Since when do you give a fuck about our hopes and dreams and shit?"

A wry smile tugged at my lips. "It was just a thought, bro."

"Well, table it until we're not holed up in the middle of nowhere and things are stable," he advised, shaking his head.

I snorted, wondering if things would ever be stable again. Wondering when I'd see Maddie or Cori or Grandpa. A slow headache started building at the base of my neck.

"I'm going to see if Ash has anything new," I muttered, turning away.

"If I *was* a doctor," Knight called, "I'd advise him to get some sleep."

I glanced over my shoulder.

He shrugged, feigning indifference, but I could see the concern in his eyes. "Your body can only take so much before it needs to rest. If Ash doesn't take a breather, his body will do it for him."

My first instinct was to tell him to shut up; it didn't matter if we all ran ourselves into the ground to find Madison, but then I realized he might be onto something. My best friend was driving himself crazy trying to unravel the mystery of where Gary had taken her.

After a beat, I nodded, acknowledging Knight's suggestion. Then I went to find my best friend.

As I wandered past Bex's open door, a frustrated groan caught my attention. I paused and stepped into her doorway.

The room Bex had chosen was full of large windows and light, amplified by the snow. It also had a desk where she'd set up a workstation to finish the rest of the semester. Getting the teachers to allow her to switch to a virtual-only option had taken some cajoling and more than a few thinly veiled threats, but it paid off.

"Calculus?" I guessed as I leaned against the wall. Last night, I'd caught her and Court studying for the class she struggled in the most.

Bex turned, her hazel eyes sad and frustrated. "No. My mom."

That made me stand up straighter. "She still pushing back about you being here?"

Bex worried her lower lip between her teeth. "Sort of. I mean, not about this. Whatever you guys said to my dad to get him to agree, worked. He told Mom it's for the best, and I'm not asking how or why she agreed. But she *is* insisting I go to Europe with her for Christmas to see my grandparents."

Getting Malcolm Whittier to agree to us pulling his daughter from Pacific Cross hadn't been hard. All we'd needed to do was threaten to expose the side deals he was making overseas to his bosses in D.C. His technology was highly sought after globally, but he'd been exclusively contracted through the Department of Defense for the past five years, ever since his CryptDuo app took off.

"Winter break is in three weeks. Maddie will be back by then." Fuck, she *had* to be. "Gary will have been handled... If you want to spend the holidays with your family, you should."

Court would throw a bitch fit, but he'd deal.

Or follow her to her grandparents' estate in France like a fucking stalker.

She nodded. "Yeah. I mean, I missed Thanksgiving because I went to Brookfield with you guys. I don't think Mom will let me skip another holiday. Besides, I miss Nana and Papa."

No mention of her father, which wasn't surprising. Betty and Malcolm's marriage had been in name only ever since Bex had been sick as a kid and Malcolm had almost gotten her killed.

Studying Bex, I noticed her hunched shoulders and the dark circles under her eyes. "Have you talked to your dad since..."

Since we'd blown up the way she perceived him. In our world, Bex's dad was one of the rare fathers who actually seemed to care about his daughter, and when we'd divulged to her that he was involved in a human trafficking ring with our fathers—it was his technology that helped them all communicate privately—she'd been gutted.

I couldn't imagine how she'd react if she found out that her father was also partially responsible for her almost dying as a kid. Yeah, he'd been played by Jasper Woods, too, but he'd ultimately given Woods what he needed to manipulate Court into some fucked up shit by using Bex as bait under the guise of a bullshit camping trip in the middle of her chemo treatments.

She shook her head, and some of the shorter pieces of her dark hair fell free of the haphazard ponytail she'd scraped it into. The streaks of green and blue she'd dyed into her hair at the beginning of the year had mostly faded now to blonde.

She licked her lips, uncertainty in her gaze. "My whole life, my parents were the two people I could count on. I mean, I know my dad never hurt me the way yours hurt you, or the way Gary hurt Maddie and her sister, but… I thought he was one of the good guys."

Maybe Maddie really did have my balls in her pocket, because that was the only explanation for me walking into the room and crouching in front of Bex's chair.

"Your dad loves you, Bex," I reminded her. "He just got caught up in some bad shit with a bunch of assholes."

She sniffled a little. "You don't have to make excuses for him, Ryan."

"I'm not," I assured her with a laugh. "I have my own shit to own up to without adding anyone else's to the mix. But I don't want you thinking any of his decisions means he loves you any less."

One corner of her mouth tipped up. "You're not the guy you used to be, you know that?"

I grimaced and stood up. "Yeah."

"It's not a *bad* thing." Bex giggled. "Maddie's been good for you. It's nice to see you—all of you—the way you used to be."

Before we'd abandoned her ass.

Fuck.

"I'm sorry about before," I apologized, meaning it.

Her eyes narrowed. "You know, I hated the way you always called me Rebecca when Maddie first came to school. It was like…"

I waited.

"… like we were just strangers." She sighed and looked down. "You guys meant the world to me at one point. And I know I was younger and annoying and—"

"You were never annoying."

She raised a brow.

"Okay, you were *sometimes* annoying," I conceded with a smile, remembering the way she used to follow us around everywhere. "But after what happened, it was easier to think of you as Rebecca. Not..."

"Becca," she whispered with a sad smile. "*He* still calls me that sometimes."

Of course Court still called her that. She'd always been *his Becca*. It was why Ash, Linc, and I had called her that, too. When Court had cut her off, he'd never had to ask if we'd do the same. We just *had*. The four of us were a team, and we couldn't be friends with her without hurting him. Back then, it was the four of us against the damn world.

"He cares about you," I said, careful not to say too much. There was a lot of history between Bex and Court; history that *they* needed to sort out.

"I hate it when he calls me that," she admitted with a harsh whisper, her lips pressed into a tight line. "I hate it... and I love it. How messed up is that?"

"Emotions are messy." I knew that better than most. "But he's trying."

"I shouldn't care." Her nose wrinkled adorably as she tried to fight what she felt for Court. "But dammit, I still do."

"He's a lucky bastard," I told her, shaking my head. "So am I. The shit I put Maddie through... I don't know why she's still with me."

"She loves you." Bex said it like that answer alone was the key to every problem in the world.

Maybe, in my world, it was.

"I'm not good for her," I confessed. "But I'm too selfish to let her go. I need her. She's everything good in me."

"That's not true. Cori alone is proof of that." Bex reached out and touched my hand. "You're not your father, Ryan. You're not a monster."

I looked at where her hand rested on mine. "A lot of people would disagree with that."

"Not the ones who matter."

The corner of my mouth hooked up. "Touché."

I heard his footsteps before he even entered the room, but it wasn't a surprise; Court didn't stray far from Bex.

"Hey." Uncertainty lingered in his voice as he looked at us, not accusing, but confused as to why I'd be alone with her. It wasn't like Bex and I were best friends. When we were kids, Court was the one she was always hanging around. I could count on my fingers the number of times I'd been alone with her, and most of the occurrences were after I'd met Maddie.

"Everything okay?" Court stared at Bex like he could see through her head and read her mind. Or like he wished he could.

"Totally fine," Bex said with a bright smile that even I could tell was forced.

Court's gaze jerked from me to her. "I thought you might want to finish going over differentials, but if you're busy…" His dark gaze snapped to me, his brows arched.

I stepped back. "I need to find Ash. We were just… catching up."

"Thanks, Ryan," Bex called as I retreated.

"Anytime," I assured her, surprised that I meant it. For so long, my world had contained only four people: Corinne, Ash, Linc, and Court. Now the circle of people I cared about was getting bigger, which meant I had a lot more support.

And a lot more to lose.

CHAPTER 19

RYAN

The house we'd bought came with a massive formal dining room. Since none of us had the time or inclination to shop for furniture, we'd bought it with everything included, which meant an eighteen-foot-long solid oak table with seating for twenty.

Ash had taken over the room as his command center, setting up routers and cables in addition to no less than five computers. I half expected to see a cot shoved into the corner.

Walking in, I wondered if maybe I should move the bed in for him. Ash looked like shit.

"Hey." He didn't look up from the screen of laptop number four as he finished off an energy drink and put the can next to more than a dozen empties.

I vaguely remembered some health article about a guy who'd had a heart attack after drinking six of those things in succession.

Pulling out the chair across from him, I slowly sank down. "I'm worried."

"I know. Me too. But I think I'm getting close to finding her," Ash muttered, his green eyes moving as he read whatever was on the screen.

"I mean about you," I clarified.

Now he glanced up. "Aw, honey. That's sweet."

"Fuck off," I retorted.

"I'm fine."

"You look like shit," I countered.

He sucked in a sharp breath through his teeth. "And *you* look like a douchebag. We all have our crosses, bro."

I rolled my eyes. "I'm serious."

"So am I."

A low growl rumbled in my chest. "Dammit, Ash—"

"What, Ryan?" He cut me off with a glare. "What do you want me to say, huh? It's my fucking... You know what? Forget it."

I leaned forward. "No, hang on. You think Maddie going missing is *your* fault?"

His jaw clenched. "He fucking outsmarted me. Gary motherfucking Cabot outsmarted *me*. Twice. What the fuck am I supposed to do with that?" He looked absolutely disgusted with himself and the situation.

"Ash—"

He shoved away from the table with a hiss. "We should've known his bitch ass would try something. I should've... I don't know. Fucking put a tracker in Maddie's ass." His eyes lifted to the ceiling. "Maybe I should do that for Bex."

"Maybe you should take a break," I suggested, knowing full well he'd never agree. I mean, I wouldn't either.

"How about *you* take a break?" he snarled, glaring at me. "You go lay down and take a nap while the rest of us worry about what Gary's doing to Maddie. I mean, at least Kindell is dead, so we know *he's* not there."

My throat tightened, and I reminded myself he was lashing out because he was tired and frustrated, like me.

Ash openly mocked me. "And we all know Kindell was the only friend Gary had that would've *loved* getting his hands on—"

With a roar, I shot to my feet. "Shut the fuck up!" My fist clenched with the need to drive it into his face. I'd never wanted to hit my best friend as much as I did at that moment.

His chest heaved as he stared at me from across the table, that eight feet of space the only thing saving him from being on the ground.

"She's out there alone." His voice cracked at the end, and he cleared his throat before looking away. "I care about her, okay? I spent the better part of a decade turning a blind eye to what my aunt and uncle were doing to Victoria. I can't fail Maddie, too."

"Victoria wasn't your fault." I blinked back my anger as I realized why he was twisting himself up over Maddie.

He looked at the table. "She had a setback."

I started and narrowed my eyes. "What?"

He swallowed hard and met my eyes, looking miserable. "I'm her emergency contact for the facility. She... she tried to kill herself two days ago."

"Jesus," I swore, stabbing my fingers through my hair. "Why didn't you say anything?"

"Because I can't help Victoria, but I *can* help Maddie," he replied.

"Ash." I blew out a hard breath. "Victoria isn't your fault, and you've done everything you can to get her the best possible help."

I knew for a fact he had. Since rescuing Victoria from his sadistic aunt and uncle, Ash had made sure she wanted for *nothing*. He'd set her up with a beachfront condo on a small island Grandpa's family owned in the Maldives.

Part of what we'd done when setting up Phoenix International was make sure we had a safe haven for people who needed it. Anyone too scared to return home or try to rejoin society. There were no extradition treaties in place for the Maldives, and with a single dock and a tiny airstrip on the island, it was easy to control access. Even still, Royal and Bishop had helped us recruit several of their former military buddies to guard the island as an extra security measure.

There was a small hospital with state-of-the-art equipment, including several therapists who'd had no problem giving up busy practices in congested cities for a fully paid cabana in paradise with a lighter case load.

Victoria had been the first resident, and she had periods where it seemed like she'd finally started moving on. But then something would trigger her, and she'd regress to the point of suicide. It wasn't the first time she'd tried to kill herself, and it likely wouldn't be the last.

The first three times, Ash had gone running to her side, feeling guilty as fuck that he hadn't seen the abuse she'd endured for so long. Finally, the psychologist told him he needed to stop coming; Victoria had fixated on him as her savior and was hurting herself for his attention.

It killed him to leave her alone, but the therapist made a convincing case that Victoria was becoming attached to him on an unhealthy level, causing her to regress. Unlike Dr. Sharon Browne, the psychologists Phoenix employed were genuinely focused on patient care.

Needless to say, Ash still felt like shit when Victoria had an episode, but he resisted running to her side.

"I know Victoria's situation isn't my fault," he muttered, shaking his head. "I just fucking hate feeling helpless."

I nodded, knowing exactly what he meant. Every breath I took felt like a betrayal to Maddie. I'd failed her and didn't deserve the oxygen filling my lungs.

A sharp chirp from one of the computers had Ash turning with a frown. He moved down to another screen and tapped a few things before whispering, "What the fuck?"

"What?" I demanded, coming around the table to see the screen. All I saw was a fuckton of numbers that made zero sense.

"No, no," he hissed, furiously tapping on the keyboard.

"Ash!" I snapped.

He ignored me and kept typing, his fingers flying across the keys until, finally, the screen turned blue and then the computer went dark.

"Fuck," he managed, his dark skin going ashy.

I clamped a hand on his shoulder, squeezing hard. "What the fuck just happened?"

He slowly turned to me. "Someone hacked Maddie's bank accounts."

My insides clenched.

"They drained every account," he finished.

I jerked back. "Gary?"

"More likely someone he hired," Ash answered. "But the money's gone from every account. All the inheritances…"

"How?" I ground out through clenched teeth. "The whole point of moving the money to offshore accounts was so that he *couldn't* access it."

"I know," Ash returned, sounding as frustrated and pissed off as I was. "But he found someone who could."

"Can't you stop it?"

He jabbed a finger at the black screen. "I tried, Ry. They blocked me and then fried my computer when I tried to back-hack them." His jaw clenched. "He found someone better than me."

Panic sliced through me like a fileting knife. Blood rushed from my head fast enough to make me grow dizzy and grab the back of Ash's chair as my knees almost buckled. "The money was the only reason he needed Maddie. Now that he has it…"

My stomach flipped hard enough that I tasted bile on my tongue.

This whole thing had started because Gary wanted that inheritance—an inheritance only Maddie could get him.

If he had the money… then he no longer needed Maddie.

"Oh, *fuck*," Ash whispered, his gaze shooting to me with apprehension.

"What now?"

He swallowed audibly. "Look, Ry, don't lose your shit, okay? But this just popped up in my alerts."

I waited, bracing myself for the worst, but when he showed me his laptop screen, nothing could've prepared me to see Maddie and Charles together, kissing.

Staggering back, I could only gape in horror. Her hands were pressed to his chest, and it definitely didn't look like she was pushing him away. He had one hand wrapped around her hip and the other cupping her face as he kissed her.

"It's fake," I managed, desperation filling my veins. It had to be. "Some sort of photoshop shit."

Ash shook his head. "I don't think it is, bro."

With a roar of rage and pain, I grabbed one of the chairs and hurled it against the wall. Chunks of plaster and drywall went flying as the chair exploded like toothpicks.

Ash was on his feet in a second. "Dude, calm down. This probably isn't what it looks like."

"It doesn't look like my girl kissing another guy?" I snarled, ready to throw a fist at his face.

"Ry," he snapped. "Think about it. Do you think Maddie is doing this because she wants to? Do you honestly think she'd fucking replace your ass?"

No.

I sucked in a deep breath, forcing myself to chill by taking deep breaths and reminding myself that Maddie wouldn't betray me. My gut told me there was more to this, even if the photo was pretty fucking damning.

It was like the engagement party all over again, but I wasn't ready to let history repeat itself.

Not until I talked to her and heard her side of things.

"Maddie wouldn't do this unless Gary was forcing her."

"I agree," Ash said.

I met his gaze. "We need to find her before he makes her do something like actually marry this fucker."

CHAPTER 20

MADDIE

Somehow I managed to sleep for over twelve hours. I blamed the drugs still lingering in my system. Waking up from a dream where Ryan and I were sitting on the beach in front of his house, his fingers lazily tangled with mine as I sat between his legs and he peppered kisses from my shoulder to jaw and I turned my head for a full kiss... only to open my eyes and realize I was still in hell?

Yeah. That sucked.

"Good, you're awake," Mom said as she burst into my room and headed for the large window to yank open the curtains. She beamed at me and clapped her hands. "Time to get ready for the day."

I couldn't help but stare at the bruise on her cheek. Not even makeup could hide the black and blue tones completely.

Sitting up, I considered trying to plead my case again, but ultimately swallowed down the argument. She'd made her choice, and it hadn't been me. Hell, at this point, we probably had matching bruises.

Planting her hands on her hips, she stared down at me. "Out of bed, lazy bones. Your father has been lenient—"

I couldn't suppress a disgusted scoff. "Right. Really patient. He waited all of, what? Twelve hours from the time he had my marriage dissolved to whore me out to someone else?"

"That's enough, Madelaine," she snapped.

I reared back, eyes wide. "What did you just call me?"

Her chin lifted a haughty notch. "Your father and I discussed it, and we think it's time you accepted that you *are* Madelaine."

My fingers curled around the soft comforter. "You've got to be kidding."

"No, we aren't," she stated. "It's who you are. It's who you *agreed* to be. And there will be less confusion or chances of slipping up if we all get used to the change now."

"Changing my name won't change who *I* am," I ground out. "It won't change the fact that *Gary* is a murderer and *you're* a junkie."

She crossed the room and slapped me across the face. "Shut up. I'm not sure why you're so damn determined to make this more difficult than it needs to be."

I lifted a hand to my stinging cheek, glaring up at her. "Because he killed my sister. He killed *Marge*."

She blinked at me. "Who?"

"Marge? The librarian I worked with? The woman who helped buy my school supplies when you spent all our money on crack," I added, unable to keep the bitterness from my tone.

Mom rolled her eyes. "That old bitch? She was constantly meddling. You're better off without her."

"God, I hate you," I whispered, looking away before I did something like get up and slap her back. I had a feeling that if I started hitting her, I wouldn't stop.

"So ungrateful," she muttered, her lip curling. "After everything I've done for you."

"What have you done, Mom?" Now I got out of bed and stood across from her, flinging my arms wide. "Please, tell me what the *hell* you've actually done for me."

She exhaled through her nose. "Charles will be here within the hour. Your father and I expect you to be presentable and courteous to him, am I understood?"

"Oh, I understand you. I just can't believe you," I muttered, rolling my eyes.

She flashed me a brittle smile. "It's a new day, sweetheart. And you could do a lot worse than Charles. He's a duke, for crying out loud."

He wasn't a duke yet, but I wasn't about to argue the semantics of titles to her. "Then *you* marry him," I shot back.

She took a small step toward me, but I refused to back down. Her brows pulled together. "Get dressed and ready. If you think you'll need help, I'll send Evan or your father in to assist you."

"Fine," I muttered, moving to storm past her for the bathroom.

She caught my arm, her acrylic nails digging into my skin. "Don't mess this up for me."

I met her gaze and held it. "You picked the wrong side, Mom."

Her brow furrowed with confusion.

"Ryan was going to help me save you. We were going to make sure you were taken care of." I jerked my arm free. "But you're on your own after this."

Triumph glimmered in her eyes. "Your idealism might actually be adorable if it wasn't so pathetically misplaced. You think Ryan Cain gives a shit about you? He's probably balls deep in the nearest pussy, because that's all you were to him. And sure, he may try to get you back, but only to prove he's better than Gary." Her gaze swept over me. "You forget, I've been where you are, honey. I bought the bullshit, and look where it got me—knocked up, and a life in a shithole with a brat I never wanted."

I shook my head. "You still don't get it, and you never will. How can someone incapable of love understand the concept? I pity you, Mom, because I got the guy and the life. I'm going to have it all, and you'll be left with nothing, just like Gary."

"As smart as you are, you really are stupid," she murmured. She reached into her pocket and pulled out her phone before tossing it at me.

The photo of Charles and I kissing was pulled up, along with a headline announcing our engagement.

"That went out this morning to every major publication." She smirked at me. "Think he's still going to want you when he realizes you've been spreading your legs for another man?"

"I didn't sleep with Charles," I muttered, pushing the phone against her chest. "Ryan trusts me."

But even as I said it, all I could think of was our engagement party and the video... and the way he'd assumed the worst. And that hadn't even been me in the video. This time, I was absolutely in the arms of another man.

Ryan would know I didn't have a choice, though.

Right?

"You're a naive little fool," Mom spat.

I shrugged, shoving down my fears. "Maybe I am. Maybe you're right, and Ryan doesn't care about me the way I think he does." I paused for a beat. "But if you're wrong? If he loves me a fraction as much as I love him? God help you and anyone else who gets in his way." Without waiting for her to reply, I swung around and went into the bathroom, closing and locking the door.

When I exited the bathroom after finishing my hair and makeup, another outfit had been selected for me. I pulled on the green dress and matching Mary Janes with a slight heel. I was just buckling the second shoe when my door opened.

I glared at Evan. "Most people would knock."

Evan nodded at me, ignoring my irritation. "Good, you listened."

"Fuck off," I replied with a bright smile.

He frowned but didn't engage. "Your fiancé is here. Your father wants you downstairs."

I tapped my finger against my chin. "And if I say no?"

"Then I'll drag you downstairs," he replied in an even tone. He shrugged. "Really doesn't make a difference to me."

"Why does that not surprise me?" I muttered, walking around him.

He caught me by the elbow. "Look, I get it, okay? You're pissed off and lashing out. But word to the wise? Gary's in a shit mood. Don't push him."

It was on the tip of my tongue to bite back with a witty retort until I saw the dead seriousness in his eyes. "Helping me? I'm surprised."

"Believe it or not, I don't take joy in watching him hurt you," Evan admitted. "I didn't like it when he did it to your sister, and I *really* don't like participating."

"Then don't do it," I snapped.

He snorted. "Go downstairs before he comes looking, and save us both the headache."

Sucking in a deep breath, I squared my shoulders and marched down the stairs, pausing when I saw Gary glaring up at me.

"You're late," he spat as the doorbell rang. An older man that I didn't recognize hurried forward to open the door.

I arched a brow. "Sounds like I'm right on time."

He grabbed my wrist off the sleek banister and ripped me forward. I cried out, losing my footing and tumbling down the last few stairs to drop in a heap on the landing.

"What the hell?" Charles's shocked voice rang out in the large foyer. "I told you not to touch her again." He hurried forward and helped me up.

"She's clumsy," Gary drawled. "And besides, I told *you* that until she was paid for, I would do whatever the hell I wanted with *my* property."

Charles glared at him. "I won't have you damaging her. I'm the future Duke of Blye, the current Marquess of Perring. She's going to be my wife, and she'll look the damned part."

My knees and hands stung where I'd hit the marble floor, but I was more embarrassed to have them discussing me like I was a sweater they were haggling over.

"And, as it stands, I'll have that money to you by the end of tomorrow," Charles added.

Gary stiffened at the same time I did.

"What?" I whispered, praying I hadn't heard him right.

Charles ignored me. "My associate freed up the funds an hour ago. We'll be transferring them by the end of the week, provided everything is set in motion for our marriage."

Gary inclined his head at the stairs. "Evan is ordained. We can perform the ceremony now."

My heart slammed painfully in my chest.

Charles gave a mirthless chuckle. "Unlike you Americans, I won't simply settle for a quickie marriage in some backyard. It will be done in England over the winter holiday, but I plan on taking Maddie home with me to meet my family first."

"When?" Gary asked, tilting his head as his gaze flicked to me.

Charles smiled benignly. "Tonight. Why wait?"

CHAPTER 21

MADDIE

My breath caught in my chest, trapped by expanding hope as I looked at Charles. He wouldn't meet my gaze, but I knew this was his way of getting me out of this hellhole. And I was all the way in.

"Well then, we should finalize things," Gary said, flashing me a gloating smile. "Let's step into my office."

I started to follow, but Gary spun and blocked my path with a cool look. "You're not needed for this. Sit and wait for your fiancé in there." He jerked his chin at the sitting room off the foyer.

"I'll collect you when we've concluded our business," Charles added, his tone just as aloof and condescending as Gary's.

Gritting my teeth, I forced a smile and spun on my heel before marching into the room that looked like it had been professionally decorated by someone who loved the color white. White carpet, white walls, white furniture, and a few gold accents that barely broke up the starkness of the space.

I perched on the edge of the sofa, twisting my fingers in my lap as I waited.

And waited.

And waited.

There was a clock on the mantle of the fireplace, and I watched as the seconds ticked into minutes that crawled into an hour. I was going crazy not knowing what was happening and how my fate was being decided.

Finally, after eighty-six minutes, Charles appeared in the doorway with Gary.

"I'll start having her things packed up," Gary told him, sparing me a look that warned me to play along. "You can pick her up as soon as the funds are fully deposited."

Charles nodded. "Do you mind if we take a walk around the property? There are some things I need to discuss with her. Expectations and stipulations."

Gary's eyes narrowed. "You're free to use this room." He waved a hand at the glass doors that led to a sitting room where it would be easy for anyone walking by to see us.

Charles looked at me carefully. "Before I finalize our deal, I want to make sure her acquiescence isn't just for show around you."

My spine stiffened. If I hadn't known Charles was on my side, this whole conversation would've been humiliating.

"Fine," Gary bit off. "Thirty minutes and I'll need her back. I, too, have things to discuss with her."

Charles held out a hand, beckoning me forward. I went to him warily, eyeing Gary and giving him as wide a berth as possible.

"Her coat?" Charles asked, quirking an eyebrow.

Sighing, Gary snapped his fingers, and the small man who had answered the door earlier appeared with a black wool coat. Charles took it from him and slipped it over my shoulders before taking my fingers in his. "We'll be back shortly."

Gary nodded slowly, his eyes narrowed as he watched us leave through the front door.

As soon as the door shut behind us, I sucked in a deep breath. It had been too long since I'd actually breathed fresh air, and the mountain air here was crisp and sharp with the impending threat of snow.

I'd forgotten how much I loved the scent of snow in the air and the silence that came with the fluffy white flakes.

"Come on," Charles murmured, tightening his hand around mine and leading me down the stairs and around the house toward the wooded area I'd seen from my bedroom.

"Where are we?" I asked after several minutes of quiet.

"Montana," he replied, glancing down at me.

Another question pressed heavily on my mind. "And the money? Did you really find it?"

A grim nod. "My cousin, Tyler, is the best in the business. Ash is good, but he never stood a chance at truly burying your accounts when Ty got involved." He shot me a sympathetic look. "I'm going to have to give Gary the money in order for this to truly work."

I sighed. "I figured as much. Honestly, I don't give a damn about the money at this point. Maybe if I'd just given it to him from the start, we could've avoided this whole mess."

"No," he argued. "This was always about more than the money. It was about proving to the Collective that he should be leading them."

"The Collective?" I echoed, frowning.

Charles hesitated. "I'd assumed Ryan told you about them. It's a network of some of the most powerful men on the globe. They make their fortunes at the misfortune of others, usually by illegal means."

"I mean, he sort of told me about his dad and some of the others," I hedged, not willing to give away Phoenix or what the guys had planned.

"It's a complicated, volatile situation," he murmured, his eyes flashing as he stared straight ahead.

"You say that like you have first-hand experience." I tugged him to a stop near the tree line.

He frowned and looked down. "Maybe I do."

"Charles—"

"But there are a few other things we need to talk about." He met my gaze. "One of the things I insisted on seeing was your medical records."

My brows shot up to my hairline.

"I told Gary that I needed to make sure you were healthy, but I also knew you'd been at Highwater and likely pumped up with an assortment of medications. I'm willing to assume you weren't privy to the medical decisions made on your behalf?" He gave me a pointed look and pulled his phone out of his pocket before unlocking it and scrolling. He handed it to me. "I didn't look, but they were sent to me. I thought you might want to know."

I took the phone, hesitant at what I'd see, but he was right. I wanted to know what had been done to me. What they'd forced into my system.

Most of the names I didn't understand and couldn't even pronounce. A few things stuck out. "They said I'm bipolar? That I was suffering from a manic episode when I married Ryan? This is bullshit."

The corner of his mouth lifted. "I mean, one could argue that you weren't in your right mind for marrying that prat."

I glared at him.

"Too soon?"

"You think?" I grumbled, scanning the rest. More words I didn't understand. A few more outright lies told by Dr. Browne. At the bottom of the report, I froze, and everything in me went ice cold.

"Maddie?" Charles touched my elbow, but I barely felt it. "You look like you're going to pass out. What is it?"

I couldn't stop staring at the line under *Procedure Complete*. An involuntary procedure that had been carried out at Highwater when I'd been unconscious the last day before my transfer order came in. A completely fabricated transfer order that brought me from Highwater to here. But not before—

"They removed my birth control," I whispered, feeling sick and violated all over.

"They did *what?*" Charles looked confused.

I stepped away from him, not wanting to be touched. I squeezed the phone in my hand as tight as possible. "I had an IUD put in a year ago. Gary had it removed."

I tossed back the phone and he caught it, looking horrified. "Why would he do that?"

"Now? I don't know. I mean, he threatened to have it taken out so that Ryan could get me pregnant because of his grandfather's will, but there's no reason for me to get pregnant *now*." I wrapped my arms around my waist, shuddering as I remembered waking up here yesterday and the ache between my legs that I'd chalked up to body aches from the drugs.

Charles's expression went ashen. "Oh, God."

"I know, right?" I raked my fingers through my hair, barely tamping down the urge to yank it out by the roots.

"No, Maddie... I think this is my fault."

"How in the world—"

He twisted away with a huff, rubbing the back of his neck. "Gary and I had several conversations over the last week. He approached me about marrying you and the money, and I... I played up what was expected of a wife in my family. When he mentioned how willful you were, I was quick to inform him that women in my world tended to not fight back once they were pregnant and had something to lose."

His admission detonated like a bomb between us. I staggered back several steps. "What the fu—"

"I was trying to make it believable," he hissed, his gaze snapping toward the back of the house. "Stop glaring at me like that before Gary comes out here. Until you're out of this house, we can't have him suspecting anything. I'm still not convinced he didn't know about..." He clenched his jaw.

"About what?" I prompted.

He took a deep breath and reached for my hand. "Keep walking with me."

"Tell me—"

"Maddie, *please*." He gave me an imploring look that didn't relent until I accepted with a huff. He pulled us farther from the house. "I have a confession."

"Okay," I spoke evenly. "I can't *wait* to hear this one. Did you have them start fertility treatments on me, too? Wait—am I already pregnant thanks to some artificial insemination when I was drugged?"

"Of course not." He stared at me, clearly repulsed by the idea, before shaking his head as if dislodging the thought. "But I think you might still hate me a bit when I tell you this."

I wasn't sure how to brace myself for whatever was about to come next. As it was, I couldn't imagine being surprised by anything at this point.

Charles stopped again, turning to face me and grabbing both of my hands as he looked down at me. His green eyes were hard and unflinching. "I knew you weren't Madelaine Cabot when I met you."

CHAPTER 22

MADDIE

I was wrong. I could still be surprised.

With a gasp, I tried to rip my hands free from Charles, but he held fast. In fact, he moved closer to me, transferring both of my hands into one of his larger ones and wrapping his free hand around the back of my neck.

"Your father is watching from the window," he murmured, his face inches from mine and entirely too close. "Don't pull away or I'll have to prove I can control you." His gaze flashed to where my cheekbone had bruised from when he'd struck me before.

"How did you... I don't..." My world was tilting on its axis.

Again.

Dammit, I was so sick of being blindsided. Of things flipping over and leaving me exposed and vulnerable when I thought I'd finally figured them out.

I closed my eyes and took a deep breath before looking at him and gritting out, "Explain."

"It's a long and complicated story that we don't have time for right now," he told me, almost gently, "but I can give you the overarching details. Madelaine knew I hated her father. She approached me in the spring about a plan she had to ruin him and asked me to meet with her in Greece. But when I arrived, the hotel had—"

"—burned to the ground," I finished for him.

He nodded, releasing my hands. "I tried to get in touch with her but couldn't find anything. Tyler was able to dig up enough surveillance footage from the camera across the street to prove she had checked into the hotel a day earlier, but that was all. We retraced her footsteps and found... *you*."

My breath caught.

"I decided to switch to Pacific Cross. I hoped to see Madelaine there, but when I met you on the quad, you had no idea who I was, and I could tell it wasn't an act." He watched me closely, but I wasn't sure what he was trying to find.

"Why didn't you say something?" My brow furrowed.

His mouth flattened. "Because I wasn't sure what you knew. And when I saw how close you and Cain had become... Maddie, your sister wasn't just trying to find something on her father. She also alluded to something Ryan and his friends were up to."

I forced myself not to react. "Oh?"

His green eyes narrowed, piercing me with a look that demanded answers. "They're mixed up in something, too. I know you think Ryan's a good guy—"

"He is." Taking a deep breath, I lifted my chin and stepped back. "I know exactly what Ryan and our friends are doing, because he told me. Now I'm part of it, too. It's why Gary's done all of this." I waved a hand in front of myself. "I don't know what Madelaine thought she knew about Ryan, but I have a feeling she thought the wrong thing."

"Did you know that Court Woods has five half-brothers?" Charles challenged. "That three of them joined the military, and once their tours were finished or ended, they disappeared? Tyler has found evidence that they're working for a company that Madelaine stumbled upon."

"Phoenix," I said simply.

He stared at me, his jaw going slack.

"I told you, Ryan and I don't have secrets. I know all about

Phoenix, and I've met Court's brothers. Royal's a bit of an asshole, but Bishop and Knight seem cool." I shrugged like it was no big deal, because it wasn't.

He frowned, looking at a loss for words. "Madelaine was sure they were starting a company with the intent to overthrow their fathers and move up the ranks in the Collective. Everything there is based on a hierarchy system. It's cutthroat and brutal, and Madelaine was determined to destroy the foundation."

"Then she should have talked to Ryan," I replied, my heart cracking a bit. "He could have helped her."

He opened his mouth to argue.

"Phoenix *is* a company the guys started to take down their fathers, but that was the sole intention. They don't want any part of the world they corrupted. They're trying to *fix* what their fathers broke. That's part of why Ryan and I got married. The engagement was a plan between Gary and Beckett Cain to cash in on a will set up by my family and Ryan's grandfather. They wanted the money to help them open up a human trafficking pipeline."

"Fuck," Charles whispered, paling a bit.

Shaking my head, I kept going. "Ryan and I got married so I would have access to the trust left to me. Ash moved it to offshore accounts so that Gary couldn't touch it." I snorted. "Until you and your friend Tyler came along. Now he gets it all, I guess."

He looked chagrined. "Suppose I've royally fucked that up, haven't I?"

"Ryan and the guys have been using Phoenix to put Cain Industries and Cabot Global out of business. Without the funds they were providing, the whole network was supposed to fall apart. Court's brothers work for Phoenix, trying to help people who've been hurt and exploited." I drew in a shuddering breath. "Madelaine had it wrong—Ryan's one of the good guys."

"Madelaine was so certain they were as nefarious as their fathers. She worked for years to get proof on them all. Some of the videos she sent me proved it."

"You've seen the videos?" I grabbed his forearm.

He nodded. "Yes. She sent them through an encrypted app."

I rolled my eyes. "I'm well aware of it."

"She said that she had more, but she had moved them to a secure facility," he went on. "She compiled videos, ledgers, and copies of emails and memos sent between members of the Collective, but she needed to store them somewhere safe that her father couldn't touch."

Pandora. Madelaine had stashed all the proof there.

Now more than ever we needed to get into that vault and see what my sister had unearthed.

This could have been so different if Lainey had trusted Ryan. If they'd worked together, this never would have happened.

And I never would have come to Pacific Cross.

"Madelaine had proof that Ryan and the others participated in their initiations," he argued. "They were willing—"

"They were no more willing to do the shit they did than you were to hit me yesterday." I touched my cheek and watched him wince at the reminder. "They did what they did because the alternative was worse. They made their choices, and I trust their intentions. Maybe my sister should have asked them instead of assuming."

Then again, why would she? Madelaine had been used and abused by almost every person in her life. It was heartbreaking.

Charles looked at the ground. "I believed what Madelaine told me. I let my own biases cloud my judgment." He lifted his gaze to mine. "It's why my father and I agreed to his proposal about marrying you."

I tilted my head, confused.

"Gary Cabot is an evil man," he began.

I glanced at the file that was proof my biological father was a psychopath. "You don't have to tell me that."

"He killed my mother," he stated, his tone hard and flat.

My hand flew up to cover my mouth. "Oh, my God."

"Not directly," he added, his jaw tight. "But he seduced her. Got her pregnant. She died because of the pregnancy."

"I don't understand," I admitted.

"My parents had an arranged marriage," he confessed. "They weren't in love, but they were good friends who grew up knowing what was expected of them. My mother struggled to conceive and, after I was born, the doctor advised against any future pregnancies because it would put her at great risk. My father agreed and had a vasectomy."

"Okay." I dragged out the word as I tried to follow along.

"Gary and my father grew up in the same world. They'd made some business deals that helped them both." He hesitated for a beat. "My father, too, is part of the Collective, but he stays on the fringes. Enough to keep our family and assets protected, but he does his best to keep all his dealings, personal and business, above reproach."

"Sounds like a great guy." Sarcasm dripped from my words.

Charles's gaze hardened. "People in our world aren't given much of a choice, Maddie. I would've thought you understood that."

"There's always a choice," I argued. "And if you hadn't told me you were on my side, you can be damn sure I'd be fighting Gary every step of the way down our fake aisle."

"That wouldn't be advisable," he said. "Gary Cabot isn't a man you cross. Do you think it was an accident that my mother got pregnant? Three years ago, Gary convinced her that they could have a child and a life together. He needed a new heir because Madelaine was proving too difficult to control."

"But he had me, so that makes no sense."

He grimaced. "Maddie, it would have been a lot easier for him to have Madelaine die in a car accident and raise a new baby to inherit. Switching you and your sister was infinitely more difficult, but necessary when my mother died with their unborn child," Charles informed me. "You were, and *are*, his last resort."

A chill trickled down my spine, its icy fingers wrapping around my bones. "Why did you really agree to marry me?"

"To get close enough to kill Gary Cabot," he admitted.

I snorted. "Get in line." I ran a hand through my hair. "But now that Gary has my money again, we're back to square one. Well, square one-point-five, I guess, since Beckett is out of the picture."

"Cabot was always smarter with his money than Cain," Charles agreed. "Cain was new money and married into wealth, but he never had the assets or connections Cabot does. Your family—"

"The Cabots aren't my family," I snapped, irritation spiking in my blood. "Family isn't supposed to hurt and use you. They're supposed to support and give a damn about your life. Ryan, Bex, Court, Linc, Ash, Cori... *They're* my family."

"And me?" He cocked a brow.

"What about you?"

"I care about you. I'll support you."

I paused, not entirely sure what he was asking for.

"My father and Tyler are all I have," he whispered.

"Tyler?"

The corner of his mouth hooked up in a fond smile. "Yeah. Tyler's my cousin. Her dad was kinda the black sheep of the family, and she grew up in the US until her parents were killed in a car accident a few years ago. She lives with my dad and I now."

"Oh. I'm sorry," I murmured.

"She's also the reason I have a shot in hell at getting you out of here. She's the brains that was able to find and transfer your money to Gary." He winced a bit at the admission.

I glowered at him, still pissed about that.

"Look, Maddie, I've kept my circle small because... Well, because it's easier to not get hurt if you minimize the people around you who can obliterate your world." His look of resolute sorrow was one of the saddest things I'd ever seen.

"But that's not living. That's hiding, Charlie."

His brow quirked. "Charlie?"

I shrugged. "Charles sounds so stuffy and formal. If we're going to be married, I need something normal to call you."

A soft smile ghosted across his lips. "Charles was my grandfather's name. My mum always called me Chase." He dipped his head, his cheeks turning a cute shade of pink. "She always complained she was forever chasing me around the house. Tyler, my dad, and my mates back home all call me that, too. You can as well. If you like."

"Chase." I tested the name out on my lips, eyeing his windblown chestnut hair and kind eyes. "I like it."

"I like hearing it," he replied.

"So, *Chase*," I began with a tiny smirk, "what do we do now?"

He swallowed. "Tyler will have completed the transfer by this evening. I'll schedule a flight to London tonight and pick you up. We'll call Ryan from the car, and hopefully he's close enough to meet us, or we'll change the flight plan and fly you to him."

"Gary will know you betrayed him," I murmured. "It's going to be hard getting close and getting your revenge if he knows you're on my side."

"Perhaps," he allowed. Sincerity shone in his eyes. "But I suppose this is *my* choice, and I'm choosing you."

CHAPTER 23

MADDIE

Watching Charles—no, wait, *Chase*—leave sucked, because I felt like I was losing my only ally, but I knew he was leaving to set things up so I would be free from Gary and this whole mess.

Turning away from the front door, I flashed the monster in question a tight smile. "Guess I'll go pack."

He laughed. "Sure, sweetheart. Go ahead and *pack*."

Something in his tone made me hesitate and my pulse quicken.

He shot me an openly mocking look. "Well? What are you waiting for? Go pack."

I frowned. "What—" My words were cut off when his hand went around my throat and shoved me against the door hard enough that the air whooshed from my lungs.

"Did you think I didn't learn my lesson?" His stormy, furious eyes searched mine. "Did you think you could have a single fucking conversation I wouldn't hear in this house? On this property?"

Oh, shitballs.

Whatever Chase had used to mask our conversation in Gary's office the day before, we hadn't considered needing outside. But apparently Gary had eyes and ears everywhere.

My horror must have shown, because he laughed, squeezing

harder and robbing me of the ability to breathe. Panicked, I clawed at his wrist, his fingers, and finally his face.

That pissed him off enough that he let my throat go only to rear back and punch me in the same cheek Chase had yesterday.

Pain exploded across my face, my vision blurring, and I fell to the ground.

"*That* is how you correct bad behavior," he sneered above me. "Not that pathetic little hit he tried to pass off."

"Why?" I croaked, my throat raw and my face throbbing. I weakly managed to push myself into a sitting position to stare up at him through the eye that wasn't swelling shut.

"Because I want what you fucking stole from me," he rasped. "Now I get my money, and *Chase* will get a matching grave next to his mother."

"No!" I cried, fear pulsing in my blood with every frantic heartbeat in my chest.

"Although," he mused, rubbing his jaw, "I suppose I no longer have a use for you." The hate in his eyes was chilling. There was nothing human in the way he scowled down at me.

But if he thought I would beg, he was dead fucking wrong. "So, kill me," I spat. "I'm done playing your twisted games. Fuck you."

"No," he replied, smiling. "I won't kill you. You're going to pay for what you did to me. What your sister did. I'm going to enjoy selling you to my friends. Maybe I'll include your mother in the deal. And when they've broken you so completely that there's nothing left to use, I'll mail the pieces of you to Ryan."

When I was ten, there had been a fifth grader who loved giving me shit every single day about anything from my mom to my ratty clothes to my trailer park. I'd taken it for weeks until, one day, I snapped.

That was how I felt then as I pushed myself to my feet and launched myself at Gary.

It was stupid and pointless, a move borne of impotent rage and dehumanizing fear, but it was freaking worth it to see the surprise in his eyes and the roar of anger when my nails dug into the side of his face. I felt the flesh score open a second before his hands grabbed my waist and slammed me into the ground.

My head hit the floor first, and the only thing that kept me from blacking out was the plush welcome mat. My neck and shoulders ached as I fought for my damn life, swinging and screaming until my throat was raw and my arms were wrenched painfully above my head.

I tried to yank them free, but Evan had finally joined the fray and held me down as Gary got to his feet.

"You stupid bitch," he raged, pressing his hand to his face as blood oozed from where I'd caught him.

I smiled, ready to embrace whatever came next and knowing I hadn't gone down without a fight.

"Boss?" Two men stood behind Evan, both dressed in the same charcoal suit as the former. I recognized one from the night of my engagement party. He'd grabbed me in the cemetery and hauled me home.

Gary glared at me, his chest heaving. "You're going to pay for that."

"Worth it," I ground out with a laugh, still struggling against Evan. I tried to get my feet under me for leverage as Gary snapped his fingers at the two goons. "Fucking hold her down."

I kicked as much as I could as they approached. It was pretty pointless, and within seconds, I was pinned to the floor and unable to move.

"I hate you," I hissed at Gary.

He slowly knelt beside me and wiped the blood on his hands onto the front of my shirt. "Not nearly as much as I hate you. But allow me to show you what the rest of your life looks like." He glanced at Evan. "Turn her over."

All three men flipped me onto my stomach, and I kept struggling, kept fighting, until I felt something cold and sharp press against my shoulder. I froze, and Gary dug the knife into my shoulder, the point cutting easily through my skin and muscle. He added more pressure, and I screamed as it scraped against bone.

I clenched my teeth and whimpered, the searing pain beyond anything I'd felt before as he twisted it once.

Twice.

I almost blacked out the third time, and, like he knew I was close to passing out, he ripped the blade from my shoulder and started slicing away my clothes before I could breath. Blood ran hot and sticky over my skin and pooled under me as I swallowed a ragged sob.

Cool air hit my exposed back and legs, and I gagged at the fear clawing up my stomach while what remained of my dress was ripped away. He left me in my underwear, and I squeezed my eyes shut, refusing to see what came next.

I hardened my heart, built a wall of brick and cement around my emotions, and vowed that whatever he did next wouldn't matter.

The clink of his belt coming unbuckled was the only warning I got before fire erupted on my lower back. I shrieked against my clenched teeth before I could swallow the sound.

The belt came cracking down again, this time against my ass. I felt my underwear rip from the force of it before the next lash hit my shoulder blades, flaying my skin and sending a new blast of pain through the place he'd stabbed me.

Every time the belt came down, fire licked across my skin until I thought I would combust. I pressed my face against the rug, my eyes closed as tight as possible as pain flared hot and cold through my body until I was just dizzy, barely able to draw a breath.

Until I finally, thankfully, passed out.

The sound of sobbing pulled me from the darkness. As flames licked up and down my back, from ass to neck, I realized the sobs were coming from *me*.

"Shhh," a soft, familiar voice admonished before a cold cloth was pressed to my shoulder.

The world went white as I cried out, fresh pain flaring across my nerve endings.

"I know it hurts," Mrs. Delancey continued, still applying pressure, "but I have to clean your wounds, Maddie."

I shuddered, the trembling of my own body sending even more ripples of agony down my spine.

"I'm going to have to stitch some of these closed," she added, her voice oddly soothing as she worked. A cool cream was gently massaged into my torn flesh, providing the barest hint of relief.

"W-why are y-y-you helping m-me?" I managed through chattering teeth. Why was I so cold?

She sniffled, and I got the impression that she was... crying? No, that couldn't be right. Mrs. Delancey had been with Gary for years. She knew what he was capable of.

"I tried to tell you," she whispered, her voice cracking. "I told you not to fight him. But you're so much like your sister. She refused to back down, too."

The mention of my twin made me blink away tears. Had she gone through this, too? Had Mrs. Delancey stitched her back together after Gary had beaten her unconscious? "*Why?*"

"Because you need help," she answered, her soft hands moving down my back to my hips.

Everything in me hurt. I couldn't tell one pain from the next, but I was aware enough to know that I was lying face down on the bed in my room, and I was naked. Terror spiked through my chest like a harpoon.

"D-did they... Was I...?" I couldn't even speak it.

She sighed. "Raped? No, honey. They didn't."

"When d-did you get here?" I asked, needing to focus on her voice and not the humiliation of being stripped and beaten. I'd done everything I could to stop him, but it hadn't been enough.

"I've been here since before you arrived," she replied. "I simply stayed out of sight. I knew you wouldn't care to see me. But when they left you in the hallway after... Well, I had someone from the kitchen help bring you upstairs."

Oh, God. How long had I been out? "What t-time—"

"It's almost six," she answered, laying a soft bandage across part of my lower back.

No, no, no.

Fear choked me as I realized that all of my plans had gone up in flames that smoldered as ashes at my feet. Gary knew Chase was on my side, which meant he was in serious trouble.

Chase was supposed to be here tonight. I had to warn him, if it wasn't already too late.

"I n-need your phone," I stammered, cracking my good eye open to look at her.

She grimaced and shook her head. "I can't."

Determination tightened my core. "He's g-going t-to—"

"I know," she interrupted, her eyes full of regret. She looked down. "Maddie, he's currently celebrating. I overheard everything that happened with your... With him. I know what Gary was planning to do, and it's already been done."

My breath caught.

He's currently celebrating.

"The money he was waiting for was transferred into his account shortly after five." She resumed covering my back with gauze. "When I went downstairs for more supplies, I heard him receive confirmation about your new..." Her lips pursed as her gaze skittered away. "There was a car accident. No survivors were found in the wreckage."

I pressed my lips together to smother a sob. *Dammit.*

I'd gotten my friend killed. He'd chosen to help me, and now he was dead.

It wasn't fucking fair.

The bad guys weren't supposed to win. They just weren't. And definitely not like this.

"You never should have come to this forsaken place," she swore. "Your sister... I can't believe she tricked you into taking her place."

"She was trying to stop him." I realized it was true even as I spoke it.

Madelaine hadn't left me holding the bag. She hadn't run off with Evan, a guy she claimed was her boyfriend. She'd been going to meet with Chase. The one guy who hated Gary Cabot as much as she did. The only chance she had at stopping him.

She'd risked it all, and he'd found out and killed her.

But even if she hadn't been in Greece, he still would have killed her. Still would have found a way to find me and force me to access the inheritance.

He'd known Adam Kindell was sneaking into his thirteen-year-old daughter's bedroom and had the freaking audacity to say Lainey had wanted it. The man was a certifiable sociopath with zero regard for anyone but himself.

He was always going to come after me.

Mrs. Delancey's hands hesitated for just a moment, and when they returned to me, there was a slight tremble. "I think..."

I swallowed roughly. "Say it."

She sighed. "It doesn't matter."

"It does to me."

"He knows he can't control you. That you're beyond... Tonight was about him unleashing his own fury, but I know that it won't be the end. I tried to tell you, he *always* wins. The threats he made... they aren't idle."

"Then let me use your phone," I begged. "We won't leave you behind. We'll help you and your son."

She sucked in a ragged breath. "I need to think about it."

I wanted to scream because *what was there to think about?*

She pulled back and exhaled. "All right, the only thing left is to stitch up some of the deeper wounds." Despair flashed in her eyes. "It's going to hurt."

My muscles tensed before I forced myself to relax. The cream she'd rubbed into my back seemed to have a bit of a numbing effect, but I suspected that would vanish as soon as she started sewing my flesh together.

"I can take it," I vowed, meaning it in every sense of the word.

I was down, but I wasn't out. It would take more than fists and belts to break me. Not while I still had everything left worth fighting for waiting for me.

CHAPTER 24

RYAN

"How are you, son?" Grandpa was one of two people I'd ever let call me that. The other was my football coach, but he wasn't exactly someone I was speaking to right now, since I'd walked off the field in the middle of our first playoff game and ended the team's season.

I exhaled, letting his concern crack the hard exterior I'd erected to keep from falling apart. I'd had to shore up those walls several times since Ash had announced Maddie's accounts had all been drained, two days earlier.

Gary officially had all of her money, which was exactly what he'd wanted. The only things he didn't get were the shares of Phoenix and Brookfield, since Grandpa was, thankfully, still alive.

The news outlets hadn't said much beyond publicizing Maddie's newest engagement, and I kept waiting for a date to be announced.

Or worse, a follow up saying they were married.

My gut twisted.

The last few days had been… "Not great."

On the other side of the video screen, Grandpa's head dipped. He'd lost even more weight in the few weeks since I'd seen him at Thanksgiving. I hadn't wanted to believe the doctor's prognosis that his disease was rapidly progressing, but there was no denying it.

He was dying, and it wouldn't be much longer.

If I lost him before I found Maddie...

I'd lose my fucking mind without either of them. If Grandpa was the anchor that kept me grounded, Maddie was the compass that kept me on course.

Without them, I was lost and adrift.

I cleared my throat, locking down my emotions. I needed to be strong for Grandpa. "Ash has narrowed down a few properties in North America where Gary might be. We're planning to split up and do recon starting tomorrow."

When Ash had relayed this info at dinner hours earlier, I'd been ready to run out the door, but Royal had adamantly shut me down. I'd argued with him, with all of them, until Bex yelled that I was being an idiot and needed to think logically, the way Maddie would want.

Seeing Bex—tiny, timid Bex—stand up and shout at us had finally gotten through to me. I hated it, but they were right. Gary had already proved he was capable of outmaneuvering us, and we needed to play this carefully to make sure Maddie wasn't caught in the crossfire.

After dinner we'd planned which locations we'd hit. Ash was going to stay behind with Bex while Royal and I went to Nevada, Court and Knight went to Montana, and Linc and Bishop hit South Dakota. All were remote properties and perfect places to hide a kidnapped girl away from the world, and all were owned by small companies that buried the name of the parent company, Cabot Global.

Unable to relax, I'd finally called Cori. After excitedly telling me about her new school and rattling off her wishlist for Christmas—a horse was now at the top—she'd asked to talk to Maddie, and I'd come up with a bullshit excuse and hung up. Then I'd called Grandpa. I'd needed to hear his voice reminding me it was going to work out.

Even if that was a lie.

"Waiting is a smart plan," he agreed. "She's a strong woman. She's going to be fine."

I scrubbed a hand over my face. "She's been through so much."

"Exactly. She's no stranger to surviving. Have faith in her," he encouraged, and broke into a rattling cough that made me flinch. Behind him, his caretaker appeared.

"It's late," Eloise chided, settling her hands on the back of his wheelchair. She gave me a sad nod. "Hello, Ryan."

"Hey." I managed a tight-lipped smile.

Eloise had been with Grandpa since shortly after his diagnosis, but she'd been a friend of the family prior to that and was someone we trusted. Hell, she'd been there when I'd married Maddie in Grandpa's living room.

"I'm so sorry," she murmured, shaking her head. "But your grandfather is correct. Maddie is—"

"Strong. I know." Irritation embedded in my tone like ground glass in pavement. I was sick of people telling me how strong my girl was. I knew, better than most, how true that was, but I also knew everyone had a breaking point. And, for fuck's sake, wasn't Maddie due a little good luck by now?

Grandpa turned and patted Eloise's hand. "Just a few more minutes, Lou."

She pursed her lips but moved out of frame, and a moment later I heard the sound of a door closing.

"She's trying to be supportive." Grandpa kept his tone mild, the censure there but also muted under his concern and empathy.

"I know," I echoed, stabbing my fingers into my hair. "It's been *weeks*. First she was at that fucked up asylum, and now she's been alone with Gary for *days*? Jesus, Grandpa. Who knows what he's—"

No, no. I couldn't finish that train of thought, or I'd be in the car, headed to the first location Ash had found before anyone could stop me.

I leaned back hard enough in my desk chair that it creaked and threatened to tip over. Drumming my fingers on the desk, I tried to silence the riot of voices and urges screaming for me to get up and do something.

"I spoke to Corinne today," Grandpa said, the soft cadence of his voice and the mention of my sister enough to pull me back from the edge.

For now.

I nodded, another twisted version of a smile moving across my lips. "She wants a horse for Christmas."

Grandpa's eyes twinkled. "I have an entire stable that she's welcome to. But if she wants her own…"

I scoffed and rolled my eyes. "You spoil the shit out of her."

"I noticed you didn't complain about how I spoiled you when you wanted a car for your sixteenth birthday," he pointed out.

I couldn't stop from smirking as I envisioned the cherry red Lykan Hypersport sitting outside on the driveway the day he'd gifted it to me. I fucking loved that car. And it sure as shit cost more than a damn horse.

"Fine," I relented.

His expression sobered. "Any word from that fuckhole of a father?"

My shoulders shook with laughter. "Tell me how you really feel."

He scowled at me. "Only thing that excused him for not being a wet spot on a bed was fathering you and Corinne. And I use that word very graciously."

"Fair enough," I murmured. "No word. Ash tracked him to Panama and has been keeping an eye on him." Unlike Gary, who'd apparently had more money and connections buried than we'd anticipated, my father was dead broke. Whatever money he had in his pockets now was from whatever he'd grabbed from the house and pawned.

But my father was a fucking cockroach, and I knew I'd eventually have to crush him beneath my heel before he scurried around long enough to annoy me.

"Good. He's—"

Whatever Grandpa was about to say was cut off by the piercing chirp of the alarm. Two doors down, I heard Bex yelp. That noise was loud as hell.

"Ryan?" Grandpa's brows slammed down with concern.

"I'll call you back," I told him, ending the chat and leaving my room. The alarm got louder in the hall, where I found Linc, his hands clapped over his ears.

"Fucking *fuck*," he griped. "Seriously, I'm kicking Bishop in the balls for this. I told him we didn't need—"

"Got your attention, didn't it?" the man in question snapped, brushing past us and heading for the stairs.

"Dude, turn off—" The alarm died before I could finish the demand. "Thanks, asshole."

He flipped me off over his shoulder, and Linc and I started to follow.

Bex poked her head out of her room, her face pale. "What's going on?"

"Not sure," I admitted, looking at my friend.

"Go." He waved me on. "I'll hang with Bex until we know what's up."

"I don't need a babysitter," she muttered.

Linc pushed her back into her bedroom with a grin. "Please. Now I have an excuse to hang out on your bed and piss off Court. Win-win, babe."

Rolling my eyes, I hurried down the stairs and met the others in the dining room.

Court's head snapped up. "Bex?"

"She's fine. Linc's keeping her company." I walked to where he, Ash, and Bishop were standing in front of a monitor that showed images from the cameras we'd set up around the property. "What tripped the alarm?"

Ash pointed at the lower right square, where a pair of headlights pierced the dark. "Company."

A growl worked its way up my throat. "We know who?"

Bishop shook his head. "Knight's checking it out. Royal went out as backup."

Bracing a hand on Ash's chair, I leaned over his shoulder. "Can you zoom in?"

He tapped a few things, and the screen enhanced to full size, giving me a good look at the beat-up Corolla. Knight was paused a few feet away, his Glock trained on the driver. He was speaking, but there was no audio.

The cameras were sharp enough that I saw surprise flit over Knight's face a second before he holstered his gun. He reached for his phone, and mine started to ring in my pocket.

"Who is it?" I demanded, my eyes fixated on the screen.

"Guy says he knows you," Knight replied, his tone clipped. "He's with some chick, but he says he knows where Maddie is."

My fingers tightened on the phone. "Who the fuck is he?"

"Charles Winthrope?"

Fire licked through my veins. "Bring him to me."

CHAPTER 25

RYAN

A bitter smirk twisted my lips as Knight and Royal dumped the Duke of Douches at my feet. Although, he didn't look much like an heir to anything with messy hair and a bruise on his shadowed jaw. Instead of the usual pressed shirt and pants, he wore jeans and a t-shirt. The whole look was super... normal.

"Where the fuck is my wife?" I snarled, more than ready to beat the answers out of him.

He opened his mouth to reply when Court brought in another person. A girl, probably Maddie or Bex's age, cursing like a damn sailor as she slapped off Court's hand and twisted away with a defiant tilt of her chin. She clutched a laptop to her chest, her white-knuckled grip around it the only sign she was scared. The defiant tilt of her chin and the glare in her eyes—a vibrant shade of blue that looked almost purple—showed she was pissed.

Ash appeared behind her, already reaching for her laptop. She spun away with a glare, holding it tighter. The dark hair she'd scraped back into a messy ponytail just missed slapping my best friend in the face.

"Don't touch my shit, asswad," she snapped.

"Tyler," Charles warned, shaking his head as he got to his feet with a grimace. He pressed a hand to his ribs. "Don't. This isn't what we're here for."

Her jaw dropped open. "Are you fucking kidding me? We shouldn't *be here* at all, Chase."

"Chase?" I arched a brow.

He gave a small shrug. "Nickname."

"Adorable," I deadpanned, barely holding onto my fury. He had three seconds before I lost what little hold I had on my shit.

His head tilted as he watched me. "Madison sure thought so."

I was on him before I registered what he'd said. His back crashed into the wall, rattling a picture free and sending it shattering against the floor as my forearm pressed across his throat. "The fuck did you just say?" I ground out. Then it penetrated, my eyes going wide before I could control the emotions spiraling in my chest. *"Madison?"*

"Let him go!" Tyler shouted, held back easily when Ash grabbed the back of her oversized hoodie in his fist. Standing more than half a foot taller than the petite girl, he looked down at her with something like amusement flickering in his green eyes while she struggled.

Charles coughed and spluttered, his face turning red. He tried to push me off, but I wasn't budging. He was in decent shape, but he didn't have the power—or rage—I did. I leaned harder against him, just because I could.

"Stop!" Tyler cried behind me.

When he was damn close to passing out, I let him go. He sucked in a ragged gasp and started coughing as he slid down the wall to the floor.

"Tell me where she is," I growled, "or next time I won't stop."

"Fucking wanker," he wheezed, glaring at me. "I came here to help *you*. For *her*."

My knuckles cracked as I made a fist at my side. "You have ten seconds to explain."

"That's generous," Royal rumbled behind me with a snort.

"How do you know—"

"Her name?" Charles cut me off, still rubbing his throat. "Because I knew Madelaine. The *real* Madelaine, and while I'd love to sit here and explain everything to you, I came here because Madison is in trouble."

"No shit," Court snapped, leaning a shoulder on the wall leading from the dining room into what would've been the formal living room if this had been a house for a normal family.

"I also happen to know exactly where she is," he replied. His gaze flickered to Tyler. "For now."

"What does that mean?" Ash asked as I demanded for the third—and final—time, "Where is she?"

Tyler twisted away from Ash and opened her laptop, balancing it in one hand as she tapped a few keys. "They're still there. For now." She scowled at me while Ash reached over her shoulder and plucked the laptop from her fingers.

"Hey!" She turned and tried to grab it, but Bishop caught her around the waist and kept her back. "Get off me, you cow-dick-sucking twatwaffle!"

"That's creative," Knight said with a chuckle. "Do cows have dicks? I thought it was the bulls."

I only had eyes for Ash as he looked at whatever she'd been seeing. His gaze lifted to mine. "It's the place in Montana." He looked at Charles. "How'd you find her?"

"Again," Charles gritted out, "it's a long story. All that matters is that Gary tried to kill me," he pointed to the bruise on his jaw, "when he realized I was there to help Maddie. It took Tyler and I two days to get here. You have to get her *now*. I cannot stress how much danger she's in."

"Especially after the fucked-up shit that pencil dick did to her," Tyler added grimly. She winced and looked at the floor.

I felt my heart plummet to my feet. "What did he do to her?"

"Not nearly as much as he will if you don't go get her." Charles stared at me. "*Now*."

"How'd you even find us?" Ash asked, looking up from the screen.

Tyler smirked. "You're kind of shitty at hiding your tracks. We'd have been here sooner, but we couldn't risk flying in case Gary was monitoring the airports."

"I told her I'd get her out," Charles whispered, sounding gutted. "I promised I'd get her back to you."

I had so many questions. So much that didn't make sense and so many answers I didn't have.

But none of that mattered right now.

I looked at Royal. "We're leaving."

He nodded and arched a brow at Charles. "Can you tell us anything about the house?"

Charles nodded and started to stand, using the wall for support. "He's got plenty of guards around, inside and out. It won't be easy."

Bishop and Royal exchanged knowing smiles, bloodlust in their eyes.

"We're not afraid of a fight," Knight told him, rolling his neck and popping the joints.

"How many guards?" Court pressed, straightening and coming into the room with a dark expression.

Tyler reached for her computer. "I hacked his security system. I can show you inside and out where everyone is in real time."

Ash's brows slammed down. "All the properties operate under a closed loop system. You'd have to have been onsite to get access."

She rolled her eyes. "Thanks for the astute observation, Captain Obvious." She wiggled her fingers. "Wanna give me my computer so I can show you what I'm talking about?"

"Give it to her," I ordered, nodding at him.

With a sigh, Ash handed the computer back. She snatched it from his hands with a glare before twisting away from him. Even still, Ash moved forward and crowded her back to peer over her shoulder.

"Jesus," she huffed, sparing him a glower over her shoulder. "Can you breathe any louder? It's like a freaking lawnmower lives in your mouth or something."

Clenching his teeth, Ash shot me a withering look.

"Here." Tyler flipped the screen so I could see the snowy outside of the house in Montana we'd already been profiling. But unlike the aerial shots that had been taken by a passing satellite three months earlier, it showed two men stationed in the front of the house. She hit a key, and I could see a third man walking down a line of trees in what looked like the backyard.

Royal rubbed his jaw. "It's too barren and exposed everywhere except the trees, but we know those back up to a cliff the house is at the bottom of. We'd need to rappel down the side in the ice and make our way on foot through the forest."

Charles made a sound of protest. "There's no—"

Royal held up a hand, not finished. "I know. There isn't time for that."

"So, we go in guns blazing," I stated, already imagining the cold weight of my gun in my hand.

"That's risky, too," Bishop pointed out. "How far away is the main road?"

"From the drive that leads to the house? A solid five miles, and most of it is in the open. No way they wouldn't see you coming," Tyler said, shaking her head. "Plus they have men guarding it to radio up to the others if anyone so much as stops and asks for directions."

"But there's a road that wraps around the top cliff," Knight said slowly, his eyes lighting up. "That old logging track is five hundred feet away."

A smile crawled across Bishop's mouth. "And it *is* a shitty time of the year to drive that stretch."

Knight shoved his hands in the pockets of his tactical pants and rocked back on his heels. "Gravel road with zero maintenance? It's an accident waiting to happen."

Royal rubbed the back of his neck, annoyance flashing on his face. "Why is the answer with you two always to blow something up?"

"Aw, c'mon, big brother," Bishop teased. "You know you love it, too."

Court sighed loudly. "You know they live for this shit."

"I'm sorry," Charles spoke up, "you're going to blow something up?" He frowned as his gaze bounced from person to person.

Knight shrugged a shoulder. "I mean, sort of?"

"Will it put Maddie at risk?" That was all I cared about.

Royal pressed his lips into a flat line, his blue eyes dark with concentration. "It minimizes the risk to her as much as possible."

"How?" Ash demanded.

"We drive one of those big ass trucks off the cliff," Bishop stated.

"And maybe add a few extra things to help it go boom when it hits the ground," Knight chimed in.

Bishop nodded. "The explosion diverts attention from the guards at the house. We time it with an assault on the guards at the front gate. Take them out and haul ass to the main house."

"And then what?" Charles looked astonished and disturbed.

Royal shot him a dark look. "Kill anyone that gets in our way." He looked at Tyler. "Can you monitor shit from the computer? Tell us where the guards are?"

She nodded, eyes wide. "Uh, sure. Inside, too. There aren't many cameras in the house, but it may help."

Fear churned in my gut. "And what happens in the five minutes it takes us to get from the main road to the house? Maddie could get hurt if Gary—"

"He won't," Tyler said, her voice soft and somber as her gaze flicked to Charles. "He's been too busy making plans to bother with her, and she hasn't left her room since…" She swallowed and looked away.

"Since *what*?" Icy slush filled my veins as my bones turned leaden.

Tyler and Charles exchanged another glance full of something that scared the shit out of me.

Tyler blew out a long breath. "I didn't get access into their system until the last time Chase was at the house." She inclined her head at Charles. "After the first time he met with Gary, he gave me an idea of the set up. I had a feeling the security system was closed off so it couldn't be hacked."

Court scoffed and looked at Ash. "Probably knew you'd hack it in minutes."

Tyler rolled her eyes. "Sure he would've."

Ash shot her an annoyed look.

"Anyway," Tyler went on, looking at me. "The second time Chase went back, I had him help me get access to the house. Most of the few cameras inside are aimed at the doors, and one is in Maddie's room."

"He wanted to make sure she didn't run," Bishop mused.

Tyler nodded. "Yeah. So, after Chase left the second time, I managed to hack their system and saw..." She trailed off, biting her lower lip. "Look, maybe it's easier if you just see it for yourself." Turning her attention back to the computer, she started clicking buttons.

"We're going to get everything ready to leave in a few minutes," Royal informed me, filling the uneasy silence that settled in the room as Tyler worked.

Court nodded. "I'll grab Linc." Then he pointed at Ash. "You good to stay back with Bex and these two?"

"Of course," Ash agreed, watching all four brothers leave the room.

"Okay," Tyler breathed, lifting her violet eyes. "For what it's worth? I'm sorry." She passed me the screen, cued up to the video.

Swallowing down my emotions, I took the computer and pressed play.

And watched my world go fucking red.

CHAPTER 26

MADDIE

My back throbbed as I slowly got out of the shower, thankful it was one I could walk into without having to step over the edge of a tub. Every movement pulled at my aching muscles. Hell, the first time the water from the shower hit my back, my legs had almost buckled, but I was sick of lying in bed and needed to wash away some of the memories of Gary's attack. The feel of strange hands pinning me down.

A shudder rolled down my spine, and I gritted my teeth against the pain. I focused on using the towel to gently dry every part of me except my back. Padding to the large mirror hanging over the double sinks, I leaned forward and wiped away some of the condensation to see my reflection. My eye wasn't swollen shut anymore, and I had actually been able to chew the soft-boiled potatoes in my dinner. The bruising was still nasty, but it was nothing compared to the rest of me.

I took a deep breath before turning around to get a look at the worst of the damage.

The bruises on my back looked even worse than when they'd been inflicted, a mottled mess of black, purple, and blue that looked like Monet's blind understudy had haphazardly slapped colors across my skin from the top of my shoulders down to my thighs. The welts, which had swelled up and pulled my skin impossibly tight, had finally started to subside. The belt Gary had used had broken my skin in only a few places, and ultimately the only injury that had needed stitches was the stab wound.

The good news was I'd have maybe a few small scars when I was done healing, but right now, when I moved, it still felt like my back had been doused in gasoline and set on fire.

I gently peeled away the waterproof bandage Mrs. Delancey had insisted on when I'd adamantly said I wanted a shower.

She was the only person who checked on me. She brought me meals and pain medication, but never the one thing I really wanted: a phone.

Tonight, as she'd set my dinner and next dose of meds on the table near my bed, she'd hesitated and studied me, and I'd hoped she was considering letting me make a call. Unless she relented, I was trapped. My door was always locked now, keeping me prisoner.

I tossed the used bandage into the trash can near the toilet and took a deep breath, readying myself to get dressed.

It took a pathetically long time, and I was out of breath once I finished pulling on my shirt. The fabric grazed my back, and I grimaced as I looked in the mirror and wondered how I'd brush my hair. Washing it had taken an eternity, and I'd skipped conditioner.

I grabbed the brush from the top drawer of the cabinet built into the sinks and trudged through my room to my bed, prepared to sit on the edge and untangle every knot in my hair. At least it was clean now.

I was a few feet from the foot of the bed when the whole house shook. The windows rattled hard enough to make me yelp. For a second, I wondered if it was an earthquake, but we weren't in California. Shouts sounded from outside, and I turned to see a massive fireball arcing up over the trees behind the house.

"Oh, my God," I whispered, changing my course and stumbling to the window. I pressed my hands to the glass and stared, mouth gaping, as the floodlights around the back of the property showed Gary's men converging in the backyard.

In the darkness, it was hard to make out much beyond the glow of the fire and the men arguing about what to do.

The fire didn't seem to be growing, the snow likely hindering it from catching hold of the trees and burning everything to the ground.

Pity.

I turned away, my face twisted with annoyance at how much easier this would be if the house caught fire and Gary burned alive.

With my luck, everyone else would get out of the house, and the only one becoming human barbeque would be *me*.

I sat on the edge of my bed and slowly worked on the tangles in my hair, focusing on breathing through the pain that throbbed in my bones with every movement. Tears burned the backs of my eyes, but I kept going, determined to finish before I lay down and slept.

Sleeping was all I did. There was nothing else to occupy my time, and it was the only reprieve I had from this living nightmare.

I finished and moved to set my brush aside, dropping it to the floor by accident. I glared at it, like the brush had jumped from my fingers onto the floor all by itself, while contemplating picking it up or kicking it under the bed because I was freaking exhausted.

Something scratched frantically at the lock in my door, and a second later, Mrs. Delancey stumbled in. Her usually neat hair was askew, and her eyes seemed wild as she searched the room before her gaze landed on me.

"Thank God," she whispered, quickly closing the door and fumbling with the key to lock it again. "We have to hurry."

"Hurry?" I echoed, curiosity and caution warring inside me. "What's going on?"

She pointed a trembling finger toward the window. "The fire."

I frowned. "It's snowing. The fire won't be able to burn through—"

"No!" she snapped, losing her composure. "There are men coming. Men with guns."

As if to confirm her suspicions, I heard the eerily familiar *pop-pop* of gunfire. Living where I had near Detroit, I was no stranger to the sound. It sent icy chills skittering across my nerves, goosebumps erupting on my skin from toes to fingers.

Mrs. Delancey screamed, dropping to her knees like the bullets were going to come zinging into the room.

My eyes went wide. "Ryan."

Mrs. Delancey shook her head. "No. Your father picked this place because it was so isolated. There's no way he could slip in and cause all this havoc."

No, *he* couldn't. Not alone. But Phoenix could.

I stood up, wringing my hands as I wrestled with going to find Ryan or staying put until he came for me.

More shots rang out, and I sat my ass down. As much as I wanted to run to him, I couldn't even run. Hell, I could barely *walk*. I'd be more of a hindrance than a help right now. The last thing I wanted was to distract any of them and cause someone to get hurt.

The knob on my door shook viciously, and I gasped, hope lodging in my throat.

It crashed right back down into my stomach as the door was kicked in by Evan, a gun in one hand. His cold eyes found me and he stalked forward, grabbing my arm around the bicep. "We're leaving." He started dragging me toward the door.

I pulled back, looking at Mrs. Delancey for help, but she stared, gaping, as he manhandled me out of the room. She didn't try to stop him.

I grabbed the doorframe in a last-ditch effort, my nails digging into the paint.

"Don't make this difficult," Evan snapped, glaring down at me. "I'll knock you out and drag you out of here if I have to."

"Then that's what you'll have to do," I hissed back.

With a growl of frustration, he changed tactics and spun me around so my back hit the wall. Pain exploded so hard and fast I thought I'd throw up. I screwed my eyes shut as my legs gave out, and my grip fell from the doorway. I couldn't *breathe*.

Grunting, Evan hauled me down the hall. "Let's go." When he turned for the stairs, I barely managed to stay upright, knowing that, if I fell down them, he'd let me go and then drag my unconscious body out by my hair.

I focused on the steps, trying not to pitch forward as tears blurred my vision.

A cold silence had settled throughout the house, and I wondered where my mother was. If she was safe or...

Now wasn't the time to think about that.

The front door was open in front of us, and Evan quickened his strides. It was too much. I stumbled as I reached the landing, my ankle rolling and my legs giving out.

"Fucking hell," Evan growled, turning to pick me up.

I scrambled back to get away, but there was nowhere to go. The stairs were behind me, and Evan was in front of me. I pushed uselessly at his hands as he reached for me.

"Let her go," a cold voice ordered from the other side of the stairs. Relief made my knees go weak because I *knew* that grumpy ass, gravelly voice.

Evan whipped around, angling his gun at the person who dared to interrupt him kidnapping me.

Through the gaps in the railing, I spotted Royal. He looked completely emotionless as he leveled his own gun at Evan. His stance was relaxed, like he was watching a tennis match instead of about to shoot someone.

"Maddie," Royal said, his tone flat and even, "can you get up and come to me?"

Evan's gaze flickered to me, and I could see the moment he realized he'd lost. Screeching tires and more gunfire echoed in the foyer, and I spied taillights flying down the drive.

"Your boss is gone," Royal went on. "Game over. Put the gun down."

"Fuck you," Evan spat, and licked his lips nervously.

I used the stairs to push myself up, my vision swimming unsteadily. "He got away?"

Royal didn't look at me. "For now." There was a hint of apology in his voice.

Evan stiffened when I took a step forward, and I realized I couldn't walk around him without being in range for him to grab me and use me as a shield. I stepped back, my heel bumping the bottom step, and then lifted myself onto it.

Evan grimaced and shook his head slightly. "Smart girl," he murmured, his gaze lingering on me. "Maybe you'll survive him yet. Good luck with that." He turned to Royal, determination on his face as his finger touched the trigger.

"No!" I shouted, the sound cut off by a single shot. My heart pounded and my ears rang as Evan fell back against the wall, blood dribbling from his forehead. The wall behind him was sprayed with blood and—

I gagged and turned away, leaning heavily on the railing.

"Maddie, look at me," Royal said gently, touching the back of my head.

Even with me a step above him, he was taller. His dark blue eyes searched mine, worry lingering there. "Can you walk?"

I nodded slowly, unsure I could open my mouth to talk without vomiting. My gaze drifted over his shoulder.

Royal moved, blocking my view of Evan. "Don't look, sweetheart, okay?" He touched his ear, and I saw the tiny device there. "I've got her. Everything clear?" He waited a beat. "Meet at the front. Let's get the fuck out of here."

"Okay," I whispered, shuddering at the cold air sweeping into the room from the open front door. I probably should have put on more clothes than a t-shirt and loose gray shorts after my shower. I could practically feel my wet hair freezing to my scalp.

"Hey, hey," Royal cajoled. "Stay with me, okay? I think you're going into shock."

"It's f-freaking freezing," I argued weakly, shaking my head as my teeth chattered.

The corner of his mouth lifted. "Because we're in the middle of Bumfuck, Montana, in December. We need to get you outside." He grimaced and looked at my bare feet. "I can carry you."

I wasn't entirely sure how he'd manage that, since my back would scream in protest. "I can make it."

"Sure you can, little warrior," he teased. "Why don't you—"

Heavy footsteps pounding up the concrete to the front of the house made him stop cold. It was like watching a curtain fall across his face. One second he was concerned and human, and the next he was a machine, whirling toward the front door with his gun trained at the person incoming.

"Put that shit away," Ryan demanded, tucking a gun in the back waistband of his pants, his bright blue eyes flashing. He didn't pause, and Royal barely had time to step back before he was in front of me.

I trembled as his cool hands came up to cradle my face, his eyes searching mine. "Maddie."

My eyes slid shut, the sound of my name on his lips what I'd been craving for weeks. Tears squeezed through my eyelids, falling down my cheeks until they hit his thumbs, where he brushed them away.

"Baby, look at me," he whispered.

I opened my eyes. "You're really here?"

"I'm really here," he vowed, leaning his forehead to mine. His lips brushed lightly over mine once, twice.

"And we really need to be leaving," Royal chimed in from behind him.

"Ready to go?" he asked against my lips.

I nodded, unable to speak as I looped my arms around his neck and held on.

He kissed my lips once more, then the tip of my nose, before gently turning around in my arms so my hands were clasped over his throat. "Climb on," he said, bending a bit so I could more easily get on his back.

I hesitated, not sure how he could've known my back was messed up. But at this point, I didn't care. I wanted to go home.

My back still protested as I maneuvered myself up, his hands hooking behind my knees as he straightened. I pressed my forehead against his shoulder and blinked at Royal, who gave me a soft smile and a nod.

"Let's go," he told us, leading the way, gun still drawn.

I turned and kissed the side of Ryan's neck. "I love you."

A shudder rippled down his spine as he turned his head a bit. "I love you, too."

"Thank you for coming for me." My voice broke a little at the end.

"Maddie, I'll always come for you."

CHAPTER 27

MADDIE

The others were waiting for us by a massive SUV parked in front of the detached garage. Ryan strode right up to them. "Hold her for a second, and watch her back," he ordered Linc, passing me to our friend like I was a baby.

"I can stand," I started to protest.

Ryan scowled at me. "It's barely twenty degrees and you don't have shoes, Mads." He turned and yanked open the back door to grab something.

"Fuck, it's good to see you, girl," Linc whispered, unusually emotional as he carefully hugged me and kissed the side of my head. Court came up beside us a second later, greeting me the same way. When Bishop went to do the same, Ryan shoved him back with a growl before working a pair of thick socks over my feet.

"What?" Bishop asked, winking at me as Linc set me down to jog to the driver's side and turn on the SUV.

"Those two I'll allow because she's hurt," Ryan ground out, "but you keep your fucking hands to yourself."

"He's been a grumpy ass since you disappeared," Bishop told me, and then his expression softened. "Glad you see you in one piece."

"Where's Ash?" I asked, looking around for my other friend. Bex's absence I expected—no way would Court or the guys let her near a situation like this.

"Waiting for us back home," Ryan answered, linking our fingers and bringing my hand to his mouth to kiss. "Let's get you in the car."

I pointed to where the flames were still visible. "This you guys?"

"Knight," Bishop replied, frowning. "Fucker gets to have all the fun."

Royal rolled his eyes, eternally annoyed with his brothers. "We need to pick his ass up on the way, so let's go."

"Wait," I said, looking back at the house. "What about my mother?"

Ryan shook his head. "Gary took her with him. Sorry, baby."

"Don't be," I said, annoyed she'd somehow skated away once again. "Mrs. Delancey's still inside."

Ryan looked surprised. "The housekeeper?"

I nodded. "She's sort of been helping me."

"I can get her," Bishop offered.

"Is there a car here she can use?" I countered, waiting for him to nod. "Then we're not bringing her. Gary has her under his thumb, and I'm not sure we can trust her."

"Okay." Ryan looked ready to pick me up again. "Let's get you out of here."

I looked at the car, wondering how this would work. The idea of sitting as we bounced over the roads made me ache all over.

"Maddie and I will take the back," Ryan announced, striding forward and opening the back door then flipping up the second row of seats and climbing into the third. He turned and held out a hand to me.

I grimaced as he helped me into the space, Court and Linc flanking me in case I fell back.

Ryan sat against one side. "Lay on your stomach," he said, watching me intently.

"How'd you know?" I asked softly, doing as he suggested and resting my head in his lap. His fingers delved into my damp hair, stroking it as Court flipped the seat in front of us upright so he and Linc could get in that row.

Royal and Bishop got in front, and Royal started the car as Linc and Court turned around to look at me. I glanced out the closest window as we drove away from the house. Pink and orange swirls were just starting to tint the horizon as we sped away.

"Charles told us," Ryan answered.

I jerked, trying to sit up, but Ryan kept my head pressed to his leg. "He's alive?"

Court answered. "Showed up at the house a few hours ago."

"I thought he was dead," I whispered, sagging in relief and feeling more tears. I was so sick of crying, but at the same time, I'd been holding in a *lot*. Eventually the little cracks in the dam holding back my emotions would crumble, and I'd fall apart.

But not right now.

Ryan's fingertips brushed my nape. "Can I…"

I swallowed and nodded, giving him permission for whatever he wanted. He moved, and the light over our seats turned on. Gently he tugged back the collar of my shirt. A breath hissed between his teeth, and all his muscles tensed as he no doubt got a glimpse at some of the damage.

I closed my eyes, feeling Court's and Linc's furious gazes lingering on me, too. "How did Charles know? He wasn't there when this happened."

"His friend, Tyler, hacked their security system. Gary had a camera pointed at the front door. She showed us the video." Ryan's fingers delved back into my hair and massaged my scalp.

Tremors rippled through my body, and I felt shame color my cheeks. They'd all seen? That was humiliating.

"Don't," Ryan murmured as someone adjusted the air vents so they blew hot air across me. "You couldn't have stopped him, Mads. You did *nothing* wrong." The protective notes in his tone were their own kind of heat, thawing some of my insides.

"I'm so tired," I uttered, drained and finally able to let my guard down.

"Get some rest," Ryan urged. "We'll be home before you know it."

My eyes were already closed, and I was falling away into sleep. But even still, I almost opened my mouth to tell him it didn't matter where we went. As long as I was with him, I was already home.

I woke up a few times. Once when we picked up Knight, who was still riding the high of his "epic boom." He jumped into the car with a *whoop* and was punched by everyone for disturbing me.

Ryan woke me up to get me to climb on Court's back to move from the car to the airport. I almost played the needy girlfriend card and insisted Ryan carry me, but I vaguely remembered Knight asking Ryan about his ribs.

But as soon as we were in the helicopter, this time with Bishop at the helm, I was draped over Ryan's lap again with my feet on Court's legs while Linc and Knight sat across from us and Royal took the copilot seat.

"Maddie?" Knight leaned forward.

"Not now," Ryan snapped. "You can check her out when we're back and she's not totally exposed."

Knight flopped back in his seat as the rotor blades started thumping overhead. "She's not the only one getting checked out, asshole. If you pulled your stitches *again—*"

I tried to look up at Ryan. "Why do you have stitches?"

He cleared his throat and stroked my hair. "Don't worry about me, baby."

I frowned, unhappy that he was brushing off my concern, but I was *so* tired. Within seconds, I was asleep again, and then we were getting out of the helicopter and transitioning to another SUV. Well, two SUVs.

Once again, Ryan and I got in the back. This time Court drove and Linc rode shotgun. The others rode behind us. I drifted in and out of consciousness.

Next thing I knew, Ryan's finger was tracing the curve of my cheek and the outline of my lips. "We're home."

"You're my home," I mumbled, still sleepy and not quite alert.

His fingers stilled. "You're my home, too, but how about if we get you out of this car and into a bed?"

Yeah, a bed sounded awesome.

I sat up slowly, Ryan carefully helping me as we turned down a long road lined with pine trees.

"This isn't California," I murmured, looking around at the towering trees dusted with snow. We were still somewhere north and cold enough that several inches of snow blanketed the ground.

"Wyoming," Court said, glancing at me in the rearview mirror. "We needed to get out of Pac Cross for a while. This place is off the grid, and we'll figure out what to do from here."

I nodded, my head still kind of foggy. "What about Bex?"

Ryan brushed some of my hair over my shoulder. "She's here, too. She's finishing the semester virtually."

My brows shot up. "Her parents agreed to that?"

"Yes," Court answered, his tone rough.

I shot Ryan a look and he shook his head, silently indicating that whatever was bugging Court was something he'd tell me about later.

My eyes slid shut and I leaned my head against his shoulder. I'd missed the way I could read him with a look. I opened my eyes in time to see the trees give way to a large, open space with the billionaire's version of a log cabin in the middle. Smoke curled up from one of the chimneys and rose into the clouds hovering overhead, and it looked like a scene from a movie.

"Whose house is this?" I asked as Court pulled around one side to a four-car garage. He hit a button to open the door and then backed in the car.

"Ours," Ryan answered, and when I shot him a stunned look, he added, "It belongs to Phoenix, technically."

"Well," Linc said, unbuckling, "a subsidiary of a subsidiary that's tucked inside a seashell—"

"What the fuck are you talking about?" Court stared at him across the console. "It's a *shell* corporation."

Linc blinked. "That's what I said."

"You said *sea*shell, dumbass."

Linc's arm shot out and clipped Court's bicep hard enough for him to grunt. My gaze bounced between them, amused and reassured by their banter.

"Fucker," Court hissed, pulling back to hit Linc.

"Enough!" Ryan snapped. "Either of you dipshits hurts Maddie goofing off, and I'll personally kick both your asses."

Linc rolled his eyes and opened his door as the other SUV backed into the spot beside ours. "So fucking touchy."

Court glanced back at me. "Sorry, Mads."

A smile pulled at my lips. "Don't be. I've missed you guys."

"We missed you, too. Especially—"

My door ripped open and Bex appeared, her hazel eyes swimming with tears. "Oh, my God! You're really back!" She started to reach for me, and quickly stopped herself. "Shit. Ash said you're hurt. Can I hug you?"

"No." Ryan's voice cracked through the air like a whip, and I felt him tense behind me. "She's seriously hurt, and she needs to rest."

Instead of backing down, Bex planted her hands on her hips and scowled at him. "Really? How are your ribs, Ryan?"

Court got out of the driver's seat and tugged Bex back. "Easy, tiger."

I turned sharply, wincing as my back pulled. "What about your ribs?"

Ryan shot Bex an annoyed look that gentled when he faced me. "Can we talk about it inside? We have a lot to catch up on."

"Debriefing in ten?" Royal asked as he walked by, a black duffel bag slung over his shoulder and black aviator glasses hiding his eyes.

"You're kidding, right?" Ryan growled. "She *just* got here."

Royal frowned. "So, twenty?"

"Fucker—"

Court placed a hand on his brother's chest. "Let's give them a few hours, bro. They need it."

Royal grunted, and I got the impression he wasn't pleased with the suggestion. But he turned and strode into the house as Bishop and Knight brought up the rear.

"I'm fucking starving," Knight whined, rubbing his stomach.

"I made breakfast," Bex said with a quick smile.

Linc came around the truck and grabbed her from behind, hugging her to his chest as he placed a noisy kiss on her cheek. "You're a goddess, B."

Bex blushed, and Court glowered at his best friend until Linc let her go and traipsed after Knight and Bishop, presumably to find food.

I used the handle above my seat to maneuver myself backwards out of the car. I heard Bex's fast intake of breath when part of my shirt rode up. Ryan's jaw tensed, and I forced myself to smile at him.

"I'll be okay," I promised.

"I'm holding you to that," he muttered, running a hand through his hair and wincing.

I finished putting my feet on the garage floor and waited for him to get out. When he walked around to meet me, he was paler than he'd been in the SUV. Or shit, maybe I hadn't noticed.

"Ryan—"

He kissed my forehead. "Inside. Food and then sleep, okay?"

"Medical, food, and *then* sleep," Knight called as we made our way into the house.

The door from the garage led into a small mudroom and then a massive kitchen that would've made a chef drool. Across the large island in the middle was a spread of food—eggs, pancakes, waffles, hash browns, bacon, sausage… And half of it was already piled onto the plates of the four men sitting at the banquette near a large window overlooking the rear of the property.

My gaze moved around the room, landing on each person and feeling the utter rightness as the pieces of my world slid back into place.

Standing in the walkway between the stove and island was Ash. He wiped his hands on a towel and smiled at me, then came around the island and kissed my forehead. "Hey, Mads. Hungry?"

I gently prodded the inside of my cheek with my tongue, suppressing a flinch when it still ached. "Maybe some eggs."

"Girl, you need protein and carbs," Bishop called.

Knight pushed his mostly eaten plate away and stood, knocking his brother across the back of the head. "Look at her face, bro. Probably hurts like a bitch to chew." He moved in front of me. "You good if I check you out now?"

I shook my head and turned to the man at my back. The man who always *had* my back. "Ryan first."

Ryan shook his head. "No, babe. I'm fine. You first."

Narrowing my eyes, I poked the side he'd been favoring.

"Fuck," he hissed, twisting away from me, jaw clenched tight enough to break teeth.

I lifted my hand to my face, stunned at the smear of blood across it. For a second it didn't make sense.

"Shit. You pulled your stitches *again*?" Knight moved around me.

I stared hard at Ryan, my heart pounding. "What happened?"

He opened his mouth, and I knew he was about to tell me it wasn't a big deal. But he was hurt and *bleeding*.

A memory surfaced. Gary had taunted me at Highwater. He'd had Ryan arrested… and attacked in prison.

"Stitches from when you were *stabbed*?" My hands balled into pointless fists at my sides, because Gary wasn't around for me to pummel.

Ryan grimaced as Knight lifted his shirt and revealed a patch of gauze-soaked crimson. "Maddie."

Holding up a hand, I shot him down before he could even try. "Uh uh. You sit your ass down and let Knight take care of you, or you can plan on spending a lot of quality time with your hand for the next decade."

It was a bluff, an outright lie. But of the two of us? I wasn't the one bleeding in the damn kitchen. And I'd say anything to get him to accept the help he needed.

He pressed his lips together, likely hiding the start of a grin. "Okay, Mads. You win." He nodded at Knight.

From behind me, Linc chuckled. "God, I've missed her."

CHAPTER 28

MADDIE

Watching Knight redo Ryan's stitches ruined any appetite I'd had. Worry churned in my gut as I sat on the edge of the bed in what I was told was my and Ryan's room.

I studied Ryan shirtless as Knight worked, and while I still got that familiar thrill at seeing all his hard lines and sculpted muscles on display, as I looked at the healing wound that would leave a scar, guilt weighed me down.

"Mads."

My gaze snapped to his to find him frowning.

"None of this is on you."

I didn't have the energy to argue. Sighing, I turned away and stared out the window. It had started to snow again.

As a kid, I'd loved snow. The trailer park I'd grown up in was rough and dated, with more weeds than plants and deep ruts in the gravel roads. But snow had always turned my world into something new and pure.

Wistfully, I tried to recapture that feeling, but it hovered just out of reach.

My world was too fucked up for even a blanket of snow to hide the trauma.

"Okay," Knight said, coming to stand in front of me. "Can I take a look at your back?"

I startled and looked at Ryan, who was pulling his shirt over his head. He gave me a supportive smile that did nothing to help me feel more at ease. As if seeing my uncertainty, his eyes narrowed.

"Uh, sure," I finally muttered, even as I wrapped the bottom of my shirt in my balled fists and held on.

Knight's brow furrowed. "Maddie—"

He was cut off by a soft knock at the door. With an annoyed huff, Ryan stalked across the room and ripped it open to reveal Chase on the other side.

I stood quickly. "You're okay."

Smiling, Chase stepped forward, only to be blocked by Ryan.

"Ry," I entreated, "Chase is a friend."

Ryan glanced over his shoulder, brow cocked. "*Chase?* He has you calling him that shit, too?"

I rolled my eyes and elbowed him. "Would you have found me without him?"

"Yes," Ryan countered. "Ash had already found three properties we were going to check out, and one of them was where you were."

"Before or after Gary had another chance to beat her or sell her to one of his friends?" Chase asked, his tone sharp.

I flinched, and Ryan growled before shoving Chase into the wall on the other side of the hallway.

"Stop!" I shouted, hurrying forward to grab Ryan's shoulders and stop him from putting Chase into the damn wall. I managed to tug him away from Chase, but Ryan stayed firmly between us, like I needed a shield from the guy who'd essentially helped Ryan save me.

"Class act as always, Cain," Chase taunted, shaking his head in disgust as he straightened his shirt. His green eyes pierced me. "Should I even attempt pleading a case for you to leave all this mess in your past? I can have us on my family's estate in Blye by tomorrow night. You'd be safe."

Ryan chuckled, the sound devoid of humor and full of venom. He took a single, threatening step toward Chase, rolling his massive shoulders as if readying for a fight. "Fucking try to take her away from me. I dare you."

Chase smirked. "Doesn't seem like much of a challenge if a wanker like Gary can manage it."

"Both of you *stop*," I snapped before Ryan could respond. "Can't you see you both matter to me?" I tugged at Ryan's arm until he turned and looked at me. "Chase is my friend. He helped you get me away from Gary. He protected me several times when Gary tried to… You know, what? It doesn't matter."

I spun away and paced into the room before whirling back and pointing a finger at Chase. "And do you really think you're helping me? All I want to do is take a minute to *breathe*. You were there. You saw what happened and what he was like firsthand."

Chase lowered his gaze, his cheeks reddening. Ryan just stared at me stonily, still keeping his body firmly planted between Chase and me.

I threw my arms up. "I'm not going with him, Ryan. We're seeing this thing through to the end, together." I turned to Knight and sighed. "Can you check me out so I can get some rest? I just want to sleep for a week."

Knight nodded, his expression calming. "Of course." His dark eyes flicked over my shoulder. "Both of you assholes get the fuck out."

Ryan snorted. "No fucking—"

"I still have the file from Gary," Chase interrupted, looking from Knight to me. "If the doctor thinks it would be beneficial."

"File?" Knight asked.

"He's not a doctor," Ryan muttered at the same time.

"Send it to Knight, but I'd also like to see it again, too," I told Chase. "I didn't have a chance to absorb everything. I want to see if…" If my father had done anything else besides have me drugged and my birth control device removed. With my luck, he probably *had* had me inseminated or something.

Shaking away the thought, I looked at Knight. "Gary had a medical file on me. All the drugs they put in my system, and procedure—"

"*Procedure?*" Ryan cut in, crossing the room and coming to stand in front of me. "What did he do?"

Chase cleared his throat. "My phone is in my room. But we should talk after you've rested. Tyler had some questions, and maybe a solution to the money issue."

Surprise zipped through me. "Tyler's *here*? I thought she was in England or something."

He shook his head. "No, she insisted on coming to the US when I decided to accept the engagement offer."

Ryan growled, the noise sounding more animal than man, and I reached out to smooth the furrow in his brow. "Fake engagement, remember?"

Chase cleared his throat. "Tyler's asleep now. We drove all night to get here and crashed." A scowl swept over his features as he pinned Ryan with an annoyed stare. "And our doors were mysteriously locked when you first arrived, or I'd have come to see you then."

"Strange," Ryan deadpanned, clearly not giving a shit.

Sighing, I rubbed my forehead, an ache settling behind my eyes.

"I'll let you rest. We'll talk later," Chase said, reaching forward and pulling the door shut.

"What procedure?" Ryan wasn't letting this go.

I faced the bed, my back to both of them, and started to pull off my shirt. Ryan's hands covered mine before I'd tugged it up half an inch, delicately removing the shirt and tossing it aside.

I lay down on the bed, curling my arms between my chest and the mattress. "Gary had my IUD removed while I was unconscious."

I felt the bed dip as Ryan sat by my head and reached under me until he'd found one of my hands to hold. He didn't offer useless apologies that wouldn't change anything now. Instead, he just held on to me.

Warm hands touched my back. "Looks like this is actually healing pretty well," Knight said, his tone quiet and his touch professional.

Ryan didn't speak, but he squeezed my hand, and I could feel the rage rippling through him as he took in my mangled back.

Knight cleared his throat and lifted the bottom of my shorts. "Looks like he only broke the skin in a few places. You're lucky."

I snorted into the mattress, my back throbbing. "Yeah, I feel lucky."

"Sorry," Knight apologized, sounding sincere. "I just mean, I've seen guys overseas who were whipped with worse than a belt. Their scars never went away, and a lot got infected. Your shoulder is bleeding a bit, but the stitches didn't tear."

I managed to turn my head and smile up at Ryan. "See? You can escape a psycho *and* keep your stitches intact."

A thin smile tugged at his mouth. "Noted." The worry in his blue eyes was undeniable.

"I'm okay," I assured him.

His jaw clenched, a muscle ticking. "Maddie, you're not seeing what I'm seeing."

Knight moved away then came back and started wrapping up my shoulder. "I have some arnica cream that will help with the swelling and bruising. I'll give it to Ryan. Massage it into her skin, but be gentle. You don't wanna aggravate what's already started healing."

"Got it," Ryan replied.

Knight finished and stepped back. "I'm going to see if Chase has that file. I don't want to miss anything. You sure you don't mind if I look at it, Maddie?"

I dipped my head in agreement. "Yeah, go ahead."

"Cream's on the dresser," Knight told Ryan. "Both of you should get some rest."

My lips twisted into a smile. "But what about Royal's debriefing?"

Knight laughed. "I'll handle big brother and check on you both later."

"Thanks, man," Ryan said, getting off the bed and following Knight as he left. He locked the door and came back to me with a heavy sigh. "Mads. I don't even know where to start."

"Then don't," I practically begged. "This isn't your fault."

"I promised to keep you safe," he argued.

"Can we please play the blame game when I'm not exhausted? If I don't sleep soon, I'm going to start crying, and you'd be amazed at the back muscles it takes to produce a solid sob." It was true. As much as I'd wanted to cry the day after my attack, I'd quickly learned that crying tensed and tugged at an array of muscles I hadn't expected. Quiet was better.

Another long sigh from Ryan, and then he grabbed the cream from the dresser. He scowled down at me as he squeezed some into his palms. "If I hurt you, tell me."

"I will," I lied. There was no way for him to touch me without hurting me, but it would be worth it. I'd endure every kind of agony under the sun to feel his hands on me.

I jolted as he first made contact, but as he massaged me, I went boneless. He worked quietly, smoothing his way down my back and pausing to tug my shorts off to finish taking care of my ass.

Ryan groaned softly. "You've seriously been running around all fucking night and day without underwear on?"

"You're lucky I had shorts on," I replied drowsily. "I'd just gotten out of the shower when you decided to stage your rescue. Maybe give a girl some notice next time, and I'll be packed and ready."

"The explosion *was* your notice," he teased.

"I'll keep that in mind for when I'm kidnapped and held captive again," I quipped.

Growling, Ryan tossed the tube away. "There won't be a next time."

"You can't promise that," I said, shaking my head.

He gave a soft hum of disapproval and stripped off his shirt. "I'm contemplating different ways to make sure it doesn't happen."

"Like?" I looked at him as he stretched out on his back beside me.

He ticked up a finger. "Sewing our skin together."

My nose wrinkled. "Gross."

"Hardwiring your bones with a tracker."

"Hard pass," I laughed.

His brow wrinkled. "Handcuffing our wrists together?"

"Might make going to the bathroom interesting."

His eyes sparkled. "But we'd get to know each other in every way."

I patted his chest. "Maybe we should save some of the mystery."

He snagged my fingers and held them over his heart. "I'll keep thinking."

I nestled closer, my head finding the perfect spot in the space between his chest and shoulder. I closed my eyes and relaxed. "You're crazy."

He was quiet for a long moment. "Mads, I need to ask you something."

I perked up, the serious note in his voice making me nervous. "Okay."

He glanced away with a soft exhale. "Baby, I saw the engagement announcement."

My heart sank.

"I saw you kissing—"

I quickly covered his mouth with my fingers, tears filling my eyes. "I didn't have a choice, Ryan, I swear. I didn't want to kiss him."

Ryan pushed my hand down and silenced me with a searing kiss. "I'm not accusing you, Maddie. I just… I guess I just needed to hear you say it."

I sniffled a little.

"Baby," he murmured, wiping away a tear, "don't cry. I fucking hate it when you cry."

I met his gaze. "I really didn't have a choice. I didn't want to kiss Chase any more than he wanted to kiss me."

He scoffed, clearly not buying the last part.

"I mean it," I insisted. "Chase is my friend, and Gary forced us to do it. But it was just a kiss. I love you."

He gazed into my eyes, nothing but trust and love in them. "I know."

"You believe me?" I whispered, hope fluttering in my chest.

"Maddie, I love you," he replied with a ferocity that spoke to my soul. "I made the mistake of not trusting you once. I swore I'd never do that again, and I'm not fucking us up. I will *always* believe you."

CHAPTER 29

RYAN

Hiding things from Maddie sucked, but when she'd bared her back to Knight and me, I had to swallow my rage. She hadn't seen the way I'd started to shake and nearly bolted for the door to track down Gary and do worse to him.

Having someone remove her fucking birth control while she was unconscious? What the actual fuck was *wrong* with this guy?

Thank God for Knight, who had kept it together and acted as a buffer. He'd taken care of Maddie while I held her damn hand, helpless to do more to fix the mess we were in.

Now that she was sleeping soundly, though, all I could do was stare at her. I was relieved that she was back, but bloodlust still simmered in my veins. It would take only a single degree to tip me into a full-blown boil.

I eased out from under her and got up, then pulled on my shirt again and went to find answers. I paused in the doorway, looking back at her, and wondered if I should just do what my heart wanted. Crawl back into bed with her and keep watching her sleeping at my side, as close to peace as either of us had come in the last few weeks.

My spine steeled and I crept from the room, closing the door soundlessly behind me.

I'd rest with her when I knew no one else was coming for us. When I knew she was really safe.

I found Ash standing in the dining room, pissed off and close to losing it as he glared over the table at Tyler.

In a rumpled top and yoga pants, Tyler looked like she'd just rolled out of bed, her hair still in a messy bun and the glasses perched on her nose emphasizing the almost violet color of her eyes.

"What's up?" I asked, pausing warily.

"Nothing except that this limp-dicked dung beetle can't admit that he's wrong," Tyler spat.

Ash rolled his eyes toward the ceiling, his hands curled tightly around the back of the chair he stood behind. "Swear to Christ, Ry, get her out of here."

"Or what?" Tyler scoffed. "What are you going to do? Keep sucking at the one thing you're supposed to be good at?"

Charles—or *Chase*, since that was apparently his new name—appeared behind Tyler in the doorway that led to the kitchen. "Everything all right?"

"Take your sidekick and bounce," I told him, jerking my chin at Tyler.

"Why don't you go sniff a moldy crotch?" Tyler countered, turning her ire on me.

My brows shot up. "I'm sorry. Is it a love connection then?"

"He's my *cousin*," she hissed. "And if anyone's the sidekick, it's him."

"I think I'm offended," Chase murmured. "Tyler, why don't you take a break?"

She gaped at him. "Chase, come on. You're going to let these dipshits push you around?"

"Does she come with an off button?" Ash demanded. "Seriously, shut up."

"Don't speak to her like that," Chase replied as Tyler cried, "Fuck off!"

"Jesus Christ," I groaned. "Can we all just act like adults for a fucking minute?" I stormed into the room and yanked out a chair before falling into it.

Chase grimaced. "As much as it pains me, I think he's right." He moved forward and sat across from me.

Snorting, Ash sat down. Tyler was last, and she sat with a huff and folded her arms.

"Now," I started calmly, looking at my best friend, "where are we at with finding Gary?"

Ash ignored Tyler when her hand shot into the air like this was a schoolroom. "None of his accounts have been touched, but he may have fled to one of the properties we flagged before that we thought Maddie could be at."

Tyler thrashed her hand back and forth.

"Yes?" I drawled, looking at her.

She smirked at Ash. "He's in Nevada. Henderson, specifically."

"How could you possibly know that?" Ash demanded.

"Because I planted a Trojan horse when I transferred the money. He handled everything on his phone, and I can track him that way. I have access to everything—his accounts, his emails and phone calls. I hacked his mic, so I know if he farts." She shot Ash a triumphant smirk.

"Other than the fact that that's gross... Not bad, newbie." Grudging respect tinged Ash's tone. He drew in what looked like a painful breath. "Can you show me? I might be able to notice something about what he's planning next."

Tyler settled back in her seat and nodded. "Of course."

"Awesome. Now that you two are playing nice, maybe *Chase* can explain how he ties into this and how he knew Madelaine." I stared at the guy in question.

He swallowed and nodded. "Madelaine reached out to me last spring."

"Why you?" I demanded.

He sighed. "Because Gary Cabot is responsible for the death of my mother and my unborn sister. They died a year earlier."

"Whoa, what?" I straightened. "Gary and... your mom?"

Chase nodded. "Yes. They had an affair. She became pregnant, against medical advice, but Gary knocked her up on purpose. Her placenta detached, and she hemorrhaged to death." His jaw clenched and he looked at his hands.

Tyler's lips pressed together. "Chase found her."

"I'm sorry." My apology was genuine. If he loved his mom half as much as I'd loved mine, then his grief was consuming. I couldn't imagine losing mom *and* Cori.

"He wanted another child so he could get rid of Madelaine," Chase added, swallowing his emotions.

"He had one. Maddie," I countered.

"And look at how much trouble it's been," Chase pointed out. "She isn't the grateful little gutter rat he plucked from the slums and gave the world to. She questions things, defies him. Sometimes in more ways than her sister ever did."

Annoyance rippled across my skin, but I could see his point. Killing Madelaine and raising a new baby would have been easier. And we'd been wrong about Gary needing the inheritance immediately; he seemed to have been operating just fine before he'd gotten ahold of it.

"I can't believe you gave him that money," I bit out, rubbing the back of my neck.

"We did it to get Maddie free," Tyler protested. She glared at her cousin. "I told you not to get emotional. But no, you *had* to tell her the truth."

Chase frowned at her. "You didn't see what I saw. Maddie needed *hope*, Tyler."

I leaned forward. "And how exactly did you get in a position to give her that hope?"

"Gary reached out to several people in his European circles about her. One of them was my father. It was a dig, mostly, to point out that my father no longer had a wife, but my father shared the message with me, and I realized Maddie was in trouble," Chase explained.

"Reached out how?" I pressed.

"He was attempting to sell her off and recoup some of what he'd lost." Chase's flat tone was jarring. "I know you're well aware of the types of men he was offering her to."

Bile rose in my throat, burning me from the inside out. That fucking cocksucker. I knew exactly the type of men he'd offered my girl up to. Men who would look at a gorgeous girl like her and crave nothing more than to break her apart the way a child pulled the wings off a fly when they were bored.

Chase nodded at me. "I offered him a better solution. In exchange for Maddie and five percent of the inheritance, Tyler would locate the money and have it transferred to him."

Tyler cringed a little in her seat. "If it helps, I think I can get the money back."

Ash cocked his head. "You can?"

She shifted in her seat. "Yeah. It'll take a little time, but I wired it through a network that I can use to backtrace it."

"Smart," Ash murmured, giving her a tiny smile of approval that turned her cheeks pink.

"Thanks."

I looked at Chase. "Okay, so back to Madelaine. What did she say?"

"That she'd been watching her father for years. That she wanted to stop him, and she thought we could help each other. The plan was for her to meet me at my family's summer house in Athens, but she never showed up."

"Because Gary had her killed," I surmised.

Chase nodded. "When she didn't show, Tyler tried to track her down. We heard about the fire, but I never connected the dots. I decided to transfer from Oxford to Pacific Cross to get close to her. When I met her that first day, it was fairly obvious she wasn't the girl I'd been working with."

I shook my head, wondering how this asshat had instantly seen what I'd missed for months. Maddie was nothing like her sister. They might have looked identical, but just talking to her should have clued me in. Hell, the first time I'd met her, I'd pinned her to the bed. Madelaine would've submitted and tried to seduce me, but Maddie had fought me for every inch.

I'd been so blinded by my hatred of Madelaine that I'd missed enjoying the first time I'd met the woman who would eventually become my entire reason for existing.

"To be fair, I tried to warn her off you," Chase added with a wry smile. "Still might, but she's convinced her sister was wrong about you lot." He pointed from me to Ash.

"Meaning what?" Ash demanded.

"Meaning," Maddie clarified as she walked into the room in a loose shirt and sleepy expression, "Madelaine also convinced him that Phoenix was another company run by entitled pricks who exploited the innocent." She paused beside my chair, an accusing look in her eyes. "Knight said we *both* needed to rest."

"Not tired," I countered.

"Funny," she chirped with false enthusiasm, "neither am I." She pulled out the chair on my other side and looked across the table. "Hey. You must be Tyler."

"Which would make you Maddie." Tyler smiled at her. "How are you feeling?"

"Alive," Maddie replied with an easy smile that tightened as she attempted to get comfortable on the chair. "And sore."

"You could be in bed resting," I told her with a sharp smile.

She returned it. "So could you."

"I'm sorry I left you there," Chase told her. "I'd give anything to go back and—"

"And what? Fight through a bunch of armed guys? You'd have died, and they wouldn't have found me as quickly." Maddie shook her head, her long blonde hair falling in soft waves around her face. "You did the right thing. I thought you were dead when he told me he'd been recording us."

Chase grimaced. "I failed you."

"You really did," I agreed.

Maddie slapped my arm. "Behave."

"Can I get you anything?" Ash offered.

Maddie started to shake her head, and then paused. "Actually, yeah. Maybe it's time we all had a meeting to talk about what happens next.

Specifically how we get what we need to take Gary down once and for all."

"You want to go to Pandora," Chase murmured, smiling. "It's brilliant."

"It's risky," I shot back.

"And it's *my* choice," Maddie concluded, turning to me and arching a brow. "Madelaine hid an arsenal of shit against Gary. Against your dad, too. Don't you want to finally end this?"

"Baby, we've discussed the risks, and it's too much. Especially right now. You can barely walk without being in pain."

She sighed and took my hand. "Then we wait a few days for me to heal and do it then."

"Pandora is in Las Vegas," Tyler said softly. "Gary is in Henderson. It's pretty close."

"Good thing I'm not going alone then, isn't it?" Maddie smiled, looking at me to validate and approve her plan.

This girl was going to drive me crazy.

I exhaled hard and looked at Ash. "Get the others."

CHAPTER 30

MADDIE

The shower cut off as I closed the door to our bedroom. With a sigh, I leaned against it and considered my next move. We'd been in Wyoming over a week, and my back was almost completely healed.

Not that Ryan had noticed.

Well, not in the *way* that I wanted Ryan to notice.

Sure, we slept in the same bed every night, and we were together all the time. I'd broken down about Gary killing Marge and my mother's new role in his life. Ryan had told me about his stint in prison. Ash and Tyler had been doing their hacker thing, when they weren't fighting, and Ash had finally gotten us a tentative time frame for when I could access Madelaine's security box at Pandora. The plan was to leave Wyoming tomorrow night.

Ryan, Linc, Court, and I would travel to Las Vegas while the others stayed behind. We figured keeping the party small would help us fly under the radar, and I was anxious to see what my sister had been hiding.

But I was even more anxious to get some alone time with Ryan. It was the middle of December now, and I was acutely aware that I hadn't been with him in weeks.

And I was pretty freaking over it.

Reaching behind me, I flipped the lock on our door and stalked with purpose to the bathroom. I nudged the door open as he was stepping from the shower, drying himself off. He looked up at me, his smile instant.

"Did you want the shower?" he asked, wrapping the towel around his waist and running a hand through his wet hair.

"No." My gaze tracked a bead of water as it rolled down his chest, across his abs, and dissolved into the towel.

He tilted his head. "Everything okay?"

"No," I said again, still watching him, wondering how I'd tell him what I wanted without bursting into flames of embarrassment.

He frowned at me. "Maddie—"

I stripped off my shirt, smirking when his gaze dropped to my tits and the way they moved beneath the sheer lacy bra I'd put on earlier. Lust swirled in his gaze for a moment before he shoved it down. He licked his lips and met my eyes. "Do you need me to look at your back? Is it bugging you?"

"What I need—" I sucked in a fortifying breath "—is *you*."

His fingers twitched at his sides. "Mads, you're still healing. I don't wanna hurt you."

I unbuttoned my jeans and peeled them off, along with my underwear. "Fine. Then I'll handle it." I turned to go to the bed. If he didn't want to fuck me, then I'd take care of myself.

Before I'd made it two steps, his arm locked around my waist and dragged me to his chest.

"Madison." The soft growl in his voice made my insides melt, and I sagged against him, loving the way my body fit with his.

I tilted back my head and looked at him over my shoulder. "I'm fine, Ryan. You are, too." Knight had removed his sutures the day before, satisfied the skin had healed enough. "I miss you. I *want* you."

His lips found mine, coaxing them open as his tongue swept inside and devoured me. The arm around my waist tightened, pinning my arms to my sides so I couldn't touch him in return. All I could do was accept what he was offering.

"I miss you, too," he murmured against my lips. "But I'll never forgive myself if I hurt you."

"Like I said," I breathed, my heart thrashing in my chest as I doubled down on my threat, "I can take care of things myself if you're not sure you can handle it."

He pulled away, a gleam entering his eyes that made my insides shiver. "Okay. Prove it."

My mouth went dry. "What?"

He let me go and stepped back, jerking his chin at the bed. "Prove to me it won't hurt. Get yourself off, and maybe I'll think about joining."

I searched his gaze. He was serious. He wanted me to…

"Okay," I murmured, taking a deep breath and squashing my inhibitions. I walked backwards to the bed, opening the front clasp of my bra and taking it off. I tossed it at his face.

With a smirk, Ryan caught it and leaned a shoulder against the bathroom doorframe. Not even the thick terry cloth of the towel could hide his arousal.

I knew my cheeks were on fire, but if he wanted a show, then I'd show him *exactly* what he was missing.

My knees hit the edge of the bed and I slowly sank onto it, running my hands up my ribs and cupping my breasts. I scraped my nails over my nipples, plucking and squeezing, before running my hands back down my body.

I watched his gaze as I stroked my fingers slowly over my labia. His blue eyes were fixed on my fingers, and he bit his lip when I slipped my middle finger between my folds.

My eyes shuttered as my back arched, the slightest brush of my fingertip against my clit sending shockwaves through my system. A soft moan slipped from my lips, and I circled my clit again.

"Show me," Ryan demanded. "I want to see how wet you are."

Chuckling, I shook my head and smirked at him. "Nope. You didn't want to play, remember?" I fell back and scooted farther up the bed so I could dig my heels into the mattress. "Fuck," I whispered, circling my entrance and feeling how soaked I was. "I forgot how good this feels."

"Madison."

"Shh," I told him, smiling to myself. He was on the verge of breaking, if the rough tone was anything to go by. "You're killing my me-time vibe." I sank two fingers inside my pussy and groaned, long and hard, playing up how turned on I was.

"Christ," he swore under his breath, and I could imagine the frustrated look on his gorgeous face. The way the muscle in his jaw would tick as he clenched his teeth, the way his eyes would flash with warning…

Just picturing Ryan hot and bothered was enough to make me shudder as I kept fucking myself. My back arched off the bed as I moved my fingers up to glide around my clit. I was so damn close. My body strained forward, aching for release.

I slipped my fingers through my wetness and back to my hole, about to add a third finger to the party when a hand slammed around my wrist and yanked it away. My eyes snapped open to see Ryan standing between my legs.

"You win, baby," he told me, the concession sounding dangerous as his gaze burned across my skin. He lifted my fingers to his mouth and sucked them clean, groaning at my taste on his tongue. He'd dropped the towel, and I felt the head of his cock nudge at my entrance.

"Doesn't feel like I'm winning yet," I said, rolling my hips and hoping he'd magically slip inside me.

His hands dropped to my hips as he flashed me a smile that lit up my heart. "Fucking temptress." He slammed inside me in one thrust that left me gasping at the sudden fullness. Shit, how had I forgotten how big he was?

"Okay?" He paused, checking to make sure, and when I nodded, he grinned. "I love this pussy." His hands tightened on my hips as he pulled out and drove back in, pounding into my body.

My back lifted off the bed as I cried out, desperate for more. But at this angle, I could barely touch his hips. He had all the power, and he used it to propel me closer and closer to the edge. Until everything in me was pulled tight, shrieking for release.

He moved a hand from my hip, never breaking his rhythm as he pressed his thumb against my clit.

I shattered with a scream of relief, my body convulsing as he kept thrusting, dragging out my orgasm until I was a twitching mess of aftershocks.

But he wasn't done. He was still hard inside me, and he somehow lifted and maneuvered my legs so my ankles were behind his neck.

"Oh, God," I whimpered, the new angle impossibly tight as he pushed in and out of me.

"Again, Maddie," he ordered, his blue eyes electric as he watched me, his thumb slicking around my clit. "You wanted me, now you have me."

I clenched around him, loving the guttural, desperate edge to his voice and the wild look in his gaze. He needed me as much as I needed him. We both needed this, and as my body arched and clenched, I wondered if this would be how I died.

Death by orgasm.

Sign me up.

I stretched my arms over my head and gave myself over to the tsunami rolling through me. My world went white for a minute as I came apart, not sure I would ever stop spasming around his cock.

With a roar, Ryan emptied himself inside me, his hips jerking against me as he rode out his own release. When he was finished, he let my legs go and fell onto the bed beside me.

My heart pounded as I tried to remember to breathe.

"Shit," I whispered, feeling the mess between my legs.

Instantly, he was alert. "What? Did I hurt you?"

"No." I laid a hand on his chest. "But my birth control isn't technically effective yet." Knight had managed to procure some pills until I could get another IUD, but he'd warned me they'd take up to seven days to be completely effective.

And I'd forgotten.

"Shit," I faltered, shooting him a guilty look.

"Mads, chill," he told me, rolling onto his side and propping himself up on one arm. His bicep bulged, and my eyes tracked the dates tattooed there. Four dates, each one a day that he needed to memorialize.

10.01

Corinne's birthday.

7.18

The day his Nana died.

2.05

When the guys decided to form Phoenix. Also the day he got the massive Phoenix tattoo on his back.

And the last one.

11.25

Our wedding.

That one made me look away, unable to bear the reality that we weren't married. That Gary had been able to undo what we'd done.

"It'll always be the day we got married," Ryan said softly, reading my mind. His warm hand splayed across my lower belly. "And I don't give a shit if you get pregnant, Mads. I want it all with you."

"Right now wouldn't be ideal," I whispered, wondering how we'd bring a baby into this chaos we were mired in.

"No," he admitted, "but we'd manage."

"You always do that," I marveled. "Always make me feel like it's going to all work out."

He reached over and tugged me across the bed to lie on his chest. His arms wound around me, protective and safe. "Because it's going to all work out. We're going to have it all, baby."

I snuggled into his side, listening to his heart beating and letting his vow wrap around my soul.

We *would* have it all.

But at what cost?

CHAPTER 31

MADDIE

Las Vegas wasn't as spectacular in the daytime as the movies made it out to be at night. But as we drove through the city limits, I still gaped at the sights. The streets were mostly empty, but it was barely after eight in the morning. We'd driven through the night, and I was sick to death of this SUV.

And a little over the people in the car, if I was being honest.

At least Linc had passed out a few hours ago. I'd been worried that Court or Ryan might've actually punched him if he hadn't stopped singing along to the radio as loud as he could. It didn't matter what station. He belted out T. Swift as easily as Papa Roach and Coldplay.

I'd brought a loaner laptop from Ash so I could try to catch up on my schoolwork, but I'd mostly slept and watched the country zip by.

Court turned the car into a carport with flashing neon lights and killed the engine before punching Linc awake.

"Motherfucker!" Linc roared, waking up swinging, but Court was already out of the car.

I giggled as Ryan rolled his eyes and opened his door to let us out while a bellhop came to the car with a bright smile and a cart.

"We've got it." Court waved him off as he popped the hatch and pulled out the bags we'd packed. He handed Ryan his and my bags and hurled Linc's at his head when he stumbled from the car.

Linc caught it. Barely. "You're grouchy after a road trip."

"And you're an annoying asshole," Court returned.

Linc frowned and came up beside me, wrapping an arm around my shoulders. "Do you think I'm annoying, Mads?"

I shot him an amused look. "Dude, you're on your own. I lost part of my hearing when you were singing the falsetto for 'Respect.'"

He laid a hand over his heart. "Aretha *is* the queen. She deserved my best interpretation of her classic."

"And you deserve to have your nuts kicked," Ryan muttered, grabbing my wrist and tugging me away from Linc.

"I'm rooming with them," Court announced.

"No, you're not." Ryan shot him down at the same time Linc asked, "Then who's gonna cuddle with me?"

I shook my head as we approached the front counter. Ryan checked us in with an alias Ash had set up, and handed keys to Linc and Court as we walked to the elevator.

"Anything from Ash?" Court leaned against the mirrored wall as the elevator doors slid shut, his eyes closing. He'd done the bulk of the driving and insisted he was fine whenever Ryan or Linc offered to take over.

Ryan shook his head. "He's waiting for the time."

Pandora wasn't like a normal security vault tucked inside a bank. No, it was a place where obscenely powerful people went to hide their deepest, darkest secrets, and it was twenty floors beneath a strip club. It was heavily guarded, and people who wanted to access their unit were given a vague window of time and then emailed details an hour before they could go.

So now we waited. The guys would hang out in the strip club while I embraced my inner Nancy Drew and tried to unravel my sister's life. Hopefully she'd stored something that would help us shut Gary down for good.

The elevator stopped on the top floor and let us out. I raised my brows as we stepped into a marble foyer with gilded chairs set by a table with fresh flowers. There were doors on either side of us.

"Where are all the other rooms?" I asked.

Linc laughed, slinging his bag over his shoulder. "I forget how new she is sometimes, bro. Call us when it's time to go."

Court smiled at me and followed Linc into the room to our left. Ryan's fingers laced with mine, and he used his keycard to unlock the one on the right.

"Ash booked us the penthouse so we'd have privacy," he explained, holding open the door for me.

I walked through, my eyes going wide as I took in massive floor-to-ceiling windows overlooking the Strip, a living area decorated in creams and golds, and a floating staircase that led to a whole other level.

"This is like a fairytale," I whispered, not sure what to look at next.

Ryan closed the door and wrapped his arms around me from behind, his chin on my shoulder. "Consider this a mini version of the honeymoon I owe you." He kissed the side of my throat. "Tired?"

I was, but sleep was the last thing on my mind.

I turned in his arms, burrowing closer into his chest. "Nope."

He grinned as I snuck my hands under his shirt. The muscles of his abs flexed beneath my touch as I glided my hands up his chest. I lightly raked my nails across his nipples, smiling when I heard the quick intake of breath hiss between his lips. He raised his arms so I could push his shirt over his head, then I dipped my mouth to suck one of his nipples between my lips.

"Fuck," he barked, a hand twisting around my ponytail and jerking my head back.

My lips left his skin with an audible *pop* as I watched him through hooded eyes.

He grinned at me, feral and devastating. "I've got something better you can suck." He pushed me to my knees and cocked a brow, waiting for me to pick up his unspoken command.

I licked my lips, anticipation singing in my veins as I studied the bulge in his jeans a moment before unbuttoning them and wrestling them down his hips and legs, along with his boxers. His cock sprang free, damn near hitting me in the face.

Without hesitating, I leaned forward and swiped the flat of my tongue up the underside of his length, teasing his slit before sucking just his tip into my mouth.

His hands tightened against my head and he thrust forward, his cock hitting the back of my throat. My eyes watered, and I gagged. He didn't let up, pressing deeper until I swallowed hard. Then he pulled out, leaving me gasping.

"Too much?" he asked mildly, almost like a dare.

I smirked. "I can take it."

He thumbed my bottom lip. "That's my girl. Hands behind your back."

I did as he said, folding my arms together at the small of my back and waiting on my knees. Pleasure shot through me as he grinned down at me, approval in his eyes.

"Open your mouth."

My mouth fell open before my brain could process the words, my body completely ready to do whatever he wanted. I loved when he got like this; bossy and dominant and so focused on the connection between us that nothing else seemed to exist.

Keeping my ponytail wrapped in his fist, he thrust into my mouth. The taste of him exploded on my tongue, salty and tangy. I worked to relax my jaw and let him all the way in. When he went deeper, I dug my nails into my forearms and forced myself to breathe through my nose.

"Fuck, I love this mouth," he rasped, picking up the pace and barely giving me time to catch my breath. Tears pricked my eyes and slid down my cheeks. His fingers caught one of my tears, and I watched through blurry eyes as he lifted it to his lips.

"You taste amazing in every single way," he murmured, grunting at the end as I hollowed my cheeks and sucked. "Shit, yeah. Do that again, baby."

I sucked hard and swallowed against his tip as it bumped the back of my throat.

"Fuck," he swore again, jerking in my mouth. His hand tightened in my hair, getting my attention. "I want you to swallow every drop. Then I'm going to spend all day fucking you until you can't walk. Sound good?"

My core clenched, wetness gathering between my thighs. I ached to rub my legs together, desperately needing to relieve the building pressure.

He laughed, the sound dark and depraved and thrilling. "Yeah, thought you'd like that." He thrust into my mouth a few more times before he came with a groan, and, just as he'd requested, I swallowed every single drop.

With a devastating grin, he pulled me off his cock. My lips gave an audible *pop* as I sucked him off until the very last second. He urged me to my feet, and as soon as my mouth was within kissing distance, his lips claimed mine.

His tongue massaged mine, the taste of his release dancing across both our mouths as he devoured me.

"I love you," he whispered against my lips, his hand cradling my sore jaw and thumb stroking my bottom lip with reverence. "So fucking hot." He kissed me again, and my insides thrummed to life with his praise.

I loved that he loved the way I was with him. That he loved every part of me.

The insistent throbbing between my thighs was reaching the point of pain as I squeezed my legs together.

"Madison," he growled, his hand once again fisting my hair and jerking me back as he scowled at me. Then, as if he realized how rough he'd been, he started to let me go.

"Don't do that," I said, narrowing my eyes. "Don't treat me like I'm made of glass."

He paused, and the corner of his mouth kicked up. "You want more?"

I nodded in jerky movements, my chest heaving and clit twitching with the need for him to touch me. "Ryan, *please.*"

His gaze darkened into something primitive and feral. He collared my throat gently with his free hand. "I love it when you beg. I wonder how much you'll beg before I give you what you want."

I huffed because all I wanted was his dick inside me while I chased my own personal form of nirvana. "Ryan—"

He shook his head, cutting me off and moving back. "Strip."

Okay, well, stripping meant good things were coming. Or, hopefully, I would be coming.

I hurried to comply, dropping all my clothes on the floor without hesitation. I stood there, waiting for the next command, but all he did was stare.

And stare.

His gaze lingered between my thighs like a physical caress. My nipples puckered and tightened as he watched me breathe. When I was finally ready to crack, he moved, but not to touch me.

He walked around me in a slow circle, a shark eyeing its prey.

Or a master surveying his property.

A shudder rippled down my spine as I felt his gaze land on my ass.

I pressed my lips together, not sure what game we were playing, but wanting to play all the same. My fingers twitched at my sides, desperately wanting to touch him.

He paused behind me. "Go stand in front of the windows. Palms on the glass, legs apart."

I drew in a shuddering breath and walked across the room on wobbly legs to do as he'd commanded.

The glass was cool under my touch, and I could see the Strip laid out beneath me. In this moment, I felt like a queen towering above the world.

I jolted as Ryan's foot touched the inside of one ankle, then the other, lightly kicking my legs farther apart. When he was satisfied, he met my eyes in the reflection of the glass. His knuckles stroked lovingly down my spine and over the swells of my ass before dragging back up.

He repeated this motion over and over, never letting his touch stray beyond my thighs. Never reaching where I was soaked and dying for him to touch.

"Ryan." I barely recognized the soft whine in my voice.

He grinned, dimples flashing. "Need something, Mads?"

"Asshole," I seethed, glaring at him.

He tilted his head and made a soft *tsk*ing sound. "That's not very nice."

I huffed out a frustrated laugh. "You can—*ouch!*" I cried out as his hand slapped my ass. I arched onto my tiptoes to escape the fire burning across my flesh. "Jesus."

His gaze met mine in the glass. "Too much?"

I knew what he was asking; was it too much like what Gary had done to me. While I'd been surprised, and it had stung, now the pain was suffusing into a glowy sort of heat that warmed my skin.

No, it wasn't too much. It wasn't enough.

I cocked a brow. "That the best you've got?"

The smirk he gave me in return was terrifying and breathtaking. I braced myself for the next time his hand hit my butt, this time cracking against the opposite cheek of my ass. He held his hand against me, letting the heat from the blow radiate between us.

Exhaling, I hung my head between my shoulders and gave myself over to just *feeling*. Amazingly, with each slap he landed, I felt my pussy clench in anticipation and worried that my arousal might actually start leaking down the insides of my thighs.

That would be embarrassing.

As if reading my mind, Ryan's hand slipped from my ass to between my legs. His fingers glided easily through my folds, and I almost came when the tip of a finger barely brushed across my over sensitive clit.

"Ryan!" I shouted his name, desperate and frantic for him to fuck me.

His fingers lazily trailed through my wetness, spreading my arousal into the crack of my ass before going back to the source for more. A blunt finger circled my entrance, and my knees trembled.

"Please," I gasped, canting my hips back and hoping I'd be able to impale myself on his finger.

The asshole splayed a hand on the small of my back to keep me still. He leaned forward, his lips grazing my ear as his chest covered my back. "Beg for me."

"Ryan," I pleaded, arching into him. "Please touch me."

He hummed, a finger sliding along the side of my clit. "Like this?"

"Harder," I begged, trembling. "Please."

A soft chuckle, and then he kissed between my shoulder blades. "I love torturing you, baby."

I lifted one hand from the glass to wind around the back of his head, turning so my face was less than an inch from his. "I need you," I whispered, feeling desperate tears well in my eyes.

His eyes searched mine a moment before he leaned in and kissed me softly. "I need you, too, baby." He gripped my hip and slammed into me, bottoming out in one thrust.

"Fuck!" I wailed, my body toppling over the edge into chaotic freefall as I clenched around him hard enough for spots to dance in my vision. His arm banded around my waist as my knees buckled.

He never stopped thrusting, grunting from the effort of holding my body up and driving into me.

My palms pressed against the glass as I squeezed my eyes shut and rode out the sensations. The hand not wrapped around my middle delved between my legs, pinching and circling my clit.

"No, no, no," I cried, my head thrashing as I tried to escape the impending second climax that I knew would decimate me.

But Ryan held me firm and steady, his grip unyielding as he drove my body higher and higher, tension spiraling in my core until I couldn't catch my breath.

His teeth nipped my throat. "Come for me again, Madison."

"Can't," I managed between clenched teeth, barely able to think.

He laughed softly against my neck. "Yes, you can. Want me to prove it?" He rubbed my clit harder, thrusting deep and hitting a magical spot that was like a factory reset on my nervous system. Everything went white and I spasmed around him, a scream ripping from my throat as I lost all control. The only thing that mattered was Ryan.

Just him.

He jerked inside me with a rough cry, burying his face against my neck as he came.

It was like an out-of-body experience, and I lost track of time. One minute I was splintering into millions of pieces, and the next, I was cradled in Ryan's lap on the couch.

I cuddled deeper against his chest, loving the safety and protection he offered.

His lips kissed the top of my head. "You okay?"

I nodded, sleepy and sated. I wasn't entirely sure I could form sentences at this point.

He chuckled, the sound rumbling from his chest. "We should try and get some sleep."

Again, I could only nod as I tried to climb off his lap. As soon as my feet touched the floor, my legs started to shake. I toppled back against him as he laughed.

I couldn't even be mad. He'd promised he'd fuck me until I couldn't walk, and he'd more than delivered.

"I've got you," he murmured, sweeping me into his arms and standing to carry me upstairs to the bedroom.

Sighing, I closed my eyes and settled against his chest, wanting this feeling to last forever but knowing it wouldn't.

It couldn't.

Not until we'd ended what Madelaine had started.

CHAPTER 32

MADDIE

"Do you think there's something wrong with me?" I murmured in the darkness as Ryan cradled me to his chest after another epic lovemaking session. Seriously, his stamina was a thing gods would envy.

I'd spent all day in bed, with the exception of going to the bathroom. Ryan had ordered food for us and insisted I stay relaxed—and naked—while he went to grab it from the door. We'd eaten in bed, slept, and I'd woken up to his tongue stroking between my legs.

After he'd gotten me off three times with his tongue and fingers, I'd insisted I was too exhausted for more. So, he'd gotten creative with the clothes we'd packed and tied me to the headboard. He owned my body and used it over and over until I was nothing but a melted pile of goo.

But now, as darkness descended and my heartbeat started to steady, I finally voiced something that had been plaguing me for weeks.

Ryan's fingers stilled in my hair. "What? Why would you ask that?"

I managed a one-shouldered shrug. "Just a thought. Don't worry about it."

He rolled me onto my back, caging me in with his massive arms as his hips settled between my legs. His eyes searched mine. "Talk to me."

I sighed and tried to look away, embarrassed and wishing I'd kept my mouth shut.

He caught my chin in his hand and refused to let me shy away. "Madison. What the hell are you talking about?"

"When we... When we're like *this*," I began with a whisper, "why is it okay?"

His brow furrowed. He wasn't getting what I was saying.

"You spank me," I muttered, feeling my cheeks flame as he grinned, "and it hurts, but when Gary hits me... That isn't okay? But what *you* do is?" I was fucking this up.

Ryan's mouth fell open and he scrambled off me so fast he nearly fell off the bed. "Maddie." He raked a hand through his hair, looking shocked and sick.

Oh, no.

I'd definitely fucked this up.

"Do you..." His voice shook, but I wasn't sure if it was from anger or emotion as his blue eyes flashed in the darkening room. "Do you think you have to... That I'd make you—"

"No!" I practically shouted, lunging forward and grabbing his arm when I thought he'd run. "I didn't mean... Dammit, I'm sorry. That's not what I meant at all." I let him go and fell back, drawing my knees to my chest and hugging them. I pressed my lips into a hard line, trying to swallow my tears. Closing my eyes, I dropped my forehead to my knees. "Can we just rewind the last five minutes and forget I said anything?"

"No," he replied, sounding baffled and worried. "Mads, you've gotta clear this up for me. Jesus, do you think I'm like Gary?"

"God, no." My head snapped up, shaking back and forth vehemently. "No. Absolutely not. I just don't understand why I feel this way with you and it's *so right*, but Gary does something similar and it's wrong."

Ryan stared at me, concern in his expression.

I shrugged again, helpless and confused. "Does that mean something's wrong with me?"

He watched me for another beat before huffing out a laugh and crawling back across the bed to pick me up and settle me in his lap. "Baby, there's nothing wrong with you or the millions of other people who like a little kink in their relationship. Just because you like me spanking your ass or fucking this perfect mouth until you choke—" he leaned in for a fast kiss "—doesn't mean anyone else gets to touch you without your consent, or hurt you."

I bit my lower lip. "Right."

"Mads, do you think I'd force you to do something if you said you wanted to stop?"

"Of course not." No way. I trusted Ryan implicitly with my heart *and* body.

He touched his forehead to mine. "There's *nothing* wrong with you, Madison. You're perfect, and you're mine."

I tipped my head back to kiss him, sinking into the feel of his lips on mine as I accepted the truth in his words. Nothing could be wrong about the way he made me feel, reckless and safe at the same time. How he kept me grounded but gave me the strength and freedom to soar.

His hand slipped up my rib cage to palm one of my breasts, his thumb stroking over the tight peak as I whimpered into his mouth. I was achy between my thighs in a way that made me want to sit on a bag of frozen peas, and yet I still felt arousal simmering in my blood.

Fuck it. I'd find the bag of peas after this one last time.

I lifted up and straddled him, my slit rubbing against his half-hard cock. I knew from experience it would take him less than a minute to get fully hard and impale me, so I grinded against him like a cat in heat, enjoying the sensations rippling from my pussy as I took my time.

His hands clamped down on my waist. "Thought you needed a break."

"Turns out I need you more." I moaned as the hard tip of his cock pressed on my clit. I'd just reached between us, ready to guide him into me, when the sharp trill of a phone pierced the quiet.

I froze, my hand wrapped around his dick as I made eye contact with him.

The phone rang again, and he swore. "It's Ash's ringtone."

I nodded, guessing as much.

He grabbed his phone from the nightstand and answered the call on speaker. "Yeah?"

"Fucking hell," Ash griped. "Don't you two check your messages? I've been texting for the last five minutes."

Ryan shot me an amused look as he replied, "We've been busy."

"Right," Ash muttered, and I could picture the exasperated look on his face. "Well, get yourselves decent. Pandora set the time for tonight."

My eyes went wide. "T-tonight?"

Ryan's eyes narrowed. "You don't have to go, Mads. We can find another way."

"No, I'm going." My pulse was racing, and I felt a little ill, but I was sure this needed to happen. I needed to see what my sister had hidden.

"What time?" Ryan demanded.

"Eleven," Ash responded.

I glanced at the clock. It was a couple minutes after ten now.

"Can you let Linc and Court know to be ready to leave in fifteen?" Ryan kept his eyes on me.

"On it." Ash hesitated. "Be careful, okay?"

"We will," I promised as Ryan hung up. I settled my hands on his shoulders. "I should get ready."

"Wait." His hands tightened on my hips, keeping me on his lap as he frowned. "Just... are you sure, Maddie? We'll stop Gary. You don't have to do this."

I laid a hand against his cheek. "Madelaine died for whatever secrets she was hiding in that vault. I need to know what they were. I owe her that much."

He scowled. "You don't owe her shit. She fucked you over, Madison."

"But if she hadn't, then I wouldn't have you, would I?" I murmured. "Face it. Without Madelaine being, well, *Madelaine*, you and I never would've met."

He rolled his eyes. "Fine. The bitch did *one* good thing."

"She's my sister, my twin." I shook my head. "I can't explain it, but I have to see this through. We've come too far."

"Fine," he muttered. "But if things go sideways—"

I leaned in and kissed the tip of his nose. "You'll bring the cavalry and save me."

He smiled viciously. "More like I'll burn this city to the motherfucking ground, but sure. Cavalry works, too."

Pandora was about what I'd expect of a strip club located several miles off the Las Vegas Strip and heading into the desert. With a tin roof and wood siding, it definitely hid the fact that several stories beneath the dirt and sand was a vault that protected the dirty secrets of the world's elite.

The club was on an isolated stretch of road, and I wasn't sure if that was intentional or not. Nothing about this place screamed super-secret vault hundreds of feet below the surface, but what did I know about running a criminal safety locker enterprise?

It looked like a barely functioning dive bar, with a neon sign advertising bare tits, and signs for half-priced drinks on Wednesdays and a wet t-shirt contest every Friday. The gravel parking lot was full of cars and motorcycles, and I felt out of place as I exited my taxi within my allotted time frame.

Surrounded by a ring of cigarette smoke, a group of men by the door eyed me like fresh meat. I straightened my shoulders and arched a brow full of boredom and disdain at them before moving toward the front door, reciting Ash's instructions in my head as I went.

I needed to find the bartender and request a private dance with Violet. I'd be shown into a private room, searched for weapons and trackers as well as listening devices, before being screened. If I passed that, then I'd be escorted into the elevator and taken more than fifteen stories underground to the vault level.

Sounded easy enough, except for the screening part. As long as Madelaine had opted for a blood sample and not a biometric scan, I'd be golden. Our DNA was identical, but our fingerprints? Not so much.

The room was smokey and the music loud, the heavy bass of the song vibrating through my bones. There were three stages, each with their own pole and girls in varying stages of undress. The crowd was predominantly male, and I resisted the urge to look for the two people I knew were already inside.

Ryan and Linc had gone ahead of me to make sure they blended in well before my arrival. Court had trailed my taxi to make sure I made it to Pandora. Ryan had damn near thrown a bitch fit when Ash said I'd need to show up alone, but ultimately, he'd agreed to the plan.

A man bumped into me from behind, his hand curving around my hip as he leaned in to ask, "What time are you on, sweetcheeks?"

My nose wrinkled. I mean, *sweetcheeks*? Really?

"Not a dancer," I informed him, pushing his paw off me.

His leering gaze swept the length of my body. Dressed in dirty jeans and an even dirtier shirt with holes in it, his handlebar mustache was longer on one side than the other. "One of the backroom girls then? Shit, Jasper sure is upping his talent lately. What's the rate?"

Oh, for fuck's sake.

"More than you can afford," I assured him. I turned to leave, and he grabbed my wrist.

"You don't need to be a bitch," he hissed.

"And you don't need to be an asshole," I snapped back, feeling a prickling awareness zip up my spine.

Dammit. If Ryan saw this, he'd lose his shit and blow our chances at getting into the vault.

I sucked in a breath and softened my approach. "Look, honey, it's my first night, okay? I'm a little overwhelmed. Can you please let me go?" I wobbled my lower lip, and the dumbass caved.

He released me. "Sure thing, sweetie. I'll let you get settled, but yell for Ned if you need anything." He winked at me. "And when you start taking private requests, don't forget I was your first friend here."

Oh, gag me.

I smiled shyly, looking up through my lashes with a giggle. "Thanks, Ned."

He sauntered off, an extra swagger in his step as I turned away with a repulsed shudder.

Yuck.

I needed to get this over with.

I marched over to the bar that spanned the length of the back wall. It had seen better days, but that didn't deter the crowd. Three women and a man handled the patrons with practiced ease, skirting the line between business and flirting.

Finally, a woman with big brown eyes and dark blonde hair came over to me with a smile. The lights caught the sequins of a bikini top that barely covered her nipples. "What can I getcha, babe?"

I cleared my throat. "I wanted to request a private dance."

Her brows shot up.

"With Violet," I added.

She covered her surprise quickly and reached beneath the bar to grab a glass of ice. She used the soda nozzle to fill it with water before pushing it to me and turning away. She walked over to the man and whispered something to him. His gaze snapped to where I stood.

Throat suddenly dry, I lifted the glass and sipped. Finally, the man gave a curt nod, his dark eyes still on me as the woman came back.

"You can wait for Violet in the blue room," she informed me with a smile, coming around from behind the bar. "I'll take you there. Can't have a pretty thing like you wandering around now, can we?"

I left my glass as she linked her arm through mine and guided me through the crowd. When a few men called her by name, she grinned and waved coyly, never faltering despite the sticky floor and her insane heels.

A curtain flanked by two guards hung at the back of the room. They looked like normal security until I spotted the guns at their hips.

Most nightclub security guards didn't come with a Glock as an accessory.

"She has an appointment with Violet," the woman said to them.

The one on the left didn't blink. He simply pulled back the heavy black curtain for us to walk though into a tiny corridor with a door at the end. The space was barely lit, but I spotted a camera above the door, a red light blinking angrily at me.

"I'm Nancy, by the way," the woman told me, approaching the door and knocking twice.

"Maddie," I murmured back, eyeing her warily as the door opened and another armed man appeared.

"She's here to see Violet. Jake said the blue room's free," Nancy told him.

The man nodded and stepped back. Nancy turned and waved me toward him. "This is as far as I go, sweetheart."

"Uh, thanks," I stammered, and walked through the doorway. The guard slammed the door, and I heard a locking mechanism engage, sealing me off from the rest of the club.

The silence here was so startling it made my ears ring. There was no music, no bass, no whistles and shouts. Just quiet.

"This way," the guard ordered, leading me down a hallway to the left with several more doors, each one closed. Dim sconces provided just enough light for me to make out the dark walls and gray wood floors. But there were no pictures, no artwork. Nothing but a row of doors.

The man stopped at the one second from the end and pressed his thumb onto a scanner above the doorknob. A moment later, the lock flashed green, and the tumblers disengaged. He opened the door and turned to me. "Purse."

I slowly handed it over.

"Phone?"

"It's in my bag."

He nodded and jerked his head at the door. "Wait inside."

The second I cleared the door, it closed behind me. Panic flared in my chest, and I tried the doorknob, my heart thrashing as I realized it was locked.

Whirling around, I looked at what was definitely a blue room. Blue velvet couches sat against navy blue walls. There was another door on the other side of the room, but it, too, was locked tight.

A red pulse of light in the corner caught my eye, and I spotted the security camera. I wondered who was on the other side. If someone was watching me freak out in this little blue box.

The last thing I needed was for them to get suspicious.

I walked over to a couch and sat down to wait.

CHAPTER 33

MADDIE

I had no idea how long I waited. I finally started humming just to break up the silence that settled around me like an oppressive blanket.

When the door I'd entered unlocked and opened suddenly, I scrambled to my feet. The man from the bar stepped inside, my purse under his arm.

"Jake?" I guessed, remembering what Nancy had called him.

He stared at me, his expression like something carved from granite. There was zero emotion as he looked me over. Finally he uttered one word that made my heart clench. "Strip."

"Excuse me?" I spluttered, folding my arms over my chest and taking a step back.

He sighed, looking utterly bored. "Strip. You know the drill."

I swallowed roughly. "Isn't there a woman who can... What about Nancy?"

He snorted. "Cute, but you still have your clothes on."

"Look, buddy, I'm not stripping for you," I snapped, irritation lacing my words.

"Then get the fuck out," he replied with an indifferent shrug. "Doesn't matter to me either way."

I shifted on my feet, not entirely sure what to do. I'd anticipated being searched, but not *strip* searched.

He rolled his eyes. "Look, unless you're hiding a third nipple, I can assure you that you haven't got something I've never seen before." He paused. "Scratch that. I've seen a third nipple before. Fuckin' weird shit."

"Are you serious?" I gaped at him.

He nodded and pointed to his ribs. "Yeah. Fucker was right here." He snapped his fingers. "Just strip so I can make sure you aren't wearing a wire or sneaking something in."

I looked down at my skinny jeans and black tank top. "Does it *look* like I'm hiding anything?"

"Sweetheart, I've seen a woman old enough to be your great-grandma come in here with a gun shoved up her cunt and a bowie knife in her ass. Why? I don't fucking know, and it ain't my job to care. It's my job to make sure that shit stays up here, which is exactly where your perky ass will be unless you *strip*." He ran a hand through his dark hair and shot me an exasperated look, his dark brown eyes full of annoyance.

"Fine," I muttered, pulling off my top and toeing off my shoes. I stripped down to my bra and panties, and when he rolled his eyes again, I stripped out of those too.

My gaze cut anxiously to the camera as it kept flashing, recording every movement.

"Turn around, bend over, and touch your toes," he ordered, twirling a finger.

Painfully aware of how vulnerable I was, I gritted my teeth and complied, wrapping my hands around the backs of my knees as I bent forward and showed him *everything*.

"You can get dressed," he told me.

I hurried to pull on my clothes.

"For what it's worth, you've got nothing to be ashamed of," he added. Weirdly enough, it didn't sound like he was being pervy or threatening, just making an honest assessment.

"Uh, thanks?"

"No problem." His smile was quick and easy as he crossed the room to the other door, passing me my purse. He kept his body angled so his back was never fully to me. Despite his relaxed stance, he was still very much alert and aware of any threat I might possess.

I quickly rifled through my bag, frowning when I didn't see my phone. "Uh, where's my—"

"You get your phone back when you leave," he informed me with a pointed look that said I should've known that, too. "Can't have you Instagramming inside the vaults."

Yeah, that made sense.

He pressed his thumb to another scanner by the door. It clicked, and a small compartment beside him opened up.

"Do you have your key?" He turned and looked at me.

Nodding, I tugged it from my pocket and handed it to him. He inserted it into the box and turned it.

"Gonna need you over here, pretty girl." He waved me over and indicated a blue light inside the box with a camera built into it.

A retinal scan? Shit. I'd done research on how *identical* identical twins needed to be, and apparently eyes were like fingerprints; they weren't the same.

My heart thrashed in my chest as I slowly approached the camera like I was walking to my execution. Which, okay, I very well might've been.

With a trembling breath, I crouched a little to bring my eyes level with the device. The lights flashed across my vision and finally, thankfully, turned green.

My knees almost gave out in relief, not sure how I'd managed to pass *that* test. It must not have been a retinal scan. Maybe facial recognition software? Since Madelaine and I had all the same bones and structure on our faces, it was a test I could pass.

Either way, I wasn't going to question it.

"Thumb," Jake told me, nodding to the scanner under the camera.

My heart thudded in my chest so loud that he had to hear it.

"Anytime," he drawled, sighing.

Licking my lips, I pressed my thumb to the device. A second later, I hissed as a sharp prick pierced my skin. Blood welled on the pad of the device.

I waited, holding my breath, until the door unlocked.

Jake grabbed the knob and yanked the door open to reveal a small elevator. "In you go." He handed me the key back, and I stared at him from inside the little space.

He leaned in and tapped a keyhole. "Key goes here."

I stared at the blank panel. "There's no buttons." Which floor was I supposed to go to? For that matter, how could I even push a button for the correct floor when there were no buttons?

"Hence the key." He raised his eyebrows, looking at me like I was an idiot.

"Right," I murmured, inserting the key and tentatively twisting it.

"See you on the other side," he called as the door shut and the elevator started its descent.

The soft hum of the elevator was my only company as I was lowered deeper and deeper under the club. Other than a single overhead light, there was no way of knowing where I was, what floor I was close to. It was disorienting in a way that was pretty genius.

But it also made me wonder what happened if there was a fire or some other emergency. God, what if the elevator broke down? There wasn't even an emergency button. I'd never been claustrophobic, but suddenly the space felt like it was shrinking around me, and I wanted out. No, I *needed* out.

I leaned my back against the wall and closed my eyes, focusing on taking deep breaths as my hands fisted at my sides.

"This'll all be over any minute," I whispered to myself.

Except for the ride back up.

I mentally rolled my eyes. My brain had zero problem torpedoing hope with reality.

When the car stopped and the door opened, I wasn't sure what I'd been expecting, but it wasn't... *this*.

I stepped into a brightly lit hallway with marble floors and gray walls trimmed in snow white paint. Elegant artwork hung along a lengthy corridor that forked almost fifty feet down.

A uniformed guard in a suit stood waiting for me with a bottle of water, which he promptly handed to me. His muscles were barely contained in the charcoal lines of his clothes, and I spotted tattoos winding up his neck and curling around his bald head. "Welcome back to Pandora, Miss Cabot. Are you ready to proceed? Or do you need something else first?"

I slowly took the bottle, eyeing the lounge area behind him with its bright floral arrangements and plush chairs. It was like I'd stumbled into the waiting room of an upscale hotel. The change was jarring from the scene upstairs.

"N-no," I finally managed. "I'm ready to proceed."

"You'll need your key." He inclined his head at the elevator.

I reached in and grabbed my key. Within seconds of my pulling it free, the door slid shut, and I heard humming as the car started back up.

"This way," the man instructed, leading me forward.

My shoes squeaked obnoxiously on the polished floors, and I tried to be aware of my movements as I went. Ash and Linc had suggested I show up in something designer that Madelaine would've worn, but I needed to know I could make a run for it if things went sideways.

Running was hard to do in a pencil skirt and heels.

I eyed my surroundings. Then again, I was God-knew-how-many stories under the desert, so where the hell was I gonna run?

At the fork, the guard took the left hall. Then he made a right at the next fork. By the fourth turn, I realized Pandora was even bigger than I'd anticipated. I was hopelessly lost, and every hallway was identical.

Same art. Same floors. Same walls.

There was no way to find my way back without a guide or dumb luck.

The guard stopped short in front of a door, turning to me. "Your key?" He used his thumb to do the same thing as Jake, opening up a small compartment in the wall next to the door so I could repeat the process again with the key, face scanner, and blood test.

Once I'd passed the tests, the door opened. No lights were on in the room.

He tapped a doorbell mounted inside the room near the door. "Ring the bell when you're ready to leave," he instructed me, and closed the door behind me. I flinched when it locked me in darkness.

"Great," I muttered, reaching out to see if there was a light switch.

The overhead lights flared to life, triggered by my motion.

"Convenient," I said to myself, getting my first look at the small room.

The space was roughly as big as my closet at Pacific Cross. With white walls, a white tiled floor, and a couple obscenely bright fluorescent lights embedded in the concrete ceiling, the room was big enough to walk around in but not do much else. And there were only three pieces of furniture.

A television mounted to the wall.

An armchair.

And a set of particle board drawers.

"Okay, Lainey, what the hell were you hiding?" I started with the drawers and wasn't disappointed. "Holy shit."

Rows of thumb drives, each painstakingly labeled with dates and initials.

There were dozens of them. Same thing in the next drawer. The third was empty, but I felt compelled to open the fourth, and when I did, my heart stuttered.

There was only one flash drive here, labeled with a single word.

MADISON.

CHAPTER 34

MADDIE

The TV had a USB port, and my hands trembled as I inserted the drive into it. The screen flickered to life and Madelaine's face appeared. The video instantly started.

She sucked in a deep breath and sat down in what looked like this room. She looked beyond the camera and smiled. "Don't go far, okay? I'll be done in a few minutes."

"Take your time, sweetheart," a rough but familiar voice told her. A second later I heard the door click shut, and my sister faced the camera.

"Hey, Madison," she started with a small smile that wobbled at the edges. "God, this sounds so pathetic to even say, but here we go. If you're seeing this, then things didn't work out the way I wanted. And I'm so fucking sorry for that."

My heart twisted as I sat down on the edge of the chair to watch my twin.

"But," she countered with a nervous laugh, "if you're here, then you're smart as hell. Maybe even smarter than me, especially since you probably pieced this shit together out of breadcrumbs. But that's not enough, big sister. You have to be better."

She sucked in a shaky breath, her gaze dropping to her lap. "I guess

I should start at the beginning, right? I left you with an absolute mess, and you deserve to know it all. Everything. Every fucking detail. Even the ones I wish I could forget, and believe me, I tried."

Her head tipped back, throat working as she blinked back tears. "Fuck, Laine, get your shit together. Stop being a bitch."

I smiled, amused that her inner voice sounded a lot like mine.

"I found out about you when I was thirteen," she admitted. Dark fury spread across her features, her mouth tightening. "My thirteenth birthday was supposed to be… I don't know. But let's just say it ended up being one of the worst days of my life, and I had this idea that I could file for emancipation from my dad."

My heart slammed painfully into my ribs, because I knew what had happened the night she turned thirteen.

Looking down, she picked at her nails for a second before realizing what she was doing and straightening her shoulders to turn her attention back to the camera. "I found my birth certificate… and yours. That's how I found out I had a twin sister." She shrugged a little at the camera. "It sounded like something from one of the mystery books I read as a kid. You know the one with the girl who's always finding random shit and solving cases?" She waved a hand. "Yeah, her. So, I decided to solve the mystery of *you*."

Madelaine's nose wrinkled as she sucked her teeth. "There wasn't a whole lot to work with. And Dad wasn't sharing. We had this whole big fight and he told me…" Her gaze shuttered. "Well, it doesn't really matter now, does it?" Her gaze snapped to the camera. "Madison, if you haven't figured it out by now, stay away from him. He's dangerous, and…"

Her fingers shook as she ran a hand through her blonde hair. "Stay away from Adam, too. He's a fucking pedophile. He's been coming into my room since the night I turned thirteen." A gruesome smile twisted her lips. "Adam told me that he'd been sent by my dad to keep me in line. That was why I needed to get my birth certificate. I *had* to get away, and I was stupid enough to think I could actually get emancipated."

She was silent for a long moment after that, and I flinched when I felt something wet hit the back of my hand. I stared in wonder at the wetness smeared across my skin, and it took a second to realize I was crying.

"For what it's worth," she added, stroking the inside of her wrist where a jagged scar lay, "I tried getting away once. I wanted it to be over. Maybe I would've tried harder, but Dad… Well, his threats can be pretty persuasive."

Madelaine sucked in a deep, fortifying breath and met my gaze through the screen. "There's enough in those drives to make sure that asshole goes away for life, and there's nothing guys in prison love more than a kiddie rapist on the block. They'll do far more damage to him than I ever could, and I gotta admit, I love the idea of him being on the receiving end of everything he did to me for years. For what he tried to do to…" She trailed off, shaking her head. "It doesn't matter. But just remember that he'll use the people you love to hurt and control you."

All emotion drained from her face. "If you don't love anyone, then they really can't hurt you. I learned that early on. I cut out every person who mattered before they could be ruined like me."

Bex. She was talking about Bex.

She rolled her neck, working out tension. "I've done a lot of shitty things, many of which you probably know about by now. I made a lot of mistakes, and I tried to fix what I could, but it wasn't enough."

My heart broke for her. All I wanted to do was reach through the screen and hug her. To wrap her up and protect her the way no one ever had either of us growing up.

It wasn't until Ryan that I'd found out what it meant to be loved and protected. To have someone willing to fight for me, no matter the cost.

"Everything you need is on those drives. It took me years to compile them all, but it's amazing the things men let slip when you're a pretty decoration in their bed or on their lap. They think you're stupid and ignorant. Long legs, nice tits, big blue eyes, blonde hair… Men will see all the parts of you as sparkly ornaments on a doll they think they own. They'll never realize each piece is another weapon in your arsenal. Use that. Let them think they've won, Madison."

She grinned at me through the screen. "And then tear their fucking hearts out."

A grim smile pulled at my lips as resolve tightened around my own heart.

She exhaled slowly. "There's one more thing. Something that... Fuck, I think I actually got it wrong. I'm *hoping* I got it wrong." She worried her lower lip between her teeth before looking down at her hands and lifting her left one, her engagement ring flashing. "Ryan Cain."

My breath caught.

"I thought he was just like his father. Like *our* father. Him and his friends, the way they acted and the shit they did. I even found out they started their own little side venture." She snorted, shaking her long hair over her shoulders. "But I think I might've been wrong. I think... Well, what I think doesn't matter. It's what I can *prove*. There's tapes on them, too, but the more I watched, the more I wondered if I just got so used to seeing bad guys that I lumped them in with the rest."

But she'd been right; Ryan and our friends were nothing like their fathers or ours. God, if she'd only trusted him...

"The plan is for you to never know this video exists," she explained. "I'm going to Europe to meet with someone I think can help me. He hates our father more than I do, which is saying something. But Charles seems like a good guy, and his cousin is some insane tech wizard. She should be able to verify that all the recordings I have are legit."

Taking a deep breath, Madelaine leaned forward. "Here's where it gets tricky, sis. As soon as you use what's on these recordings, you're going to piss off a lot of powerful people. There's nothing old white men hate more than when a smart woman takes them down with their own hubris. Make sure you're protected before you start taking shots."

She glanced down again, looking lost and oddly vulnerable. "I never did that. I never found someone who would protect me. A person I could trust. Well, I might've found him, but… It's too late for that, I guess." She lifted a shoulder with a wry smile. "Maybe that's because, in a perfect world, *you* would have been that person. My twin. The other half of my soul."

With a sharp laugh, she wiped under her eyes. "And now I'm getting emotional, so clearly it's time to end this shit."

Don't go, I wanted to beg. I wanted more. I wanted to hear every story, know every secret from her own lips.

I'd never have the chance.

"I'm sorry I left you with such a mess, Madison. I'm so fucking sorry." She rolled her bottom lip between her teeth before giving me a sad smile full of heartbreak and fear. "I really hope that five years from now, we're cracking up watching this video and drinking to see how dramatic my ass is, but if you're watching this, then I guess I won't be there."

Her blue eyes, identical to mine in so many ways but somehow so much older and tired, met mine through the screen. "I never loved anyone, Madison, but I think I could have loved you. I'm sorry I'll never know."

A sob ripped from my throat as she stood up on camera and leaned forward. A second later, the video feed went dark. I buried my hands in my face and cried, desperately wishing for the one person I could never have.

CHAPTER 35

MADDIE

I sat until the lights flickered off. Only then did I stand and wipe away the last of my tears, vowing to get the justice my sister and I both deserved. With the lights back on thanks to my movement, I pulled the thumb drive from the TV and tucked it into my pocket before gathering up the rest.

By the time I was done stuffing them in my purse, it bulged and barely zipped. I triple checked to make sure I'd grabbed everything from all the drawers, knowing I wouldn't be coming back here.

I glanced around the room, looking for any last traces of Madelaine and disappointed when there were none to be found.

The door opened behind me, and I turned with a forced smile. "I'm ready to—oh." I stared at Jake as he filled the doorway a moment before pushing inside and not quite closing the door.

"Uh," I started, backing up and wondering if I could make it past him. "Where's the guard? I thought he was—"

"She's really gone then?"

His question stunned me for a heavy beat, and then I realized why the voice on Madelaine's tape was so familiar. It was Jake's. The bartender?

"You knew my sister," I managed to get out, still working past my shock.

He nodded, jaw tight. "Laine's... She's dead?"

I nodded, my movements sluggish as my body and brain tried to reconnect.

"Fuck," he hissed, his expression full of pain as he landed hard against the door. "I told her to be careful. That she was too close."

"What did she tell you?" I asked, edging closer to him as if proximity could make her memory more tangible. "How did you—"

He shook his head. "There isn't time to talk. You need to get out of here, Madison."

"You know who I am."

A wry smile tilted up one corner of his mouth. "In that outfit? No way were you Laine. Plus, using the main club entrance instead of the back one for the vaults was a pretty big fucking giveaway. You're lucky I was here tonight."

I gaped at him. "Uh..."

He shot me a rueful smirk. "You don't really think you got in here on your own merit, did you? I bypassed some of the checkpoints so you could get down here."

I could only stare at him.

He raked a hand through his tousled locks, shooting me a look of pitying disbelief. "Shit, you really are as innocent as Laine said."

"She told you about me?" I managed to croak out.

He gave a grim nod. "Yeah. She told me about you. I knew all about her plans to meet up with some British guy and ask him for help taking down her father." A muscle ticked in his jaw. "I told her she needed to slow down, that she was being reckless. But that was just how she was."

I glanced down at my full purse. "You know about the tapes?"

"Yeah."

"Do you know what she was going to do with them?" I whispered.

He gave an indifferent shrug. "She wanted to buy her freedom and then unleash them on as many media outlets as possible. Show the world what all those greedy assholes were really doing."

I swallowed hard, watching him closely. "You cared about her."

His eyes hardened, his jaw going tight.

"You helped her record the video," I pointed out. "You helped *me*."

His gaze jerked away. "It doesn't matter now."

"But—"

He huffed. "Look, Madison, you've got to go, okay? Gary's on his way here."

My spine stiffened. "For me?"

"No, to access his own vault," Jake replied. "He has no idea you're here, and I'd like to keep it that way. I told your sister I'd do what I could to help you."

I had so many questions, too many questions. "How did you—"

"*Really* can't talk right now," he told me through gritted teeth. He held out a hand. "Let's get you out of here before he shows up. His appointment is in a couple hours, but he sometimes shows up early for a private dance before he goes into the vault. I have a car waiting to take you back to your hotel. I'm assuming you're not in Vegas alone?"

I shook my head.

"Good. Gary has no idea that Laine had a vault here or what she was up to." He guided me out of the room, closing it and handing me my key. I slipped it into the pocket with Madelaine's message for me.

Jake walked faster than the guard, his steps sure as he navigated the maze of halls with ease. When we arrived at an elevator, it wasn't the same one I'd come down in, which meant there were multiple ways to access the vaults.

Maybe then that meant—

"No," Jake said sharply, slamming his hand down on the biometric scanner. The screen flashed green and the doors opened. He guided me inside and didn't speak until they were closed. "You can't break in and figure out what Gary's darkest secrets are."

My brows rose. "I wasn't going to."

He snorted. "Sure, you weren't. How do you think I met your sister? That was *her* original plan, too. This car is strictly for staff. Five people have access. Several of the private rooms have elevators and each takes you to a different spot in the vault. They don't all access the same floors, and I'm sure you noticed the halls are all identical?"

I nodded.

"You'd have no clue where you were or where you were going." His voice roughened. "And if someone other than me found you wandering around down here, you'd be in deep shit. The secrets buried in here could decimate democracies and upend the fucking world."

I scoffed. "And yet all I spotted were two guards."

He bared his teeth. "Every single person who works here is a guard."

I blinked at him.

He gave an amused snort. "From the bartenders to the dancers to the waitresses. Every single person who works here is trained to kill a man a dozen ways with their bare hands. There are weapons hidden everywhere around here."

"Shit." I bit down on my lower lip.

He arched his brow. "Why do you think we're in the middle of the fucking desert? It's the perfect spot for a fucking graveyard. Pandora sits in the middle of a hundred acres of desolate, barren *nothing*. It's monitored by the best security systems known to man and guarded by people who make the secret service look like amateurs."

I could barely breathe as I watched him and the gravity of where I was finally settled on my shoulders. A chill swept my skin, leaving goosebumps in its wake.

He turned to me fully. "The vault levels were originally a bomb shelter that was expanded on. The world could explode in a nuclear war and this place wouldn't ever be touched. You're three hundred feet below street level, insulated by ten-foot-deep layers of steel, concrete, and tungsten. And even then? There's a six-inch layer of graphene surrounding the vaults, which are on more levels than you can imagine."

My breath whooshed out of me.

"Yeah. You aren't getting in, and you'll die trying," he confirmed.

MAD LOVE

Sullen, I leaned against the wall as we continued our ascent. "Six inches doesn't seem like much."

He laughed softly. "Graphene is stronger than diamonds and can be stretched. Trust me, six inches is enough if you know how to use it."

"Speaking from experience?" I quipped, my stress bleeding out in the form of being a smart-ass.

The amusement in his eyes died. "I'd say ask your sister, but..."

"Oh."

"Yeah. *Oh*," he echoed.

We finished the rest of the trip in silence, and when the doors opened, it was to a small space with two doors where Nancy waited with my phone.

"Here you go," she said, handing it to me with a smile. Her gaze moved to Jake. "Victor said—"

"Vic can go fuck himself," Jake growled, ending her comment and sending her brows shooting up.

She sucked on her teeth. "Your funeral, babe." Then she turned and walked away, disappearing behind a door at the end.

Turning to me, Jake raked a hand through his messy hair. "Car's waiting out back. It'll take you straight to your hotel."

"How do you know what hotel I'm at?" That was a little unnerving.

"Because Pandora, contrary to the name, doesn't like secrets."

My nose wrinkled. "Pandora's a strip club and whatever those vaults are. You make it sound like it's a person."

"Nah. People you can kill. Pandora never dies." He winked at me and jerked his chin at the phone in my hand. "I programmed my number into that. You need something—anything—call me. I'll do whatever I can. For Laine."

"Thank you," I murmured, my fingers tightening around the device.

"Take care, Madison," he murmured, watching as I slipped out the back door and into the car he'd arranged. Once we started driving away, I texted Ryan to let him know I was safe and on my way to the hotel. He replied back instantly that he was on his way to meet me.

Then I settled back against the seat and tried to keep my head from exploding from all the revelations of the night.

The drive back was quiet, the driver not bothering to speak or play the radio. I let the thoughts tumble in my mind like a broken dryer that wouldn't stop.

I beat the guys back to the hotel room. While I waited, I scrubbed the makeup off my face and slipped into one of Ryan's t-shirts and a pair of yoga pants before tucking myself into a corner of the massive sectional sofa across from the gorgeous lights of the city below. In my fist, I clutched Madelaine's message, unwilling to let it go just yet.

"Mads!" Ryan's sharp voice cracked through the air before the door was even open.

And I was on my feet, running to him before he'd fully stepped into the room. He caught me with an *oomph*, staggering back as I wrapped my arms around his neck and my legs around his waist. His hands caught me under my thighs, walking us into the room as Linc and Court filed in.

Relief made my bones heavy as I trembled against him, finally cracking under the pressure and stress of the night.

A hand smoothed up my back, as much checking for injuries as it was trying to comfort. "Are you okay? Did something happen?"

"No. Yes. No." I couldn't settle on an answer, and I could see the frustrated lines of his face pulling into a frown as he sat on the sofa with me straddling him.

"Maddie, talk to me," he urged, finally able to put both hands on my face and pull me far enough back to look in my eyes.

"I will," I promise, "but right now, I just need to kind of absorb everything, and I want to do that while you're holding me. Is that okay?"

His eyes softened. "Of course it's okay, baby." He settled my head on the spot between his shoulder and chest, near his heart, that I'd secretly dubbed *mine*.

The cushions beside us moved, and I peeked over to see Court sitting down. He gave me a tight, tired smile while Linc paced a bit behind the sectional.

"Do you want a drink?" Linc offered.

I shook my head. All I wanted was exactly what I had.

My fist squeezed around the flash drive.

Well, almost everything I wanted.

Court eyed my fist. "Whatcha got there, Mads?"

Ryan stiffened a little under me, but never stopped rubbing my back.

Finally, I unfurled my hand so they could see.

"A thumb drive?" Linc scowled at it.

Ryan sighed. "More footage?"

"A message," I replied, closing my fingers around it again. "From Madelaine. She left it for me."

Court sucked in a sharp breath, his gaze snapping from Ryan to Linc and then me. "Shit. Seriously?"

I nodded and offered it to him. "Watch it. You'll see. My laptop is by the door." I hadn't bothered with it since Ryan and I had first entered this suite. So much for catching up on my missing assignments. I was *so* going to fail this semester.

Court eyed my outstretched hand before taking the drive. He looked it over before exchanging a look with Ryan. Then he tossed it to Linc. "Let's see what she has to say."

Linc retrieved my laptop and positioned it on the glass coffee table in front of the sofa. I turned my head and watched with them as Madelaine appeared, tears filling my eyes once again.

None of them spoke as the video played, but their expressions shifted from wariness to disbelief to… sadness?

"Holy shit," Linc breathed as it ended, folding his hands behind his head and looking stunned.

"There's more recordings?" Court looked at me.

I nodded. "So many. They're all labeled, but I didn't have a chance to really look them over or play them. I figured Ash could start cataloging them and we'd figure out our next moves."

Ryan nodded, his chin bumping against my head as his arms tightened around me, anchoring me through this storm. "We'll leave whenever you want, Maddie."

"Now?" I posed the answer like a question. We'd been in Vegas for less than twenty-four hours, but it felt like I was finally at the point where we had the power to swing momentum in our favor. Besides...

"Gary's at Pandora," I added.

"Jesus, Mads. Fucking lead with that shit." Linc threw his hands up in the air.

Ryan tugged my head back by my hair. "Did you see him?"

"No," I answered, quick to soothe his worry. "But a friend let me know he was arriving to check on something in his own vault."

Court got up. "I'll get the car. Ready to leave in five." He and Linc left the suite to gather their things.

Ryan stared at me, his expression hard. "A *friend*?"

"I'll explain it all on the way." I leaned in and kissed him softly, loving the feel of his lips pressed to mine. "Let's go home."

CHAPTER 36

RYAN

Madison fell asleep not long after we crossed the Nevada/Utah border.

As we'd pulled away from our hotel, she hadn't said anything about being worried, but there was no denying the way she'd kept looking out the back window like something was chasing us.

Or she was leaving something behind.

After telling us about the rest of her trip to Pandora, she'd settled against me, tracing lazy patterns on my jeans-clad thigh. I didn't think she was aware of what she was doing, and I'd caught Court checking on her in the rearview mirror as well as Linc twisting around in the front seat occasionally to make sure she was okay.

It seemed like we were all waiting to see when she would break. When the stress of the last few months would finally wreck her and send her into a tailspin. I mean, how could it not?

"She's really out," Linc whispered now, turning to look at her again, a soft expression on his face.

I smoothed some of the silky blonde hair from her forehead. She'd put her head in my lap and curled up on the bench seat to sleep almost an hour ago, and hadn't moved since.

As I watched her, my heart expanded, threatening to break

through my rib cage. I realized, not for the first time, the lengths I'd go to if it meant protecting her. I'd never thought I'd fall in love, and I'd sure as hell never it expected to feel like *this*.

It was as terrifying as it was liberating. Like knowing I had it all, but being painfully aware of how quickly it could all vanish.

"I asked Royal to start making a plan to go after Gary," I said, keeping my voice low and even so as not to risk waking Maddie.

I didn't want her involved in what came next.

Court's dark gaze met mine in the rearview mirror. "You want to move on him in Henderson?"

I nodded. "I'm done waiting. If Royal and Ash think Gary's house will give us the best shot at ending this, then I'm in."

"Fuck, yeah," Linc cheered softly from the front, a savage grin on his face as he glanced at me. The facade he frequently wore was good, and I often forgot that, under the comedic relief and playboy persona he showed the world, he was quite possibly the most fucked up of my friends. He had demons shackled to his soul.

"What about Maddie?" Court asked.

My eyes narrowed. "What about her?"

"Planning on telling her where we're really going when it happens?" Court's eyes challenged me to lie to the woman I loved.

Sighing, I looked down at her again. "I'm not lying to her."

"Are you planning on bringing her?"

"Are you fucking serious, bro?" I glared at him.

Court shrugged. "It's her fucking father, man. He put her and her sister through the wringer. She has a right to see it through to the end."

"She's been tainted enough by this bullshit," I spat. "I don't want her in the same zip code as that asswipe ever again. She can stay behind with Bex."

Linc snorted. "Oh, they're gonna love that. Hope your dick enjoyed the action in Vegas, because it'll be a while before it sees anything more than your hand when she finds out you're planning to leave her behind to play hero."

"Fuck off," I muttered, glancing back down at her. A tiny frown creased her brow, and my heart twisted at the mere thought of her having a bad dream. I stroked my thumb over the worry lines until they smoothed out and she sighed softly, snuggling against me.

This girl, man. I was so fucking gone for her it wasn't funny. It was downright dangerous how much I loved her. The kind of love that set the world on fire and demolished kingdoms in mythology. Those stories had never made sense until Madison Porter tumbled into my life.

"I want Gary Cabot dead," I murmured, venom in my tone. I more than wanted him dead; I wanted him suffering and writhing in agony as everything he'd done to her, I did to him, tenfold. I wanted him begging for death before I put a bullet in his head.

"He will be," Linc assured me, the same fire in his gaze as he grinned at me.

Court nodded in agreement. "His days are numbered, but I'm not sure I like the idea of splitting our resources. If the place in Henderson is as fortified as the one in Wyoming, we'll need all seven of us to get in and out."

"Or we could let your brothers blow something up again," Linc suggested.

Court snorted a laugh. "I'm not crazy about leaving Bex and Maddie alone, though."

"We could always leave a few people behind," I pointed out. Maybe there was a way to split our forces up because Court was right—I didn't want to leave either of them exposed just in case. "Maybe Ash."

Court shook his head. "No, we'll need him for communications."

I gritted my teeth. "There has to be someone we can spare."

Linc shot me a smirk. "What about your new buddy, *Chase*? Think the future duke is up to protecting the girls?"

"Fuck no," I huffed, irritation rippling across my skin. I hated that fucker. He annoyed the shit out of me and was constantly finding a reason to be around Maddie. And I hadn't forgotten their fake engagement.

Asshat had probably loved that, even if it was for show.

"The Rippers owe us a favor," I hedged, wondering if now was the right time to cash in on that. MCs weren't exactly known for their subtlety, but I wasn't sure I cared if it meant Maddie being rid of her father once and for all.

Linc gave a low whistle. "That'd be ballsy, but we don't know how those guys operate. It's kinda soon to rely on them."

"We'll see," I murmured, dismissing the idea for now. "I'll wait until Royal's run all the options before we figure that shit out."

"Big brother sure loves planning a mission." Court smirked, affection in his eyes. For years, he and Royal had struggled to connect. It had taken a long time for Royal to accept that Court wasn't like their father. The man didn't trust easy, but when he did, he was loyal to the bitter end. It was why I knew I could always count on him.

I exhaled and leaned against the seat, my fingers sifting through Maddie's long hair. "Where are we with the legal shit?"

Court scoffed at the way I dismissed the hoops he and Linus were jumping through to make things right. Starting with the fact that me being this close to Maddie was currently a fucking crime.

"There's no undoing the marriage being annulled," he started, and I grimaced. "Sorry, bro."

"Doesn't change shit," I replied. "A piece of paper isn't going to tell me whether or not Maddie's mine."

"If we can prove Gary was manipulating Maddie and the courts, the restraining order will be easy to overturn." Court shot me a wry look. "I don't have to tell you that it doesn't help your case that you technically kidnapped her from her court-appointed guardian."

"Her court-appointed guardian was a sadistic fuck intent on selling her to the highest bidder," I growled. "He locked her up in an asylum, pumped her full of drugs, and removed her fucking birth control. Who *does* that?"

Linc ticked up a finger. "Sadistic fucks?"

If Maddie hadn't been sprawled on my lap, I'd have kicked his seat into the dash. Instead, I settled for flipping him off.

"We need *proof*," Court stressed. "That's what matters. And right now, on paper, Gary makes a compelling case."

I glanced at the purse on the floor. Maddie hadn't been willing to pack it in the back with the rest of our stuff. She needed to keep the drives close until she handed them over to Ash.

"Hopefully Madelaine can help us out with that." I barely believed I'd said that with a straight face.

Linc's jaw tightened. "Is it weird I feel kinda bad for her?"

"I don't know," I muttered, not sure where I stood on the matter of my ex-fiancée anymore. That video Maddie had shown us had definitely given me more perspective, and shit, yeah, I felt kinda bad for her. On the other hand...

Court practically snarled at us. "She made Bex's life a living hell, remember?"

"This is true," Linc agreed. "But I'm questioning her motives."

Court made a strangled sound of disbelief. "What possible motive could there be for destroying the life of a girl who was nothing but innocent?"

Ah, shit.

"Fuck," Court whispered, realizing his misstep as he glanced at Linc. "Dude, you know I didn't mean—"

Linc held up a hand, his voice hard. "We're not talking about that."

"I'm sorry," Court offered. "You know none of us blame you."

"What part of *we aren't talking about it* aren't you understanding?" Linc snapped, glaring across the console. "Christ."

Court sighed. "If anything, it's me."

I shot him a curious look. "Huh?"

"I isolated Bex," he explained. "It was my decision for everyone to cut her out of their life after what my father did. I thought a clean break would be easiest. If I ignored her, she'd be safe."

"She almost died, dude," Linc grumbled. "You did what you thought was best to keep her alive."

"Yeah, and look where that got her," Court replied, his tone full of self-loathing. "I was so fucked up by what happened that I put her out of my mind. I ignored that Madelaine was tormenting her for years."

"That's not fair," I protested. "She's three years younger than us. After that summer, we never ran in the same circles. We went to a different school most of the time, and our schedules sure as fuck didn't overlap. How were you supposed to know what was going on in her life?"

Court shook his head. "All I've ever wanted was for her to be safe. Do you know what it's like to realize you're the one who fucked that up?"

"Yeah," I confessed, looking at Maddie again. "I'm well aware."

Court winced. "Fair."

"This trip has turned into such a bitchfest," Linc muttered. He pointed at Court. "You need to man up and grab onto the chance Bex is giving you." He turned and aimed a finger at me. "And you need to accept that Maddie's stronger than you think. And *both* your whining asses need to stop blaming yourself for not being all-knowing gods who can control the fucking universe. Life happens."

"Dick." I rolled my eyes.

"Fine, I'm a dick," Linc agreed. "Now can we try to enjoy the rest of the damn trip before we get back to the house and start planning all the ways we're going to kill Gary?"

Court snickered and shook his head. "Whatever you want, man."

Linc perked up. "Whatever I want, huh?"

Worry tugged at me. "If you turn on the radio and start singing, I'll make sure every single girl who crosses paths with you for the rest of your life knows you have an incurable case of crotch rot that's highly contagious."

Linc actually pouted, but he pulled his hand back from where he'd been about to turn on the radio. "You guys suck ass."

CHAPTER 37

MADDIE

"Holy shit," Ash breathed as I piled the flash drives on the dining room table.

Chase moved to look over my shoulder, but Ryan positioned himself at my back, his hands settling possessively on my hips. I turned my head to kiss his jaw while he shot Chase a glare that would've made most men run.

Chase rolled his eyes and moved to my other side, but I noticed he didn't touch me. "This is insanity."

"I'm impressed," Tyler admitted, picking up one drive and then the next before starting to arrange them. "She dated them and everything."

Ash walked around to where Tyler had begun laying the drives out in order, and braced one hand on the table and the other on the back of her chair as she worked. He watched the way Tyler's fingers trembled before she got ahold of herself and focused on the task at hand.

Bex stood off to one side with Court and Linc. "What does all this mean?"

"We won't know until we start looking," Ash admitted, repositioning one of the drives Tyler had sorted. He smirked when she scowled at him, likely annoyed he was butting into her task. "But this is a fucking amazing start. Some of these names I recognize."

"So, that's...good?" I asked. I leaned against Ryan's chest, still tired and craving sleep that wasn't in the backseat of a car. I loved Ryan, but his thighs had way too much muscle to be comfortable for more than a nap.

Knight leaned in from the far end of the table, the only other brother present as Bishop and Royal were taking their turns checking the perimeter and the security feeds. "Does that say *P. Henderson?*" He gaped in disbelief.

I looked at the drive he was talking about. "As in former Vice President of the United States Peter Henderson?" My eyes rounded.

"Your sister was a badass," Tyler whispered, looking at me. "Possibly psychotic and a raging bitch, but a badass. I mean, how she even got all this stuff is beyond me. These aren't people who just let themselves be recorded or followed."

It's amazing the things men let slip when you're a pretty decoration in their bed or on their lap.

She'd sold pieces of herself to get everything sitting here.

"Fuck me," Court whispered, pushing off the wall. He grabbed one from the pile. "Coach King." He flipped the label toward Ryan.

Ryan stiffened at my back. "What the..." He took the drive, and I turned in his arms. "Why would she have one on him?"

Bex made a tiny noise of distress, and everyone turned to her. She bit her lower lip. "After he got fired from PC," she hedged, wrapping her arms around herself, "there were some rumors in the girls' dorms."

"Rumors?" Court stared at her.

She nodded. "Apparently Madelaine wasn't the only student he'd been sleeping with, but she was definitely the oldest. Some of the freshmen girls said that he'd... You know." She blushed. "Coach King supplemented part of his coaching salary with being a part-time phys-ed teacher at the academy."

"Motherfucker." Ryan shook his head. He tossed the flash drive back into the pile, looking disgusted.

I touched his hand, not sure how to help. For some insane reason I wanted to apologize, but I wasn't sure why. Because Madelaine had betrayed him? Because a man he'd trusted had not only screwed him over but had been messing around with underage girls?

He met my eyes, his expression telling me he knew exactly where my head was and that there wasn't anything I could do. So, I slipped my arms around his waist and hugged him.

Ash spread out the pile of drives so Tyler could continue sorting. "There's CEOs, congressmen, and entertainers in here. Actors and singers. Goddamn."

Tyler nodded and kept sorting, getting stuck on a drive. "This one doesn't have a date, just a name, but I don't recognize it."

Ash took it from her and shook his head, puzzled. "No idea. We'll figure it out later." He tossed it aside, letting it slide away from what they were working on.

Bex inhaled sharply.

"You okay?" I asked, worried when her face paled. "Bex?"

She walked to the table like she was in a trance and picked up the discarded drive. "Beeps," she whispered, smoothing her thumb over the label.

Court crowded around her back. "What—"

"It's what Madelaine used to call me." Bex swallowed hard. "It was a stupid nickname. I… When Madelaine used to laugh really hard, she'd make this weird, squeaky noise." A sad smile tipped up the corner of her mouth as she looked at me. "I called her Squeaks, and she said my name should be Beeps."

I hadn't had a chance to sit down and tell Bex that, in her video to me, Madelaine might have been trying to explain why she'd cut Bex off, but this kinda confirmed my suspicions. "Do you want to watch it?"

"I don't know," she confessed.

"You don't have to." Court's eyes flashed protectively as he glared at the thumb drive like it might grow legs and attack her.

Linc cleared his throat. "But it might give you some answers."

Court glared at him. "Or not."

"Still her choice," Knight pointed out with a shrug.

Court turned his annoyed look at his brother.

"Bex, it's whatever you want," I told her softly. "Zero pressure."

"I wanna know," Bex said, her voice trembling. "I *need* to know."

Shaking his head, Court didn't look convinced. "She spent the last few years making your life hell, Becca."

"I know." She clutched the drive in her fist as she looked up at him, uncertain. "But it might give me some answers."

He brushed back some of her dark hair from her face, his touch lingering. "I don't want to see you get hurt."

Her lips twitched into a small smile. "I love that you want to protect me, but I'd rather know the truth. Even if it hurts."

Court flinched and jerked his hand back, and I remembered that Bex still had no idea that Court was holding back the real reason he and the guys had stopped being her friend when they were kids.

"Do you want to watch it alone?" I asked her, making a mental note to tell Court to man up and tell her the truth soon, or I'd do it for him.

"Actually, would you mind coming with me?" Her hazel eyes focused squarely on me.

Behind me, Ryan cleared his throat, his hands settling on my shoulders. "You guys should use the den. We have a few things to discuss with Royal, Bishop, and Knight."

Suspicious, I accepted the quick kiss he gave me before he left the room with Linc, Knight, and a reluctant Court.

Ash looked at Tyler. "You good?"

She nodded, not looking up as she started on a new row of the drives. "I'm going to check a few just to make sure there isn't any malware before we start looking at them."

Ash smiled, looking mildly amused, before following the others.

Tyler let out a sigh. "Guess there's men-talk to be had, and us girls can't be part of it."

I started laughing as Chase frowned. "I'm a man."

Tyler lifted her eyes and gave him a patronizing smile. "Sure you are, Chasey."

He glared at her. "You're becoming a prat, Tyler. Don't make me send you back to London."

She scoffed under her breath. "I'd like to see you try."

His brows slammed down. "What did you—"

"The boys are plotting someone's demise, I'm trying to work, Maddie and Bex are going to uncover the last great secrets of Madelaine—" Tyler sucked in a deep breath "—and what exactly are *you* doing to help?"

Chase glared at her while Bex and I exchanged amused glances.

"Maybe try making dinner?" Tyler suggested.

Chase looked more than a little uncomfortable. "I don't think anyone delivers this far into the mountains."

I laughed and wrapped an arm around Bex's shoulders before looking at Tyler. "You can handle him?"

"I suppose," Tyler muttered, shaking her head. "Spoiled rich kid."

Chase threw up his arms. "So, it's my fault I was raised by servants and had a full staff cooking my meals?"

"Yes," the three of us answered in unison. Tyler and Chase were still bickering as Bex and I left them and wandered down the hall to the den.

With a large flat-screen TV and two massive sectional sofas, the room was where we'd all frequently ended up at night, hanging out and watching movies while Ryan and I were both recovering from our injuries.

I walked down the short flight of steps into the sunken-in room and turned to face Bex, who was staring hesitantly at the flat-screen. "I don't think I want to watch whatever this is like it's a movie. I mean, if it's a highlight of Madelaine's greatest hits against me…" A nervous laugh escaped her.

"For what it's worth? I really don't think that's what this is," I told her.

"Neither do I," she admitted. "And that actually scares me more." She walked around the backs of the couches and grabbed her laptop from a side table, then came back and sat down.

"Ready?" I asked, slipping onto the spot beside her.

"No." But Bex turned on the screen and inserted the flash drive. A second later, a series of folders popped up.

Bex's eyes narrowed as we silently read the file names, but the most important seemed like a video file marked with her nickname again. When she double-clicked the file, a video of Madelaine started the same way mine had.

Madelaine was in the same clothes and room as in the message she'd left me, which made me think she'd filmed the videos back to back. She wiped her palms on her pants as she sat across from the camera with a stiff face.

"Uh, hey, Beeps," she started with a husky laugh. "Shit, no. You like Bex now, right? Bex. Got it. I swear I'll try not to be an asshole on this, but we both know bitch mode is my default setting."

Bex rolled her eyes in agreement.

"I've spent a lot of time thinking about how I'd apologize to you, and I swear if I get a chance to do it in person, I'm going to." She smiled weakly. "You were the best friend I ever had. Hell, you were my *only* friend. At least in the ways that mattered."

I laced my fingers with Bex's and leaned my head on her shoulder as Madelaine continued.

"That's why I had to let you go," Madelaine whispered. "Gary knew how much you mattered to me, and… I wasn't going to let him hurt you, too. But you—dammit, Beeps, every time I tried to push you away for your own good, you just held on tighter."

Madelaine bit her thumbnail and shook her head. "Why couldn't you just— No. This isn't on you, it's on me. But that's why I did the things I did. I had to make sure it was obvious I didn't care about you. I had to prove to him that you were nothing, when really, you were everything. You were my best friend, B, and I'm sorry for the way I repaid that."

I glanced at Bex, not surprised to find her crying. Tears rolled down her cheeks as she watched Madelaine's confession. "That stupid bitch," Bex hissed, sniffling as she looked at me. "I would've stuck by her no matter what, Maddie."

"I'm an idiot, I know," Madelaine muttered on screen, confirming what Bex had said. "Look, if you're seeing this then I hope that means you met Madison. You were with me when I found out about her, and it's only right if you're there with her after I'm gone."

We shot each other watery smiles, squeezing our hands together.

Madelaine leaned forward. "I know I don't have any right to ask, but... look out for her, would you? The way you tried to do for me? She's going to need someone real and true, and you're the best person I've ever met, Beeps." She drew in a slow breath. "Which makes what else I have to tell you suck even more."

Bex sat up straighter, and worry curled in my gut.

Madelaine grimaced at the screen. "I figured it out, I think. I didn't even mean to, it just kinda happened, and I don't have all the facts, but I included what I could on this drive." She swallowed hard. "B, your dad isn't the guy you think he is. And *he's* the reason Court stopped being your friend when you were little. I think he's also responsible for those night terrors you used to have."

I swung my head and looked at my best friend. "Night terrors?"

Bex wet her lips. "After my treatments. I used to have these crazy nightmares. Everyone told me it was because of the chemo and shit. I had these weird ass dreams. I haven't had one in a long time, but when Lainey and I were still close, I had them pretty often."

"All the stuff I found is on here. I didn't add your dad's name to the others because, well, he's your dad. What you do with the info is up to you," Madelaine said, pressing her lips together. "But here's what I think happened between you and Court..."

CHAPTER 38

MADDIE

"Court!" Bex's shout echoed off the walls and ceiling of the house as she stormed through it, red-faced and out for blood.

I chased after her. "Bex, maybe you should calm—"

She whirled and stabbed a finger toward my face. "*Don't* tell me to calm down, Maddie!"

I held up my hands, surrendering, as she spun away from me and continued the hunt. A pit opened in my stomach, threatening to upend the contents, and I trailed Bex into the kitchen.

This was bad. So bad.

Madelaine had mostly been guessing, but she hadn't been too far off in her suspicions. My twin had missed her calling as a PI, because the history of shit she'd unearthed in her seventeen years was amazing.

"What's going on?" Chase asked, standing wide-eyed in front of the sink filling a pot with water.

"Where is he?" Bex growled, sounding like a feral kitten.

Court, I mouthed behind her back.

Chase pointed at the mudroom that led to the garage. "Pretty sure they're all out there."

Bex took off without any further encouragement.

"What the hell?" Chase stared at me.

I shook my head as Tyler emerged from the dining room and asked, "Is she good?"

"Not even close," I muttered, running a hand through my hair and following my best friend.

Sure enough, the guys were crowded around a table, deep in thought, until Bex yelled for Court again. Court's head snapped up, concern filling his eyes as he left our friends and came to Bex, meeting her in the middle of an open bay.

"What's wrong?" His hands reached for her arms, like he needed to touch her to make sure she was all right and unharmed.

Bex knocked his hands away and shoved him back a step. "I want the truth, and I want it right the fuck now."

Court looked at me, confused, before turning back to the spitfire. "Okay. Maybe it would help if I knew the question, though."

"Why did you stop being friends with me?" Bex demanded, her tiny hands squeezing into fists at her sides.

Court's expression went from worried to stony in seconds. "I told you. I was an asshole. I was starting middle school and thought I didn't want you tagging along anymore. We grew up, and I—"

Bex's hand cracked across his face so fast I thought I was seeing things. But the sharp slap echoed off the concrete floors and made everyone turn to stare.

"Bex," I whispered, stepping forward.

To her credit, Bex staggered back, staring at her hand like it had been possessed. "I didn't mean… Oh, my God. I *hit* you."

Court rubbed his jaw, his cheek red. "Yeah, you did."

"I'm sorry." Bex shook her head, trembling from head to toe. "I don't know why I did that. I've never hit anyone in my life and—"

"It's fine," Court told her with a heavy sigh.

"No, it's not, but I can't…" She pulled on the ends of her hair. "Why are you lying to me? Just tell me the truth for fucking once! Do you even know how to do that?"

"I told you—"

"Liar!" She screamed the accusation at him with enough force that he stepped back.

Breaking away from the group, Linc tried approaching her from the other side. "Bex, what's going on?"

"What's going on is that I thought I was going crazy for *years*," Bex hissed. "Did you know I had to see a therapist? That I still sometimes have to take anxiety medication for something I thought was a dream?"

Court's eyes went wide. "What?"

Bex shook her head. "I had night terrors. Everyone told me it was a side effect of the chemo. That it was normal to have anxiety after having cancer. But that didn't explain the dreams and why, when I woke up, I was always screaming for *you*." She glared at Court, who looked more than a little helpless.

"Becca," he whispered, looking gutted. "I didn't... Shit, I didn't know that."

"How could you?" She threw her hands in the air. "You *left* me. You forgot I existed, and I thought it was all some horrible nightmare that I'd made up because I had such a high fever during treatment. But it wasn't, was it? The cabin was real."

Slowly, heartbreakingly, Court nodded once. "What do you remember?"

"Why don't you just tell me what happened? Or is the truth something so far out of reach for you that you can't handle the concept?"

Court stared at the ground and exhaled. "Okay. Why don't we go—"

"I'm not going anywhere with you until you give me answers." Bex folded her arms under her chest. "What the hell happened?"

Rubbing the back of his neck, Court fumed silently for a beat before lifting his eyes to me. "Did you tell her? Couldn't you just let it fucking alone?"

"What? No," Bex retorted, her face twisting in bafflement. "Madelaine was the one who... Why would Maddie know?"

I sighed heavily and stared at Ryan, who looked ready to intervene. I shook my head at him, because we were so far past burying this.

The betrayal in Bex's eyes was heartbreaking and one hundred percent my fault. "You *knew?*"

Ryan left the table and came to my side. "I told her."

Bex looked around, horror on her face. "You all knew? And no one told *me?*" Her accusing gaze landed on Linc.

"Court asked us to keep it a secret." Linc shoved his hands into the pockets of his jeans. "To protect you."

"How kind of him to make all these decisions for me." The sarcasm in her tone fooled no one; she was hurt and about to start crying.

A muscle ticked in Court's jaw as he clenched his teeth. "I did what I thought was necessary to keep you safe."

"And who the hell gave you that right?"

"I gave it to myself after you almost *died* because of me," he snapped. "After it became obvious that your pencil dick of a father cared more about his business than keeping you safe, and after it became more than fucking apparent that my dad was willing to kill you if it meant keeping my ass in line!"

Bex stared at him.

"I'd already lost a brother. I wasn't losing you, too, Becca," he finished. "Does it make me an asshole? Sure. Fine. Call me an asshole, but you're alive, aren't you? He never used you to bait me again, did he?"

"Maybe we should give you two time to talk," I suggested, my gaze flickering between them.

"No," Bex finally said, her voice strangled. "You know what? I'm done talking. You guys do whatever the hell you want. I mean, why should things like my feelings or wants be a consideration when you've already figured it out."

"Becca," Court growled as she turned to leave, "fucking stop."

"You got exactly what you wanted, Court," she told him, looking over her shoulder. "No one can use me to hurt you, because I'm out of your life. Let's keep it that way."

"Bex," Linc sighed. "It's not—"

"Seriously, Lincoln, don't waste your breath," she sneered, icicles dripping from her words. "I never meant anything to any of you.

That's pretty fucking obvious, given it was so easy for you to discard me." Bex paused as she passed me, tears in her eyes. "But I thought you were different."

I took a step toward her. "I'm so sorry. I should've told you."

"Why didn't you?" Her gaze moved past me to Ryan. "Because he asked you not to? *Ordered* you not to?"

I pressed my lips together, unsure what to say to fix this. I knew my silence would come at a cost, but this was beyond what I'd imagined. Her hurt cut deeper than her anger ever could, and knowing that I was part of it sucked beyond the telling.

"Right. Look, I'll talk to you later, Maddie, but right now I want to be alone." Her gaze cut to Court. "The way I'm supposed to be, right?" Her mocking stare proved too much, and he flinched away. With a scoff, Bex walked back inside.

"You realize you handled that terribly, right?" Knight drawled from the other side of the space.

"Why didn't you just tell her the truth?" Bishop asked, frowning at his brother.

Royal was still staring at the table and didn't seem inclined to get involved at all.

Ash stepped around him and clapped a hand on Court's shoulder. "She's upset, man. She'll cool down and—"

"And what?" I interrupted, curious more than anything. "Forgive him a third time? Forgive all of us when we've all proven that we'll keep lying to her?" I shook my head and looked at Ryan. "I'm sorry, but I should've told her everything from the start. I never should've agreed to keep this secret."

"I shouldn't have asked you to," Ryan admitted. "I'm sorry, Mads."

I turned to Court. "Pick a side and stay there, Court."

He frowned at me.

"Either you want her in your life or you don't, but you can't half-ass it. Hell, you're not even partially assing it. Tell her the truth or let her go. But whatever this thing is between you guys, it isn't healthy for her *or* for you." I looked at the table they'd been gathered around. "Is this something I need to know about?"

Indecision warred on Ryan's face for a split second, and I saw the very moment he decided not to hide the truth.

"We're planning on going after Gary."

"When?" I demanded.

He ground his teeth. "Two days."

"Were you going to tell me?" I folded my arms over my chest.

His gaze jerked away from a second, his throat working. "Not exactly."

"Am I part of this plan?"

"Absolutely not," he said firmly, his gaze snapping back to mine. "I don't want you near him if I can help it. I won't apologize for protecting you, Mads. We both know I'll do shit that you may not like because my end goal is making sure you're safe. Can you live with that?"

I couldn't exactly get pissed that he was being honest with me when I'd asked. Deciding this wasn't a battle I needed on my plate, I exhaled and nodded. "I can live with that as long as you don't lie to me about it."

I spun on my heel and grimaced at Court. "See? Communication. It can actually work. Now, if you all will excuse me, I'm going to make sure Chase isn't trying to serve us boiled water for dinner before begging my bestie's forgiveness." I leaned over and smacked a kiss to Ryan's lips before leaving.

I entered the mudroom cursing, but when I entered the kitchen, it was all I could do not to burst into laughter.

Water bubbled over the rim of the massive pot and splashed onto the stovetop with a hiss as Chase... waved a damn hand over the steam.

I rushed over and turned down the heat, then lifted the pot for a few seconds for the bubbles to settle. When I set it back, it still simmered, but the bubbles weren't threatening to spill over the edges. "What the hell?" I laughed as I looked at Chase.

Red-faced, and probably not because of the heat, he groaned. "I thought I'd make soup. I mean, it's just water and whatever shite you throw in to make it taste good, right?"

"Right," I deadpanned. "That's all it is. Did you even look at what ingredients we have?"

A sheepish expression crawled across his face. "Uh, I assumed I'd find something in the pantry that would suffice."

"Awesome. I'll tell everyone we're having pantry soup for dinner." I rolled my eyes and turned to the far wall, where built-in stainless-steel doors covered two full-size refrigerators and a freezer.

I opened the freezer door and pointed to a stack of frozen pizzas. "These have instructions that are fairly idiot proof."

"That may not do," Chase teased, pointing to the text on the box. "It doesn't even have pictures, and we've both established I'm more than fairly an idiot. Some might even call it full-blown idiocy."

"I would!" Tyler called from the other room.

I giggled and pulled out the pizzas. Hopefully six was enough, otherwise we'd be having pantry soup, too. I took the water off the stove and set it aside, and then showed him how to operate the ovens.

As the second oven started to preheat, he looked at me. "Is Rebecca all right? She seemed upset when she ran through here."

I exhaled and dumped the cooling water down the drain. "She will be. It's just... There's a lot of history here."

"Well, if it ever gets to be too much, say the word," Chase offered with a small smile.

Curious, I leaned a hip on the counter. "Meaning?"

"Meaning whatever you want it to mean." He met my gaze, something that I couldn't quite figure out glimmering in his green eyes. "If you, or Rebecca, want to leave, you have options. My family is more than equipped to help you escape your father and see that he's brought to justice."

"I think we've got it handled. But thank you," I added as an afterthought.

He nodded. "Just know the option is always there, should you need it. I had my family's jet moved to a nearby airport just in case."

"Aren't you worried about Gary knowing you aren't dead?"

He frowned and leaned against the opposite counter. "I'm certain he already knows. But the only reason he tried to kill me was so I couldn't help you, which I did."

"You did." I smiled. "Did I say thank you?"

"No thanks are ever needed, Madison," he assured me with a grin.

"Well, thanks all the same," I replied, straightening. "I'm gonna go check on Bex. You've got this, right?" I waved a hand at the ovens and boxes.

"So, I just put the boxes in and let them cook," Chase surmised, glancing from the boxes to the oven as it preheated.

My jaw dropped. "No, dumbass. You have to take the pizzas *out*—" I stopped when he started laughing. "You're a jerk and probably going to kill us all in one meal."

"Apologies," he said, still chuckling as he tweaked my nose, "but you were simply too adorable in your horror."

I gave him a playful push, and he caught my wrists in his hands. I tried to twist away with another giggle.

"Thought you were checking on Bex." Ryan's sharp voice cut into my laughter.

This time when I pulled back, Chase let me go. I smiled at Ryan, blatantly ignoring the hard look in his eyes as he watched us from the other side of the counter. "I had to teach Chase how to work the ovens, and he almost burned the water for his pantry soup."

Chase snickered at my back. "It would've been delicious."

Ryan's eyes narrowed. "I bet. Chase is all about helping out, isn't he?"

Uneasiness swirled in my stomach. "Ryan, we were just joking around."

"I'm sure," he said. "I mean, I'm sure *you* were, but I'm not so sure about Chase."

"Meaning what, mate?" Chase asked.

"Meaning I see the way you look at my wife," Ryan ground out, glaring at him.

"Ryan!" I gasped, gaping at him.

Chase smirked. "Funny, because I'm fairly certain she's *not* your wife anymore. Not your fiancée, either."

Ryan started to round the counter and I intervened, blocking him. "Ry, stop. Come on. He didn't mean it like that."

"I think he did," Ryan seethed, still looking behind me.

"Maybe I did," Chase admitted, causing me to spin around. He cocked a brow at me. "I meant what I said, Maddie. You have options. And they're not all tied to men who will order you around."

My jaw dropped as I whirled to stare at Chase. "That's *not* what's happening here."

Chase met my eyes. "Trust me. I'm well aware of what's *not* happening here." With that cryptic statement, he turned and walked out of the room.

"What just happened?" I murmured, stunned.

"Seriously?" Ryan snorted at my back. "Come on, Mads. You can't tell me you haven't noticed the way he's always finding reasons to be near you. The guy's fucking obsessed with you."

"No, he isn't," I denied, shaking my head as I looked at him.

"Don't be stupid," he told me.

I backed up a step. "I'm sorry. What did you just say to me?"

Ryan rolled his eyes. "Maddie, you know what I meant."

"Yeah, I do, and you better check the attitude," I warned him.

"What do you expect, when I walk into a room and he's all over you?" he demanded.

I ticked up a finger. "One, I expect you to see that I wasn't doing anything with my *friend* that I haven't done with Linc or Ash or Court. It's okay for me to joke with them, but Chase is a hard line?"

"My friends don't want to fuck you," he answered, arching a brow.

I held up a second finger. "Still not done, okay? Most importantly, I thought you trusted me."

He sighed. "I do."

Yeah, that didn't sound convincing at all.

"Wow, maybe try meaning it when you say it." I shook my head in disbelief. "I cannot believe that we're back to square one."

"That's not what this is," he insisted.

"No? Because it sure as hell seems like it, Ryan." I pointed at the garage. "You're keeping things from me *again*, and you think I'd, what?

Screw Chase amongst the frozen pizza boxes while you guys could walk in for front row seats to live porn? Have I not convinced you enough that you're it for me? What else do you need me to do?" I threw my hands in the air, frustrated to the point that I wanted to scream.

Guilt flashed in his eyes as he reached for me. "Nothing, okay? Baby, it's me. I'm sorry. Of course I trust you."

My head landed against his hard chest, but I didn't hug him back.

"Maddie," he whispered, his lips brushing the top of my head. "I'm sorry."

Reluctantly, I lifted my hands to his waist, looping my fingers in the front pockets of his jeans. "I know you love me, but it doesn't mean shit unless you trust me, too."

"I do trust you," he replied. "I don't trust *him*."

Scoffing, I looked up at him, unimpressed by the answer.

"I'm sorry," he repeated, staring into my eyes. "I have my own shit to work through, and it's not fair to put that on you. Forgive me, please?"

Now I wrapped my arms around his waist, accepting his apology. "Of course I forgive you. But you chased out the cook, so that means *you're* making dinner."

CHAPTER 39

MADDIE

I knocked softly on Bex's door, and when she didn't answer, I tested the knob. Surprisingly, it twisted open. I peeked in, my gaze sweeping the room until it landed on her, curled up on the queen-size bed and facing the window as more snow fell.

"Can I come in?" I asked, hating to disturb her, but also needing to fix the hole in my heart caused by her pain.

Sighing, Bex waved a hand, indicating I was free to enter, so I did. Once the door was closed, I walked across the room and sat on the edge of her bed. "I'm really sorry, Bex."

"You should be," she muttered, still not looking at me. "I thought you had my back."

"I do," I insisted. "When Ryan told me, I said that he needed to talk to Court and have Court tell you the truth. That it wasn't fair. I also said I wouldn't keep their secret indefinitely, but then everything went to shit, and I honestly forgot."

Another heavy breath. "It's not your fault. Not really."

I touched her ankle. "I'm your best friend, and I should've had your back. Do you want me to fill in the blanks?"

Madelaine's video had made several right assumptions, but there were also a few things I knew from Ryan that my twin hadn't known. Bex had to still have questions.

"No," Bex finally said, flipping onto her back and looking at me. "I want Court to tell me."

"I can go get him," I offered.

"No," she repeated, shaking her head as her mouth turned downward. "I want him to *want* to tell me. I want him to realize that I'm worth the freaking truth, Mads."

I nodded, understanding her point. "Okay. But I don't know if he'll ever be ready for that."

"Then he doesn't care about me the way I thought he did," she murmured. "Not the way I want him to."

"Do you remember what you told me when Ryan hurt me after the engagement party?" I raised my brows until she gave a short nod. "Same thing applies now with Court. I don't think he's trying to hurt you. In his way, he's trying to protect you."

"It's a bullshit excuse," she told me, sitting up and drawing her knees to her chest. "I don't need to be protected, and neither do you."

"Tell that to the half dozen alpha males downstairs," I teased with a weak grin. "They think protecting us little girls is their sole purpose in life."

Bex's face darkened into a scowl. "Well, this little girl's about to nut punch all of them if they don't cut it out."

I cracked up, unable to hold my laughter at the visual of tiny Bex doing just that. "Let me know before you do, okay? I totally want to record that."

A wry smile twisted her lips. "Deal." Then the happy light in her eyes vanished. "Madelaine recorded stuff about my dad on those drives. Do you think I should watch it?"

"I don't know," I admitted. "The guys already told you he was involved in some of the shadier shit, but not nearly to the extent their dads were."

She looked down, wrapping her arms around her legs. "I don't want my dad to go to prison, Maddie. I mean, he's my *dad*."

I smothered a wince. "Okay."

"He's the guy who taught me how to ride a bike. Who spent the night in the hospital with me when I was sick," she went on. "I know he's done some bad things, but…"

"Then don't," I answered. "Bex, your dad might not be innocent, but he's far from Gary Cabot's level of dirty. And it seems like every time he did something, it was because his hand was forced."

Not that it absolved him of guilt, but I guessed it was something. And right now, Bex needed to cling to that hope.

Besides, Malcolm Whittier hadn't known that, when he'd agreed to Bex "going away" with Jasper Woods, she was really being kidnapped to manipulate Court. The Whittier and Woods families had been friends for years, vacationing together before their kids were even born. Madelaine's original guess in the video was that Malcolm had sold out his daughter for seed money for the startup that would eventually be CryptDuo. But Malcolm wasn't a monster. He was just an idiot who had trusted a man he thought was his friend.

Still, his mistake had nearly cost Bex her life, and it had absolutely been the start of his marriage decaying. Betty and Malcolm were married in name only now, something Bex had pointed out multiple times since I'd met her. But they both loved Bex more than anything.

Couldn't say the same for my parents. They'd both proven, repeatedly, that I was for sale to the highest bidder or for the next fix.

"Hey." Bex touched my hand. "Where'd your head go that has you looking all sad?"

"Just wondering what life would've been like with parents that actually cared about me." I flashed her a forced smile and tried to shrug it off.

Her expression morphed into something fierce. "It's their loss, Maddie. Screw them both for not seeing how amazing you are."

"I hate that Gary won," I confessed. "He got the money, and Madelaine's dead. It's not right."

"Maybe Ash and Tyler will find something on the drives that'll help," she suggested. "And you know Ryan isn't going to let him waltz off into the sunset."

Judging by the planning in the garage, she was right.

"Speaking of Ryan, he's making dinner. Are you hungry?"

Her brows shot up. "Ryan *Cain* is making dinner?"

Suppressing a grin, I nodded. "Originally it was Chase, but Ryan pissed him off, so I told Ryan that he's stuck making it instead."

"Is it wrong that I kinda want to watch and see how bad he messes up?" Bex's hazel eyes sparkled with mischief.

I smirked. "Nope. Let's go."

Disappointingly, Ryan was actually handling dinner okay. Nothing was burning, and while he looked annoyed to be stuck as our chef, he also wasn't bitching about it.

"Hey." Ryan greeted Bex with obvious caution, eyeing her as she rounded the island to grab one of the barstools. "Everything okay?"

"No," she replied, her tone curt. "Everything okay with you?"

He lifted a brow. "Not especially. Look, I'm sorry—"

Bex held up a hand. "Save it. If you were sorry, you would've told me the truth years ago."

Ryan winced and nodded. "You're right. But, Bex, we *do* care about you."

"Not enough," she replied, blunt and unforgiving. "Right now, I'm here for Maddie, and that's it. As soon as all of this is over, I'm going home, and I want all of you out of my life as much as possible."

Court, who had been coming in from the garage with Linc and Ash, froze. Linc found his voice first, trying to play it off by moving around his friend and slinging an arm across Bex's shoulder. "C'mon, B, you don't mean that."

She shrugged him off with a pointed glare, ignoring Court completely as he stared at her. "Don't touch me. And yes, I'm serious."

Ash sighed and walked over to stand near Ryan. "Bex, please don't take this personally."

Her brows shot up. "Uh, what other way is there to take it? You four deliberately kept something massive from me. You've lied to me for *years*. None of you had the balls to tell me the truth. I mean, you still don't."

Court made a strangled sound in the back of his throat before storming to Bex and whirling her seat around to face him. "I said I'll tell you now, Becca. You're the one who stormed off like a child."

I winced, because that really wasn't the right way to handle this.

Bex folded her arms. "Too late. I don't care anymore."

"Bullshit," Court spat. "Don't lie to yourself, sweetheart. We both know you care, or you wouldn't be pissed at me."

An icy mask fell over her face. "I'm not pissed, Court. I'm not *anything*. Sort of like how I'm not anything to you."

Growling, Court caged her in against the counter, bracing a hand on either side of her body. "You know that isn't true. I think it's time you and I finally had this out, baby girl."

Her cheeks turned pink, but her mouth was still set in a mulish line. "Fuck off, Court."

His head tilted to the side. "Fuck off? Or fuck you?"

I jerked my gaze away from where they looked to be a second away from beating the shit out of each other or tearing each other's clothes off. Ryan met my eyes and smirked a little, but I noticed Ash had wandered out of the kitchen. Only Linc was watching like this was free pay-per-view.

Bex sneered. "You wish."

Court leaned in more, his tone going softer and darker. "Oh, I really fucking do. You and I have been dancing around this for months now. Why don't we just get everything out in the open so I can prove what we both know?"

"Which is?" Bex's breath hitched.

"That you've always belonged to me," he said, his voice like liquid sin.

Ryan cleared his throat, busying himself with staring at the oven timer as it ticked down the last few seconds. I felt like Linc—powerless to look away.

Bex leaned in a little, her lips less than an inch from Court's. "Is that what you think?"

Court's chuckle was deep and full of promise. "We both know it. Call it fate, destiny, whatever. It was always meant to be you and me, Becca. I was your first kiss, remember? I was meant to be your first everything."

Bex watched him, and for a heartbeat, I thought she was about to melt. But at the last second, she leaned back with a smug look. "I'll give you that you were my first kiss, but you weren't my first."

Court jolted like she'd slapped him.

"Or my second." Bex made a soft *tsk*ing sound under her breath. "Not my third either." She patted his cheek in a patronizing manner. "But it's cute you think I spent the last several years waiting for you to come back and claim me while you fucked every girl with a willing hole." Her gaze slid to Linc. "Sometimes with your bestie, too, right?"

"Shit," Linc whispered, backing away from Court, who looked ready to explode like a nuclear bomb.

Court's eyes narrowed. "*Who?*"

"Uh, pretty sure Linc's your bestie, isn't he? Or have you been sharing girls with more than him? I really hope you wrapped your shit up." Bex played dumb.

"Stop playing games. Who were you *with?*" Court ground out, and I wondered if Knight's medical skills extended to dentistry, because Court might need it, the way he was grinding his teeth.

Bex rolled her eyes. "I'm not doing this with you. We're done, Court, okay? We're not friends, we're not anything." She turned her stool back to face the other way as Court seethed at her back.

"We'll see about that," he growled before stalking out of the room. Moments later a door slammed somewhere in the house hard enough to rattle the pictures on the walls.

The timer buzzed, and I was pretty sure I heard Ryan say "Thank fuck" as he grabbed the first two pizzas from the ovens. He set the second pizza aside and put two more in the ovens before resetting the timer and looking at me. "Why don't you—"

A sharp cry from the dining room cut him off, and we all scrambled through the doorway between the two rooms to see what was wrong.

Tyler looked up, her eyes finding me without hesitation, a massive smile spreading across her face.

"Jesus, girl," Ash hissed, "what the fuck is wrong with you?"

Tyler didn't pay him any attention. "I did it!"

"Did *what?*" I asked, my heart still pounding. I mean, seriously.

With a triumphant flourish, Tyler flipped around her laptop, showing us the screen. "I managed to transfer every single cent back into Madison's accounts." She eyed Ash with smug satisfaction. "*And* I made sure no one could hack her accounts again."

Ash rolled his eyes as I gaped at her. "You got back the inheritance?"

Gary was going to lose his shit.

Tyler bit her lower lip, looking like she might explode from excitement. "Well, not exactly."

Ash moved around the table and examined the screen. After a beat, his jaw literally dropped. "You did this?"

Tyler nodded.

"God*damn*," Ash whispered, awed.

"What'd she do?" I asked.

Tyler smiled at me. "I wiped out every single account of Gary's that I could find. All his liquid assets are now *yours*, Maddie."

I stepped back, bumping into Ryan, who steadied me by putting his hands on my hips. "When you say wiped out, you mean…"

"I mean Gary Cabot can't even buy a freaking cup of coffee at McDonalds. He's dead-ass broke."

"Holy shit," I whispered, a slow smile starting to spread across my face.

"You're rich, baby." Ryan chuckled as he hugged me to his chest.

I turned to him. "Do we need it?"

He frowned. "Need what? The money?"

I nodded.

He looked at me like I was crazy. "No, of course not. Phoenix has plenty of ventures that make more money than any of us could ever spend in a lifetime. Plus, there's Brookfield."

Dragging in a deep breath, I looked at Tyler. "Donate it."

MAD LOVE

Her brows shot up. "What?"

"Donate it. Every single penny."

"Uh, are you sure?" She glanced at the computer and then me. "It's a *lot* of money. I mean, we're talking—"

I shook my head. "I don't want to know. It doesn't matter. He's hurt so many people... maybe this will counter some of that."

"Any place in particular you want the money to go?" Tyler sat down in front of the screen and waited.

"Something for domestic abuse victims," I murmured. Ryan's arms tightened around me as he rested his chin on my shoulder. Bex gave me a supportive smile.

"Okay," Tyler agreed. "Want me to make it anonymous?"

A slow smile spread across my face. "No. Make sure the entire world knows Gary Cabot donated it. I don't want him trying to weasel the money back. If the public knows, then he'll have to let it go to save face."

Tyler cackled. "I love it."

Inspiration struck me. "One more thing? Make sure you mention that it's been donated in honor of Madison Porter."

CHAPTER 40

RYAN

I was addicted to the way Maddie smiled. Her whole face lit up, and her eyes did this cute little crinkly thing that made my heart—and my dick—swell.

"Stop looking like you're about to bend her over the table in front of everyone," Ash murmured from my other side.

"Asshole," I snapped, but there was zero heat to my tone as I elbowed him.

Ash chuckled, watching as Maddie used her hands to describe something to Bishop while we finished off the last of the pizzas. She had everyone's attention except Court, who was still glowering about Bex, and Royal, who was working out logistics on his phone as he chewed his fourth slice of pizza.

Glancing around the table, I leaned back in my seat and twirled a lock of Maddie's hair in my fingers. Almost everyone I cared about was sitting in this room right this second. I'd kill for these people, die for each of them.

Okay, maybe not for Chase, because I was still pretty sure he was into my girl. Fucker hadn't stopped making moon eyes at her all night. Him I might sidestep a bullet for.

As if sensing my thoughts, Chase glanced at me. I took the opportunity to remind him that he could fantasize about Maddie all he wanted, but every night she was in *my* bed, screaming *my* name.

I hooked a foot on the leg of her chair and dragged it flush with mine, then wrapped an arm around her shoulders. Her conversation stuttered, and she looked at me with surprise that quickly turned into a warm smile as she leaned against my chest. I shot a smug look at Chase, amused to see him look at his plate like he'd just learned what pizza was.

Nails dug into my thigh, alerting me to the fact that Maddie wasn't oblivious to what I was doing, but she kept talking to our friends.

My phone buzzed in my back pocket, but I ignored it. I had special ringtones set up for my grandfather and sister, and short of a message from them, I wasn't letting go of the woman at my side.

But then Ash's phone went off, followed by Court's and then Linc's. All three glanced at their screens, and their gazes instantly snapped to me.

"What?" Maddie asked, catching the tension as the conversation around us died out.

Trepidation churned in my gut as I pulled out my phone and unlocked it to see a message from Gary. I bit back a snort, wondering what the fucker could want. Probably more threats about us stealing his money.

I opened the message and didn't understand the embedded link, but when I clicked on it, a news article popped up about the most recent victim of an overdose, citing a bad batch of heroin that had been sweeping across Los Angeles.

Another message from Gary popped up, and I hit it with my thumb before the notification could vanish.

A photo filled my screen. A woman, lying amongst a pile of garbage, a needle sticking out of her arm. Her face was slack-jawed and pale, at odds with the designer clothes. But there was something familiar—

With a gasp, Maddie ripped the phone from my hand. "No, no."

Panic squeezed my chest as she went pale and made a low, keening sound that shredded my insides. "Babe—"

"It's my mom," she whispered, clutching the phone to her chest and slamming her eyes shut. "Oh, my God. What have I done?"

Bex shoved her chair back from the table with a screech, coming around to Maddie's side and kneeling. "Maddie, it's okay."

"He *killed* her," Maddie choked out.

I looked at my friends, who all looked as shell-shocked as I felt.

Tyler looked a little sick. "I'm so sorry, Maddie. If I hadn't taken all the money…"

"This isn't your fault either," Chase told her, wrapping an arm around his cousin's shoulders. "Madison, if there's anything I can do—"

I swallowed my irritation, because it wasn't what my girl needed right now.

Abruptly, Maddie stood. "I need to be alone right now, okay?" She didn't wait for an answer as she fled the room.

I pushed back and got up, tossing my napkin on the table.

"She asked for space, mate," Chase said in a nearly benign tone, but I caught the undercurrent of smug annoyance. "Best let her be."

I laughed, the sound utterly devoid of humor. "The day I take advice from you about what *my* girl needs is the day I roll over in my grave."

Taking the stairs two at a time, I headed for our bedroom. Sure enough, Maddie was curled up on her side in the middle of the large bed. Without hesitation, I slid in beside her, wrapping her in my arms and snuggling her to my chest.

Her shoulders relaxed as soon as I touched her, tension draining from her body like I was the comfort she needed.

"Did I do this?" she whispered, tracing a vein on my forearm.

"No," I said as firmly as possible.

She rolled onto her back and looked at me, eyes glassy. "Ryan… God, I'm a terrible person."

"Bullshit." I shook my head. "Mads, you're the best person I know."

"Not because of what Gary did." She swallowed and blinked, the tears falling free. "I'm *relieved*."

I wiped away her tears with my thumb and let her continue at her own pace.

"My mom has been like an anvil around my neck for as long as I can remember," she admitted. "I've always cleaned up her messes, and when she took Gary's side… I don't know. I guess something in me broke, and I finally stopped seeing her as the woman who raised me. She was another person who was using me to better herself."

"She was," I agreed, stroking Maddie's hair away from her face. "Not seeing your worth… Baby, that's on her. And there's nothing wrong with how you feel."

"What daughter feels freaking relieved that her mother died?" she cried, eyes wide with disbelief.

"One who's been put through the fucking wringer because the one person who was supposed to give a shit cared more about her next fix than her daughter," I answered, fury for her vibrating in my words. "Angela Porter was your egg donor, baby. She wasn't a mother. Not in any way that ever counted. Feeling relieved she can't hurt you or betray you doesn't make you a monster—it makes you human."

Sniffling, Maddie handed me my phone back. "There was another message from Gary. He said for you to tell me that this was the price for my betrayal."

"Fuck Gary. He knows his days are numbered, and he's lashing out." I cupped her face, feeling the familiar ache of want echo in my bones as I caressed her soft skin. "He's out of options, and he knows it. He knows we've won."

"I hate him." Her lower lip wobbled. "I want him…"

"What?" I whispered, coaxing the truth out of her.

Her blue eyes flashed fire. "I want him dead. I want this over, Ryan."

I leaned in and kissed her slowly, loving the taste of vengeance and fury on her tongue as I teased it with my own. "I told you once that I'd give you the world. I'll give you whatever you want, Madison."

Understanding lit her eyes, and she wrapped her arms around my neck. "I love you, you know that, right?"

I hummed under my breath as I shifted to be on top of her. Her thighs naturally fell open to cradle my hips, fitting us together like we'd been created for each other. "Feel like reminding me?"

Things like fate and destiny had always seemed like a load of crap until I met this woman. Until I realized she was the other half that I'd been missing, the light to counter my darkness.

"I plan on reminding you for the rest of our lives," she swore, the sweet promise banding around my heart like an ironclad vow that I intended to remind her of until I was dead.

CHAPTER 41

MADDIE

I wasn't aware Ryan had left our bed until I felt him return to it hours later. Naked and sleepy, I rolled over and reached for him. "Where'd you go?" I yawned around my words.

With a warm chuckle, he pulled me to his chest, which was offensively covered by a shirt. He'd definitely been naked when he'd fucked me unconscious—I squinted at the clock across the room—four hours ago.

"Royal needed to see me," he murmured, his lips whispering against my hair as his hand drifted down my hip and squeezed my ass.

I propped myself up on his chest. "Should I be worried that Royal can get you to leave me when I'm naked in our bed?"

His smile was a thing of terrifying beauty. "Absolutely not." His adept fingers slid down the crack of my ass and stroked between my legs.

I considered clamping my legs shut, but honestly, who was I kidding? Wantonly, I spread them to give him more access.

He grunted in satisfaction as he easily slipped two fingers inside me while his thumb stroked my clit in a lazy way that was just enough to send shockwaves rippling across my body, but not enough to actually get me anywhere in a hurry.

"Ryan," I whined, trying to grind against his fingers.

The jerk chuckled, the warm sound rumbling between us as he took his time exploring me like it was his right. Which, okay, it totally was. A right I'd given him over and over and planned to for the rest of our lives.

"Please," I begged, needing more.

His lips found mine in a languid kiss that did nothing to ease the inferno between my thighs. His tongue stroked mine, sure and unhurried, as my nails scratched his chest. When I pulled my mouth away to suck on one of his flat nipples, he groaned and pushed his fingers deeper into me on reflex.

I smirked inwardly, pleased that I could make him crack. But my triumph was short lived when he rolled me onto my back and straddled my waist, then took both my wrists in one large hand and pinned them above my head.

"Cheater," he murmured, leaning down to nip my bottom lip as his cock pressed hard and heavy against my stomach.

I writhed under him, tugging uselessly to free myself. Finally, I fell back with a huff and a glare. "Let me go."

His head cocked. "Nah. Don't think I will. I think I want to take my time, and you're going to let me."

I snorted. "That's what you think, huh?" Brave words for a girl who was practically melting at the way his eyes were devouring me.

"Don't move," he whispered, his thumb sweeping along the inside of my wrist before he climbed off me and the bed.

I started to sit up. "Ry—"

He glared at me. "I said, don't move, Madison."

Okay, the growly way he ordered me around really shouldn't have been as hot as it was, but I found myself exhaling and lying down. I reached back up and looped my fingers around the slats of the headboard, holding on because I didn't trust myself not to accidentally reach between my legs and finish what he'd started.

Ryan was back seconds later, a pair of handcuffs dangling from a finger. He arched a questioning brow at me.

Oh, hell. Those things again?

Arousal shimmered in my stomach and leaked from my center. I shivered and nodded, licking my suddenly parched lips.

Ryan's responding grin made my heart flip. "That's my girl," he murmured, his voice a caress that slid over my heated skin like a satin sheet. He handcuffed me to the bed, and I realized these cuffs were lined with a soft, supple leather that didn't hurt my wrists at all. Even still, Ryan ran his pinkie along the edge to make sure it wasn't hurting me.

I tugged at the restraints, a thrill shooting straight down to my core as I realized how helpless this left me.

Ryan stood beside the bed and fisted his cock in his hand, giving it a hard stroke before his thumb swirled around the pearly drop of fluid at the tip. My mouth freaking watered, remembering the way he tasted on my tongue and wanting it.

A slow grin spread on his face. "Do you have any idea how gorgeous you are, baby? Looking like you're starving for my cock?"

I bit my lower lip, but it wasn't enough to hold back the needy whimper of want.

He kneeled over my chest and touched my jaw. "Open."

Like it was just another thing for him to command, my lips parted instantly. He pushed into my mouth slowly, and I forced myself to relax as he nudged the back of my throat.

"Fuck, your mouth is amazing," he uttered, bracing a hand above the headboard for leverage as he started to withdraw.

I hollowed my cheeks, sucking hard as he thrust in and out of my mouth. His taste, familiar and salty, exploded on my tastebuds, and I hummed as he fucked my mouth. His free hand traced my jaw as he stared down at my lips stretched around him.

"Gonna swallow every drop, right, baby?"

I hummed again in agreement, redoubling my efforts and smirking internally while he grunted and jerked on my tongue.

"Fuck, Maddie," he groaned. "So fucking good." His eyes closed, his head falling back in ecstasy as he pumped into my throat. The vein on the underside of his cock pulsed a second before he came in my mouth with a grunt.

I sucked him through his orgasm, swallowing every drop and even licking my lips when he finally pulled out, to make sure I didn't miss anything.

"You're amazing," he praised, his gaze soft and full of love as he leaned down and kissed me, tangling our tongues as our lips slotted together. A hand brushed across my breasts, tweaking one nipple and then the next until I arched off the bed with a breathy cry.

"I've got you," Ryan promised, his voice rough and full of sin as he moved to the foot of the bed. Moments later, he was crawling between my spread legs, his wide shoulders a tight fit as he pressed a kiss to each hip before nuzzling against my center. "God, I love the way you smell." He licked a stripe up my slit, and my back came off the bed. "The way you fucking taste." He groaned in approval, splaying a hand across my lower belly to hold me still as he feasted on my pussy.

His fingers sank into me and curled, rubbing against the front of my pussy. I clenched my teeth to swallow a scream as he massaged my G-spot.

"So tight," he murmured, approval in his gruff tone as he pumped a third finger into me. His lips fastened around my clit, lashing it with his tongue before sucking it into his mouth.

My body spasmed as I came with a low, almost wailing, cry. He kept rubbing that spot inside of me as his lips sucked at my clit. The sensations were too much and before my first orgasm had finished, I was rolling into a second that made my chest ache from the force of it. I forgot how to breathe as everything in me seized up, clenching and throbbing as I shattered.

I tugged uselessly at the headboard, needing to push him off before I blacked out from the pleasure. I couldn't close my legs or move away from sensations so perfect they bordered on painful.

"N-no more," I gasped, my head thrashing back and forth.

He lifted his head, his lips and chin shiny. "But we're just getting started, Maddie." He dragged a blunt finger through my slit, and I flinched when he rubbed against the side of my swollen clit. "Ready?"

I shook my head, mindless. "Can't."

He kissed the inside of my thigh almost reverently. "Yes, you can."

"Seriously might die," I muttered, squeezing my eyes shut.

He laughed, the sound warm and full of lust and love. "Not a chance. I plan on torturing this sweet body for years to come." He circled my entrance, and I moaned as my pussy tried to clench around him.

"See?" His lips kissed the top of my pussy like a reward for being a good girl. "I knew you had more in you. Besides, this part is when it really gets fun."

"F-fun?" I stammered, my eyes flying open in alarm to see him reaching over my leg for something he'd tossed onto the bed.

With a grin, he held up a silicon plug with a bulbous head. "This is bigger than the last plug, but not nearly as big as me." He winked. "But this'll help us work up to me taking this ass." As he spoke, his fingers brushed against my asshole.

With a sharp gasp, I tried to twist away, even as new sensations that weren't unpleasant at all rippled across my nerve endings. "Wh-where the hell did you even get that thing?"

He smirked at me. "I had Court pick it up when he went into town the other day."

I gaped at him. "Seriously?" I wouldn't be able to look Court in the eye ever again without blushing like crazy.

Ryan made an amused sound. "Trust me, asking him to buy a butt plug and handcuffs is like asking him to pick up birthday candles. He's a kinky fucker."

"I don't know what to even say to that," I admitted.

"How about you stop saying anything unless it's *yes, Ryan* or *harder, Ryan*."

I glared at him until his fingers probed my back hole again, and then my whole body shuddered. On instinct, I tried to twist away from the forbidden sensations.

His eyes narrowed. "Want me to tie down your legs, too?"

"No," I whispered, stilling beneath him.

The corner of his mouth hooked up in a smug grin. "Good girl."

Heat suffused my cheeks, and something in me ached for more of his praise. Pleasing him made me happy in a way I'd never be able to put into words. Maybe it was stupid, or fucked up, but I craved the way it felt when I did something to please him.

Ryan rubbed the plug between my legs, using my own arousal and release as lube before dragging the object back and pressing it against my ass.

"Relax," he said, his voice soft and cajoling. "You can take it."

Taking a deep breath, I relaxed and let him push the foreign object past the ring of muscle. The stretch burned through me, and my hands curled around the wooden slats of the headboard until I was sure my nails had gouged chunks out of it. I felt impossibly full and overwhelmed.

He twisted the plug, gently tapping on it and lighting up a whole new cascade of sensations that made my eyes roll back in my head as I gasped.

Satisfied the plug was secure, he crawled up my body and reached up to release my hands. Instantly, my arms came around his neck as his cock nudged my entrance.

"I love you," he murmured, his lips against mine, as he slid a hand down my side and under my thigh until my leg was hooked over his waist.

I kissed him, my fingers delving into his short hair. "Prove it."

He grinned against my mouth and slammed himself into me.

Of, fucking fuckity fuck.

He was already big, and with the plug, the fit was relentlessly tight, so much that I struggled to suck in a breath. I cried out, my neck arching as he withdrew and pushed back in, setting a frantic rhythm. All I could do was wrap my arms and legs around him and hold on as he pounded into me.

"Ryan," I gasped as my pussy rippled around his cock and my eyes squeezed shut.

"You're so fucking perfect, Maddie," he praised, his face pressed against the side of my throat. "Hang on, baby. You're gonna love this."

A second later the plug in my ass started to vibrate.

My cry bordered on a shriek as I clawed at Ryan's back. *Oh, God.* It was too much. Way too much. I couldn't figure out where the pleasure started and ended.

I came hard, clenching around him as wave after wave of ecstasy rolled through me, until I was twitching in his arms as he kept thrusting, kept moving. Raking my nails down his spine, I felt Ryan shudder. He was close, so fucking close.

With the last bit of energy I had, I clamped my pussy hard around him. He came with a strangled cry, his hips jerking against me as his release painted my insides. He stopped the plug's vibrations a moment later and collapsed on my chest, his breath coming in pants.

Stroking his sweaty hair as he softened inside of me, I let myself ask the question I hadn't wanted to when he'd slipped back into our bed. "What happened?"

He sighed, kissing the side of my breast. "Royal thinks our best bet is to hit Gary at his Henderson house while he's still there. Eventually he'll find a way to liquidate some assets and could disappear."

"When do you leave?" Worry carved a hollow pit in my stomach.

He hesitated and turned to look at me, his chin on my sternum. "Later today."

I nodded, absorbing that. "You'll be safe?"

"As safe as we can be," he promised, and lifted off me so our faces were closer together. He pushed my hair back from my forehead. "Do you think anything in the world could stop me from coming back to you?"

"No," I admitted, even as fear twisted my heart into knots.

His eyes softened. "I'm coming home, Maddie."

I sniffled a little. "You know, at some point, we really need to figure out where *home* is. We can't stay here indefinitely."

"I agree," he replied, a crease forming between his brows. "But, Mads, I already told you that where we live is just a house. *You're* my home." He settled his hand over my heart. "This is the place I'll always come back to."

CHAPTER 42

MADDIE

Morning was cold and gray, with swollen clouds threatening to dump another several inches of snow across the region. I was starting to miss the California sunshine.

I stood in the cold garage, wrapped in one of Ryan's PCU Knights hoodies, as the guys finished loading the SUVs that would take them to Henderson. The plan was for them to arrive in the middle of the night for a hard, fast strike that Gary wouldn't see coming.

I'd insisted on not knowing more details than that. All I needed to know was when it was done, and that all of my guys were safe.

"It'll be fine," Ash assured me, pausing in front of me with a duffel slung over one shoulder and a laptop tucked under his arm.

My gaze cut to where Ryan and Royal were huddled under the open hatch of the trunk, discussing something. "I can't lose him, Ash."

He dropped his bag and ducked to meet my eyes. "You won't, Mads. I promise. I've got his back."

Forcing a smile, I nodded. "I know."

As if he sensed my distress from across the room, Ryan's bright blue eyes found mine. The corner of his mouth hooked up, flashing a dimple as he looked at me in a way that settled some of my jangling nerves.

Hands came down on my shoulders from behind. "Geez, Mads, we're going to kill your fuckface of a dad, not going off to war. Stop looking so sad," Linc teased before he kissed the side of my head, then stepped around me and tossed his bag in the trunk of the SUV. He climbed into the back seat next to Knight.

Bishop opened the driver's door of the other SUV and stood on the step rail. "Time to go, assholes. Load up." He winked at me before ducking back inside the cab.

Ryan came up in front of me, his hands framing my face. "We've got this, Maddie. Don't worry."

Snorting, I arched a brow. "You're kidding, right? The only thing I can do is worry."

He kissed my forehead, then the tip of my nose, and finally my mouth. My toes curled as I wrapped my arms around his neck, our kiss going from sweet to an inferno in seconds. I would never get enough of this man. He was my forever.

"I love you," I whispered, my forehead touching his.

"Don't do that," he murmured. "Don't say it like you're saying goodbye."

I nodded. "Okay." Squaring my shoulders, I lifted my chin and met his gaze. "I love you, and I'll see you when you get home."

He grinned, making my tummy flip. "Damn, I love you." He kissed me again, hard and fast. "I'll call you when I can, okay?"

"Be safe," I said as he stepped away. My gaze swept over the two SUVs, and I raised my voice. "All of you be safe."

"Yes, ma'am," Knight teased from the back seat as he smiled at me.

With one last look, Ryan got into the front passenger seat of the SUV that Court was driving. Court had been silent most of the morning, and Bex hadn't come out to say goodbye.

I watched the cars back out of the garage and waited until they disappeared around a bend in the snow-covered drive before closing the garage doors and trudging back inside with a sigh. It would take them nearly twelve hours to drive to Henderson, a few hours to handle Gary and whatever men he was using for security, and then another twelve hours back.

It was going to be a long couple of days.

I kicked off my shoes in the mudroom and decided to make breakfast for the rest of us instead of crawling back into bed and cuddling Ryan's pillow to inhale his scent.

Staying busy would be better.

Chase ambled into the kitchen about twenty minutes later, looking sleepy in a t-shirt and pair of flannel pajama bottoms. He blinked in surprise at seeing me juggling a skillet full of cheesy scrambled eggs and the waffle iron. "You cook."

"I do," I confirmed. "Hungry?"

"Yes, thank you. Can I help?" He hesitated, looking nervous that I might take him up on the offer.

I snorted a laugh. "*Can* you help?"

"I can keep you company," he countered.

"Deal." I pointed at a seat across from me at the island. "Pull up a chair."

"Have you thought about what comes next?" he asked, already going for the heavy questions before I'd finished my first cup of coffee.

"Meaning?" I didn't turn around as I worked on the eggs.

He cleared his throat. "Well, once Gary is taken care of, you're free. Granted, you had Tyler donate all that money, but you're still the sole heir to a lot of lucrative companies. You could do whatever you want. Go wherever you like."

I slowly set down the spatula and turned to face him. "Who says I'm not exactly where I want to be?"

Chase frowned. "I just meant—"

"I know what you meant." I held his gaze. "Chase, I appreciate you wanting to look out for me and be my friend, but if you *are* my friend, you have to accept that Ryan is a big part of my life. I love him. I'm not walking away from him now, and especially not when we finally have a chance to have our happily ever after. Get on board, or get out of the way."

He opened his mouth to say something, but then wisely closed it.

I flashed him a smile as he conceded my point. Or, at least, accepted it. Ryan wasn't going anywhere. And if he did? I was the barnacle attached to his ass for the rest of his life. Gary annulling our marriage didn't change the fact that he was mine in every single way.

Once I'd plated the eggs, I turned off the stove and checked the last of the waffles. "I'll get Bex and Tyler so we can eat." I'd turned on my heel to do so when Bex literally slid into the kitchen with wide eyes.

"Where is C—where is everyone?" she demanded, her gaze pinging around the room like they were hiding in the cabinets.

"They left," I said slowly, looking at her disheveled hair and pale face. "What's wrong?"

She clutched her cell phone to her chest. "It's my mom. She... She was in a really bad car accident. I need to get back to Los Angeles."

"Oh, God." I quickly wrapped my arms around her, hugging her hard.

Chase stood up. "They took both cars."

"What? *No*," Bex cried, pulling away from me. "I need to get to her. My dad called and said I... Dammit." Tears spilled over, and she swiped furiously at her eyes.

"Let me make a few calls," Chase offered, his tone soothing. "I can have a car here to get you within the hour, and you're welcome to my plane."

Bex's shoulders sagged. "Really?"

Chase nodded. "Of course." He patted her back as he walked out of the room, pulling out his phone.

"Okay," I started, not sure what to say or do. "What do you need, babe?"

She pressed her lips into a flat line. "I just... I need to get home, Maddie."

"All right." I sucked in a breath. "Let's go pack our stuff."

"Our?" Hope shone in her eyes.

"Of course. I'm coming with you," I said. Did she think I'd let her deal with this alone?

"What about Gary?"

I sighed. "The guys are on their way to... You know. Beckett's left the damn country. The only real problem still is the restraining order, and it's not like Ryan will be with me."

"You're sure?" she pressed.

I touched her face. "I'm sure. You're my best friend, Bex."

She leaned in and gave me a tight hug. "Thanks, Maddie."

I hugged her back, shoving down the guilty feeling welling in my gut. I'd call Ryan from the plane and tell him about our change in plans. I mean, he couldn't tell me not to go if I was already in the air, right?

Right.

As Bex and I headed upstairs to pack, I could already imagine how pissed he was going to be, but he'd have to suck it up. Ryan owned my heart, but Bex was the sister of my soul, and she needed me. He would have to understand.

CHAPTER 43

RYAN

"Don't be mad."

Was there ever a conversation in the history of the world that started with that sentence that didn't end in someone being pissed the fuck off?

"What's wrong?" I demanded, my hand gripping the phone at my ear hard enough for the casing to crack.

Court's head whipped around, and he stared at me from the driver's side as Knight and Linc leaned forward from the back.

"Bex's mom was in a really bad accident. She's in the hospital, and it doesn't look good," Maddie told me.

"Shit," I swore. "Is Bex okay?"

Now I had Court's full attention, and I mouthed what had happened to him. He looked torn, ready to turn the car around.

"Yeah. She just needs to see her mom."

I nodded. "Okay. Tell her as soon as we're back, we'll get her home."

The silence that followed sent my bullshit meter through the roof.

"Madison?" I growled her name, already knowing whatever she said next would be bad. When Maddie got quiet, it usually meant I had fucked up, or she had. Either way? It wasn't good.

She cleared her throat, the sound almost delicate. "So, Chase offered to fly her back to Los Angeles."

"Tell Bex not to get on that damn plane," I ordered, annoyed they'd even consider stepping foot back in California without us until Gary was handled. "She can't go back there alone right now."

"I mean, I agree." She huffed a nervous laugh.

My eyes closed, and I focused on not losing my shit as what she *wasn't* saying registered. *God dammit.* "Tell me you're not going back with her."

"I would, but we made that promise not to lie to each other," she said, and I could imagine the way she was nervously biting her lower lip, waiting for me to explode.

The last thing I'd ever want to do is not live up to her expectations.

"Madison!" I barked her name loud enough that Court swerved the car. Someone honked from the lane next to us. "Don't even fucking think about it."

Another soft sigh. "Ry, I'm calling you from the plane. We already took off. But Chase and Tyler are with us," she added quickly. "Chase said his dad is going to have some hired security guys meet us at the airport."

Why wasn't I surprised that Chase was the fucking hero, riding in to save them both?

I pinched the bridge of my nose, panic and fear spiraling me into a stratosphere of anxiety I didn't know existed. The only reason I'd felt confident going after Gary was because I'd known Maddie was safe and sound in Wyoming. "Are you sitting down?"

She hesitated, and I could practically see the confusion that would be lining her pretty face. "Yes?"

"Enjoy it," I ground out. "I swear to fuck, when I see you, you won't sit for another goddamn month without feeling the imprint of my hand on your ass."

She made a cute little squeaking sound that in any other situation would've made my dick harder than steel. Turned out her tiny noises stopped being sexy when her life was in danger.

"Ryan, come on. She's my best friend," Maddie tried. "And you're going after Gary right now, so there's no real threat to me."

"You're kidding, right? Dammit, Maddie, you're not safe until Gary's six feet under and being spit-roasted in hell where he belongs," I argued. I looked back at Knight. "Call Royal. We're going to L.A."

"What? No," Maddie argued, her voice jumping an octave. "Ryan, you have a plan—stick to it. We'll be okay. Chase—"

"If you mention that asshole to me one more time, I'll kill him on principle," I threatened. Maybe I was being irrational, but the idea of Maddie being hours away, walking into a situation I hadn't fully vetted, scared the piss out of me. Sure, we knew where Gary was, but it wasn't like Gary was the only enemy we had.

I caught Court's gaze and knew he was worried about the same thing. Jasper Woods had been quiet—too quiet—lately. He'd gone off the grid, along with Ash's and Linc's fathers, when Beckett and Gary had gone down. It wasn't out of the realm of possibility that they could come after Maddie or Bex to get at us.

Maddie went quiet for a beat, my first warning a storm was brewing. "He's helping me, Ryan."

"I'll just bet he is," I drawled, the insinuation heavy in my words. "He's probably loving every second of this."

Knight tapped my shoulder with a grim look. "Royal says if we cancel now, we'll lose our window. Ash has been monitoring his accounts. Gary managed to get enough cash to get him out of the country tomorrow night. He's already booked a private plane. It's now or never, Ry."

"Fuck," I hissed, slamming my head back against the seat rest.

"Ryan," Maddie started.

"Not right now," I snapped, shushing her as I turned to Knight. "What if we split up?"

Knight and Linc exchanged uneasy looks. Yeah, I'd known it was a shit idea as soon as I'd said it. Ash's intel placed ten guys guarding Gary, and odds were they'd been loaned to him by Jasper Woods. That meant ex-military machines, trained to kill first and ask questions never. Cutting our manpower in half was risky, especially if we wanted to get in and out without this turning into a media circus.

Gary Cabot's place in Henderson was smack dab in the middle of one of the state's wealthiest suburbs, a gated community with guards in addition to his personal detail. We'd have to be stealthy and quiet, and that meant no drawn-out fights.

"I'm sorry." Maddie's soft voice filled my ear, and I wanted to tie her ass up and lock her in a cage for the rest of her life to make sure she never pulled a stunt like this again. "Ryan, it's her *mom*. I couldn't let her go alone. Bex is a mess, and she needs me."

I stabbed my fingers into my hair. "Mads, what if Gary set this up to draw you out? I mean, a car accident? Seems pretty convenient."

She was quiet for a moment. "That still wouldn't change the fact that Bex needs to go see her mom. And I can't just let her go by herself, Ryan."

"Fuck," I barked, slamming a fist against the door as helplessness surged in my chest. I didn't know what to do.

"Ry, we'll stay in public at all times. Gary can't kidnap me in the middle of a hospital," Maddie reasoned. "Chase has security guys waiting for us as soon as we get off the plane, and I promise I'll stay with them."

Court looked at me, seeming grimly resigned. "It's your call, bro." He looked away, knowing that he didn't have a right to get pissed at Bex or demand she do what he wanted.

"Let me talk to Chase," I said with an aggrieved sigh.

"Why?" Suspicion clouded her tone.

I gritted my teeth. "Because I want to make sure he understands all the ways I'm going to kill him if anything happens to either of you."

"Um, okay." There was a soft rustling as she passed the phone to the Duke of Douches.

Chase immediately started in. "Look, I know you're pissed, mate, but—"

"Shut the fuck up and listen to me." My tone was sharp enough to split a diamond. "If anything happens to Madison or Bex, I'm holding you personally responsible."

"I know." His tone seemed serious, but he didn't know the sheer hell I would rain down on his ass if he made a mistake when it came to her.

"I don't think you do, so let me break it down for you, asshat. If you fuck this up, I'll spend years taking you apart piece by piece and make sure you're conscious the entire time." I was already imagining the dark, dank warehouse where I'd spend countless hours torturing and killing him if something happened to Maddie.

Chase bristled. "I'm not an idiot."

"That's yet to be determined," I muttered, running a hand through my hair and yanking on the strands. "Let me talk to my girl."

He snorted. "You realize she's not livestock that you own, right? She's her own person, capable of making her own decisions."

A cold smile twisted my lips. "Every single perfect inch of her belongs to me, and if you haven't realized that by now, you're a bigger dumbass than I thought."

With a hiss, he gave the phone back to Maddie.

"I really don't want you to be mad," she said, her tone the kind you'd use when soothing a rabid animal poised to attack.

"Too late," I replied, shoving down my rage because I really didn't want things to be strained between us when I was so far away and unable to reassure myself she was all right in person. "Just… stay with Bex and Chase. Don't go *anywhere* by yourself, okay?"

"Okay," she agreed. "I'll see you soon. I love you."

The small tremor in the way she said that cracked a fissure wide open in my heart. She said it in an utterly vulnerable way, like she thought I'd be too mad at her to say it back.

That would never, ever be the case.

"I love you, too, baby," I responded, my tone gentle in a way that made Linc pretend to crack a whip over my head as Knight laughed. "*Please* be safe."

"You, too," she breathed before hanging up.

I hurled my phone at the dash with a grunt. "Fuck!"

Linc touched my shoulder from behind. "She's a smart girl, and she isn't alone."

I wiped a hand over my mouth, surprised to feel my fingers shaking. "If anything happens to her…"

"You can't think like that," Knight warned me. "Get your head in the game, Cain."

I didn't say anything as I turned to stare out the windshield and watch the mountains go by. He didn't get it. How could he?

Maddie *was* the game. She was my endgame, and nothing we did mattered if she wasn't waiting for me when it was all over.

CHAPTER 44

MADDIE

The smell of a hospital was one of my least favorite scents in the world. Like antiseptic, desperation, and sorrow. At least, that was the vibe I got when we walked past the ICU to a private waiting room while Bex was taken to her mom.

We'd gotten off the plane and been met by Chase's security, who'd driven us to Los Angeles General. One of them stayed with us at the hospital while the other drove Tyler to Chase's house.

"So, you have a house? I thought you stayed on campus." I frowned, looking at Chase as he scrolled through his phone.

He glanced up, a small pout pulling at his mouth. "No offense, Maddie, but I'm not exactly accustomed to sharing a building with a bunch of randy, sex-crazed men." He shuddered. "I like my peace and quiet."

I rolled my eyes. "Apologies, your grace."

He smirked. "That's my father's title."

"And what's yours?" I crossed my legs, glancing at the door.

"Technically the Marquess of Perring," he replied, his tone formal and stiff. "The proper term would be, *my lord*."

I couldn't help but giggle. "Wow. That's so crazy. You're practically royalty."

He shrugged, but a small blush stole across his freckled cheeks. "It's a title, nothing more. The nobility doesn't mean what it used to five hundred years ago."

"It's kinda cool," I teased. "You're a—what? A lord?"

He nodded.

"Lord Winthrope," I said, pitching my voice with a false British accent.

Amused, he shook his head with silent laughter. "It's Lord Perring, but Chase is fine, if you please."

I huffed with fake annoyance. "It does *not*, in fact, please me, your lordship."

"Bloody hell," he groaned, but smiled.

My laughter dimmed as I looked at the door again. "I wonder how Bex is." It had been over an hour since she'd gone back to be with her mom.

"The doctors said that they think Mrs. Whittier will make a full recovery," Chase said gently.

I turned and smiled a little. "I know. I just worry about Bex."

"I worry about you both," Chase replied, his brow furrowed. "Honestly, Madison, I was hoping you'd get a little perspective here and see that this isn't normal."

"*This?*" I echoed, disdain dripping from the word.

"Needing permission to go somewhere? Armed guards watching your every move?" He shook his head. "It's not healthy."

"Maybe not," I agreed. "But it's what I've chosen, and I'm not going back."

After a heavy sigh, he held up his hands. "All right. Whatever you wish."

The door to the waiting room cracked open and Bex stepped inside, her eyes swollen and red from crying. My heart sank as I stood up, expecting the worst.

"She's gonna be okay," Bex told me, her voice cracking. "She broke a couple ribs and her ankle, and she has a pretty bad concussion, but they think she'll make a full recovery."

"Thank God," I whispered, my shoulders sagging as I hugged her. "Did they say how it happened?"

"Drunk driver," she replied. "He drove through a red light and slammed right into her. He didn't have a freaking scratch on him. He's in jail."

"Okay." I took a deep breath and forced a smile. "That's good news."

Bex sniffled against me. "Yeah. Right now she needs her rest, but the doctors said I could come back in the morning."

Malcolm Whittier appeared in the doorway, looking stressed in a rumpled gray suit and a wrinkled shirt with several buttons undone. His dark hair, the color of Bex's, stuck up in various places where he'd likely been running his hands through it.

"Dad got us a hotel nearby," Bex added, pulling away. "Maybe you should head back to PC? I mean, you don't have to stay—"

"I'm staying." I took her hands in mine. "No way would I leave you alone right now."

She smiled, gratitude shining in her eyes. She glanced at her dad. "Maddie can stay with us, right?"

He cleared his throat and nodded. "Of course, sweetheart."

"I'll get my own room," Chase added, his eyes meeting mine. "My... friends and I will stay nearby in case either of you need anything." He looked at Malcolm and strode forward, hand outstretched. "Forgive me, I don't believe we've met. Charles Winthrope, but my friends call me Chase."

"Malcolm Whittier." He shook Chase's hand and then backed away. "Ready to go, sweet pea?"

Bex nodded and laced her fingers with mine. She leaned against my shoulder as we walked out of the waiting room.

RYAN: We're an hour out. Going radio silent. I love you.

My heart squeezed as I stared at the message. I was sitting

cross-legged on Bex's bed wearing one of Ryan's old shirts while Bex finished in the bathroom.

MADDIE: I love you. Be safe.

There was no reply, and I set aside my phone with a heavy heart only to hear it chirp with another incoming message. Hope surged in my chest as I scrambled to look.

COURT: Is she ok?

A sad smile touched the corners of my mouth as I tapped out a reply.

MADDIE: She's doing all right. I'll take care of her.

Text bubbles appeared and then disappeared before he finally answered.

COURT: Thanks

"Ryan?" Bex guessed as she towel-dried her hair in the doorway.

"And Court," I admitted.

There was no missing the mix of emotions playing on her face. "What did he want?"

"To make sure you're okay," I replied. "He's worried, B."

"Whatever," she muttered, tossing the towel across a chair near the desk and coming over to sit by me on the king-size bed we'd be sharing. Malcolm had reserved a two-bedroom suite at an upscale hotel near the hospital, and Chase and Tyler, along with the security guards, were a few doors down from us on the same floor.

"I really think you should hear him out," I told her as gently as possible.

She looked away, her features pulled tight. "No. He's had years to come clean, Maddie. I'm done spending time with a guy who obviously doesn't give a shit about me."

"Okay, we *both* know that's a lie." I shot her a knowing look. "If you knew the whole truth—"

"I don't want to talk about it." She got off the bed and stalked to the dresser for her brush before ripping it through her dark strands. "Once your dad is out of the picture, I'm done with them."

Hurt panged against my heart. "You realize I'm part of *them*, right?"

She sighed. "Maddie, you're my best friend, and that won't change.

I just mean, I'm done holding out for something that can never happen. I wasn't lying—Court might've been my first kiss when we were kids, but only because Linc was an asshole and dared him to kiss me."

I smothered a smile. Somehow I doubted a dare from Linc was what made Court kiss Bex, but sure. She could delude herself all she wanted.

"But Court Woods wasn't the first or second guy I slept with. Maybe it's time I start dating again. Or at least hook up with someone before my vagina dries up for good," she muttered.

I snorted. "I think you're a few decades away from that, babe."

"I mean it," she insisted with a smile. "When we get back to PC, I'm going to be Bex two-point-oh. I'm going to date and flirt and have fun. *Horizontal* fun."

I made a face as I shrugged. "I don't recommend limiting yourself to just horizontal." A wicked grin spread across my face as she laughed and hurled a pillow at me.

I caught the pillow and hugged it to my chest. "Just make sure that whatever you do, you do it for you, and not to prove something to him."

Sighing, she tossed the brush aside and sat down. "I don't want to think about him."

I nodded in sympathy, because I got it. When I'd come back to PC after Ryan screwed me over, I'd wanted to lash out and hurt him, but ultimately, I would've hurt myself more. "It's okay to take your time, is all I'm saying. Do things you want for *you*. Not for the guy who can't get out of his own way to see how freaking amazing you are."

"Emotions suck," Bex declared with a huff, her lips pulling down as someone knocked at the door. "You can come in."

Malcolm stuck his head in, his expression somber. "Becky."

She was instantly on her feet. "What?"

He cleared his throat, tugging on the collar of the shirt he'd changed into. "The hospital just called. Your mother developed a clot, and they're taking her back into surgery. I was going to head back—"

"I'm coming, too," she declared, already throwing on a hoodie over her pajamas and shoving her feet into shoes.

"Sweet pea, there won't be much you can do," he murmured, shaking his head.

"She's my mother," Bex snapped, close to tears. "I'm going."

"Want me to come too?" I offered.

She looked at me and shook her head. "No. I'll call when there's news, okay?"

I nodded and watched her go, my heart heavy for my friend. A moment later, the front door to the suite closed, and I was alone in the silence.

CHAPTER 45

RYAN

Movement caught my eye as Royal signaled us to move forward.

It had taken a little more work to get inside the community than we'd anticipated, especially when someone had decided that the perfect place to let their fluffy poodles take a midnight shit was right in front of the bushes we'd been hiding in.

We'd left the SUVs and gone on foot through the streets, keeping to the shadows and staying as hidden as possible. Ash handled everything, checking for blind spots and hacking the pathetic excuses for security systems the houses around here had. They might've been top of the line for the public, but they were no match for my best friend's hacking skills. Once he put the digital footage on a continuous loop feed, we could've walked down the middle of the road, and all the security tapes would've shown the next day was an empty street.

Working in the dark, we moved as a unit. The unit Jasper Woods had always wanted his sons to be; efficient, tactical, and lethal. Surrounding the two-story brick house at the end of a nondescript cul-de-sac, we took up positions and got ready to hit hard and fast.

Adrenaline churned in my blood, heightening my senses as I prepared to end my former father-in-law once and for all. The only regret I had was that it would be quick. I wouldn't have time to carve him into pieces the way I craved, the way vengeance demanded.

Three guards wandered around the backyard, looking bored but alert as they scanned the eight-foot-tall hedges we'd hidden behind. They weren't idiots; they'd been trained by one of the most ruthless killers the United States military had ever created. The only people I'd met more dangerous than Jasper Woods and the men he commanded were his own sons.

Most of whom were standing with me tonight, about to help me take down the monster who had nearly killed the woman I loved.

Thunder rumbled overhead, ominous and providing the perfect cover for our plan.

"Thirty seconds," Ash warned, his voice crackling across the com in my ear.

I drew in a deep, slow breath, waiting for the moment we'd all agreed upon. Part of the reason Royal had insisted we strike tonight was the storm that was rolling in. It would muffle some of the sounds of whatever fight happened and give us the perfect excuse for—

A bolt of lightning split the dark sky a second before the world plunged into darkness as Ash cut the power to the entire community.

The three guards were immediately alert, reaching for their radios, but it was pointless; part of Ash's blackout included a jammer that rendered their technology useless.

"Go," Royal whispered, his voice a sharp command as we surged forward from the shadows as a unit.

Court, Linc, and Bishop were on the other side of the house from Royal, Knight, and myself.

Our dark clothes concealed us as we stepped through the hedges and moved fast. Heavy clouds that blotted out the moon and stars split open, and rain began to fall in sheets around us.

Satisfaction surged in my gut as the rain provided even more cover. I reached the man closest to us. His back was turned. My hands went to his jaw and the back of his head, twisting with a sharp *crack* that was swallowed up by the rumble of thunder.

Another guard cried out, the shout of surprise dying fast as Knight snapped his neck, too. Royal had already handled his guy and was staring at us like we were taking too long. "Three down," he reported to us all.

I flipped him off as we went to the back door and Knight quickly picked the lock.

We stepped into the dark kitchen. A bolt of lightning illuminated the room for a split second, but we didn't pause as we moved for the back stairs connected to the room. Royal went first, then me, and Knight went last, walking backward up the steps to ensure no one snuck up on our six.

"Two down." Court's voice broke the silence, and I pictured my friends entering the front of the house as we'd planned.

That left five scattered somewhere inside.

"I've got two heat signatures in the front hall," Ash informed us.

I finished going up the stairs as Linc's voice said, "Not anymore. Two more down."

Three guards left.

The door closest to us opened and Royal spun, his gun firing at the same time as another shot rang out. Drywall and plaster exploded in a cloud behind Royal as he ducked the shot that should've gone through his skull. The crack of the shot echoed in my ears.

"One down," Royal muttered, looking pissed that the guy he'd shot had had the audacity to fire at him first.

"They know we're here," Knight muttered at my back.

"Three left," Ash told us. "Looks like they're in the master bedroom."

I bit back a snort. Of course Gary was hiding in his room with a couple guards.

He could have an entire Navy SEAL team in there, and it wouldn't change the way tonight was going to end. He was going to die.

Adrenaline flooded my veins as I anticipated the moment I finally looked him in the eye and watched the defeat register. He'd lost.

From the other side of the hall, Court, Linc, and Bishop materialized from the darkness, and we all paused by the set of double doors that led into the master bedroom.

"You've got less than five minutes," Ash warned. "Finish this up and get the fuck out."

Royal stepped forward, ever the leader, and nodded at Bishop. He kicked in the door and spun out of the way as bullets immediately fired into the hallway. Bishop and Court returned fire, and I heard a grunt from inside the room as someone went down.

"Keep your panties on, Ash," Linc told him with a dark chuckle. He stepped around Court and fired into the room, taking out another guard.

A shot rang out, and Linc was flung back into the wall with a grunt. My pulse spiked as he slid to the ground, a hand clutching his chest.

Royal and I moved in, firing our guns until the clips were damn near empty and the third man, hiding behind the bed of all fucking places, fell. The acrid scents of smoke and gunpowder filled my nostrils as I looked around the room for anyone else.

"Linc?" I snapped his name, not turning as Royal and Knight checked the en suite bathroom and closets, clearing them.

"Bullet hit the vest," Court reported. "Knocked the wind outta him, but he'll be fine."

Royal stepped out of the bathroom, his expression tight.

I glanced around the room. "Where the fuck is Cabot?"

"Not in here," Knight declared, stepping out of the second closet. He bent and actually looked under the bed.

"What the fuck?" I whispered. "Ash?"

"I had only three heat signatures in the bedroom," he confirmed.

I was looking at three very dead guards, none of whom was Gary Cabot.

"Neighbors have reported the shots," Ash informed us. "You guys need to move."

"Is he somewhere else in the house?" I demanded.

Ash was only silent for a moment. "Every heat signature I pinged, you guys took care of. There were eleven total."

We'd assumed the eleven meant the ten guards and Gary.

But it was eleven guards and *no* Gary.

"He was never here," I murmured. "How the fuck did we miss this?" What hadn't we seen? Was there a tunnel or something that led out of here? We'd seen him on surveillance videos here hours earlier.

Royal's lips pressed into a sharp line. "He knew we were coming."

"How?" Knight wondered. "And where the fuck did he go?"

"Something isn't right," I murmured as Linc groaned behind me.

Ash cut into our confusion. "Seriously, guys, get the fuck out *now*. Police are less than three minutes away."

Bishop clapped a hand on my shoulder. "We gotta go, Ry."

"Everyone clear out," Royal agreed, his voice a rumbling order. Court helped Linc to his feet. They headed for the back stairs, and I turned back around to look inside the room once more.

My gaze skipped over the three dead bodies, and confusion mingled with worry as I realized I had no idea where Gary was.

And Madison was in California, unprotected.

Part of me wanted to believe that Gary had made a run for it. That he was holed up in some foreign country, laughing about getting away from us. But Gary wasn't my father. He wouldn't be satisfied with simply getting away.

No, if he was going down, he'd take everything and everyone with him. He'd burn down the world he'd helped create before he ever surrendered it.

Which meant I needed to get to Maddie as fast as possible.

CHAPTER 46

MADDIE

I lasted fifteen minutes on my own before texting Chase and Tyler to see if they'd keep me company. I was worried about Bex. I was terrified for the guys.

In short, I needed a distraction.

But I never imagined it would come in the form of Tyler telling me stories about Chase growing up in England and all the trouble he'd gotten into.

Sometimes Chase smiled, but a lot of the time, he blushed and looked ready to kill her.

In short, it was hysterical.

"His father was *livid*," Tyler finished, wrapping up a story about how, on a bet, fourteen-year-old Chase had raced his father's most valuable car and totaled it.

"In my defense," Chase said, also laughing, "I wasn't aware that they'd only made thirty-nine of that particular model of Ferrari."

I leaned back on the couch. I sat at one end and Tyler was at the other, dressed in fuzzy pajamas with rubber duckies on them, while Chase sat in a chair across from us. He looked almost normal in a pair of black sweats and an old band t-shirt.

"Have you two always been close?" I asked, my gaze pinging between them.

Tyler shook her head. "Not until I came to live with them a few years ago."

Chase shot her a fond look. "She became the little sister I never wanted."

Tyler rolled her eyes. "I think he used to be terrified of me when we'd come visit the *family estate*." She wrinkled her nose. "My father hated it there."

"Why?" I asked, curious.

"He was the black sheep of the family," Tyler explained. "And when he married my mom—an *American*—he never moved back to England."

"So, Americans are beneath the Brits?" I teased.

Chase rolled his eyes. "It was a different era, and there were different expectations."

Tyler snorted. "For you, maybe, but Nana and Papa always loved you and your dad the most. And they definitely liked your mom more than mine."

Chase made a face but didn't disagree.

"Because your mom was American?" I frowned, not sure I got it.

"Worse." Tyler's eyes sparkled. "She was a single mom, who'd had to—please hold your gasps of shock and horror—*work for a living*. God forbid a woman have any sort of less-than-stellar pedigree. I mean, she was a labor and delivery nurse, for crying out loud. It's not like she was pulling tricks at a truck stop. Not that there's anything wrong with someone willingly entering the sex trade if that's their choice," she quickly added.

"Right," I said slowly, trying to keep up.

At my confused expression, she went on, "My dad legally adopted me when I was two. I never knew my bio-dad. My mom said he was a deadbeat and a criminal, and we were much better off without him. Besides, my dad was my dad in every way that mattered."

"Gotcha." I definitely understood that blood and biology didn't make a family.

"Anyway, we'd still go to England sometimes when my grandmother guilted my dad into it, but when it became pretty damn clear that Grandmother was still pushing for my dad to leave his family in America where they belonged and come back to the motherland to find a proper wife, we stopped going."

"She was wrong," Chase muttered. His gaze flicked to me. "Still is."

Tyler shrugged. "I avoid them whenever I can. Grandmother's a bitch."

"She is," Chase agreed, but he smiled at Tyler. "But you know that Father and I love having you live with us."

"I know." Tyler looked young and vulnerable as she grinned back with a touch of sadness. "I just miss my mom and dad."

My lips tightened, and Tyler gasped. "Shit, Maddie. I'm sorry. I forgot about your mom and—"

I waved her off and cleared my throat. "Honestly? My mom was dead to me long before she stopped breathing. Maybe now she can find some peace."

Tyler studied her hands. "I was always really close to my parents," she admitted. "They were amazing, and losing them…" She blew out a long breath, looking rattled. "I mean, it's been three years, but I still remember what my dad's hugs felt like, and the way my mom smelled."

"I'm sorry you lost them." A part of me ached to know what having two parents love you above and beyond all else would feel like. Hating the macabre turn of topic, I glanced at my phone atop the glass coffee table. "I wonder how Bex is."

"I could hack the hospital system and see how her mom's doing," Tyler suggested, brightening.

Chase rubbed his forehead. "Or we could attempt a less-invasive approach and wait for her to call."

Tyler frowned. "That's a horrible plan."

"No, hacking a hospital's database is a horrible plan. And a criminal one," he pointed out.

"You didn't care what I hacked to help you find Maddie when she was missing," Tyler countered with a smug smirk.

Was it my imagination, or did Chase's cheeks turn kinda pink?

"Her life was at stake," Chase argued.

"But seriously, I owe you guys big time," I said, cutting them off before they could start to bicker. They argued like they'd been siblings all their lives. "You *both* saved my ass."

Chase smiled at me while Tyler shrugged and ducked her head, seeming embarrassed at the praise.

"I can assure you," Chase told me, "that it was truly our pleasure."

Tyler rolled her eyes and made a gagging sound. "She's still... What are you? Married? Engaged?"

I sighed and shook my head. "I have no idea anymore."

Tyler perked up. "Want me to hack the L.A. courts and have your annulment papers disappear?"

I gaped at her. "You can do that?"

"I can try," she said, frowning as she considered the challenge.

Chase sighed, exasperated. "Please, Tillie. No hacking unless it's vital to our survival."

She glared at him. "Don't call me that."

"What?" He shot her an innocent look. *"Tillie?"*

With a growl, she launched herself at him. He caught her wrists easily and stood, swinging her around so she landed in the seat he'd been occupying. The chair rocked back on two legs as he laughed at her trying to get up.

"Would you two—" The ringing of my phone cut me off, and I scrambled to answer it. My fingers shook as I swiped the green button without looking at the ID. "Ryan?"

Silence filled the line.

I frowned and glanced down at the phone, but the number was listed as private. I put it back to my ear. "Ry?"

A soft whimper sent chills skittering down my spine. "Maddie?" The voice broke into a ragged sob and then a howl of pain.

I shoved to my feet, shaking. "Bex!"

Chase and Tyler were instantly on their feet, eyes wide.

"Bex, honey," I tried, my mind spiraling to the worst-case scenario. Her mom was dead. "What happened? Is your mom—"

Another sharp, almost desperate scream rang through the line, etching itself into my bones and nearly making me drop the phone. Then silence deadened the line.

I glanced at the phone in my hand, confused and scared, to see the call had ended, but a message was waiting for me.

"What happened?" Chase demanded, coming to my side and putting a hand on my shoulder. I was sure he meant it to be comforting, but I flinched away, my skin feeling like a raw, open wound that I didn't want him touching.

"I don't know," I muttered, shaking my head as I opened the message.

The sound of my gasp ripped through the room a second before the phone slipped from my fingers. My world went fuzzy, sounds rolling together into a buzz that simply didn't make sense. I didn't feel Chase grab my fingers, or register Tyler asking me what was wrong.

My knees folded and I collapsed onto the couch as the screen of the phone stared up at me.

The picture of Bex was recent; I recognized the clothes as what she'd been wearing when she'd left less than two hours earlier. But the blood on her lips and the swollen eyes were new. Tied to a chair, she hung limp with her head slumped sideways, like she'd given up.

Or was unconscious.

Fear curdled in my stomach like sour milk on a sweltering hot summer day. Nausea rolled through me, and I thought I'd pass out.

Chase's fingers dug into my shoulders as he shook me, hard enough to click my teeth together. "Maddie!"

I could only look at the phone as the screen dimmed and then lit up with a new, incoming call.

This time, the screen displayed the name I needed to see as much as I needed my next breath.

I knocked Chase's hands off me and dove for the phone, my voice cracking. "Ryan?"

"Are you safe?" he demanded, worry apparent in his voice.

"I…" My throat closed with emotion until all that could slip free was a sob.

"Mads, baby, settle down." Ryan's voice was soft and calm, gently soothing me the best way he could. "Tell me what's going on."

"Bex," I croaked, the image seared into my brain. She must be so scared.

"What happened?" Ryan picked his words carefully, and I had the feeling he was intentionally staying vague. Maybe because Court was nearby, and he didn't want to worry him.

"He has her," I whispered. "Gary took Bex."

"Fuck," he whispered. "Maddie, we're on our way, okay? We'll be there in a couple hours. Royal's getting us transport."

I shook my head, but he couldn't possibly see that. "It's too late."

"Is—" His breathing hitched. "Maddie, is she—"

"No. But I have to go." My insides withered and died along with the future I'd been planning.

"Go where?" He sounded confused and concerned.

I cleared my throat and closed my eyes. "He wants *me*. He'll let her go if he has me, Ryan."

He was silent, and then exploded at once. "Don't even fucking *think* about it, Madison. I swear to *Christ*—"

"I need to go now, Ryan," I whispered, my heart already aching for the loss of him.

"Maddie!" he roared with fury so potent I could taste it.

"I love you," I finished and hung up. Almost instantly my phone started ringing, but I ignored it, and turned to Chase. "I need a ride."

His green eyes were huge. "What in the hell is going on?"

"Gary took Bex," I explained, my tone even and almost… placid. A numbness had settled in my bones as icy slush filled my veins. "I'm going to go get her back."

His brows drew together. "He won't just *give* her back."

"Maybe not," I agreed, "but I have to try."

Behind me, Tyler was furiously typing on her laptop. "I have Bex on the hospital's cameras leaving her mom's room. She turned a corner into a blind spot, and then nothing. Wait. Hang on. Shit. I think I have her on the parking garage feed." She looked a little sick. "Two guys are carrying… Well, she doesn't look conscious."

My phone stopped ringing and started up again almost instantly.

"When will Ryan be here?" Chase asked, his tone urgent as he took my cold hand in his.

"Not for a couple hours."

He exhaled. "It isn't ideal, but we can wait for them. I'll call in favors from my father. I'm sure we can get additional security."

I shook my head. "There was a text with the photo. I have thirty minutes to get to his house, or he'll—" I shuddered and swallowed down a wave of bile burning up the back of my throat. "I need to get there."

Chase gaped at me. "He'll kill you."

"Probably." I was a little amazed at how calmly I was discussing my own impending death.

Shock, a little voice whispered in my head. *I'm in shock.*

"But I have to try," I finished. The odds of Bex and I escaping this unscathed were about the odds of a pegasus showing up to fly me to Neverland, but I wasn't going to let her go through this alone. Gary was *my* problem, and I'd dragged her into this mess.

Chase gnawed on his lower lip. "I'll come with you. The men my father sent can take us—"

"You'll all be shot!" Tyler cried, standing up. "Chase, *no*."

"She's right. He'll kill you on sight," I agreed. "Just me."

Gary wouldn't kill me. Not right away, anyway. And maybe that would give me enough time to help Bex somehow.

Yeah, that sounded unrealistic, but it was all I could do. I had to try something.

The text made it blisteringly clear: if I didn't show up at Gary's in the next—I checked the clock—twenty-four minutes, he'd start cutting off pieces of Bex.

Again, my phone started ringing.

I stared at Chase. "Will you give me a ride? Or am I calling a taxi?"

"Maddie," he murmured, shaking his head.

"You said that I should be able to make my own decisions," I pointed out. "Changing your mind now?"

He looked so damn frustrated. "Of course not."

"Then let's go," I said, curling my nails into my palms. The sharp bite of pain barely registered as resolve tightened in my gut. I glanced at Tyler. "Tell Ryan that I'm sorry, okay?"

She nodded once, tears shimmering in her eyes.

I squared my shoulders and looked one more time at the four missed calls notification before the phone started ringing again.

My heart gave a violent squeeze, and I wanted to tuck myself into a ball and bawl my damn eyes out. It wasn't fair.

But then again, it had *never* been fair, so why would fate give me a break now?

CHAPTER 47

MADDIE

The house at the top of the hill was all lit up. The only sign that something was amiss was the two men who greeted the car when we slowed to a stop in front of the gated driveway. Their stony expressions gave nothing away, but they both looked like they'd been plucked from the front lines of the military complete with buzz cuts and massive muscles.

The guards who had driven us seemed even more on edge, and while I knew they were both armed, we were clearly at the disadvantage in the car.

Beside me in the back seat, Chase covered my hand with his. "Maddie... I don't know what to say."

"Promise you won't let this be for nothing." I searched his eyes. "Promise me that you and Tyler will get the truth out there."

"I promise," he agreed, squeezing my hand as my door opened. One of the men reached inside to grab my arm and pull me out.

"Hey!" Chase shouted. "She'll get—" He swallowed his objections when a gun was leveled at his face by the man yanking me out of the vehicle.

"It's fine," I assured him, even as fear sent my pulse spiking. "Just go."

The man holding me chuckled. "Smart girl." He kicked the door shut and dragged me back as his friend unlocked the gate.

Chase's car didn't move even as I was dragged backward up the drive.

"I can walk," I snapped, trying to pull away and find my own footing. I looked back, expecting to see Chase's car leaving, but it stayed put. In fact, the interior lights were on, and I could see Chase and his guards being forced out of the car as more men materialized from the shadows with guns aimed at them.

"Wait—let them go!" I cried, trying to run back.

The guy holding me let out an amused snort. "They're the least of your problems right now, princess," he sneered while keeping his hand on my arm, his grip bruising, and twisted my ponytail around his other fist, yanking hard. "Fucking move." He shoved me, and I barely caught myself from sprawling on the asphalt.

The second guard laughed, the sound wheezy and raspy, like he smoked a carton a day.

Lanterns lit the driveway as we trudged to the spectacular Spanish-style mansion that sat at the top of the road. Built at the highest point of the community, it sat like a beacon of wealth and power, looking down on the city of Los Angeles.

Months ago, I'd been awed by the beauty of this house. By the lush grounds that I'd actually spent a summer helping to garden. The rows of flowers I had planted then were still thriving…unlike me.

They would last long after I'd gone, a silent reminder that I'd been here.

As the front doors loomed closer, I remembered the last time I'd been hauled to this house, propped up between guards sent to retrieve me. Maybe I should've just given Gary what he'd wanted then. Been compliant and docile.

The memory of Ryan's electric blue eyes surfaced, and I knew it never would have worked.

Since the day Madelaine and I had switched places, I'd been on a collision course with Ryan Cain. We were destined to end up together, our relationship forged by chaos and violence and more love than I'd ever thought possible.

As much as I was grateful he was hours away from Gary, I wished he was with me. Instead, I pretended he was walking right beside me.

Don't let them see you scared, baby.

I lifted my chin as we walked up the steps to the house and went inside. The doors closed behind me, the sound echoing in the vast space. I looked around at the place that had been my sister's home.

No, her prison. Then mine.

A bitter smile twisted my lips, because I knew Ryan would raze it to the ground before the night was over. Sure, Gary might kill me, but if I could make him drag it out, Ryan would catch him.

An idea snagged on my mind.

Two hours.

Less than that now, and Ryan would be here.

Could I hold on for two hours? Survive whatever Gary had planned?

For Ryan, I would sure as hell try.

"He's waiting in the ballroom," the man behind me huffed, shoving my shoulder.

I resisted the urge to roll my eyes, not needing to give them any added incentive to hurt me. But seriously, the *ballroom*? It never stopped sounding utterly ridiculous.

The room was situated just off the foyer, with gleaming crystal and gold chandeliers and gilded crown molding around the vaulted ceiling. Floor-to-ceiling windows showcased the Los Angeles skyline, making it appear that the city was at our feet.

Fucking pretentious asshole.

In the middle of the vast space, Bex was tied to a chair. Unlike her picture, she was alert now. Her hazel eyes were filled with a mix of terror and fury, and they widened when she saw me. She struggled against her restraints, her cries muffled by the gag in her mouth.

Without thinking, I rushed forward only to be jerked back by the asshole who seemed to think my ponytail was a set of reins. The momentum dropped me onto my ass, my hands and tailbone absorbing most of the jarring impact with the gleaming hardwood floor.

Gary's biting laugh echoed off the walls, crawling across my skin and leaving goosebumps in its wake. He stepped out of the shadows like a damn villain in a movie.

"Welcome home, sweetheart," he greeted with absolutely zero affection.

I glanced around the space and shrugged. "I think I'll pass. I've seen trailers nicer than this."

He hissed and jerked his chin at the man behind me. Again, I was lifted up by my hair, my eyes watering as pain splintered along my scalp.

"Jesus," I seethed, my chest heaving as I got my feet under me. I glared at the jerk. "It's not a handle, you know."

The man's plain brown eyes flicked over my shoulder, likely for approval. Next thing I knew, I was back on the ground, and my cheek was on fire from where he'd backhanded me.

Oh, shit, ow.

That hurt like a bitch.

I wished I was wearing a watch so I could track the time. Maybe seeing the two hours ticking away would've helped me endure whatever came next.

"Did you search her?" Gary drawled.

Rough hands scrubbed over my body, and I gritted my teeth as I resisted the urge to fight back. It would only earn me another a slap.

"She's clean," one of the guys declared as his hands finished squeezing my ass. "Has on a vest, though."

I winced. The bulletproof vest had been Chase's, and when we'd first gotten to the car, he'd royally pissed off his guards by insisting I wear it under my t-shirt before berating them for not having one for me. Now I felt like an asshole, because he probably needed it.

Gary sighed. "Get it off her."

My shirt was ripped open from the back and the vest roughly pulled off my body, leaving me in a thin camisole and my bra.

Gary grinned at me, his teeth flashing. "Perfect. Now I can shoot you in the back if you try to run."

I glared at Gary. "I'm here, like you wanted. I'm not running, asshole, so let her go."

He tilted his head. "No, I don't think I will. You see, you cost me a lot of money, Madison. And I think Rebecca will help me recoup some of that." He patted the top of her head, smirking when she tried to shrink away with nowhere to go. "I know of a shitty little brothel in Thailand that would love some fresh American cunt."

"No—" An arm wrapped around my middle as a hand clamped across my mouth, silencing me.

Gary held up a finger with an aggrieved sigh. "I wasn't done speaking yet, dear." He shook his head as if disappointed. "I suppose I can't be too surprised, considering your upbringing."

He walked away from Bex, the heels of his shiny shoes clicking across the floors, until he was inches from me. He observed me the way someone would look at a penguin in the zoo. "I could have given you the world, you know."

I shook my head behind the hand that muzzled me, hoping my eyes conveyed all the ways I was trying to say *Fuck you*.

"I considered sending you with your friend, but honestly? I'd rather lose a few million than have to deal with you any longer." He reached behind his back and pulled out a silver gun, the lights glinting off it as he aimed it at my head.

Abruptly, I was let go, and the creep holding me moved away, probably worried he'd get blood on his suit.

"Any last words?" Gary cocked the trigger and smiled at me as Bex struggled behind him, screaming around her gag.

Everything in me wanted to panic, but I forced myself to stay calm and *think*.

"Killing me won't change what's already been set in motion," I told him. "My sister was a lot smarter than you gave her credit for. And she hated you a lot more than I did."

His eye twitched, the curious tick giving him away. He was intrigued and possibly... concerned?

I drew in a deep breath. "Pandora is a pretty wild place."

His eyes widened. "What did you say?"

"Pandora?" I grinned at him. "It's a place where my sister hid all the footage of you and your asshole friends doing all sorts of illegal things."

"Where are the recordings?" His face was an odd combination of pale and red, like he wasn't sure if he was furious or going to shit his pants.

I shrugged. "A friend has them." I smirked, thinking of Tyler working on the drives at this very minute. Maybe a little lie wouldn't hurt. "Madelaine had a lot of shit on you, you know. And if something happens to me or Bex? She's sending everything to every major news outlet."

Fury twisted his features into something inhuman. He lunged forward, wrapping his hands around my neck and shaking me. "Tell me where they are!"

This close, I could see the panic in his eyes. We hadn't finished going over everything my twin had discovered, but it stood to argue she had a lot of dirt on our father. And based on his reaction, there were things he didn't want getting out.

My nails dug into his wrists, trying to pry him off, but he was too strong. When I was close to blacking out, spots dancing across my blurry vision, he shoved me to the ground and whirled, jabbing a finger in Bex's direction.

"Get her up," he snapped, barking orders like a madman.

The two men jumped to do his bidding as I coughed and choked on the floor, rubbing my raw throat. I tried to protest as they cut through the ropes binding Bex to the chair and jerked her upright. She looked terrified, but she didn't make a sound as she met my eyes.

Gary sneered. "Get rid of her gag, too. I want my daughter to hear her friend's screams."

As soon as the gag was gone, Bex quickly rushed out, "Don't tell him *anything*, Maddie."

Gary growled in frustration and flicked a finger. A moment later, one of the guards punched Bex in the stomach. She doubled over with a pained wheeze.

"Stop!" I cried, unable to watch them hurt Bex.

Shit, shit, shit. I hadn't thought this through.

Pressing the barrel of the gun under my jaw, Gary tipped my head back to the point of pain. "Unless you want to watch those men take turns breaking her in for the trip ahead, I suggest you start telling me what I want to know."

I met Bex's terrified eyes. She slowly shook her head.

My hesitation cost us both.

The sound of her shirt ripping made me jolt. "Stop, okay? I'll tell you."

"Maddie, no!" Bex stared at me from across the room, her shirt gaping open where they'd split it down the middle and exposed her pale torso and pink bra. "I can take—"

A roaring sound filled my ears, and I wanted to scream, but I started to shake instead.

"Fuck!" someone yelled, and I realized it wasn't me who was shaking; the whole damn room was shuddering. The crystals of the chandeliers tinkled as they bounced until, with a booming crash, one fell just feet from Bex and the guys holding her.

As a crack spread across the ceiling, they backed away from Bex and fled the vicinity. "Earthquake!" one of them roared, running for cover.

Gary just stood there and gaped, and I used the moment of surprise to push him aside as the floor under us trembled violently and began to break apart. I pitched forward and tripped toward Bex.

"Get back here!" Gary yelled, and amidst the sound of shattering glass, a louder *crack* sounded. Something whizzed past my ear as I tackled Bex to the floor.

"We need to get out of here," Bex gasped, looking around desperately.

Gary was on his knees now, and the gun had slid several feet away. I saw it the same time he did, and determination licked a fiery path through my soul. I scrambled for the gun as he began crawling toward it.

"Maddie, *stop!*" Bex's sharp cry made me freeze in time to glance up and see another chandelier break free, along with chunks of plaster and wood from the beams above.

I rolled away, covering my head, and the world crashed down around me.

CHAPTER 48

MADDIE

The silence was almost as deafening as the roar of the earthquake had been. In the distance, I could hear car alarms blaring, but it was mostly quiet.

Quiet and... dark.

My head was killing me as I lifted it off the floor and looked around to see the room silhouetted in shadows and debris. I gasped when I looked at where the windows should have been. The entire wall was *gone*. Hell, a good chunk of the floor was, too. It had broken off and gone down the side of the mountain. The entire city was dark, just a bunch of shapeless ridges and lines against the moonlight.

Bex.

I needed to find my best friend. I reached into my back pocket for my cell phone and turned it on, frustrated when I saw there was no service. The screen was cracked from how I'd landed on it, but the flashlight app worked.

Turning to look for Bex, I sent the light glancing over a lump near the door. My stomach roiled as I realized it was one of the guards, but his head had been partially caved in when part of the ceiling fell. His sightless eyes stared at me until I lowered the light.

Bex. I need to find Bex.

I tripped over pieces of floor and ceiling as I made my way to where I thought I'd left her.

"Bex?" I whispered, trying to discern a girl-shaped bump from a rubble-shaped one as I slipped on a large chunk of crystal and nearly wiped out. "Shit."

A soft moan came from in front of me. "Mads?"

I pushed through the rest of the way and dropped to my knees beside her, helping her sit up. "Are you okay?"

She blinked and focused on my face, dust in her brown hair. "You're bleeding."

I touched my forehead, surprised to find it wet with blood. No wonder my head was pounding. "Did you get hurt?"

She looked over herself. "I think I'm okay. Just a few cuts and bruises, but I'm not sure how much of that was from the earthquake." She gave a nervous, breathy chuckle and looked at my phone. "Tell me you can call for help."

I shook my head. "No service." I looked down again. At least the clock worked, and it was showing that the two hours I'd been waiting for Ryan had been more than cut in half.

That was if they could land a plane somewhere following an earthquake.

Hopelessness started bubbling up in me, but I pushed it back. I had to get Bex and I out of here.

"Where's Gary?" she asked, grunting as I helped her to her feet. "Ouch. I think I sprained my ankle."

I wrapped her arm around my shoulders so she could use me for support. "I don't know," I admitted.

"Okay." Bex's teeth were chattering as she tried to hold it together. "Let's see if we can get the hell out of this deathtrap." She glanced around, and, as if to prove her point, another piece of the ceiling broke free and fell a few feet away with a crash and cloud of dust.

I couldn't make out the foyer or front door beyond this room, and the only other option was rappelling down the side of the cliff the house had once sat on top of.

Ironic.

This place had been designed to showcase power and wealth, and it was because of that very thing that it was on the precipice of falling into the valley. If I wasn't in mortal danger of this monstrosity of a house falling down on my head, I'd take a few pictures to gloat.

Speaking of monsters... I kept my gaze moving, searching for Gary in case he was hiding somewhere. I would've liked to think that a natural disaster might've tempered his desire to kill me, but the man had already proven he was laser focused on my death, so I wasn't planning to stick around and tempt fate.

I huffed a breath as we made our way across the uneven floor. "I can't believe we just got our asses saved by an earthquake."

The corner of Bex's mouth turned up. "Well, at least Mother Nature's on your side."

I snorted. "About time I had a mom that gave a damn."

She laughed, the sound soft but strained. "Seriously, Maddie? You're going to joke about that now?"

I glanced around. "If you can't laugh during a natural disaster, then when can you?"

Sighing, Bex kept pushing forward until her foot caught on something and we both almost went down. I struggled to keep us upright, the pain in my temples throbbing even harder in protest as my head dipped.

"Shit, sorry," she apologized.

"We're almost there," I said, my gaze fixed on the spot where the doors to the hallway were. I just prayed there wasn't anything blocking them. "I thought all Los Angeles buildings were earthquake proof."

"Yeah, but when half the side of a cliff gives way, the house on top doesn't really stand a chance," she pointed out, panting as we finished crossing the floor.

"Moment of truth," I murmured, surprised when I pushed on the door and it swung open easily.

The foyer was a mess, from what I could see. The windows in here were blown out, too, and there was glass scattered across the cracked marble from where yet another chandelier had fallen.

Chandeliers were clearly a major problem in earthquakes.

"I feel like we woke up in a dystopian novel," Bex whispered.

I had to agree as my gaze traveled around the darkened space. The front doors were gaping open, showing the dark semi-circle of the driveway. Pictures that had lined the curved staircase had fallen off the walls. Splinters of cracked frames and broken glass littered the steps.

The place looked like a damn war zone.

Anxiety tightened my stomach as we moved forward. Where were Gary and the other guard? Or the ones from outside? Shit, was Chase okay?

Approaching footsteps made us both freeze. I looked around, desperate for a place to hide. I was about to pull Bex back into the ballroom when a light flashed across the opening of the house and landed squarely on us.

"Maddie?" Chase called, stepping inside with two more people.

I sagged in relief at the sight of our friend and his guards. "Here," I called.

Chase and the guards quickly made their way to us, and one of the guards took Bex. Chase's arms wrapped around me in a crushing hug. "You're all right," he breathed into my hair.

I awkwardly patted his back. "What about the other guards?"

Chase grinned. "Seamus and Brennan took them out when the earthquake started. It was the perfect diversion."

"Oh, good," I deadpanned. "Thank God for natural disasters."

"We should get out of here, sir," the man not helping Bex said in a clipped tone.

"Where are your father and his men?" Chase asked.

I swallowed. "One of them is dead. I don't know where Gary or the other guy are."

Chase's eyes narrowed and he looked at the man with Bex. "Right. Brennan, you get the ladies out of here." He nodded to the other guy. "Seamus and I will see if we can locate the others."

My eyes went wide. "What? No. We *all* need to get out of here."

Seamus looked more than a little unhappy at the suggestion. "Sir—"

"You take your orders from *me*," Chase snapped, sounding every inch a lord in that moment.

"Yes, sir," Seamus ground out, his jaw taut.

Chase's hand cupped my face in a familiar way that almost made me pull back. "Madison, I need to find Gary and see if he's dead."

"And if he isn't?" I pointed out.

His green eyes heated. "Then I'll handle him myself. For my mother and sister."

I looked at Bex and Brennan. "You two go." I turned to Chase. "I'm coming with you. I need to know if I'm spending the next decade looking over my shoulder for Gary or not."

Chase nodded. "If that's what you want, then of course."

"Maddie, you should come with *us*," Bex insisted. "We need to get out of here."

"No, you should," I countered. "This isn't your fight, Bex. I'm sorry he dragged you into it."

Bex looked ready to strangle me. "Maddie, *no*. Let's get out and regroup with the others."

She was probably right, but something in me needed to see this finished. I didn't want to wake up wondering if today was the day Gary Cabot stormed back into my life and ruined it. If he got away now, who knew when he would resurface?

Best-case scenario, he was crushed under a pile of something.

Worst case, he'd escaped like the cockroach he was.

"This is a bad idea," Bex warned, shaking her head.

"I'll be fine," I promised, not sure if I was lying or not. I flashed her a tight smile. "Ryan and the guys should be here soon. They were on their way."

Bex looked like she had more to say, but a tremor rippled through the room as an aftershock hit.

"If we're doing this, we need to do it now," Seamus advised Chase. He looked around the room. "This structure is unstable."

"Please keep her safe," I begged Brennan.

He nodded. "I'll take her to the car." Without waiting for confirmation, he swung Bex into his arms like she weighed nothing.

She let out a pained squeak before shooting me one last imploring look. "Maddie, come with me."

"I'll see you soon." I watched as Brennan carried her away, her accusing hazel eyes fixed on me until the darkness swallowed them up. Then I looked at Chase and Seamus. "Let's do this."

Chase smiled at me, holding out a hand. I took it with a frown, using him as support as we went back inside.

"Stay behind me," Seamus ordered quietly, moving in front of us and angling his flashlight under his gun as he walked into the destroyed ballroom. I turned away as his light shone on the dead guard.

"One down," Seamus muttered.

Chase squeezed my hand, I assumed to offer comfort, but I was seconds away from letting him go. Unease crawled over my skin like thousands of ants, and I didn't want anyone touching me as I looked for my father's body.

How awful did it make me that I was hoping we'd find it?

We carefully made our way through the rubble to where I'd last seen Gary, lunging for the gun at the same time as me.

Seamus moved forward. "Second body," he reported, looking over a piece of broken metal from the chandelier.

I grimaced at seeing the second guard with a delicate swirl of the chandelier protruding from his chest.

"Any sign of Cabot?" Chase demanded, shining his own flashlight around the space and illuminating more destruction.

"Not yet," Seamus replied, moving closer to the edge of the room that looked out over the valley. "Maybe—"

A *crack* echoed through the space, and Seamus jerked and turned, firing his own weapon in a wild arc before toppling backwards into the dark.

"No!" I cried, running forward like I could stop him from falling, but I was too far away, and Chase gripped my hand, yanking me back.

"Stay where you are," Gary snapped, the gun trained on us as he stood up from behind a pile of rubble.

Chase pushed me behind him. "I'm going to kill you with my bare hands," he hissed, fury bunching up the muscles of his shoulders.

Gary chuckled. "Somehow I doubt that. You're just as useless as your father." He tilted his head, and in the silvery moonlight, I saw blood covering one side of his face.

"Fuck you," Chase spat. "You're a murderer."

"I am," Gary agreed with a smile. "Want me to prove it?"

A second shot rang out, and Chase collapsed in front of me with a grunt.

"Chase!" I dropped to my knees and pressed my hands against his shoulder as blood gushed from the wound. "Oh, God. Hold on, okay?"

"S-sorry," he whispered, his face shockingly pale as he blinked up at me, his gaze unable to focus.

"Don't, okay? Just fucking don't," I snapped, panic setting is as blood seeped from between my fingers. "You're gonna be fine."

He opened his mouth but couldn't seem to get any words out.

"And then there were two," Gary mused, limping closer. "To think, you almost got away. Thanks for coming back and saving me the trouble of tracking you down."

I glared at Gary, channeling as much venom as I could into my eyes. "I *hate* you."

"The feeling is entirely mutual," he assured me, cocking the gun. "Say hello to your sister for me, would you?"

I refused to close my eyes or blink. I wanted him to see my eyes as I died, to see the defiance and fight and live with that memory until the day he went straight to hell.

The *bang* of the shot made me jerk... and then the world went deathly silent.

CHAPTER 49

MADDIE

I expected a searing pain that stole my breath, but that didn't happen. Nothing in me hurt any more than the other wounds I'd sustained this night. Maybe I was in shock?

Oh, hell.

Maybe I was dead. Could the dead feel pain?

The thumping in my head answered a resounding *yes*, but I didn't feel... shot.

"Maddie!"

I shook my head, my ears ringing even as blood *whoosh*ed through them. I touched my chest, expecting to feel a hole in my chest.

"*Madison!*"

Dead. I had to be dead. Because that was the only way to explain the voice and—

Strong hands grabbed my shoulders and shook me once. "Maddie, fucking *look at me*."

Dazed, I lifted my eyes, surprised to see a startling blue pair boring into mine with a desperation that bordered on manic.

"Baby, say something," Ryan pleaded, his hands moving to my neck, my face. His expression turned lethal when he touched the cut on my head.

It took a second for me to remember how to speak. "Ryan?"

Relief crashed over his expression a second before he hauled me against his chest. "Thank fuck."

My arms slowly lifted, wrapping around him tentatively as if he was a phantom that just might dissipate when I touched him. When all I felt was solid muscle and strength, I inhaled a deep breath and buried my face against his neck.

"You're here?" I whimpered, my mind starting to piece together reality. "How did you get here?"

"That's a fun story for another day," a familiar voice told me.

I opened my eyes to see Knight kneeling next to us by Chase, his expression grim. "Shit, he's lost a lot of blood."

I swallowed a sob, my nails digging into Ryan's back as I watched Knight work. "Is he dead?"

Knight met my eyes and shook his head. "No, but we need to get him to the helicopter before that changes."

"Gary?" I whispered, trying to look around Ryan's massive shoulder to where a few other people seemed to be.

"Royal?" Ryan called over his shoulder, not letting me go.

"Dead," he replied with a hint of a smile. "Nice shot, Cain."

"You killed him?" I murmured, starting to shake.

Ryan stood up, bringing me with him as he moved me away from Chase. "Yeah, baby. I killed him."

"Thank you." It seemed like such a stupid thing to say, but it was all I had. "Bex is—"

"Court and Linc are with her," Ryan cut me off, one hand rubbing my back. "We ran into them on our way in."

My teeth chattered as I snuggled closer to his chest, freezing and seeking warmth. "I think I messed up. Are you mad at me?"

"Furious," he answered gently, kissing the side of my head as he looked in Royal's direction. "She's going into shock."

"Who's going into shock?" My tone was slurred, like I'd drunk a bottle of tequila. Except I hated tequila. The idea that I'd drink a whole bottle of that shit was hysterical for some reason, and I started laughing uncontrollably.

"Can you get her out of here?" Royal asked over my head. "Bishop and I can help Knight with Winthrope."

"Where's Ash?" I asked, worrying that he hadn't been mentioned.

"With the helicopter," Ryan assured me. "Let's go see him, okay?"

"Okay," I agreed, numbness and exhaustion making my brain buzz as my adrenaline crashed. It was as though someone had filled my limbs with lead, and I could barely keep my eyes open. The entire room was spinning while blurring in and out of focus.

Ryan picked me up, cradling me in his arms.

"I'm too heavy," I protested.

He snorted, like the idea was utterly ridiculous, and carried me out of the ballroom and then the house. Once we were outside, I took a deep breath and looked around with wide eyes. "Ryan."

"Yeah, babe?"

"There's a monster on the front lawn," I mumbled, wrapping my arm tighter around his neck as I tried to make out the wonky shape in the distance.

"It's the helicopter, Mads," he assured me. "No more monsters here."

"Because you killed the monster," I whispered.

He turned his head and met my gaze, his expression soft. "Yeah, baby."

I gulped back a sob as tears filled my eyes. "Can we go home now?"

"Back to PC?"

I shook my head. "Can we go to Brookfield?"

He exhaled a long breath. "Yeah. As soon as we get you checked out, okay?"

"Chase, too?" I pressed.

He growled slightly. "Fine. That asshole, too."

"And Bex?"

"And Bex," he confirmed before arching a brow. "Anyone else?"

"Does anyone else need help?" I frowned, trying to remember if anyone else had been hurt, but my memories were scrambled like a jigsaw puzzle.

"Don't worry about that right now," he told me as we closed the distance to the helicopter.

As we got closer, I heard Bex's sharp gasp. "Oh, my God. Is Maddie hurt?"

"Goddamn it, Becca," Court snarled, "would you stay the fuck still? You need that ankle looked at by a fucking doctor."

I lifted my head to see Bex trying to jump down from the helicopter as Court grabbed her waist and pulled her back. Linc and Ash were waiting near the helicopter as if they were guarding it. Both stepped toward us.

"She okay?" Ash asked Ryan.

"I think she's in shock," he answered, his worried eyes glancing down at me.

I frowned. Was I in shock? I mean, I was cold and felt a little off, but… "I'm f-fine."

Linc chuckled and reached over to push my hair out of my eyes. "Try saying that without shivering, Mads."

"It's cold," I argue.

"It's seventy degrees," he pointed out with a grimace. "Just relax, girl. Where's the rest?"

"On their way." Ryan helped maneuver me into the helicopter with the help of Court. "Winthrope was shot."

"Chase?" Bex gasped. "Is he okay?"

"Not sure." Ryan tried to put me on the seat, but I made it stupidly difficult by not letting him go. My arms wouldn't unwind, and my fingers were clamped to the point of cramping where I gripped his shirt. "Maddie, I need to help the others."

"I know." I still couldn't seem to make my damn arms work. Panic swelled in my chest like a tsunami, and my bones ached as I started to shiver harder.

"Fuck," Ryan murmured, turning so he was sitting on the seat with me on his lap. He nuzzled the side of my face with his nose, peppering kisses from my jaw to hairline. "I'll stay with you, okay?"

I nodded and closed my eyes, breathing in his scent as I tried to settle down. Everything felt wrong and chaotic, like my nerves had been stripped bare and exposed to a hurricane. The only thing that made sense was Ryan and the way I felt in his arms, so I sank into that feeling as the world moved on around me.

"I'll go help the duke of dicks," Linc muttered before jogging toward the house.

Bex reached across the space between the rows of seats and touched my hand. "Are you okay?"

"I think so," I said, picking my words carefully, because I definitely didn't feel *right*, but I didn't think I was hurt.

A shudder rippled down her frame. "When I heard those shots... Jesus, Maddie."

I forced a smile across my numb lips as Ryan's thumb stroked the exposed skin above my hip.

"Ash," Ryan's voice rumbled, "grab some gauze for her forehead."

I frowned as Ash came closer and pressed a white bandage to my head. He flashed me a small smile. "How you doing, Mads?"

"Tired," I answered honestly, yawning to punctuate the response.

Ash lifted concerned eyes to Ryan. "She might have a concussion."

Ryan growled. "We need to go. How's Bex's ankle?"

"I don't think it's broken," Court replied.

"Where's... Brandon?" I tried to remember the name of the other guy who had been with Chase and Seamus.

"Brennan went back inside," Bex told me.

Ryan's arms tightened around me. "He was with Royal and Bishop. You probably didn't notice because it was so dark."

"He killed Seamus," I whispered, remembering the way the guard's body had jerked before he disappeared over the edge. I screwed my eyes shut and shivered.

"Who?" Ryan sounded confused.

Bex helped him out by adding, "The guard who went inside with Maddie and Chase."

Ryan made an unhappy sound. "Fucking idiots."

I peered up at him, wondering who was an idiot. Before I could ask, the others rushed up carrying Chase between them. There was a bit of shuffling as Bishop jumped in the cockpit seat and started flipping buttons and Ash got into the seat beside him. Brennan and Knight loaded Chase onto the floor of the helicopter, blood continuing to seep from his wound. He looked gray.

Knight pushed into the space and looked at Brennan. "Get out."

Brennan narrowed his eyes. "Fuck off. I'm not leaving him unprotected."

"Too much weight," Bishop barked from the front, spinning around and looking at Brennan. "Get the fuck out."

Brennan looked ready to argue when the tell-tale click of a gun being cocked made him freeze.

Court didn't blink as he aimed the gun at Brennan. "Get out on your own, or we'll roll your body out."

"Court!" Bex stared at him with huge eyes.

With a snarl, Brennan backed out of the cabin.

Royal leaned around the frame, Linc at his side. "We'll meet you at the hospital." He thumped the side of the helicopter and jogged backwards as the blades started spinning.

The noise made the thumping in my head even louder, and I burrowed against Ryan and tried to block out everything else as we lifted into the night.

It wasn't a surprise that the hospital was full of people.

What *was* surprising was how quickly we were all seen. The doctors rushed Chase into surgery while Bex and I were taken back and seen almost instantly, despite the crush of people waiting.

The earthquake had hit Los Angeles hard, and a lot of people were hurt.

Court followed Bex and an orderly to radiology to check out her leg while I was taken up a few floors.

Without an available gurney. Ryan carried me, following on the heels of a nurse I'd watched him slip a handful of bills.

Even in a catastrophe, money was still king.

"There are people who need a doctor more than we do," I whispered as Ryan stepped into a room.

He looked down at me, completely unapologetic. "I don't give a fuck about other people. *You* matter the most to me."

"That isn't fair," I protested, even as he set me on the bed.

He leaned down, looking in my eyes. "I don't care, Madison." His large hands framed my face. "Let me take care of you, okay?"

I nodded and leaned back as the nurse stepped around the other side of the bed. "Do you know your name, honey?"

I started to nod again, but realized I needed to give verbal answers. "Yes."

"What is it?"

I met Ryan's eyes and sighed a little. "Madelaine Cabot." The name tasted bitter on my tongue.

"Do you know what day it is?" A tiny furrow appeared in her brow as she watched me.

"December fifteenth," I replied, then frowned. "Or sixteenth. What time is it?"

She smiled a bit. "Three in the morning." She winked. "Honestly, I'm not sure I'd have gotten that right either."

I breathed a tiny laugh, my gaze flashing to Ryan. Arms folded over his chest and feet braced apart, he was dressed in all black tactical clothes that clung to his muscular frame like a second skin I really wanted to peel off with my teeth. As if sensing the direction of my thoughts, he arched a brow before rolling his eyes.

Glancing away, I smirked inwardly and finished answering the barrage of questions from the nurse until she was satisfied.

"Dr. Rice will be here to check you out in a few minutes, but I don't think you have a concussion. We'll get you stitched up and maybe keep you overnight for observation—"

"Do I have to stay?" I interrupted, anxiety welling in me again. "I really just want to go home, and I'm sure there're other people who can use this room."

Ryan's eyes narrowed, as if he was ready to argue.

"That's not my call," the nurse said, "but I'll pass along your request to Dr. Rice." She gave me a warm smile and stepped out.

With a heavy breath, Ryan moved forward and perched on the edge of my bed, not nearly close enough for me. He reached forward and held my hand, tangling our fingers together. "Gotta admit, Mads, I'm torn between screaming at you and kissing the shit out of you."

"I vote for kissing," I said as seriously as I could manage, even as the corners of my mouth turned up.

"I'm serious, Madison." His thumb stroked the back of my hand. "Tonight... Fuck, you could've been killed."

"But I wasn't," I felt the need to point out.

"Saving Bex, I get," he admitted, looking down for a second before meeting my eyes. "But going back in after Gary? With fucking *Chase*?"

"And a guard," I muttered, but that sounded weak. "I just had to see for myself if he was dead."

"He wasn't," Ryan snapped, heat flashing in his eyes. "And if we hadn't shown up when we did..."

I lifted my other hand and touched his face. "Did I say thank you for saving my life?"

He looked annoyed and frustrated. "I shouldn't have *had* to save your life. You should've been *safe*."

Sighing, I shook my head. "I told you before that if you want the girl who's going to sit back and let you handle everything because you have a penis and I have a vagina, you need to look for someone who isn't me."

A low growl worked its way out of his throat. "This has nothing to do with the fact that you're a girl, babe. I'm pissed because you went into a situation where you *knew* you'd be hurt. You fucking hung up on me when I was miles away. Do you honestly think that's fucking fair?"

I shrank back a little as guilt settled in my gut.

"And then, by the grace of fucking God, you actually had a shot at getting free, and you went *back inside*." Now he was really pissed. "I was seconds away from being too late, Maddie."

"I'm sorry," I whispered, a tear sliding down my face. "Please don't be mad at me."

With a groan, he leaned forward and hugged me. "I'm not mad, baby. I was fucking terrified. I still am. It's gonna take a little while for me not to see you standing there with a gun aimed at your head."

I wrapped my arms around his back as a tremor rippled down his spine and across his frame. I kissed the side of his neck and added a soft, "I'm sorry."

He exhaled hard and drew back to look me in the eye. "I know."

I tipped my head to the side. "Still feel like kissing me?"

The intense expression melted a bit, and the side of his mouth kicked up before he leaned in to brush his lips across mine. "Always."

CHAPTER 50

MADDIE

Ryan might not have been mad at *me*, but he was sure as hell taking it out on anyone else who dared come near.

First it was Dr. Rice, who declared I *probably* didn't have a concussion, but the only way to be a hundred percent sure was if they did a scan of my head. Problem was, the earthquake had caused a lot of injuries and there were people who needed the machines more than me, so there was a massive backup.

They'd used a portable X-ray machine on Bex to determine her ankle was sprained, not broken, and she'd gone upstairs with Court to see her mother and father, who'd been losing his mind wondering where she'd gone. Thankfully the hospital had been spared any real damage from the quake, and her mom's surgery had gone off without a hitch.

Ryan had all but bitten off the nurse's head when she'd come back to stitch up my wounds and I'd flinched before the numbing cream fully set in. I tried to apologize for his behavior, but his glaring wasn't helping her finish any faster. I tried to distract her by asking questions about Chase's condition.

There was no official word yet, but from what we'd been able to find out, the bullet had just barely missed his heart. She'd left, and then Bishop, Ash, and Knight were crammed into the small couch and chair we'd squeezed into my room. They'd all checked in on me, but didn't come closer, considering the guard dog wearing a path into the floor.

I could hear chaos outside my door as Ryan paced in front of it. With every revolution he took around the walkable space in my room, my anxiety ticked higher and higher.

"Dude, sit down," Knight finally muttered, rubbing his jaw. "You're making *me* anxious."

Ryan flipped him off.

I sighed and looked at Ash. "Any luck reaching Tyler?"

He grimaced and shook his head. "No. The whole system is fucked right now. Phones are down, and so's the internet."

I frowned, worrying about Tyler all alone in the hotel, probably going nuts trying to find out if Chase was okay. It seemed like most of the damage to the city had been residential and power outages. Ash had confirmed Tyler's hotel was fine, but phone lines were a mess since a few towers had gone down.

"Okay," Ryan finally snapped, "I'm going to find the doctor—"

"No, you aren't," I cut him off firmly. "They're doing the best they can, and the last thing they need is you bugging them about discharge papers."

He glared at me.

Knight ticked up a finger. "I mean, we could just leave."

We all stared at him, and he shrugged. "What? Maddie doesn't have a concussion. They closed up the cut on her head. We're waiting for pain meds—which we have—and a piece of paper saying to keep an eye on her if things change. Again, something we can do."

Ryan rubbed his jaw and looked at me. "Wanna get out of here?"

"*Yes*," I said as emphatically as I could, wanting to shower and crawl into bed. The sun was starting to peek up over the horizon, and it had been a long-ass night. I was still in the same torn, dirty clothes from earlier.

He rubbed the back of his neck with a decisive nod. "Okay. Let's get you out of here."

"What about Bex?" I asked, swinging my legs over the side of the bed.

He grimaced at me before looking at Bishop, who stood from the plastic couch and offered, "I'll go see what she and Court are thinking. Back in a few."

I bit my lower lip as I thought of someone else. "What about Chase?"

"What about him?" Ryan didn't seem concerned in the slightest.

"Someone should be here for him when he wakes up," I said, exasperated.

He still didn't seem to care. "Not our problem, babe."

"He was shot protecting me," I argued.

"No," Ryan retorted through clenched teeth, "he was shot because he was a dumbass who went back inside when his main goal should've been taking you somewhere safe."

A frown tugged at my mouth. "He was trying to avenge his mom and sister."

"Again, not our problem." Ryan gave an indifferent shrug.

"Sometimes I want to slap you," I muttered, rolling my eyes.

His eyes narrowed as he stepped closer to me, his lips brushing the shell of my ear. "The only slapping that'll happen is my hand on your perky little ass when you're feeling better. I wasn't kidding before, Mads. You're not gonna be able to sit for a fucking week."

I opened my mouth, but he pressed a finger to it. His icy blue eyes warned me against fighting him right now, so I did the mature thing and bit the tip of his finger. He snorted, unperturbed, and kissed my forehead.

"You two are so weird," Ash muttered, standing up. "Our coms are still working, so I'll tell Linc and Royal we're heading to Brookfield and they can meet us there."

That still didn't address the Chase issue. "But—"

"And I'll tell Chase's guard to come here and sit by his master's side," Ash added with a smile. "Hell, I'll even mention picking up Tyler on the way."

"Tyler has the drives," I added. "She was still working on them at the hotel."

Ash nodded. "I'll have Royal get them from her before they leave. And I'll make sure she has a way to get in touch with us if she needs to, okay?"

I smiled at him before glaring at Ryan. "Was that so hard?"

"Yes," he replied, his tone flat. He looked at Knight. "Can you meet Bishop and get the chopper ready?"

Knight gave him a mock salute. "Aye-aye, Captain."

"Fucking idiot," Ryan muttered as Knight and Ash left.

I cocked my head to the side. "Where exactly *did* you park a helicopter?"

"Parking garage across the street," he answered. "The roof was empty, so Bishop left it there after we dropped you guys off on the roof access to the hospital."

"Do I want to know where you got a helicopter from?" I asked, giving him a long look.

His mouth flattened. "Probably not. But we'll give it back when we're done."

"But we can take it to Brookfield?" I leaned against the bed, suddenly exhausted.

Ryan moved closer and wrapped me in his arms. "Yeah. We'll probably have to stop to refuel on the way, but we'll do it outside of L.A. From here it should take less than two hours."

"How bad is it out there?" I murmured, turning my head against his chest to look out the window. This room had a view of the building beside it and the H-VAC units, so there was no way to tell what damage the city had sustained.

He stroked my back as he answered. "It was a six-point-five."

My nose wrinkled. "Explain that to the person who didn't grow up in a place where the earth routinely shakes."

He snorted a laugh. "It was strong and did some damage, but overall, it wasn't catastrophic."

I lifted my head, my chin on his chest. "Uh, I beg to differ. Gary's house literally broke in half." I'd sorta been able to make out the shape of the house from the flood lights under the chopper as it had carried us away, and I'd been stunned to see most of its left side was *gone*. Trees had toppled, and there was a giant crack running through the backyard up to the foundation.

"Well, that's because the cliffside broke free," he replied. "The majority of the neighborhood didn't have a ton of damage."

A bitter laugh escaped me. "Leave it to Gary to be destroyed because he *had* to have the house at the top."

"It *is* rather poetic, isn't it?" Ryan smiled against my forehead.

"He's really dead?" Somehow it just didn't seem believable that the monster was finally slayed.

Ryan tilted my head back to look in my eyes. "He's really dead, baby. He'll never hurt you, or anyone else, ever again."

I exhaled a breath I hadn't realized I'd been holding. My hands tightened on the waist of his pants. "Will you get in trouble?"

He snorted like the idea was amusing as hell. "Not a chance. There were plenty of us in the room to attest he was about to…" He trailed off, tensing again as the memory seemed to wash over him. His fingers curled around me, like he was trying to make sure I was still there in front of him, all right and whole.

I turned my face up, brushing my lips on the underside of his scruffy jaw. "Hey, I'm fine. We're both fine."

He nodded slowly and found my lips with his. What started a sweet, soft kiss of reassurance quickly turned into something hotter and more primal. His hands spanned my waist as he crowded me against the side of the bed. I sank onto the edge, my legs opening so he could step between them.

I gasped as he pressed against me, and I wanted desperately to rock my hips, arousal sharp and potent as it soared between us. Something deep inside me craved this connection between us, needed it to reaffirm that we really were both on the other side of this and okay.

Which was, of course, when the door to my room opened.

"Seriously? You two couldn't wait?" Ash sounded a mix of bemused and exasperated.

I peeked over Ryan's shoulder and hid a smile against his shoulder. "Any word from Linc and Royal?"

He nodded and closed the door as he stepped into the room. "They'll meet us at Brookfield. I also saw Bishop in the hall. Bex is good, but she wants to stay here with her mom and dad."

"Court staying?" Ryan guessed.

Ash grimaced. "No. Bex told him to go, and Malcolm threatened to call security if he didn't leave Bex alone." He sighed and shook his head. "Sometimes I don't think those two will ever get their shit straight. Court's going to meet us at the chopper."

My lips bunched to the side as I considered my best friend. "Maybe I should check in with her before we go."

Ryan framed my face in his big hands. "Mads, I'm sure phones will be back up by the end of the day, and if they aren't, Ash will figure out a way for you to talk to Bex. Right now, you need to rest."

I nodded reluctantly, but looked at Ash, wanting confirmation of what Ryan had said. When he gave a quick nod, I relented. "Then let's get out of here."

CHAPTER 51

RYAN

There were very few moments in my life that I could remember being absolutely petrified. The night my mom died, and when Beckett had first mentioned selling off Corinne if I refused to marry Madelaine, but neither moment held a candle to seeing Gary pointing a gun at Maddie, a split-second away from pulling the trigger.

A heartbeat was all the time I'd had to analyze the moment and react. I owed Court and Royal for all the hours they'd drilled marksmanship into me, all the hours spent at the gun range.

Even still, my hands shook a little as I looked at the woman sleeping next to me. After we'd arrived at Brookfield, I'd taken Maddie up to our room and helped her shower. She was practically a zombie, the adrenaline and shock of the night leaving her weak and fragile in a way I'd never seen.

I'd tucked her into bed and waited for her to fall asleep before I tried to get up to find Grandpa. I knew he'd have a lot of questions, and I needed to give him answers. But as soon as I started to move away, Maddie rolled toward me and fisted my shirt in her small hands, drawing me back into the bed.

The soft whimpers she made, so close to cries, broke my heart and didn't stop until I wrapped her in my arms. Once she was settled against my chest, I finally felt the knot of tension that had been wound around my heart start to loosen.

I couldn't stop touching her, my fingertips skimming over every curve and piece of soft skin I could reach. She was here and whole. We'd both survived Gary, and we both needed this moment.

Sleep came in fitful spurts. I was unable to completely relax as my body was attuned to every sharp intake of breath and sigh Maddie made when she moved.

I woke up again when the door to our room opened. Sunlight was streaming through the windows; Maddie had insisted on leaving the curtains and blinds open before going to sleep. But it wasn't morning; the golden-orange tones told me the sun was starting to set.

Grandpa appeared in the doorway, his expression somber. Eloise, his nurse, was behind his wheelchair.

"May I come in?" Grandpa asked quietly, looking more frail than I remembered. The change was startling and made my pulse pound in concern even as I nodded.

Eloise moved silently as she pushed him to the edge of the bed. Before she stepped away, her gaze swept across Maddie and softened. "Do either of you need anything?" she asked.

"No, thank you," I murmured with a small smile.

She ducked her head and nodded before leaving.

Grandpa sighed, looking at Maddie. "I'm sorry, my boy, I waited as long as I could, but I wanted to see that you were both all right before I went to bed."

My brows shot up. "What time is it?"

"A few minutes after five," he answered with a tired smile. "You'll have to forgive me—these days sleep seems to be the only thing I can manage with any sort of success, but I wanted to check on both of you."

I glanced at Maddie, at the perfect pink shade of her full lips, which matched the natural flush of her cheeks. "She's going to be okay."

"And you?" Grandpa was never one to let things slide, and the old man saw way too much.

"I can't stop imagining what would've happened if I hesitated a second or if my aim had been off," I admitted, my arms tightening reflexively around Madison.

"But you didn't, and it wasn't." He fixed me with a hard stare. "Worrying about outcomes that never happened won't help either of you."

"I know," I replied. "But it's hard."

Grandpa's gaze dropped to Madison, his expression similar to when he looked at Cori. "I'm glad you've found her."

"Me, too." My chest constricted as I watched her for a moment. This girl was part of my soul, and I couldn't live without her. I refused to live without her.

Maddie stirred in my arms, her lashes fluttering as her eyes opened. If she was surprised to see my grandfather sitting across from her, she didn't show it. She gave him a slow, lazy smile and mumbled, "Hi, Grandpa."

He beamed at her like she'd given him the greatest present in the world. He reached forward, his hand shaking as he touched hers. "How are you, my dear?"

Maddie's gaze flicked to me before responding. "Good, I think. Is everything okay?"

He patted her hand with a reassuring smile. "Everything is just fine."

Maddie gasped and started to sit up. "Cori—was her school hit by the earthquake?"

Fuck me, how had I forgotten about my sister? Then again, if something had been wrong, Grandpa would've told me immediately.

"She's just fine," he told us both. "Barely felt a thing. When I spoke to her, all she could talk about was coming here next week for the holidays."

Maddie blanched. "I forgot the holidays were so close."

"It's no wonder," Grandpa said with a rattling wheeze that turned into a bone-wracking cough.

Maddie swung out of bed and grabbed the box of tissues on the dresser even as the door opened and Eloise strode in. I sat up, watching as Maddie passed him a handful of tissues, and we exchanged glances as the coughs subsided and he lowered the tissues, now speckled with blood.

Eloise flashed us a tight smile that didn't meet her eyes. "I think it's time for you to rest, sir."

He nodded, looking more pale than when he'd come in. "I think you're right." He tried to force his lips into a grin for Maddie and me. "I'll see you both at breakfast in the morning, yes?"

I nodded, answering for us both. "Of course."

Grandpa's smile slipped as Eloise wheeled him out of the room. Maddie watched them go, looking like she wanted to help but didn't know how. Instead, she settled for closing the door and crawling back into bed with me, an unhappy frown pulling at her mouth.

Immediately I opened my arms and pulled her against my chest, then rolled onto my back so she was sprawled over me.

"He's worse." She sounded close to tears, and my heart constricted as I felt the same pain.

"Yeah," I admitted, my tone rough. "The doctors said he likely wouldn't make it to next year…"

Her lower lip trembled. "It's not fair."

I smoothed a lock of hair over her shoulder. "No, it isn't." I searched her eyes. "Hungry?"

"Sorta," she mumbled, ducking her head to lie on my bare chest as I traced lazy circles over her back.

I lost track of time, letting my thoughts wander to what lay ahead and relishing this moment of quiet with the woman I loved safe and sound.

Until she sat up and straddled my waist. I shot her a questioning look even as my cock woke up at the feel of her rubbing against me.

A small frown pulled at her brow as her lips twisted into a determined line. "Still mad at me?"

Honestly, I was too relieved to be mad at her, but another sort of fire burned in my gut as her warm center pressed against my abs. My hands went to her hips as I just barely resisted the urge to push her lower and grind my dick against her pussy.

She leaned over me, her golden hair falling like a silky curtain around her shoulders. I ached to wrap it in my fist. "I think I owe you an apology." The husky pitch of her voice had my cock twitching in my boxers.

A smirk pulled at my mouth, loving where her brain was going until I remembered that she'd been through hell the last few hours and I should really be thinking with a different head.

Fucking conscience.

I touched her jaw as her fingers curled into the waistband of my boxers. "Mads, hold up."

She paused, the uncertain look in her eyes breaking my heart a little. "You don't... want me?" The nervous way she bit her lower lip almost made me come in my boxers like a preteen.

With a low rumble, I pushed her down to feel how hard I was for her. Always for her. "Does this seem like I don't want you?"

The prettiest blush turned her cheeks pink. "Then what's the problem?"

I feathered my touch across the bandage on her forehead. "I just don't want you to push yourself."

Her hands splayed across my chest as she leaned over me, looking like a fucking goddess. "Maybe I *need* to be pushed right now. Maybe I just need you to remind me that we're alive and that I'm yours."

Goddamn. Her words were like a machete to my self-control. I was barely holding on.

"You were hurt," I protested, but it sounded weak.

Her lips curled in a deliciously deceptive way as she rocked herself lower against my cock. "No. I'm *hurting*, and you can help me out." Those wide blue eyes blinked at me with the most intoxicating mixture of innocence and love.

I groaned, feeling how damp she was through our clothes. "You're not fighting fair."

"I learned from the best," she teased, licking her lips as she gazed down at me.

Sighing, I folded my arms behind my head and shot her a daring look. If she wanted me, she had me. Always. "Do your worst, baby."

The grin she shot me was enough to test all my restraint. I wanted to flip her over and devour every fucking inch of her skin, to feel her taste on my tongue as she writhed against me before I drove inside her.

But my girl wanted *me*, so this was her show.

I was just along for the ride.

For now.

CHAPTER 52

MADDIE

I loved Ryan Cain with a sort of reverence that sometimes stole my breath. But now, staring down at him as he watched me and gave me total control, all I wanted to do was ride him like a pony at the damn derby.

I cringed at my internal monologue, because that *so* wasn't my best stuff, but all this skin and muscle on display would've short-circuited Einstein's brain, too. Seriously, what was a girl to do with her every fantasy available at her fingertips? This man was everything I'd ever wanted, and a lot I hadn't dared hope for. And now, we finally got to have our happily ever after.

I leaned down and captured his mouth with mine, enjoying the silky slide of our lips moving in tandem. I gave a soft moan, wrapping a hand around the back of his neck as I changed the angle to deepen the kiss.

His arms shook with restraint as he fought his natural instinct to take over. To dominate and own my body the way he craved. It said a lot that he was willing to give me free rein to explore him at my own pace.

I traced each divot and ridge of his pecs and abs, teasing the lines of his textbook perfect Adonis belt before running the tip of my finger around the edge of his waistband.

His tongue stroked mine in languid pulls that belied the energy starting to crackle around us. I panted above him, already feeling a sharp ache between my thighs where he belonged.

With a sigh, I moved my lips from his, peppering kisses across his jaw and down his throat while keeping my eyes raised to meet his gaze. I nipped and licked and kissed my way across his chest, enjoying the flash of fire in his eyes when my teeth grazed his nipples. Arms tucked behind his head, he looked utterly at ease... except for the way his body was drawn tight.

"Madison." The deep rumble of his voice chased shivers down my spine. I peered up at him through a fringe of lashes as I tongued the lines of his abdominal muscles and went lower still. He shifted his legs open to allow me space to kneel between them as I hooked my thumbs into the edges of his boxers and tugged them off.

He smirked as he lifted his hips to help me, his cock bobbing up to hit his stomach. I swallowed hard, already imagining the taste of him in my mouth as he stretched my lips wide.

"What I wouldn't give to know what you're thinking," he murmured, finally breaking the no-contact rule by reaching down and stroking my jaw.

My eyes lifted to his, unblinking. "I was thinking about how good you're going to taste."

His gaze turned fiery and the muscles of his chest seemed to spasm. "Fuck, I love you."

I grinned and turned my attention to his thick length. It twitched under my gaze before I even reached out to trace the angry looking vein on the underside of his shaft with a featherlight touch.

He groaned, the sound low and devastatingly masculine in a way that sent a fresh wave of arousal straight through my pussy. I rubbed my legs together, seeking some way to assuage the need to impale myself on his cock and take care of my needs first.

But no. I owed him an apology, and I wanted to make sure it was one that *really* conveyed how sorry I was for making him worry.

Dipping my head, I licked up the length of him before swirling my tongue around the head of his cock and sucking up the pearl of precum leaking from the tip.

"Fuck," he barked, arching back against the pillows, the muscles of his neck straining as he fisted his hands over his head.

I smirked. The powerful feeling of having him splayed beneath me, mine for the taking, was heady.

And I could do this for the rest of our lives.

Grinning to myself, I dove back in, sucking and licking in earnest until his hips started to lift and try to find my rhythm. As soon as he moved, I changed tactics until a light sheen of sweat glistened on his body.

"Maddie." His tone was a warning growl, letting me know he was seconds from snapping.

I hollowed my cheeks as I sucked him deep, his tip hitting the back of my throat. I swallowed around my gag reflex and felt him jerk on my tongue as I cupped his balls and squeezed gently.

"Christ," he hissed, hands suddenly tangling in my hair and holding me where he wanted so he could fuck my mouth and throat.

Everything in me softened as I let my defenses drop. There was something insanely sexy about witnessing him losing control and taking me the way he wanted. The way he *needed*.

When I was sure he was about to come in my mouth, he pulled me off his cock with an audible *pop* to tug me up his body. He manhandled me until my knees were sprawled on either side of his face, and then his mouth attacked my pussy without any preamble.

"Shit," I gasped, my hands flying to the headboard as I scrambled to find something to hold on to as his tongue speared deep inside me in rough, ragged thrusts.

"So fucking perfect," he muttered, his voice muffled. He sucked my clit into his mouth with a sharp tug that sent me careening headfirst into a blazing orgasm. I clenched my jaw, trying not to cry out, because there were other people in the house.

Ryan worked two fingers into my wet heat, rubbing my sensitive walls before hooking his fingers and caressing that soft spot that made my entire body clench. "Don't you dare hide those screams from me." He rubbed *that spot* again as his lips fastened around my clit, and it was too much.

A wholly uncontrolled shriek left my throat as I tried to scramble away from him, the pleasure so bright it bordered on painful. His hands locked on my thighs, holding my pussy to his face as he continued to ruin me.

I was a writhing, panting mess. My entire world was in flames as I rocked against him, the stubble of his jaw abrading the insides of my thighs. I slapped a palm on the wall as I shattered around him, coming again in hard waves that left spots dancing in my vision.

"Hands on the headboard," Ryan ordered, moving from between my legs and coming around behind me on the bed.

My fingers wrapped around the top of the headboard, my body always willing to obey even when I wasn't entirely sure I remembered how to breathe.

He tugged at my legs, positioning me just how he wanted, with my ass angled enough for him to fit himself against my opening. He nipped at my shoulder before whispering, "Don't let go, baby." Then he slammed inside of me with a guttural groan that made my toes curl.

He was impossibly large and big, and my swollen pussy rippled around him as I stretched to accommodate his invasion. He withdrew only to thrust back inside. The pace was brutal, and all I could do was feel as I surrendered every ounce of control to him.

His hands gripped my hips with enough force to bruise, and some primal part of me desperately wanted to wear those marks like a badge of honor. I wanted to look in the mirror and see the evidence of where he'd held me, reminding me that I belonged to him.

One hand slipped up my torso to roll and pinch one nipple and then the other. My back arched as I squeezed my eyes shut, giving myself over to the sensations he was wringing from my body as another orgasm started to coil low in my stomach.

I moaned, knowing this one would wreck me. Ruin me.

The hand kneading my breast slipped between my thighs and stroked my clit in firm circles.

"Too much," I whimpered, my head shaking back and forth as my legs started to tremble.

He kissed the side of my neck. "No, Maddie, it's never enough." He pinched my clit gently, and the scream I let loose was the byproduct of my soul leaving my damn body. I clamped down on his cock, feeling him jerk and pulse inside me as he came with his own hoarse cry.

My body twitched and shook as he rode me through the orgasm, and he caught me around the waist when I lost all control and collapsed. With exquisite care, he lowered me back onto the bed and lay down beside me as tears pricked at my eyes.

"Mads." He wiped one away with his thumb.

It had started as a game, but now, in this moment, the reality of what I'd done—what I'd *risked*—was crashing over me like a tidal wave, dragging me across a rocky and brittle bottom before sucking me out to sea.

"I'm sorry," I gasped around a ragged sob.

His lips pressed together in an unhappy line as he held me. "I know."

But the words fell from my lips unchecked, and borderline hysterical. "It was so stupid. I don't know why I had to go back in... And, Jesus, if you hadn't shown up..."

Holy shit.

I'd almost *died*.

Had literally been a breath away from a bullet to the head.

"I just needed it to be over. I couldn't spend the rest of our lives wondering when and if he'd show up." A slightly maniacal laugh bubbled out of me as the weight of what had happened crashed around me. "I couldn't stand him hurting you or Bex or anyone else ever again."

"Shhh," he murmured, his arms strong and solid as they anchored me to this moment. "You're okay. *We're* okay."

"I'm sorry," I blubbered again, sniffling as I looked up at him with blurry eyes.

He sighed and shook his head before pressing his hand in the flat space between my breasts. "It's who you are, Maddie. Sometimes you're reckless, but you do it because of *this*." He tapped his index finger against my skin. "Your heart is so big, baby, and that's one of the things I love about you. I'd never change that, okay? Ever."

"Even when I do stupid shit?" I whispered.

He snorted. "I think we can both agree that *your* stupid shit doesn't hold a candle to mine."

A soft laugh eased some of the tension in my chest as I curled into him.

"But," he added, "I'd *really* appreciate it if you'd keep the *almost being killed by a psychopath* tally to just one, deal?"

I kissed his chest and nodded, suddenly sleepy again. "Deal."

CHAPTER 53

MADDIE

Mrs. Flounders wrapped her arms around me the moment I stepped into the kitchen the next morning. Ryan had grabbed us a quick snack the night before, but I'd been too wrung out —emotionally *and* physically—to do more than pick at a few things before falling asleep again. We'd showered before coming downstairs... which, because we were us, led to a lot more than loofahs being rubbed over each other's skin. But by the time we were done, I was starving.

Judging by the array of food on the island and the pack of ravenous man-boys crowded around, I wasn't the only one.

As soon as she let me go to return to the stove, Mrs. Beechum, the house manager, stepped in to grab me into another bone-crushing and soul-affirming hug. After a moment, she held me away from her body, checking me over for herself with a stern eye. She made an unhappy noise when she spotted my bandage and then each a new bruise. Then she turned her annoyed look at Ryan, who hovered at my back. "It's your job to keep her safe."

Ryan's hand settled on my hip, firm and reassuring. "Yes, ma'am."

I gave a small, unhappy sigh at the displeasure in his tone, because I knew he stupidly blamed himself for me being hurt.

Seriously, was there anything more sad than an alpha male who believed he'd failed his little woman?

I bit back a snort, because judging by the testosterone-heavy vibe in this room, that joke wouldn't land well. I needed Bex back. And maybe Tyler.

"I have to check on some things, but you tell me if you need absolutely anything," Mrs. Beechum ordered me.

I nodded. "I will. Thanks."

She scoffed. "No, you won't." She pointed at each guy. "I expected *all* of you to watch out for her."

She was met by a chorus of "yes, ma'am's" that seemed to appease her before she left.

"Has anyone heard anything about Chase?" I asked.

Bishop shot me a smile from where he sat at the kitchen table near the bank of windows overlooking the backyard. "Made it out of surgery fine. Looks like he'll make a full recovery."

"Tyler said her uncle is already talking about having them flown back to London," Ash added, sitting across from Bishop with a plate piled high with food.

It took seconds for the stacks of pancakes, waffles, eggs, sausage, hash browns, and bacon to be decimated by these guys as Knight, Linc, and Royal finished filling their plates and joined the others at the table.

Ryan nudged me forward, indicating I should get my own plate. I didn't need any further prompting as I grabbed some of everything, deeply inhaling the scent of my favorite breakfast foods. "And Bex?"

"Court says she's fine. Her mom's doing good, too. Probably be discharged tomorrow." Linc popped a piece of bacon into his mouth.

"Where is he?" I asked, looking around for our missing friend and wondering if he somehow stayed behind to watch out for—or stalk—Bex.

"Meeting with Linus," Bishop replied. "With all the shit that went down, it's a bit of a legal clusterfuck, so they're dealing with it."

Ryan went to the coffee machine and poured himself a cup, then got me an orange juice.

I eyed the plate of bacon, wondering how pissed Ryan would be if I took what was left for myself. With an inward sigh, I left half of it for him.

Because true love was sharing the last strips of bacon on the plate instead of eating them all yourself.

"Court will be here in a few hours," Knight told us, and sipped his own coffee. He looked at me. "He's got a plan for how you can get rid of the whole restraining order thing and start getting your life back to normal."

I dropped into the seat beside Ash with a snort. "What's even normal anymore? Back to the trailer park?"

"Cute," Ryan remarked, setting my juice and his coffee down before getting his own plate.

Mrs. Flounders hovered in the background. "Does anyone want more? I always forget how much you boys eat." She shook her head, amused. "And I have no idea where you put it."

"I think we're good," Ryan assured her, even going as far as to give her a small, one-armed hug.

She blushed and patted her apron. "Well, I have some things to look after, but just leave your dishes in the sink when you're finished." Her steely eyed gaze landed on me, her brows arching. "That means you, young lady. You need your rest. I'll handle the cleanup."

I mean, all I had done was make everyone clean up after themselves after Thanksgiving a few weeks earlier. Although, it had been pretty hilarious, watching the guys awkwardly juggle dishes and look unsure about where things went when I led them into the kitchen after the meal.

I ducked my head as Linc muttered, "Kiss ass." So, of course, I kicked his shin under the table and smirked when he winced and sucked in a sharp breath.

Ryan sat down beside me and started eating. "The sooner we get that shit handled, the better I'll feel." He looked at Royal. "Are you guys staying stateside for the holidays?"

Royal nodded, holding a mug of coffee in his hands. "Yeah. We want to stay close since we don't know what's happening with Grandpa, and Kent's been quiet lately."

Linc grimaced. "Yeah, my dad stopped returning my calls. I have no idea what the fucker's planning next, but he's gotta know things are closing in around them. I mean, Beckett ran, and Gary's dead. That leaves him and Jasper holding the bag, and there's a fuckton of Russian Bratva looking for them to deliver on shit they can't."

Knight rolled his eyes. "That's redundant, dude."

"Huh?"

"Bratva *is* the Russian mafia. Saying Russian Bratva is like saying the same thing twice."

"Whatever," Linc muttered, waving a dismissive fork. "Point is, they're laying low, and we might actually have a few weeks before you guys are needed… elsewhere."

I looked around at Court's half-brothers. "How often are you guys away?"

"Often enough." Royal's cagey answer was compounded by a flinty stare that dared me to ask any more questions he couldn't—or wouldn't—answer. If the guy wasn't so amazing with Cori, and hadn't saved my ass, I'd have kicked him in the nuts weeks ago.

"A few weeks would be nice," Ash admitted, rubbing the back of his neck. He looked exhausted. "We need to handle the flash drives, the restraining order, find a new house, and Gary's estate—"

"The estate that's currently halfway in the valley?" I quipped, popping a bite of egg into my mouth.

Bishop laughed. "Sure, but he had houses in several other countries, as well as investments that we didn't fully eliminate, and that means that *you* are his sole heir, Madison."

"Yeah, but no way did he leave everything to me," I argued.

"Don't be so sure," Ash warned. "A lot of the inheritance by-laws in our families say it has to go to a living blood relative. You're the last one standing, Mads. Even if Gary had wanted to cut you out, he couldn't."

I tensed. "Can't I just give it all away? Again?"

Ryan inclined his head. "You can. I mean, we certainly don't need the money, but there's also nothing wrong with holding on to things for a little while. There's no rush anymore. You can take your time, and some of those places have been in the Cabot family for generations, baby."

I shrugged, not wanting to show that the history of my family *did* intrigue me a little. I mean, they couldn't all be as maniacal and fucked up as Gary had been... right?

I'd always liked history, so maybe it could be kind of fun to learn some of my own.

Suddenly, I groaned. "Shit. I guess at this point I should plan on repeating my senior year, huh?"

Ash grinned at me. "Nah. There was an earthquake, and while the school wasn't damaged, people are already calling in with their excuses. The school board already said all finals will be done remotely over winter break."

"And you were ahead in a lot of your classes," Ryan chimed in, a note of praise in his voice. "You'll be fine."

"Or, if you fail, Ash can just give you whatever grade you want," Linc finished with a smirk.

I flipped him off.

"What?" Linc looked confused around a mouthful of food, but Royal just shook his head before he looked at me with a bit more respect.

I straightened my shoulders and arched a brow, because fuck him if he thought I would be happy to coast by. I'd earned every single one of my good grades, and they meant something.

Ryan wrapped an arm around the back of my seat, almost unconsciously, as he kept eating with one hand.

"So, what's the plan for today?" I asked, looking around the group. It felt weird not to have something looming over my head.

Ryan shot me a look. "You're resting."

I wrinkled my nose and rolled my eyes. "I rested plenty."

"Don't argue with him," Ash begged, shaking his head. "Just let him play Florence Nightingale and take care of you, okay? Otherwise he'll be up *our* asses."

"First, fuck off," Ryan snapped, but there was little heat behind his words as he played with the ends of my hair. "And second, I'd make a fucking amazing nurse."

I patted his leg. "You totally do, babe."

He narrowed his eyes at me. "You didn't seem to have a problem with me taking care of you last night." His gaze heated. "Or this morning."

Bishop choked on his juice as the other grinned. I felt my cheeks and ears heat as I ducked my chin.

Ash pushed away from the table. "Cool, so we'll all just do our own thing and meet up when Court's back, yeah?" He didn't wait for an answer as he grabbed his coffee and took off. Within seconds, the others vanished as well.

I turned and arched a brow at Ryan. "You know how to clear a room."

He smirked, angling his body to face mine. "Got you alone, didn't I?" He leaned in and kissed me, tasting like coffee and bacon, and all I could do was give a happy little sigh because this? This was everything.

When Court showed up several hours later, he was all business, and if I hadn't known he was on my side, I'd have probably headed for the barn. He definitely wasn't a happy man, and I suspected it had everything to do with my best friend and the way she was icing him out of her life.

Spreading a few stacks of folders on the coffee table in the parlor, Court sat across from Ryan and I in a large armchair.

"The courts will be back up and running on Monday," he started, jumping in headlong. "Linus and I set up a meeting first thing to have the restraining order vacated."

I couldn't hide my surprise. "L.A. just got hit by an earthquake, and they're already reopening things?"

Court smirked a bit. "Yeah, it's not our first quake, Maddie. Structurally, downtown is fine. The power grids and cell towers have all been restored, and we have a tiny window to get your shit handled before the courts close for the holidays."

I sucked in a deep breath and nodded. I definitely wanted this handled sooner rather than later. I'd like to go into the next year without worrying about Ryan being arrested for holding my hand in public.

"Any word on charges being filed?" Ryan asked the question casually, but my heart immediately slammed against my ribs.

"You'll all need to go to the police station and make a formal statement, but when we compile it with the evidence of the shit he was having done to Maddie at Highwater and she makes her own statement, I can't see the police pressing charges." Court rolled his massive shoulders in a shrug that made it seem like this was just another day at the office.

"But Ryan shot Gary," I murmured, shuddering at the memory.

"And Gary was going to shoot *you*," Court replied gently. "It's justifiable homicide. We have plenty of witnesses who can back that up. He kidnapped Bex, manipulated you to come to him, shot Chase and that other guard he was with." He shook his head. "It's pretty clear cut, Maddie."

"Okay," I said, my voice tiny as I forced myself to trust what he was saying as truth.

Court grabbed another folder and held it out to me. I took it with caution, then flipped it open and saw a bunch of documents that made me frown. "What's this?"

"Deeds to the properties Gary owned around the globe," he replied.

Shit. There were several pages, and I realized there were also estimates on the property values. With each page I turned, my eyes got bigger.

"I own all of this?" My voice trembled, and I felt Ryan shift beside me so his thigh was pressed to mine, silently offering comfort and support.

Court nodded. "Well, not officially. The morgue will release the death certificate in the next few days, then we can start the claims procedures, but for all intents and purposes, yes. You own these properties outright, Maddie."

"Damn," I whispered, stunned. I could sell them and live off that money for the next hundred years without lifting a finger.

"You don't have to decide anything right now," Ryan reminded me, his tone gentle and firm.

I met his eyes and felt relief trickle down my veins. I wasn't alone; I didn't have to sort this out by myself. "Right. What else?"

Court hesitated, his fingers brushing another file. "These are Gary's business assets. Partnerships and shares he holds. We figured out a few weeks ago, when he took you, that he was hiding some things, and I think I found most of it. He filed a lot of the paperwork in Madelaine's name."

I frowned, confused. "Why?"

"Probably to keep his connections buried a little more, but we'll never really know. The thing is, *you're* legally Madelaine, and you're eighteen. So, almost everything is yours, and that might not be a good thing," he admitted, his dark eyes flashing to Ryan for a beat.

Ryan sighed heavily. "How bad?"

I watched them with anxiety niggling in my gut. Clearly they both knew something I didn't.

Court grimaced. "Enough to cause problems."

"Fuck," Ryan grunted, his jaw tight.

I raised a tentative hand. "One of you want to clue me in?"

"Gary invested in some shady shit under your sister's name. That way, if things went wrong, his name wouldn't be on the line. *He couldn't be arrested.*" Court gave me a hard look.

"Illegal stuff?"

He nodded. "There's two ways to handle it. The first is the easiest —we dump all your shares and get the name Madelaine Cabot removed from any and everything involved in the barely legal and outright illegal venues."

"How illegal are we talking?" I asked, afraid of the answer.

"A few massage parlors across Europe and Asia with less than willing workers," Court replied. "Some factories that are violating child labor laws set up by the foreign trade commissions."

I felt sick. "But can't we just… shut them down?"

Ryan covered my hand with his. "It's not that easy, baby."

My head swung to him. "Make it that easy. Can't Phoenix do something?"

He squeezed my icy fingers. "We can and we will, but it'll take time."

I opened my mouth to protest, but Court cut me off.

"He's right, Maddie. We'll add it to the list of things Phoenix will handle, but we can't just go in guns blazing. That's how people die. Dismantling organizations like these take time, or else they pop right back up." He gave me a steady look. "But in the meantime, we don't want you being pulled into a legal nightmare if things go public."

"You said there were two options. What's the other?" I pressed.

He pressed his mouth into a hard line. "You come clean to the world about who you are. We have enough proof that you're Madison Porter. You can be *you* again, but that also comes with its own complications."

"Such as?" My gaze flicked back and forth between them.

Court rubbed the back of his neck. "We'll have to have Madelaine legally declared dead, which makes everything in *her* name a lot more complicated. Everything you've done has been as your twin, Maddie. Everything in Gary's and Madelaine's names will be under scrutiny while shit gets sorted in the legal system."

"How long would it take?" Ryan asked, swiping his thumb over his bottom lip as he stared at the folders in front of us.

"Years?" Court guessed, leaning back against his seat. "The problem is, those companies in Madelaine's name might decide to cut their losses or worse."

Well, *that* didn't sound good at all. "I'm afraid to ask."

Court exhaled hard and looked at me. "A lot of these businesses Gary helped set up in your sister's name might decide it's easier to set a fire and burn everything to the ground before moving on. And by everything, I mean everything and every*one*."

Horror wrapped around my throat like the unyielding fingers of death, squeezing the air from my lungs. "They'd kill the people they're abusing?"

Ryan wrapped an arm around my shoulders. "Yeah. It's what they do, Mads."

"So, my choices are to keep living as my dead twin but potentially keep other people safe until we can free them," I looked at them both for nods of confirmation before adding, "or take my life back and potentially threaten the lives of countless other people?"

"I guess the real question is," Court summarized, "how much does being Madison Porter mean to you? Or can you live with being Madelaine Cabot for the rest of your life?"

CHAPTER 54

MADDIE

I needed a break, so I left Court and Ryan to hash out a few more Phoenix things with the others. I knew Ryan would've come with me in a heartbeat, but I wanted a few minutes to think things over for myself.

It should've been an easy decision. I'd been Madelaine Cabot for months already, and it was the safest option all around. The path of least resistance.

But I'd be lying if I didn't admit that there was a big part of me that just wanted to be Madison Porter. For people to realize that I wasn't the girl who had done the unspeakable things my twin had done. And an even bigger part of me that wanted to be completely done with the name *Cabot*.

I was wandering aimlessly through the downstairs when I heard Grandpa call me from the half-open door of his study. Without missing a beat, I poked my head in a smiled. "Did you need something?"

His face relaxed into an easy grin from the other side of his desk in a way that reminded me of Ryan and Cori. "I simply wanted to know if there was something I could do for *you*? You've wandered past my office twice now."

I frowned. Shit, had I? God, this house was big.

He chuckled and waved a hand. "Please, come in and sit, my dear. Keep an old man company."

I rolled my eyes and stepped inside. "You're not that old."

He shot me a pointed look before sighing. "Some days I feel much older than I ever imagined possible."

I sat down in one of the chairs across from his desk and tried not to be obvious in the way I studied him. In the four weeks since I'd seen him, he seemed to have lost even more weight he couldn't afford to. His skin had a sunken, gray pallor, and his eyes seemed even more bleary.

Barbed wire wrapped around my heart and squeezed as I realized that Ryan was right; he was dying.

He made a soft sound of discontent. "Don't look at me like that, dear. I'm not in my grave quite yet."

"I'm sorry," I apologized quickly, feeling like an ass. "I didn't mean—"

"I know you didn't." He cut me off with a fond look. "But that doesn't mean it won't be soon."

I stayed quiet, sensing that he wasn't finished.

Looking out the window that overlooked the vineyard, he sighed. "I wish I could have one more season. The fields are vibrant and full of life in a way that's centering. You'll find that out for yourself."

"I hope so," I confessed. "When I asked Ryan to take me home… this was the only place I could think of that felt like that."

A wobbly smile tipped up the corners of his mouth. "I'm glad to hear that. This is your home, Madison, for as long as you like. My wife said the same thing to me, that this land always felt like *home*. I want you to be as happy here as we were."

"I'd like that." Emotion lodged in my throat.

"Now, care to tell me what has you so upset that you're pacing holes in the floors?" A tiny sparkle lit his eyes. "If it's that grandson of mine, he's not too old for me to set him straight."

The idea of Grandpa laying into Ryan was amusing, and I warred with the smile trying to pull at my mouth. "No, he's been great." I regarded him for a moment. "You raised him well."

He ducked his head in appreciation.

"Court was giving me my options," I explained, quickly laying out what we'd discussed.

Grandpa listened attentively, frowning and nodding as I told him everything and why I was struggling. "Not to quote Shakespeare, but it *is* just a name."

"I know." I huffed a breath. "I'm being stupid, aren't I?"

"I didn't say that," he replied. "I can see why you want to distance yourself from your father's legacy. He caused a lot of pain, as did your sister. By carrying on that name, you'll inherit all their shame to some degree. It's unavoidable. The same way Ryan will always be known, to an extent, as Beckett Cain's son."

I paused. "I never thought of it that way."

"Why not?" Grandpa arched a brow.

"Because Ryan's more than that, and so is the Cain name." I frowned. "He started Phoenix, and he's doing everything in his power to change the way the world views his last name and his family."

Grandpa smiled, like I'd just given the correct answer to ace this test.

"The name doesn't matter," I murmured, folding my hands on my lap. "It doesn't matter what they did—it matters what I *do*."

"You have the power to make the Cabot name mean something genuine and true again," he added. "Not all Cabots were horrible humans. Besides, do you honestly think my grandson will let you run around with the last name Cabot again for very long?"

I giggled. "Probably not." I looked at my barren left finger. "I don't even know what happened to my rings," I whispered. Somewhere in the shuffle of being kidnapped and locked away, the rings had been stripped away. Who knew if I'd ever get them back?

That loss hit deep, and it was all I could do to blink back tears. I was so tired of *losing* things. Maybe it was time to reclaim them on my terms.

"Do you know what made those rings so special?" Grandpa asked.

"Ryan said that you got them when you both had nothing," I replied. "It meant that your love meant more than material items."

"True, but they were special because of the people who wore them. Those rings symbolized the love I had for my wife, and she for me." He met my eyes with a steady, reassuring gaze. "Perhaps it's time for you and Ryan to find your own symbols to represent *you* and what you share."

"You always know just what to say," I murmured, shaking my head in awe. "How do you do that?"

"I lived a life full of love," he answered. "And I've found that all the answers to every question can usually be discovered in that foundation." He started to reach for a pen, but his fingers shook too hard to grasp it.

I slowly stood. "Do you want me to—"

"If you wouldn't mind," he said, lowering his hand with a tired smile, "would you please get Eloise? I think I'll take a quick rest."

"Of course." I turned for the door.

"Madison?"

I turned back, expectant. "Yes?"

The gratitude in his eyes was humbling, staggering. "Thank you for everything you've done for my family."

"They're my family, too," I reminded him.

He nodded and smiled. "Right you are, my girl. Right you are."

CHAPTER 55

MADDIE

After getting Eloise for Grandpa, I wandered out the back door and toward the barn and the sounds of playful puppy yips. I was greeted with waves and smiles from the stable staff, and I stayed out of the way as they led some of the horses out to a pasture for exercise.

The cool air whipped into the open barn, but it couldn't quite chase away the lingering warmth left over from all the animals it housed. I followed the sounds of the puppies to a stall at the end of a row.

The mother, a gorgeous chocolate Labrador with golden eyes, looked up at me from where she stood with no less than nine puppies jumping around her. She seemed to give me a look that said *and you think you have problems*.

Smiling, I let myself into the space and sat down. It wasn't a second before the puppies scampered to me, abandoning their mother in favor of a new chew toy. With a huff, the mother lay down and closed her eyes.

I lost track of time as I played with the puppies, watching them roll and pounce with adorable awkwardness until, one by one, they crawled over to their mother and snuggled against her to sleep. Eventually I was left with a single puppy, who seemed more content to sleep on my lap while I stroked his fur.

Resting my head against the wall, I let my eyes drift shut as I petted the innocent life in my lap.

"Should I be offended that you think a barn floor is more comfortable than our bed?" Ryan teased, unlatching the door and stepping inside the stall to kneel beside me.

I lazily opened my eyes with a smile. "Our bed doesn't have puppies."

An odd look crossed his face, and he looked at the puppy I was holding. "You want a dog?"

I glanced down at the sleeping thing. "One day? Maybe?" I shrugged. "I never really had a pet. There was this old alley cat that I used to think was mine. I fed him scraps from dinner and breakfast. Then he bit me, and I needed a tetanus shot."

Ryan snorted and shook his head as he sat beside me. "Jesus, Maddie."

"Did you have pets growing up?" I asked, curious. We didn't talk about his childhood much, and I knew it was a sore topic.

He scoffed in disbelief. "Please, have you *met* my father? That's a hard no. But Mom would bring us here, and there was always something furry to play with." He reached over and rubbed the puppy's muzzle. "But having a dog might be cool." He nudged my shoulder with a smile. "One day."

I leaned my head against his shoulder and exhaled, happy just to be with him.

"I hate to push, but have you thought about what Court said?" he asked, almost hesitant. It was always strange when he sounded anything less than utterly confident.

I nodded. "I actually talked to Grandpa about it before I came out here."

"He's usually my go-to for advice, too," he admitted, tracing the puppy's tail with a finger. "What'd he say?"

"A lot," I replied, "but I think the most important takeaway was that no matter what name I pick, the history attached to it doesn't matter. What matters is us moving forward." I turned and looked him in the eye. "I'm keeping Madelaine's name. It makes the most sense. And, in a lot of ways, Madison Porter did die months ago. I can't go back to who I used to be, even if I wanted to."

"I don't care what your name is on a piece of paper. And Grandpa's right, baby, it doesn't matter."

"But it could," I added. "I could make the Cabot name mean something good, right?"

The corner of his mouth lifted in a smirk. "You think you're keeping that last name for much longer? I got rid of it once, and I have every intention of doing it again."

"I might hold you to that," I said, only half-teasing. "But I think we both have enough going on right now without worrying about resurrecting me from the dead and all the paperwork it entails. Especially not if more innocent people could get hurt."

"You're sure?"

"Yeah. I mean, at the end of the day, I'm still me, right?" I made a soft, dismissive noise as the idea fully settled with me. "But there is something I'd like to do, if that's okay."

"Name it," he replied without a second thought.

"I don't give a fuck about Gary, but I want to bury my mom," I confessed. "It doesn't have to be anything formal or fancy, but she... She had a hard life. I'd like to give her whatever peace she might be able to find in death."

Ryan studied me for a moment before leaning in and brushing his lips against my forehead. "You're something pretty fucking spectacular, Maddie."

Two days later, I'd just finished slipping a pearl stud into my earlobe when my phone rang. I reached for it and smiled when I saw Bex's name on the display. "Hey," I greeted as I paused getting ready to talk to her.

"Seriously, I'm the worst best friend," she started. "Maddie, I should be there."

"Bex, you didn't even know my mom," I said with a soft laugh. "And *your* mom just got out of the hospital, remember?"

She made a grumbling noise. "I'm *well* aware. She's... Well, she was always really intense, but this accident seems to have done something else to her."

"Meaning?" I frowned.

"I don't know," she rushed out, and I could hear the frustration in her tone. "But she kicked my dad out, and I'm pretty sure she's hired a divorce attorney. She's supposed to be resting, but she seems to be totally focused on *something*. I just don't know what."

"I'm sorry," I murmured, wishing things were easier for her. "How's your ankle?"

"Sore," she muttered. "But I'm hoping I can ditch the walking boot in a couple days, since the swelling is going down."

"See? You need to rest your foot, not be up here when I bury my mom." My voice cracked a little at the end.

Bex sighed. "Babe, seriously. I can be there in a few hours."

I cleared my throat as the shower turned off in the en suite. "No. Besides, we're coming back after the funeral, so we'll be at the courthouse first thing tomorrow."

"You ready for that?" she asked.

No. I'd have to give a formal deposition about the night of the earthquake and all the shit my father had done. Ash had spent the last two days compiling video and digital proof to back up everything I had to confess to the police.

My stomach twisted in knots at the idea of reliving the worst moments of the last several months. But the thing that still bugged me was that Gary would get away with the crime I most desperately wanted him to pay for: murdering my twin sister.

"It'll be fine," I finally said. "Court and Linus will be with me the whole time, and I know they'll make sure everything goes according to plan."

"Are we still on for dinner?" she asked. Since we'd be back in Los

Angeles, we'd all decided to meet up for dinner somewhere local to see her.

"Yeah," I replied as Ryan stepped out of the bathroom. My gaze couldn't help but linger on all the wet skin and muscles he was showing, a white towel wrapped low around his hips. He paused on the way to his dresser, arching a telling brow.

I huffed and turned away, averting my gaze before I could do something like hang up on my bestie and climb him like a jungle gym.

Besides, I'd already done that this morning.

Twice.

The fiery phoenix tattoo on his back rippled with each movement he made, tempting and taunting me to come closer and feel the warmth of the skin beneath the flames.

"Maddie?" Bex prompted.

I'd missed whatever she'd said. Crap. "Sorry. I got… distracted."

Ryan chuckled, the low sound sending a bolt of heat straight to my core. Without turning, I flipped him off over my shoulder. Asshole knew exactly what he was doing.

"Right," Bex drawled, not needing to be here to read between the lines. "Look, call me later if you aren't busy, okay?"

I laughed. "Zero promises. Thanks for calling, B."

"Anytime, Mads." She hung up, and I tossed the phone aside and turned around. I was mildly disappointed when I saw Ryan already had on a pair of black pants and was working on buttoning up a white shirt that made his skin look golden.

"Bex?" He glanced at me and tucked in his shirt.

"Yeah. She was checking in." I watched his hands get dangerously close to where—

I groaned and turned away.

"You good, baby?" He was laughing at me.

"There's got to be something wrong with me," I muttered, putting in the other earring. "I'm about to bury my mom and all I can think about is—"

His arms came around me from behind, hugging my back to his chest. "Think about what?"

A shiver rolled down my spine. I loved when he used that rough, growly tone with me. It made everything in me come alive.

But seriously, I needed to get my hormones under control.

Sighing, I turned and stepped back. "How do I look?"

"Stunning," he replied, reaching around to anchor his fingers around the back of my neck. "Mads, there's no pressure for today, all right?"

"Why am I nervous?" I tugged at the hem of my black dress. It was new; I'd had to go into town yesterday to buy a funeral dress while my mother's ashes were brought up to Northern California. The plan was to drive out to a small, rocky bay forty-five minutes northeast to spread her ashes.

My stomach twisted. She'd been cremated before I'd had a chance to claim her body. Ash had tracked down her remains to a mortuary several hundred miles away, where what was left would've been destroyed if she'd been left there indefinitely.

Ryan sighed and watched me, and I could see him struggling with how to comfort me. He didn't get it. His mother had been his world at one point, and he still mourned her to some extent. But Beckett was gone, and Ryan wouldn't have lifted a finger to recover *any* remains of his father's.

My mom had hurt me in more ways than I could count. She'd been a horrible excuse for a mother, but there was still this bond that just wouldn't let me leave her to rot in some unknown locker until she was disposed of with a bunch of other unnamed, unclaimed people.

"This is depressing," I muttered, edging backward until my legs hit the bed and I sat down.

Ryan came to stand in front of me. "It's a funeral, babe. They're not exactly known for their party atmosphere."

"Am I doing the right thing?" I tipped up my head and looked at him.

"Maddie, I gave up trying to figure out why you do the things you do," he admitted.

My jaw dropped. "Thanks."

"Stop." He held my face in his hands. "I just mean, there's a goodness in you that I'll never understand. I'm not built that way, but I love that you are. I love that you're compassionate and forgiving. In fact, I *really* love how forgiving you are."

I rolled my eyes and lightly punched his stomach.

"Just because I wouldn't do this doesn't mean it's wrong," he finished. "It just means you've got a big heart, and I hope that never changes."

I stood and wrapped my arms around his waist. "Thank you."

He kissed the top of my head as someone knocked on the door before pushing it open. Ash stuck his head inside. "The, uh, car just dropped off... We can leave whenever you're ready." He shot me a tight smile.

"Ready to go?" Ryan asked me, leaning back to look in my eyes.

"Yeah." I took in a deep breath and exhaled hard, feeling another chip I'd been carrying around start to break free. Maybe one day they'd all be gone, but for right now, it was a start.

CHAPTER 56

MADDIE

"A toast," Linc declared the following night, standing up like the ridiculous host of what he was calling our biggest win. He raised his beer bottle and pointed it at me across the table. "To Maddie, for being an absolute badass."

Ryan's fingers traced a loose pattern on my shoulder, the arm he'd draped around me a comfort anchoring me in the moment. We were dining in the back of some fancy restaurant high above the Los Angeles skyline as the sun set in the background. It was like something out of a movie, but I was too tired to really care.

The day had begun with a long, drawn-out court session featuring a lot of big words. But ultimately the restraining order against Ryan was declared null and void. When I'd finished hashing out everything Gary had done to me, the judge—not the same one Gary had paid off—looked more than a little ashamed at how the legal system had failed me.

Then we'd spent several hours at the police station as I gave my account of what had happened the night Gary was shot. It had taken forever, and I was wrung out by the end, even though Linus and Court sat with me the entire time, interjecting on my behalf when the questions became a little too probing.

I'd been given the option to wait at Bex's house with her while Ryan and the others went in for questioning, but I'd been determined to stay put in case they needed me. Hours in a hard, plastic chair had left my butt numb and my lower back aching.

Now, with everything out in the open and the police and lawyers agreeing that Ryan's shooting was justifiable homicide, it felt like I could actually take a deep breath. Some of the iron bands that had been shackled around my chest, constricting my air for weeks, were finally unlocked. And while what I really wanted was to crawl into the massive bed in the suite Ryan had reserved for us in some overpriced hotel, I knew my friends had been looking forward to a celebratory dinner. Bex had even smiled at Court when she'd walked in.

Well, until she'd realized her lips were moving without her permission. Then she'd spun away and hugged me to cover it up.

Now, seated in the private room in a place with no prices on the menu, surrounded by Ryan, Bex, Ash, Linc, and Court, I was trying to enjoy myself even though it felt like hours past my bedtime. I could totally handle this for an hour. Maybe two.

Linc tipped back his drink, taking a long sip. "We should hit some clubs after this."

Oh, *hell* no.

"Maybe you can carry on the party without us," Ryan suggested in a wry tone, his knowing gaze drifting over me in a way that always made me feel seen and valued.

I shot him a grateful smile.

"Ah," Linc hummed, nodding, "you two planning your own private party to celebrate the fact that you're allowed to legally be together?" He waggled his eyebrows.

I picked up an artfully crafted dinner roll and lobbed it at his head.

He caught it and ripped a big bite out with his teeth even as Ash leaned over from the other side and cuffed the back of his head.

Linc yelped and ducked, looking wounded. "Dude. The fuck was that for?"

"For you being a tactless dumbass," Ash muttered, rolling his eyes.

I cleared my throat. "Did you talk to Tyler?" He'd planned on reaching out today after we'd learned from the police that they'd already spoken to Chase at the hospital.

Ash nodded. "Yeah. Chase is cleared to fly, so they're leaving tomorrow morning to go back to England."

Disappointment settled low in my gut. I'd hoped for the chance to talk to Chase in person and thank him for trying to help me.

As if reading my thoughts, Ryan made an annoyed sound in his throat, still blaming Chase for the fact that I was in that room with Gary in the first place. I was pretty certain Ryan was under the impression that Chase's bullet wound was penance for putting me at risk.

Linc sighed and signaled the waiter to bring him another beer. Seriously, there was a waiter hovering by the entrance of our space, just waiting for people to give him commands. When I'd been a server, I'd juggled several tables at a time and prayed I made enough in tips to cover our trailer's rent.

"I'm down for going out after," Court said with a shrug. His sharp gaze danced over to Bex, like he was daring her to either join in or call him out.

Linc grinned and clapped a hand on his shoulder. "Hell yes. It's been a while since you were my wingman, bro. You're an awesome sidekick."

Court scoffed. "Please. I've never been the Robin to your Batman, asshole."

Linc's eyes glittered, and he looked across the table to Bex, who sat at my left. "What do you say, B? Wanna see what kind of trouble we can get into?"

She shot him a withering look. "Yeah, because this boot screams *fuck me, big boy*."

Linc blinked slowly. "Is that what you… need?"

She smirked a little. "Wouldn't you like to know."

I was pretty certain I heard Court's teeth crack from how hard he was clenching his jaw. I exchanged a look with Ryan, but he didn't seem concerned.

"And I can't," Bex said with a heavy breath. "I have to pack."

"Pack?" I echoed, looking at her in surprise.

She nodded, her expression rueful. "Yeah. My mom is insisting we spend the holiday break with my grandparents in Europe."

My heart sank. "Seriously?" I'd known it was a possibility, but I hated the idea of my bestie being so far away for *weeks*.

Bex's lips flattened into a grim sort of smile. "Yeah. I mean, it won't be *all* bad. Shopping in Paris and Milan, visiting some of the coolest museums." She nudged me. "You could come and spend some time with me."

That *did* sound kind of fun, but I knew this holiday was important to Ryan because of Grandpa. Besides, it was Cori's first Christmas without her dad, and she seemed to be struggling with that.

Beckett Cain sucked as a father, but Corinne's kindness and innocence quickly let her forget and rewrite the history so he wasn't always a massive twatwaffle to her. As other kids in her school got excited about going home to see their parents for Christmas, Corinne had started saying she couldn't wait to see her daddy, too.

Grandpa and Ryan had been talking about it last night, and I knew they were worried about her. Part of Corinne's disabilities made her guileless and way too forgiving of past wrongs. It was easy to see how Beckett had been able to manipulate her. All she wanted was to be loved, and she would've done anything to gain her father's acceptance.

"Maybe," I hedged, giving Bex a tiny smile for an answer.

Her face fell a little, because we both knew that this year, I wouldn't be running around Europe with her.

"But you'll have fun," I said, forcing myself to be happy for her.

She sighed. "I'd stay here, but Mom has been really weird lately, and I think she needs this break."

"Is your dad going?"

She shook her head. "No. She hit him with divorce papers today."

"Shit," Linc murmured. "Seriously?"

Bex looked less than happy. "Yeah. I mean, I know it's for the best. They've hated each other for years, but it's still weird, you know? I'm pretty sure my dad will move to the East Coast to be closer to work, since his government contracts were renewed."

"Makes sense," Ash said. "Sorry, Bex."

"It is what it is," she declared, taking a drink of her soda.

"All the more reason you should come party with us tonight," Linc told her with a grin.

Court grunted and glared at his best friend. "She said no."

Bex narrowed her eyes at him.

"Besides," Court added, his features hardening, "it's hard to get laid if it looks like our little sister is tagging along."

Bex winced like she'd been slapped.

"Dude," I snapped, annoyed that he was being an asshat. "Seriously?"

Court drained the rest of his beer. "Sorry. I mean, you should come if you want to." Yeah, that sounded totally sincere.

Looked like these two were back to being solely antagonistic. That was always fun.

"You're pretty quiet over there, Ry," Linc pointed out. "All good?"

Ryan nodded, the movement almost lazy. "It's just nice to have a minute to fucking breathe." He scowled at Linc. "Even if your crazy ass can't sit still."

Linc scoffed. "All I'm saying is we should take advantage of a night in the city. Recent circumstances have been difficult on us all, but I'd like to remind my dick that the world has a lot more options than my hand."

I choked on my water. "Ugh, gross, Linc."

He didn't look ashamed at all. "Mads, I love you, but unless you and Ryan are planning to open your relationship—"

"Fucker," Ryan muttered, wiping a hand over his mouth.

"—or Bex decides she's suddenly willing to give us a shot…" Linc shot her a suggestive look.

Bex laughed. "More like I'd castrate you with a rusty razor laced with ebola."

Linc moved to guard his junk even under the table. "See? My only other options are dickwad one or two." He hooked his thumbs at Court and then Ash.

"I'd borrow Bex's razor," Ash told him flatly, looking disturbed.

Court let out a dark chuckle and lifted his beer to Linc. "I've seen your dick enough to know I wouldn't touch it with Brylee's vag."

Curiosity tugged at me, since I remembered it was pretty well-known that Court and Linc had a history of sharing girls. In fact, at one point, I'd kinda thought Bex might've been into them both. But then she seemed to be attracted only to Court, and now she was doing her best to ignore him.

"Gross," I muttered, shuddering at the image Court had dredged up. I'd been so busy worrying about not dying that I'd all but forgotten my high school nemesis. "I wonder if she's still sitting at the kiddie table." The guys had punished Brylee and her friends for bullying me by taking away her coveted lunch table and replacing it with shit made for children. They'd humiliated her in a way that still made me laugh.

Ash cracked a smile, as if he was thinking the same thing.

"It feels like a lifetime ago that Brylee was my biggest issue," I marveled, shaking my head. "I guess she still will be when we go back to PC in a few weeks." With the campus closed early for the holidays thanks to the earthquake, students weren't expected back until the middle of January.

Unlike my public high school experience, where we got off a week for the holidays, Pacific Cross ensured students ample time to rest and rejuvenate before coming back to tackle their spring semester. I figured that was code for rich people taking elaborate vacations.

"Welcome to the new normal, baby," Ryan teased, a glint in his eye.

I gave a fake, dramatic sigh. "You mean all I have to worry about are mean girls and actual schoolwork? How will I ever survive?"

"If it helps," Ryan teased, "we still have my father to find, Court's and Linc's dads to control. An international company to run. Women and children to save… You mentioned wanting a puppy, too, at some point, right?"

"Is that all?" I laughed, shaking my head. Yeah, so much for *normal*.

Ryan was saved from answering me when his phone rang. He pulled it out of his pocket and frowned. "It's Knight." Flipping it open, he quickly asked, "What's up?"

Conversation died as we all watched Ryan. Worry twisted my nerves into a jangling knot as his expression went hard and then flat before he gave a slow exhale.

"Got it. Thanks, man. We'll head right back." Ryan hung up the phone and tossed it onto the table with a clatter. It knocked over a water glass, but I reached for his leg instead of moving to save the phone.

"What happened?"

He met my gaze, his blue eyes a turbulent riot of emotions as he said one word. "Grandpa."

CHAPTER 57

RYAN

As I stepped through the front door hours later, Maddie's fingers were the only thing I could focus on. They were tangled with mine, just as they'd been since we'd left the restaurant. We'd abandoned dinner and all driven straight here. It had taken so long.

Too long.

But the whole time, she'd held my hand. She didn't speak or try to make me feel better, which I appreciated. All I could think was how I should've been there.

Mrs. Beechum opened the front door for us, her eyes rimmed with red and face splotchy as she sobbed. She immediately drew me in for a hug that I had to remind myself to return with the one arm I had free, because I sure as shit wasn't letting go of Maddie.

She was the only thing that made fucking sense.

"I'm so sorry," Mrs. Beechum whispered, her ample body shuddering with sobs as she hugged me and then moved on to Maddie before the others.

Knight appeared at the top of the stairs before jogging down and giving me a heavy look. "I'm sorry, man."

I nodded, not sure what to say. Was there something I was supposed to say? Or do? Shit. What about the…

Fuck, I couldn't go there.

But Maddie could, and did. She stepped up to my side, right where she belonged, and looked at Knight before asking, "What do we do now?"

"The medical examiner was already here," Knight murmured. "We left him in his room, in case you wanted to see him."

I could only nod again. "Uh, yeah. Thanks, man."

He clapped a hand on my shoulder. "I'm so sorry, bro. You know he meant the world to us all."

It was like I'd lost the ability to speak. My words were all locked up in my fucking throat, drowning me, as I realized I wasn't even fucking *here*. I should've been, and I wasn't.

He was alone when—

"Ryan." Maddie stood in front of me, blocking out the world so all I could see was her. "Do you want to go upstairs?"

Oh, fuck. A sudden thought flew into my brain.

"Cori," I muttered.

Maddie rolled back her shoulders before looking at Knight. "Where's Royal? He should pick her up."

No, I'm her brother, it should be me. I scowled at her, ready to argue, when Maddie laid her palm against my cheek. "It's okay to let others help right now, Ry. We're your family, and we've got this."

"It's late," Knight pointed out. "Should we wait until morning to get her?"

Maddie nodded slowly. "Yeah. But I'd like Royal there first thing. Will Grandpa's death make headlines?"

"Shit, yeah," Ash murmured. "I mean, I can try and block people from reporting, but he's well-known. It'll be news."

Maddie's lips pressed together. "I don't want Corinne finding out about this from strangers. She's going to need a lot of support, and she needs to be with people she trusts."

"I should go," I muttered, rubbing the back of my neck and surprised by how clammy it felt. "She's my sister."

"She is," Maddie agreed, "and she's going to need you when she gets here. You need some time to process tonight for yourself, Ryan. Let us help."

"Royal and Bishop can bring her back. They'll be there before classes start, and they can bring her here so you can break the news," Linc added. "I mean, the plan was to pick her up from school in two days for break anyway, so you're just bumping it up."

"And we all know Cori will be happy to see Royal," Knight agreed.

It was amusing how attached my little sister was to the asshole mercenary who'd spent years perfecting the art of killing a man with his bare hands and a fun assortment of weapons. I sometimes forgot Royal was even human until I watched him talking to Cori about her stuffed animals or a princess movie.

The fucker would even watch that shit with her, completely at ease with kissing cartoons if it made my sister smile.

"Thanks, guys," I managed. "I need to see my grandfather."

"We're here if you need us," Court reminded me.

"Can I get anyone anything?" Mrs. Beechum pressed, fretting around us as she herded everyone toward the kitchen. We hadn't eaten, but I was pretty sure we'd all lost our appetites.

I stayed still until it was just Maddie and I left in the foyer.

She squeezed my hand. "Do you need to be alone?"

An unfamiliar sense of unease wrapped around my throat, strangling me as I shook my head. "Don't go."

She stepped closer to me, and I breathed in her familiar peppermint and lavender scent. "I'm right here, Ryan. I'm not going anywhere."

Still numb inside, I started up the stairs. With each step I ascended, I gripped her fingers tighter. At some point it must've hurt, but she didn't complain. She just held on and let me take what I needed from her.

This day was supposed to end so differently.

I thought back to the surprise I'd planned for us after dinner. The ring I'd left in our hotel room for her, all but forgotten for now. The rose petals, the champagne on ice... It was all romantic shit I knew the guys would give me hell for if they knew, but Maddie was worth every fucking second of it.

I'd wanted to end today by asking her again to be mine. I'd lost count of my proposals, but I had a feeling I'd be asking—begging—her to stay by my side for the rest of my life.

Just the way she was now.

Fucking hell.

The door to Grandpa's bedroom appeared at the end of the hall, and for a second, I wasn't sure I could do it. I wasn't sure I could confront this new truth.

I was a kid again, my dad telling me my mother was dead before shutting himself off in his library with whatever secretary still thought she had a chance in his bed.

I'd been alone that night, a kid unable to process what was going on until Grandpa and Nana had shown up. They'd stormed into my dad's house, and Nana had grabbed me and Cori to take us to the car while Grandpa yelled at my dad.

I'd spent weeks with them, and we'd grieved together.

But now... Now there was just me.

Maddie squeezed my fingers, startling me back to the present.

No, there wasn't just me. There was *us*.

"I'm ready," I whispered, not entirely sure I meant it, but I forced myself to close the distance to the door and turn the knob before I chickened out.

I paused, my eyes adjusting to the dimmer lighting before sweeping the room and landing on my grandfather. Emotion choked me in a stranglehold as I edged my way inside, Maddie with me every step.

"He looks like he's sleeping." I hadn't even realized I was speaking.

Maddie wrapped her hand around my bicep and leaned against me. "He looks at peace."

He did. The lines of constant stress and strain were gone, and the bottles of pills and cartons of tissues had been removed. The scene looked almost normal, except that his bed was clearly medical grade.

Taking a deep breath, I moved forward until I was at his side.

There were a million questions I suddenly wanted to ask, a thousand things I wanted to say. So many ways I wanted to express my gratitude for the role he'd played in my life.

Maddie reached around me and touched his hand. "Thank you."

I jolted, wondering if she'd read my mind.

She gave me a watery smile, tears shimmering in her gorgeous eyes. "He's the reason you're *you*. And I'll owe him forever for that."

I blinked, stunned when I felt something wet and hot land on my cheek. Fuck, I hadn't cried in... I didn't even know.

Maddie didn't hesitate. She wrapped her arms around me, anchoring me the way she always said I did for her.

"I've got you," she murmured. "I'm right here, and I'm not going anywhere."

I wound my arms around her, crushing her to my chest as I let myself fall.

CHAPTER 58

MADDIE

Comforting Ryan felt strange and achingly perfect. It was hard seeing this man who had always appeared so indestructible break down. All I could do was hold him and let him know he wasn't alone, that I wasn't going anywhere.

I stayed as he said goodbye to Grandpa, and then the others slowly trickled in to say their goodbyes. I stood at his side as the coroner's office came to collect the body, and then I followed Ryan into our bedroom and curled around him as he tried to fall asleep.

It had taken hours, but finally, he slept.

I didn't.

I stayed up, replaying how we'd gone from such a high to such a low in less than a day. I replayed my last conversation with Grandpa and shed a few silent tears for losing a man who had shown me more love than any other adult ever had. In this world, there were so few adults who were actually worth mourning, and Grandpa was at the top of the list.

In a lot of ways, I felt his loss deeper than that of my mom. I felt no loss at all for Gary.

I'd been asked by the police what I wanted done with my father's remains, and I'd shrugged before walking out. I didn't care at all beyond setting his body on fire, but I had a feeling that wouldn't have won me any favors with the police department.

As the light started trickling in through the window across the room, I propped myself up on one arm and watched Ryan sleep. He looked boyish, his dark blond hair disheveled from raking his fingers through it most of the night. His hard jaw was relaxed, and his full lips looked way too tempting as he slumbered.

With a soft rumble, he turned onto his side and nuzzled his face against my chest. My heart kicked up at the nearness, and I couldn't stop myself from caressing the curve of his shoulder with my fingertips. It was a compulsion, the need to constantly touch him and memorize the way his skin felt beneath mine.

My love of him bordered on obsession. It was consuming, the way I needed to be with him. Sometimes the depth of my feelings terrified me.

I inhaled deeply, letting myself revel in this moment as I realized his lips were moving against the upper swell of my breast. I wasn't sure if it was intentional or because he was asleep until the hand carelessly resting on my hip tightened and then moved to the front of my yoga pants to cup my pussy possessively.

A shudder rolled down my back as my body instantly softened for him, a low ache throbbing between my legs.

Looking down, I saw his sleepy gaze on me. "Ry—"

He shook his head, signaling me to shut up. Without another word, he slipped his hand down the front of my pants, inside my underwear, and traced my slit with a blunt finger.

My teeth caught my bottom lip as I barely suppressed a whimper of need, my thighs parting on instinct to give him more room to work.

His mouth moved lower as his fingers circled my clit and then lightly trailed down to my opening, collecting the wetness seeping from me. His lips fastened around a taut nipple, biting it gently over the material of my shit.

"Fuck," I whimpered, squeezing my eyes shut.

Using his shoulders, he rolled me onto my back and switched his mouth to my other breast as he slipped two fingers into me and curled them.

I placed my hands on his head and tugged him up my body, needing his lips on mine.

I expected a hungry, desperate kiss, but what he gave me could only be described as sweet and gentle. His mouth slanted over me, his tongue lazily stroking mine as he pumped his fingers into me. The heel of his hand lightly ground against my clit, but it wasn't enough pressure to tip me over the edge.

In fact, he didn't seem in a hurry at all as he worked me up with agonizing slowness. Arousal curled low in my stomach, a warmth that seeped into my veins and limbs as I kissed him, letting him have full control over the pace.

"I need you," he murmured against my skin, peppering kisses across my jaw and starting down my throat.

"I'm right here," I breathed, turning my head and giving him all the access he wanted.

A hand pushed up my shirt, exposing my breasts to the cool air. My nipples pebbled as he kissed around them, never quite making contact. I fisted my hand in his hair, barely able to keep from moving his head where I wanted him.

Usually we bordered on feral in bed. He loved to push my limits and drive me crazy until I was a squirming, panting mess. Our love was messy and consuming, and that always translated into how he fucked me.

But now he was almost reverent as he worshiped my body, his touch precise and restrained.

His thumb slipped over my clit as he added a third finger, stretching me. I rippled around him, wanting more, but also enjoying the quiet ease of this time together.

Sex, I got.

Fucking, I loved.

But this was more. This was a reminder that we were connected on a soul-deep level. That while we had passion and fire in spades, there was still something deeper happening.

This was making love.

It sounded stupid and sappy, and I'd always cringed when people used that phrase, but it suddenly made sense.

"I love you," I murmured, feeling his smile against my chest.

He lifted himself up, fingers still buried deep inside me, and hovered over me. His eyes searched mine, turbulent and troubled. "I love you."

I clamped down as he withdrew his fingers, desperately trying to hold on to him. With a small smile, he stripped my pajama pants and underwear at the same time before pushing down his sweats enough to free his cock. He moved between my legs and lifted one to wrap around his waist before steadily sinking into me.

I felt every glorious moment of his cock splitting me wide open. My pussy throbbed, needy and achy, as he bottomed out in me with a low moan.

He pulled out just as languidly, the sensual drag of his cock against my walls making my eyes roll back in my head as I whimpered and dug my nails into his shoulders. He pushed back inside, grinding against my clit.

I wanted to buck under him, to push myself harder and faster, chasing the slow build of my orgasm.

As if sensing my patience was close to snapping, Ryan readjusted us and pulled my leg higher, until it was over his shoulder. The new position left me exposed and vulnerable as he drove his cock into me. There was no way to get enough leverage to meet his thrusts, since I was practically doing the splits beneath him.

My thigh burned as he pumped in and out of me, his gaze focused on mine every second. The wicked look of satisfaction in his eyes stole my breath, and I cried out when the new angle let him hit a deeper spot inside me that made my entire body jerk.

"Ryan," I whimpered his name on a broken plea, desperate for more, as my orgasm coiled tighter.

"I've got you, baby," he whispered, repeating my words from last night as he moved just a little faster.

It was better, but still just not quite enough to tip me over the edge.

But this wasn't about me; this was about Ryan taking what he needed from me. And I was beyond willing to give him that.

Taking a deep breath, I reached for him again, needing his mouth on mine. The moment our lips touched, I felt his restraint start to slip. His hips snapped against me a little harder, driving me harder into the bed.

He did it again.

And again.

And again.

I broke our kiss, panting as his thrusts increased as he raced to claim me.

"You feel so perfect," he praised, eyes hot. "So tight and wet around my cock."

His words were like a direct line to my core as I felt my walls clench around him.

"That's my girl," he added, leaving hot, open-mouthed kisses against my neck. "I want to feel you come for me, baby. Squeeze that pretty cunt on my dick." When he moved a hand between us and drew tight circles around my clit, my orgasm rolled over me in waves that never seemed to end, blurring the lines of reality as I cried out.

Ryan jerked inside me with a rough groan, finding his release and riding me through the end of mine.

He collapsed against my chest, pressing small kisses against my damp skin as I moved my leg into a less awkward position, my muscles burning from the stretch.

Not that I had a single damn complaint.

Ryan worked his arms under me, hugging me even as he deposited all his weight on me. It was hard to breathe, but I wouldn't have changed a thing about this moment. I was only sorry it would have to end, and we'd need to face the rest of the day.

Watching the guys plan Grandpa's funeral made me realize how much went into it. It was a lot more than I'd done for my mom. There were viewings and a burial to schedule, estate details to go over, people to invite, a reception to arrange...

It seemed exhausting, and my heart broke for Ryan as he stoically took on each responsibility.

Around ten, Royal and Bishop arrived with Cori. As we'd suspected, news of Grandpa's death had made local papers, but thankfully they'd been able to grab Cori before she learned the truth.

Ryan wanted to tell her himself.

I felt his stress as my own as he paced in the living room, listening as the car's engine died and a few seconds later, Corinne threw open the front door with a squeal. Her tiny footsteps thumped through the foyer, drawing closer.

Ryan's shoulders bunched up, apprehension filling his face as each bounce drew his sister closer.

Cori burst through the door with a grin and yelled, "Ryan!" She launched herself at him like a hug-seeking-missile. But no sooner did he hug her than she was scrambling away to throw herself at me for another hug.

I held her tight, absorbing her energy and happiness while it lasted.

Cori bounced away. Literally *bounced* on her tiptoes. "I have to see my puppy. How big do you think she is? Can we go to the store and get her a treat—"

Ryan cleared his throat. "Hey, kiddo, can you sit down for a minute?"

Cori frowned. Reluctantly, she picked a chair and sat down. Her eyes moved around the room. "Wait—where's Grandpa? He always sees me first because I'm his favorite girl."

Ryan winced, and the look of pain in his expression made me shift closer to him. Letting out an uneasy breath, Ryan went and sat on the edge of the coffee table across from his sister, their knees nearly touching. "Actually, Cor, we need to talk about Grandpa."

She gave him a puzzled look. "Is he not feeling good?"

Ryan's throat worked for a moment, trying to control his emotion. "You know he's been really sick, right?"

She gave a small nod. "But he has doctors and Miss Eloise and Mrs. Beechum. They take care of him."

His back stiffened as he leaned forward, his hands dangling between his spread legs. "I know, but something happened last night, Cor."

Her lower lip wobbled for a second. "But he's okay, right?"

He exhaled, his gaze sliding to me for a minute, and I so wanted to take this hit for him. To spare him this agony.

"I can fix it." Cori jumped up, her face tight with determination. "I always make him feel better—he tells me so."

"Cor." Ryan caught her small hand as she tried to slip by him. "Cori, Grandpa died last night."

She stared at him so long that I wondered if she even understood what he meant, but then tears filled her big blue eyes and she let out a wail that sliced right through my heart. Ryan pulled her in for a hug as she sobbed.

Her tiny body shook as she cried, and I finally moved forward to sit in the seat she'd vacated so I could hug her from the other side. Ryan caught my gaze over her shaking shoulder, looking wildly unsure about how to fix this. He was Cori's hero, but this was a demon he couldn't slay, a wound he couldn't heal.

Movement caught the corner of my eye, and I looked over to see Royal standing in the open doorway. He looked gutted, watching Corinne cry, his hands clenching and releasing reflexively as he, too, tried to figure out what to do to fix her pain. Eventually, his big shoulders fell, and he walked away, leaving Corinne to us.

"I w-want Grandpa," Cori begged, pulling back from Ryan with a face full of tears and snot. "I wanna see him."

Ryan shook his head. "He's gone, Cor. I'm sorry."

That only made her wail harder, but when Ryan tried to pull her back in, she pushed at him. Her little arms weren't enough to actually stop him physically, but it definitely caught him off guard.

"This is all *your* fault!" Corinne shouted.

Ryan looked stricken, and he jerked back like she'd stabbed him. "Cori."

I wrapped my arms around the trembling girl from behind. "Honey, Ryan didn't—"

"He did!" She spun and looked at me, blue eyes wild and red. "First, he made Daddy leave, and now Grandpa. It's all his fault."

Ryan stared at me, and I watched his heart break as his little sister threw herself at my chest and cried her heart out.

I shook my head, trying to convey that she didn't mean it; she was a little girl and didn't understand.

But none of that seemed to matter as Ryan stood up on wooden legs and left the room, looking absolutely devastated.

CHAPTER 59

MADDIE

"Cori," I said as her sobs started to wane, "Ryan didn't do this."

She buried her face against my neck and refused to look up.

Sighing, I smoothed a hand up and down her back. "Grandpa was sick, sweetie. He was sick for a long time, and his body just couldn't handle being sick anymore. But that's not Ryan's fault."

She sniffled and pulled back to look me in the eye. "But I want Grandpa *here*."

I wiped away her tears. "Me, too. But he can't be, and now he's not sick anymore."

"I miss him," she whispered, huge tears suspended on the edges of her lashes. "Daddy left and now Grandpa left."

Fuck you, Beckett, I mentally snarled.

"Cori, your dad left because..." Well, I couldn't give her the real reason. "Because he needed to take a break."

"From me?" She looked crushed.

"From choices he made," I said carefully. "But none of that is your fault, and it isn't Ryan's either."

"But Ryan always fought with Daddy," she added.

"He did," I agreed, not willing to lie to her. "But they're adults, and sometimes adults fight. I fight with Ryan, too."

Her eyes got big. "You do?"

I nodded, my hands going to her waist. "I do. And I promise, I'm not going anywhere."

"Then why did Daddy leave?"

My lips mashed together. "Because your dad had a lot of problems, and he thought the best way to handle them was to go away. But none of that is because of you, Corinne."

She stared at me, looking helpless and lost. "But who will take care of me now?"

"Ryan will," I promised. "And so will I."

"Me, too," Royal commented from the doorway.

Cori turned and her face crumpled again before she ran to Royal for comfort. He caught her easily, swinging her up into his arms. Her sobs were muffled against his massive chest.

"Shh," Royal soothed, rubbing her back. "I've got you, princess." His dark blue eyes flicked to me. "Ryan's in Grandpa's office."

I stood up and wiped my hands on my jeans. As I left, I touched Cori's back.

"Does Ryan hate me?" Cori asked, her voice trembling.

"Never," I swore, linking our pinkies and squeezing hers. "Ryan loves you more than anything."

"I didn't mean it," she whimpered, surprising me when she shoved her thumb in her mouth and started sucking. "I love him," she added around the digit.

"He knows that," I assured her. "Are you good with Royal for a few minutes?"

She nodded, her head looking so tiny against his massive chest. "I wanna see my puppy."

"Okay," he agreed easily. "We'll go see your puppy. Then maybe we can get a snack from Mrs. Beechum, deal?"

She nodded once more, sucking her thumb harder and closing her eyes.

Royal flashed me a tight smile. "I've got her, okay?"

"Thanks," I murmured before going to find Ryan.

He was in Grandpa's office, as Royal had said. Sitting behind the desk, he was looking at a stack of papers while Court sat across from him with an open laptop.

Ryan's gaze lifted when I came in. He dropped to the papers. "Court was telling me that you'll have to sign some forms, since Brookfield is yours now. There're other things that—"

I laid a hand on Court's shoulder. "Give us a minute?"

Court nodded, looking a little more than grateful as he hurried from the room and closed the door in his wake.

Ryan wouldn't meet my gaze. "There's so much shit left to do. Linus said we'll have the will read after the funeral is done, but it's a formality. We all know—"

I stepped around the desk, forcing myself between him and the edge until he had to roll the chair back.

He stabbed his fingers into his hair with a sigh. "She hates me, and I can't blame her."

I leaned against the desk. "No, she doesn't."

His eyes flashed. "You heard her, Maddie."

"I heard a little girl who just had her world rocked *again*," I countered, shaking my head. "She was lashing out at the only safe space she has left."

He leaned back in the chair, his jaw tight. "Mads."

"No," I cut him off sharply. "Not *Mads*. Trust me, Ryan. The last thing she said to me just now was asking if you hated her because of what she'd said."

He looked stricken by the idea.

I placed my hands on his shoulders to stop him from jumping up. "I told her that of course you don't. That you love her and always will. That both of us will always be there for her."

His chest seemed to cave in as he exhaled. "Fuck, Maddie, I can't do this. Grandpa always held it all together. How the fuck am I supposed to live up to that?"

I moved forward, straddling him in the chair. With the wheels and arms, it was a precarious balancing act, and I was pretty damn proud of myself for not tipping the chair over and knocking both our asses to the floor.

Immediately, his arms came around my waist.

"Listen to me, Ryan Cain," I demanded, looping my arms around his neck and making sure I had total eye contact before going on. "No one expects you to be your grandfather. Not me, not the guys, not Corinne. All we need is for you to be *you*. You're the guy we trust, the guy we lean on. You have a house full of people who have your back, because you learned how to be a man watching your grandfather."

His eyes began to shine as he listened to me.

"I love you," I finished, with all the ferocity I could muster in my tone. "Corinne loves you. The guys, too. You are not alone. Not yesterday, not now, not ever. We'll get through this together."

He leaned in and kissed me. "I couldn't do this without you."

"You could," I answered. "But I love that I get to be by your side."

"Always," he swore, pulling me against his chest.

I lay my head over his heart, my body molded around his in the chair as we simply breathed the same air for a few minutes, letting the moment settle around us.

"Royal took Corinne to see the puppies," I told him after a long pause.

He nodded, his jaw brushing the top of my head. "Good. Cori loves them."

"Has she always sucked her thumb?"

He stilled for a beat. "Not since she was a little kid."

I made a noncommittal humming sound. "Well, her world has been upset. It's probably a comfort thing."

"We'll need to keep an eye on her," he reasoned. "She's had a lot of upheaval this year, and I don't want her regressing if we can avoid it."

I wasn't an expert on autism, but I knew that it came in a multi-pack of variations, and it never seemed to affect anyone the same way. Corinne was higher functioning, but she had a few other disabilities to contend with in addition to her spectrum diagnosis.

"We'll all keep an eye on her," I promised him, tracing a star pattern on his chest.

"With my father gone, Grandpa was her guardian," Ryan said. "I told Court to file the paperwork to have that shifted to me, but I'm also going to formally adopt her."

I sat up and nodded. "Okay. You were always more of a father to her than Beckett was anyway."

He grimaced. "Mads, that means Cori's always going to be a big part of our lives."

I tilted my head, not sure what he was getting at.

He slipped a hand under the back of my shirt, his wide palm spanning most of my lower back. "She's not going to grow up, go away to college, and get married the way most adults would. She'll be a constant, major part of my life forever."

My eyes narrowed. "What are you trying to say?"

His gaze lowered. "That I don't expect you to—"

I pressed a hand over his mouth, scowling. "You better not even be thinking about saying what I think you were going to, Ryan Cain. I swear, I'll beat your ass." I glared at him. "We've already talked about Cori. If you think I'm going to feel burdened by her or some other shit, then you better think the fuck again."

He chuckled, the low sound soothing as he pushed my hand down. "Easy, killer. I just wanted to make sure you were good with this."

"I love your sister," I snapped, annoyed he'd think that I'd push her off like an inconvenience for a single second. "I'm all in for the rest of our lives. I'm the one who told *you* that we'd need a house with room for her."

"Saying it is one thing, but now it's a reality," he pointed out.

I shook my head. "I'm going to have Mrs. Beechum lace all your food with the strongest laxatives known to man if you ever bring this up again, so hear me now—I'd adopt Corinne with you tomorrow if the courts would let us. I *love* that girl, and I always will."

A smile twitched on his lips. "Okay, baby. I hear you."

"You freaking better," I grumbled, still glaring. "I know that losing Grandpa is, like, the worst thing that could've happened to you, but that doesn't give you a pass to ever think I'm not a thousand percent with you *and* Cori."

He nodded, lips pressed together as he held back a grin.

I jabbed his chest with a finger. "And seriously, the next time you even insinuate I would consider walking away, I'm strapping *you* to the bed and shoving a giant dildo up your ass."

His eyes lit up, wicked and curious. "Is that a fantasy you have? Because turnabout is fair play, baby. If we're talking bondage and dildos, I've got some ideas myself."

"That's your takeaway from my threat?" I stared at him, jaw open.

His gaze dropped to my mouth. "You know how I feel about an open mouth, Mads."

I snapped it shut with an annoyed look that softened when he laughed, the sound warm and rumbling as it eased some of the tension in the room.

"Fuck, I love you," he murmured fiercely, pulling me against his chest once more.

CHAPTER 60

MADDIE

The house was overwhelmingly packed with well-wishers who had attended the funeral and returned to Brookfield to pay their last respects. Michael Harris had been a pillar of the community for years, and people came from across the globe to attend the funeral.

I'd tried to convince Mrs. Flounders to let us cater the event so she could take the time to grieve herself, but she'd swatted me away, offended at the notion that anyone could handle this house and kitchen better than her.

She *had* relented to us bringing in extra staff to help. They now mingled amongst the attendees, carrying trays of finger foods and alcohol. The longer the reception went on, the more a part of me wished I could hide in the kitchens alongside Mrs. Flounders.

Mrs. Beechum flitted around the room, intent on making sure the wake was up to the standard Michael Harris deserved. I watched as she effortlessly handed a woman tissues while continuing to talk to an older man.

Word had hit the papers that Gary Cabot had been shot and killed by his former son-in-law. The gawkers and onlookers were here just as much to see Ryan and me as they were to pay their respects. I was getting tired of ignoring the stares and whispers every time I walked by. Some were even bold enough to ask questions.

How was I doing? How was Ryan doing?

My favorite was when people tried to dig up information about whether or not Ryan would entertain bids for Brookfield.

Each time, I clenched my teeth and replied that he'd handle it his own way, but the vultures were circling, just as Ash had warned they would. It wasn't just because of Grandpa's death or the world-renowned company left hanging in the balance.

There'd never been a hint of interest on Ryan's part about taking over this side of his family's business. As far as the world knew, he was destined to rule the boardroom of Cain Industries, a mantle he'd already assumed.

But Brookfield... It was a veritable goldmine, and a lot of people knew it.

The funeral had been relatively short. Ryan had insisted that Grandpa wouldn't have wanted some long, drawn-out thing with endless eulogies and hymns. Even still, the cathedral where it was held was packed, and the procession to the burial plot seemed to never end.

I stayed between Ryan and Corinne all day, the others creating a buffer around us to keep people from getting too close. The only additional person I'd truly wanted to see was Bex, who had shown up for the funeral but had needed to leave immediately after for her flight to Paris.

Sighing, I set my now-empty glass of wine on the tray of a passing waiter and excused myself from an old woman who reeked of mothballs and was telling me why the 1979 cabernet had been the worst wine Brookfield had ever produced.

I didn't have to look far for Ryan; he was surrounded by men telling stories of his grandfather. I arched a brow, wondering if he needed a save, but he gave a small shake of his head.

Okay, seriously, maybe I could regroup in the kitchen for a few minutes and breathe.

"It's a lot isn't it?" Ash murmured as he came up to stand beside me.

I nodded and contemplated reaching for another glass of alcohol.

Ash sipped a tumbler of bourbon. "A few more hours and it'll all be over."

"Hours?" I wanted to groan. My feet were aching in these heels.

Ash shrugged a shoulder. "Never underestimate the need for people to get all the gossip at the expense of others' pain, Maddie."

I scowled. "Those people better stay the hell away from Ryan, or I'll give them some pain of their own to deal with."

He chuckled. "Down girl. Ryan can handle himself." He glanced across the room where Linc was surrounded by a flock of older women, charming them with ease. "What do you wanna bet he fucks one of them before this is over?"

My jaw dropped. "No way. They're all old enough to be his mother."

Ash sucked a breath through his teeth. "Thousand bucks says he picks up the Karen to the left."

I looked at the woman—short, bleached blonde hair, a smile that was ten shades too white to be natural, a tan that bordered on orange, and a black minidress—before wrinkling my nose. The woman looked more than interested in the guy more than a decade her junior, despite the rock glittering on her left hand. "Ew."

Ash leaned in. "Three."

Linc turned and faced the woman and *winked*. I swore I watched her panties dissolve from here.

"Two."

She giggled and laid a hand against his chest, pushing her tits out and licking her lips while Linc set his empty glass down on the buffet table.

Ash laughed. "One."

Linc stepped back and gave the woman a subtle *come here* nod with his head and turned to leave.

"Motherfucker," I swore. "He is *not* screwing some woman in the powder room."

"It's your house now, Maddie." He grinned at me and lifted his cup in their direction. "Go stop him."

Rolling my eyes, I chased them across the room and into the hallway, where I heard high-pitched giggles. When I rounded the corner where the bathroom was, the woman had Linc pressed against the wall, her lips suctioned to his neck as she shoved a hand down his pants.

"Lincoln," I snapped. "A word?"

The woman startled and turned to me with a sneer. "Who's this bitch?"

Linc shook his head and removed her hand from his pants. "Now you've gotta leave, Brenda."

She gaped at him. "It's *Bristol*."

"Totally what I said," Linc muttered.

Bristol eyed me with contempt. "Who the fuck is this cheap whore?"

"Someone who means a shitload more than you," Linc snarled, pushing off the wall. It was scary how fast he went from docile and amused to furious and vengeful. "Now take your fake tits and your plastic ass and get the fuck out."

A nervous laugh tittered out of her. "I'll just go find my husband—"

"I'll let him know we kicked your ass out for being a cunt." Linc flicked a finger. "Go."

With an indignant squeak, she stomped away.

Linc leaned against the wall, a lazy smile suddenly spreading on his face. "Maddie!"

I closed the distance between us and nearly recoiled from the smell. "You're drunk."

"I prefer the term *wasted*, but sure. We'll go with drunk." His navy eyes were glassy as he watched me.

"Linc." I softened my tone. "I know you're missing Grandpa, too, but this isn't—"

He waved a hand, nearly hitting me. "Ah, it's fine. It's a party, right?"

"It's a *wake*," I corrected, wondering if I should get help.

"Wonder why they call it that," he mumbled, shaking his head. "Maybe 'cause we're all awake and he's not?"

I sighed and tried again. "Linc—"

"I'm not sure if I should thank you or give you shit for the cockblock, Mads," he slurred. "She had that trophy wife look."

"Meaning?"

He tapped his temple. "They give the best head. They spend years perfecting the art of the blow job to land the biggest whale, babe."

"That's disgusting." I made a face.

"That's fact," he countered with a heavy sigh. "But whatever. I'll go get a drink and find another person to play with."

I blocked him when he went to pass me. "Linc, this isn't you. What's going on?"

He stared at me from where he towered over me by several inches. "Nothing. You should go be with Ry. He needs you."

I moved again to cut him off. "And you're my friend. What's going on?"

He rolled his eyes. "Look, Maddie, just…"

Raising my brows, I waited for him to finish.

"Just leave me alone, okay?" He shook his head, and this time when I tried to block him, he physically picked me up and moved me to the side, carefully setting me on my feet. I went to chase after him, but he turned away from the party and went toward the back of the house.

What the hell was that about?

I was debating whether or not to go after him or find one of the guys when it sounded like all hell broke loose in the other room. I rushed back to the party as a woman screeched at the top of her lungs.

Something furry rushed past me, zipping deeper into the crowded room.

"It's a rat!" The woman wailed, clutching at the nearest man.

Okay, she was an idiot, because it was clearly one of the puppies.

I spun to see another puppy run by, and then I spotted Cori running into the room with tears in her eyes.

After the funeral, some of the stable staff who knew Corinne had offered to keep an eye on her so she could play with the puppies and even go for a horseback ride. We'd all assumed keeping her away would be the right call; in the last two days, Cori had started to regress, just as Ryan had feared.

She constantly sucked her thumb now, usually not bothering to remove it from her mouth when speaking. Her speech had become stilted, and a lisp she'd overcome years ago seemed back in full force. She also had become extremely dependent on a threadbare stuffed pony that had once belonged to her mother, which Grandpa had saved. The one night we couldn't find it before bed, she'd had a full-blown meltdown, complete with hyperventilating.

Eleven adults had spent three hours scouring every inch of Brookfield to find the pony, which had been left in a stall in the barn.

That set off another round of hysterics when Corinne declared she was a horrible girl for forgetting her most important friend.

It was heartbreaking.

Ryan and I had planned to spend the holidays in Brookfield with Corinne, but now we were considering going to the beach house instead so she could have a break from this estate.

"Puppy!" Corinne screeched, barreling into the room and hitting a serving platter close to the edge of the buffet table. It went flying, throwing canapés into the air. "Come back!"

Ryan moved to intervene, but Corinne ducked between a group of adults gaping at her like she was a sideshow freak.

"Cor, wait," Ryan called.

I moved to intercept her, and she tripped over a man's shoe. She went sprawling into me, and I lost my footing in these damn heels. We both crashed into the ground, my back hitting the edge of a table, but considering the alternative was Cori's head getting cracked open, I'd take it.

I hissed out a breath, pain lancing through me as people moved to help us up.

Cori's thumb went back into her mouth, her big blue eyes staring up at me with fear and pain. "Sorry, Maddie. Cori is sorry."

My eyes went wide, because talking about herself in the third-person was new.

"It's okay, sweetie," I assured her, smiling.

A man I didn't recognize bent and lifted Corinne off me with a gentle smile. "Here you go, honey. Right as—"

Corinne screamed so loud I thought my eardrums would bust.

The man let her go and fell back in surprise as Ryan swooped in with a glare. "What the fuck did you do to her?"

"N-nothing," the man stammered, eyes huge as they bounced from me to Corinne to Ryan. Cori kept screaming.

"He just helped her up," I added, getting to my feet with Ash's help.

Ryan picked Corinne up and grunted as she started kicking and flailing. "Cor, it's me. Settle down, honey."

It didn't work. Corinne wasn't registering that she was with Ryan, or that Royal was suddenly standing at her side. That I was there, or even Mrs. Beechum, who had pushed her way into the room.

And she definitely didn't see the room full of gaping strangers. Several curled their lips at her, shaking their heads and muttering.

Ryan shot me a worried look and, with Royal's help, took Corinne from the room. But her shrieks echoed in the air.

"My goodness," the woman who had declared a dog a rat muttered, waving a gloved hand in front of her face. "Someone needs to teach that child some manners. What a disgrace to Michael's memory."

I saw red.

Fuck. This.

I turned to Ash and saw Court behind him. Both looked a mix of stricken and furious.

"Maddie." Mrs. Beechum touched my elbow, looking as angry as I felt.

I met her eyes. "Get everyone out of here. Party's over."

CHAPTER 61

MADDIE

Corinne's sobs broke my heart.

After leaving the guys and Mrs. Beechum to get rid of everyone downstairs, I walked down the hall to her room. I could hear Ryan and Royal trying to calm her down, but it seemed only to make her cry harder.

Stepping into her doorway, I saw her curled on her bed, her hands clamped over her ears. Dirt from her shoes streaked the pale pink comforter. Ryan sat on the edge of her bed, speaking in soft tones while Royal stood on one side, looking frustrated that he didn't have anyone to hit to make this better.

I leaned against the doorframe, not sure how to help.

"Cori sorry. Cori sorry. Cori sorry." Her whispered chant before hiccupping sobs was like a plea. Like she was terrified we'd go off on her.

The way Beckett would have.

Royal turned and looked at me, the pain in his pale gray eyes staggering. He shook his head and folded his arms over his wide chest.

I walked in, unable to stand by and do nothing. I touched Ryan's shoulder and went to the other side of Cori's bed. I let instinct guide me as I got onto the bed behind her and molded my body around hers, wrapping an arm around her waist as I kissed her tangled, sweaty head.

Her breathing hitched, and I worried she'd pull away, but she relaxed the tiniest amount and pressed deeper against me. "Cori sorry."

I kissed her head again before laying my cheek against her hair. "You have nothing to be sorry for, sweet girl." I met Ryan's eyes and saw the same fear I felt reflected. "Everything is fine, Cor."

"Cori w-was bad," she stammered.

"No, you weren't," I corrected, cuddling her as close as I could. "No one is mad at you, honey."

Royal knelt in front of her face and gave her a small, crooked smile. "Who could ever be mad at you, princess?" He laid his hand on the bed, palm up.

She didn't say anything, but eventually she reached a tiny hand out and rested it in his. The other she used to pop a thumb in her mouth.

Ryan's head dipped, and I could see how he was struggling to know what to do for his sister next.

"The guys are helping clean up downstairs," I said casually, stroking Cori's hair away from her face.

Gratitude shimmered in his eyes. "Good. Cor, I need to check on something, okay? But Royal and Maddie are going to stay with you."

She gave the tiniest of nods.

His mouth flattened as his eyes turned to me. I gave him a sad smile that I hoped conveyed that I had this. I'd take care of Corinne.

Exhaling heavily, Ryan stood up and left the room.

Royal shifted into a more comfortable position, and when his hand moved a few inches, Cori's fingers wrapped around it. She let out a small whimper.

"Easy, baby girl," Royal soothed, much like he'd say to a spooked animal. "I'm not going anywhere. I'm here as long as you need me."

Sniffling, Cori sucked in a shaky breath and her fingers relaxed infinitesimally. Slowly, her small frame started to relax. At some point, I started to hum under my breath.

Royal met my eyes and dipped his head, the acknowledgement

conveying a wealth of information. Gratitude, respect, and understanding.

My eyes blinked sluggishly, fatigue tugging at my mind as I felt Corinne go limp and finally fall into a sound sleep.

"She's out," Royal uttered, jaw still tight.

I swallowed a yawn. "It's been a long day."

"You're good with her."

"So are you," I countered.

A ghost of a smile touched his mouth. "I have four younger brothers. I've had practice with kids."

I managed to shake my head a bit. "It's more than that. Don't sell yourself short."

He shrugged one massive shoulder, the fabric of his button-up white shirt pulled taut around his muscles to the point I wondered if the seams would burst. "She's easy to love."

I glanced down at her, my chest filling with emotion. "Yeah, she is."

Someone cleared their throat in the doorway and we both looked over to see Ryan. He'd shed his suit jacket and tie, rolled up his sleeves, and undone the top few buttons of his shirt. His gaze landed on his sister and softened before turning to me. "Can we talk?"

I glanced at Royal, who nodded. "I'll stay with her."

Carefully, I extracted myself from where I'd wrapped around Cori, and rolled off the edge of the bed. Ryan drew me into the hall and to our bedroom next door, but left the door cracked before pulling me into his arms. I ran a hand down his back as he shuddered.

"It's okay," I assured him, hugging him as tight as I could. "She's gonna be okay."

Shaking his head, he pulled away from me and crossed the room to sit on the end of the bed. "I called Ms. Wallace."

Hope trickled in as I was relieved that he'd reached out to the woman who had been Cori's caregiver when she lived with Beckett. She was trained in dealing with children who had autism, but more specifically, she knew Cori.

I walked forward to stand in front of him. "Are you planning to hire her back?" When Cori had been enrolled in her private school,

Ms. Wallace had retired to spend time with her family. Corinne had round-the-clock care and attention at school, so she no longer needed a daily aide.

He nodded. "I asked her if she'd be willing to come back for a little while."

"She said yes?"

"Sort of." He grimaced. "Her daughter just had a new baby, and she can't leave until after New Year's."

"Shit," I murmured. Not that I wanted to push Cori onto someone else, but Ms. Wallace was trained to help her. She knew her disabilities and triggers. She would have, at the very least, been able to help us navigate the next few weeks to make Cori's life less chaotic.

"I told her about the thumb sucking, the third person... She said Cori's regressing." Ryan looked absolutely gutted, like he'd personally failed his little sister.

I rested my hands on his shoulders. "Okay, but what does that mean?"

He tipped his head back and looked up at me. "She's struggling. The third person thing..." Fury hardened his features. "She said that my father used to tell her how useless and bad she was. It's called illeism. Apparently it's not always a bad thing, but in Cori's case, she used it as a coping mechanism for when Beckett was cruel."

Hatred filled my veins. That man... God, he needed to be shot.

Ryan cleared his throat. "Basically her brain separates her personality from her body. She views herself as a fucking object or a thing. The way *he* did."

My fingers dug into his shoulders. "Your father is a cunt."

He snorted. "Zero disagreements from me, babe."

I blew out a breath. "How do we help Corinne?"

Ryan linked his arms behind my thighs, pulling me closer. "Ms. Wallace said Cori needs to go somewhere familiar, safe. It might help her process things. There's also a therapist in L.A. we've used before who will start working with her again."

I glanced around the room. "She's in Brookfield. Isn't that soothing enough? She loves it here. The horses, the staff, the dogs..."

He nodded. "But without Grandpa, it's not the same, and she's acutely aware of that. Everyone here is in mourning. Cori's a sensitive kid. Even if we all act like it's normal, she'll see through it."

"All right. Then we leave. We can spend the holidays at the beach house—"

"Cori doesn't know the beach house," he admitted. "She's only been there once or twice. Honestly? The best place is to take her back to the home she knows."

My brows shot up. "Seriously? Even though it's where Beckett was a dick to her?"

He looked at me helplessly. "Ms. Wallace said it's the place that Cori knows best. At least Beckett won't be there to harass her. And most of her stuff is there. She'll feel safe."

"Then that's where we take her," I decided.

"That's what I figured. I'll have to go back and forth the next few days to finalize things here. The will reading needs to be attended—"

"Ry, you can't drive back and forth each day. You'll drive yourself nuts."

He scowled at me. "I can handle being tired, Maddie."

I sighed and brushed my fingers through his mussed hair. "Why don't you and the guys stay here? Linus and Court can move up the official reading of the will, and you can wrap up what needs to be handled before coming to L.A."

He frowned at me, but I could see him starting to relent. Brookfield and the shares of Phoenix had been left to me, but there was still an official reading of the will that needed to happen that outlined where all of Grandpa's personal assets were designated. Someone from the family had to be present for that, and Ryan was the obvious choice.

"I'll go to your old house with Cori," I added. "We'll take Royal. The three of us will be fine for a few days until you get there. Then we'll all spend Christmas together."

"Shit." He dropped his forehead against my stomach. "Christmas. I need to buy stuff for Cori—"

"I'll handle the shopping," I assured him.

"Seriously?"

I nodded. "Are you kidding? I'll live out all my little girl dreams buying her everything in the damn world."

He grinned up at me. "You're sure?"

I leaned down and kissed him. "Absolutely."

"God, I love you." He stood up, his body rubbing against the front of mine with a delicious sort of friction. His hands spanned my waist, holding me tight as he leaned in and kissed the side of my throat.

I smiled and wrapped my arms around his neck. "I love you, too."

CHAPTER 62

MADDIE

The Cain Estate loomed at the end of the drive, massive and imposing. Despite the automatic lights chasing away the shadows of the dark, it still looked ominous and sent a small tendril of fear curling around my gut.

But as Royal pulled our car to a stop in front of the main doors, Corinne seemed to breathe easier. When Ryan and I had mentioned the idea of coming here to Corinne, she'd burst into tears—this time the good kind. Relief had flooded her red face, and she'd asked to go home immediately.

Royal hadn't hesitated, and within an hour, we'd packed up and were driving down the coast toward Los Angeles. The closer we got to her home, the more Cori seemed to settle. As much as I hated being away from Ryan—and I *really* hated that—Cori actually found solace in *this* place. I could see that the change was good for her.

Once he'd parked, Royal turned and looked at Cori. "Ready to go inside, pretty girl?"

She nodded, her blue eyes gaining a bit of the sparkle that had vanished the last few days. She pushed open the door and tumbled out as Royal and I joined her on the stone-paved drive. Cori rushed ahead of us, and Royal went to the back and pulled out our overnight bags.

"Cor, wait," I called as she twisted the knob and the door opened easily. Must be nice to live in a gated community where you didn't need to worry about things like locks.

Then again, the massive wrought-iron gate we'd had to punch a code to get through, along with the guard booth at the front of the community, were probably good deterrents for burglars.

Royal grumbled something under his breath, his cold gaze sweeping the area for threats.

"You good?" I arched a brow at him.

He shook his head, looking nauseated. "I hate places like this. Fucking rich assholes showing how small their dicks are by the size of their house."

"Tell me how you really feel."

He smirked at me before gesturing for me to head into the house first. I noticed that he locked the door after us and even tested it by jiggling the handle. Judging by the annoyed scoff, it didn't meet his security standards. "I'm upgrading that if we're staying here. Shit, the whole place is a security nightmare with these big windows and multiple doors."

"Doesn't it have a security system?" I wrinkled my nose and looked around.

Royal scoffed. "No. Fucking Beckett always thought he was untouchable. He had a basic one, but Ash disabled it before we got here."

"Cori?" I called, my voice echoing around the large foyer as I tried to figure out where she'd gone.

A giggle reached my ears first, the sound making me sigh in relief, as Cori appeared at the end of the hall where I knew the kitchen was. "I'm hungry!" She whirled and disappeared.

Chuckling, I glanced at Royal as he tossed our bags by the front door. "Guess I should see what's around to cook."

"We can always order in," he added, following me down the hall to the kitchen.

Right before I stepped into the kitchen, Corinne jumped out in front of me and yelled, "Boo!"

I bit my lip to keep from swearing in front of her, practically falling backward into Royal. He caught my biceps and steadied me as I gasped.

"That wasn't nice," Royal chastised, which might've meant more if he didn't sound like he was smiling.

"I got you, Maddie!" Corinne singsonged, twirling away and yanking open the refrigerator door. "Didn't I get her good, Royal?"

"Sure did, shortcake," he agreed with a rumbling laugh.

I elbowed his hard stomach, pretty sure I did more damage to myself than him. "Jerk."

"Can we have pancakes?" Corinne asked, turning to look at us with big eyes. "Or mac and cheese? The kind from the box?"

I frowned. "You want pancakes *and* mac and cheese?"

She blinked at me, uncertainty in her eyes. "Yes?"

I huffed a laugh and stepped around her to start opening doors to the pantry. "Let's see what we've got, kiddo."

Nothing.

We had a whole lot of nothing, which wasn't exactly surprising since no one had lived here in over a month. Hell, most of the lighting fixtures and surfaces had a layer of dust on them. The few things left in the fridge were old and growing colorful spots.

Royal leaned a hip against the island countertop. "Order in?"

I nodded slowly. "Yeah, I guess so."

Corinne's face fell. "But they never have the good mac and cheese."

I had to agree; the boxed kind was pretty superior, even if the cheese was powdered.

"I can make a quick run to the grocery store," Royal offered.

Cori's entire face lit up. "Really?"

He nodded. "Sure." He looked at me. "We're gonna need groceries anyway. I mean, I'm guessing there isn't anything in here that isn't expired or spoiled. We'll need milk and shit for breakfast."

"That's a bad word," Corinne told Royal, her face utterly serious.

Royal winced. "You're right. Sorry, Cor."

"Juniper Forrest's daddy has a swear jar," Cori informed him, climbing up onto a stool.

His face screwed up. "Who names their kid *Juniper?*" He shook his head. "Freaking rich people."

"Whatever you say, *Royal,*" I teased.

"Exactly my point," he retorted with a heavy breath. "Okay, and special requests from the store?"

"Gummy worms!" Cori cried, punching her fists in the air.

"Pancake mix, mac and cheese, and gummy worms." Royal let out a snort. "Do I even want to try getting you to consider a veggie or protein?"

Corinne frowned, considering. "Cheeseburgers?"

Royal's head dropped back with a groan.

"I like cheeseburgers." I high-fived Corinne.

"Anything for you?" Royal looked at me.

I shook my head. "No, but I'm allergic to peanuts, so if you could avoid those, that'd be great."

"Got it." He reached into his pocket and twirled his keys. "I'll be back in a bit. Call or text if you think of anything else, okay?"

I nodded and listened to his footsteps echo through the empty house before turning to Cori. Placing my hands on the island, I wrinkled my nose at the grimy feeling. "Okay, Cor, how would you feel about watching TV while I clean up?"

At the very least, the kitchen needed to be scrubbed down before I could consider cooking or eating on any of these surfaces.

Corinne shrugged. "Can I play upstairs in my room?"

"Sure," I agreed, watching with a smile as she ran off. Her happy squeals bounced off the walls as my phone started to ring.

I smiled when I saw Ryan's name on the screen and immediately accepted the call. "Hey."

"Hey back," he greeted. "How is she?"

"Really good, Ry," I admitted, listening to her footsteps thump across the floor above me. "As soon as she saw the house, she lit up. She went upstairs to play in her room while I do some cleaning. Royal went to make a food run."

"Fuck," he grunted. "I should've thought of that. I didn't even consider that no one's been there in weeks. I can send a delivery service and hire a maid—"

"Calm down," I laughed. "Royal and I can handle it. Unlike *some* people, we're used to doing the normal, boring human things like grocery shopping and cleaning counters."

"Ha fucking ha," he grumbled. "I'll have you know that I've learned other life skills that are just as valuable."

"Like?"

"How to fuck you with my tongue," he replied bluntly.

I sucked in a sharp breath that turned into a whine. "Dammit, Ryan. No fair saying shit like that when you're *there* and I'm *here*."

He chuckled. "So, if I were to suggest you video chat me after Cori's gone to bed…"

"I'd say hell yes," I muttered, not even bothering trying to hide the fact that I always wanted him.

"Thought so." Smugness radiated from his tone. He knew he had me by the pussy.

"So," I started, looking around the vast space, "any idea where the cleaning supplies would be?"

He guided me through the house to the mudroom off the garage where there was a small closet full of lemon-scented cleaning products.

"Awesome," I said, grabbing a few bottles.

"Mads, thank you," he said softly.

I let out an exasperated laugh. "You don't have to thank me, Ryan. Cori's my family, too. And seeing her smile was totally worth it."

"Still," he murmured. "It means a lot."

"You can show me how grateful you are when I see you in person," I teased.

He groaned. "Hell yes, baby. I'll talk to you later, okay?"

"Okay. Bye, babe." I hung up the phone and tucked it into my back pocket before looking on the shelves for a bucket.

Of course there wasn't one.

"If I were a bucket, where would I be?" I muttered, looking around like a bucket would pop out like a damn Disney character and start mopping for me.

I opened the garage door and flicked on the lights. There was a small fleet of vehicles still in their bays, like they were waiting for someone to jump in and drive them. But along the wall, I spotted several buckets.

I hooked a pail around my elbow and went back into the mudroom to load it with supplies. In the kitchen, I turned on the hot water and started mixing up what I'd needed to clean the space.

A loud thump from above made me jump, and I hissed as my arm touched the stream of hot water. "Shit." I turned off the water and abandoned my current mission to make sure Corrine wasn't upstairs destroying something priceless.

Then again, maybe I'd help her trash the entire house. It might be a therapeutic *fuck you* to Beckett Cain.

I paused at the bottom of the steps and yelled up. "Cori! Everything okay?"

It took a few minutes, but Cori's head appeared at the top landing with an impish grin. "Yes!"

"Did you drop something?" I asked.

She shook her head. "Wasn't me."

I shot her a suspicious look but didn't want to push the issue since she was doing so well. "Okay. Just... shout if you need me."

Shaking my head, I turned and walked back to the kitchen, prepared to tackle the month's worth of dust and dirt. Then again, if every room was this filthy, I might take Ryan up on the cleaning service offer so I wouldn't still be polishing floors at Christmas.

Which reminded me, I needed to pick Cori's brain at dinner for gift ideas. Ryan had given me a black credit card and told me to buy whatever I wanted for her and for myself.

I already had a few ideas for things I could buy that Ryan and I would both enjoy.

A grin pulled at my mouth as I stepped into the kitchen. I made it two steps before something grabbed the back of my hair and yanked me off my feet.

Fuck, not something.

Some*one*.

My back hit the floor and the air whooshed out of my lungs as I blinked up, trying to focus on the person looming over me. Spots dotted my vision as I tried to inhale and couldn't. Finally, just when I was about to pass out, I managed to suck in a deep breath.

Coughing, I blinked and my eyes focused. My stomach dropped as my world tilted.

Beckett Cain smirked above me, his eyes practically glowing. "Well, well. Isn't this a nice surprise?"

CHAPTER 63

MADDIE

As far as any of us had known, Beckett had tucked tail and run when Ryan and I toppled his empire. Ash had tracked him to somewhere in the Caribbean, but we'd all kind of back-burnered finding him because we were busy dealing with other shit. Somehow we'd designated him as the lesser threat.

Mistake.

Such a motherfucking mistake.

"Get up," Beckett growled, grabbing me by my hair and wrist to yank me up. My socked feet slid against the floor. I cried out as pain lanced across my scalp and tears pricked my eyes as he squeezed hard enough to grind the delicate bones of my wrist together.

"Up, bitch," he hissed, his hot breath fanning across my face as he got me on my feet only to throw me against the wall. My teeth clicked together as he crowded against me, an arm pressed across my chest to hold me in place.

"What the fuck are you doing here?" I demanded, absolute terror washing over me as I realized Cori was upstairs and we were on our own.

Whatever happened next, all that mattered was Corinne surviving this.

Please don't come down here.

My gaze shot to the clock on the microwave, and I realized it had been only thirty minutes since Royal left. He probably wouldn't be back for at least that long still.

Dammit.

"I live here," he sneered at me. "Maybe you and my cumstain of a son forgot that, but this is *my* home."

"Last I checked," I ground out, "Ryan and I owned everything that was ever in your name."

His eyes flashed with a maniacal glint a second before he drove his fist into my stomach. The air was crushed from my lungs again as I struggled to breathe. Nausea rolled through me in waves, fear and physical pain a toxic cocktail that damn near sent me to my knees.

"Where is he?" Beckett demanded.

It took a second to get enough oxygen to reply, and I used the moment to really look at him.

Gone was the posh, sophisticated man who stormed around in power suits and thousand-dollar haircuts. His blue eyes, the same shade as Ryan's and Cori's, were wild and bloodshot. His hair was messy, and he was in jeans and a t-shirt that looked like something a last-minute tourist bought at an airport.

I lingered on my assessment too long and his open palm cracked across my face. "Where *is* he?"

Fuck it. I was going to lie my ass off.

"On his way," I snapped, holding a hand to my throbbing cheek. "He'll be here any second with the others."

Beckett stared at me. "You're lying."

"Am I?" I challenged, arching a brow like my life wasn't literally hanging in the balance. "By all means, stick around. I'm sure Ryan will love seeing you again."

He hissed out a breath. "Guess that means I'll have to work fast, huh?"

My heart pounded in my chest as I looked for a way out. *Any* way out.

Beckett had backed up to hit me, which put a little room between us. There were knives in a butcher block on the other side of the island, if I could get to it.

"Pity I'll be long gone," he added, a cruel taunt in his tone. "I'd love to see the look on his face when he finds your body and his precious little sister's. Maybe I'll lay you out in the foyer... or hide your bodies in different rooms so he can try and find you."

The sound of my phone ringing in my back pocket made both of us jolt, but I recovered faster. I ran forward, slamming my hands against his chest and pushing him back with all the strength I had as I made a run for it.

Beckett crashed back into the barstools at the island while I took off at a sprint, not willing to risk my shot at freedom for the dicey chance at grabbing a knife before he could overpower me.

As I ran, I fumbled for my phone and nearly dropped it. Royal's name flashed across the screen as I heard Beckett thundering behind me.

I hit the answer button and screamed, "Royal! Beckett is—"

He crashed into me from behind, sending me flying into the opening of the foyer. The phone hit the door several feet away.

I kicked out blindly, struggling to crawl to the phone as Beckett pulled at me, trying to roll me onto my back and pin me down.

"Get *off*!" I shrieked, turning my full attention to him instead of the phone. I punched and kicked, raining blows down on him. My knee landed on something soft, and he roared, rolling off me to cup his dick.

I shot to my feet and ran for the stairs, ignoring the phone as I took them two at a time.

Cori. I had to get to Cori.

"Bitch! Get back here!"

Yeah, because *that* sounded like a good time.

My feet slipped as I hit the second-floor landing, and I nearly went to my knees as I ran for Cori's room with everything I had. I hit her door and flew through it before slamming it shut and bracing my back against it. Reaching back, I flipped the lock but had a feeling that wasn't going to do shit.

Corinne's eyes were huge as she looked at me from where she'd been drawing at her desk. "Maddie?"

My chest heaved with ragged pants. "Cor, you've gotta hide."

She stood slowly. "Why—"

"You're dead, bitch!" Beckett shouted.

Corinne let out a plaintive whimper and sank into a crouch, covering her ears with her hands. "No, no, no."

I wanted to scream, but I forced myself to take a deep breath. "Cori, honey, look at me."

She continued to rock back and forth.

"Corinne!" I snapped, my voice cracking through the room with desperation.

She lifted her head, tears in her eyes.

I forced myself to settle. "Honey, bring me your chair, okay? Hurry."

She managed to stand and drag her chair over to me. I snatched it from her grasp and wedged it under the doorknob as Beckett started to turn the knob. When the door didn't move, he punched it.

"Open the fucking door!"

I pushed Corinne behind me and looked around for something—anything—to defend us with. No way would a chair and a door hold him back for long.

Cori grabbed the back of my shirt. "Maddie."

I spun and bent to look her in the eye. "I'm not going to let him touch you, Cor, okay?"

She nodded, her eyes big and glassy.

My eyes swept the room, landing on the bathroom. I gently pushed her toward it as Beckett kept hitting the door. "In here, sweetie."

Once we were inside, I slapped a hand over the switch, bathing the room in light. I turned and locked that door, too.

"Shit, shit," I whispered.

The bathroom connected to Corinne's closet, but that was it. We were trapped. I stumbled into the closet area and looked around for where I could hide Cori. Maybe I could shatter the bathroom mirror and use a shard as a weapon?

MAD LOVE

But I'd still need to hide Cori somewhere.

Behind me, Cori started to sob softly.

I looked up, ready to pray to anyone listening for intervention when I spotted something on the ceiling. "Cor, is that access to the attic?"

She nodded.

"Is it the only one in the house?"

She shook her head. "N-no. There's one in a g-guest room and M-Mommy's room."

My eyes slid shut in relief. I was so parking my ass in a pew this Sunday to give thanks to baby Jesus and all the angels.

Even better, Cori's room had one of those ostentatious cabinets in the middle for extra shelving. I jumped up on it and stretched up to my tiptoes to push the square to the side. I grunted as I reached, my fingertips managing to knock the access tile aside inch by inch.

There was a crash in the bedroom that sounded too much like a door being cracked.

Jumping up, I managed to get a decent grip on the ledge. I'd never really been into upper body strength beyond what was needed for cheerleading, so I blamed everything on adrenaline as I managed to pull myself up into the attic space.

I rolled on my stomach and looked down at Cori. "Come on, Cor." I reached out a hand for her.

She looked terrified as she climbed up on the small table and reached for me. She was a couple inches away. "I can't!"

I leaned forward, balancing my hips on the ledge. "Yes, you can. You need to jump, Cori."

She looked unsure as she started to shake her head.

Another *bang* from the bedroom and I knew we had only seconds before Beckett kicked in the bathroom door.

"Cori! Jump *now*!"

Eyes wide, she did as I commanded, and my hands caught her wrists. I grunted and strained as she kicked her legs in the air. Inch by inch, I pulled her up to me.

"Don't let go, Maddie!" she cried, looking up at me with so much fear and so much trust.

"I won't," I vowed, pulling her the rest of the way as something hard slammed into the bathroom door.

I pulled her free of the access and laid the tile back over it.

Not that Beckett wouldn't realize exactly where we'd gone, but anything to slow him down was necessary at this point. I could hear Beckett throwing things in Cori's room, and I held her against my side, covering her exposed ear with my hand so she wouldn't hear him.

Footsteps stomped into the closet, and my heart stopped as I waited for Beckett to come after us.

But he never did.

My ears strained to hear him, but all I heard was Cori's ragged breaths and the violent thumping of my heart.

Why wasn't he trying to get up here? What the hell was he doing?

Fear made me dizzy and my stomach roil. One thing I knew in my gut; we needed to get somewhere safe.

"Where's your Mommy's room?" I whispered, my eyes struggling to adjust to the dark. Dormer windows spaced out across the roof of the house let in shafts of moonlight.

Cori pointed toward the other end of the house, and I carefully pulled her along the beams of wood. When she stumbled, I knew I had to slow down or risk us both falling through the ceiling.

I looked around, cursing how long this freaking house was, and spotted an access tile. "There?" I asked, pointing.

"Think so," Cori managed.

I let her go and edged forward to pull back the tile. The dark space below looked like another closet. Unlike Cori's, I didn't see something to jump onto, so I'd have to catch her.

Or leave her up here while I took on her father myself. Maybe I could draw Beckett away from the house long enough for Royal to show up.

Looking back at her terrified face, I beckoned her forward. She came, her trust in me absolute.

"Okay, honey, I need you to listen to me." I met her eyes. "I need you to stay up here."

She opened her mouth to protest.

"Cor, I need you to be safe while I go find your father." I pressed a trembling hand against her pale cheek. "You'll be safe up here. Royal's on his way."

Fuck me, I hoped he'd heard me and was tearing through the suburban streets to get here as fast as he could.

"Then stay with me," she begged, grabbing my hand. "Don't leave."

I let my eyes slide shut for a moment. If I stayed here with her, Beckett would know where we were. Eventually he'd find us. There was only one way out of that closet.

If I went down there, I could at least distract him until Royal showed up.

Hopefully.

"Cori, you've gotta stay here," I murmured, "and I've gotta go down there. You'll be safe here."

"He'll hurt you," she mumbled, throwing herself at my chest.

I wrapped my arms around her. "He'll try, but I can take him."

Probably not, but a little false bravado might not be the worst thing right now.

Sucking in a deep breath, I tried to steady my nerves as I prepared to jump down into the open space.

Cori's hands tightened around me. "Maddie. *Listen.*"

I paused and realized I couldn't hear much of anything aside from my ragged heartbeat throbbing in my ears. It took several seconds, but then I heard it.

The faint wail of sirens.

Holy shit. Maybe Royal had called in the cavalry.

I waited for another beat as they grew louder, shrieking through the night and alerting everyone in the neighborhood that they were coming. Then I saw swirls of light bouncing around the ceiling as they came to the front of the house.

"Thank God," I whispered, hugging Cori again.

"Maddie?"

"Yeah, honey?"

"What's that smell?"

I froze and inhaled, and the acrid scent of smoke reached my nose.

Jerking back, I looked down at the dark closet but didn't see anything.

"Stay here," I ordered, jumping down without a second thought.

"Maddie!" Cori leaned over the edge as I hit the floor and rolled.

Planting my palms on the hardwood, I started to push myself up and realized the floor was hot.

And not in a rich-people-have-heated-floors kind of way.

"Motherfucker," I swore, a new wave of panic cresting over me as I realized why Beckett hadn't chased us up into the attic.

The asshole had set the house on fire.

CHAPTER 64

MADDIE

It was almost laughable how fast my biggest fear could go from Beckett finding and killing us to being burned alive. I had no idea how far the fire had spread, but it couldn't be a coincidence.

How better to get away than have everyone focused on a giant, burning mansion?

"Cori, come on!" I called up, reaching for her.

She shook her head. "I'm scared!"

Deep breaths. "I know." *So am I.* "But we need to go *now*, Cor."

She backed away from the edge. "No!"

"Please, Cori," I practically begged. "If the police are here, that means Royal's probably here, too."

"He'll come up and get me," she countered.

I resisted the urge to ball my hands into fists. "Cori, I know you're scared, but you need to be really brave and trust me." I could feel the heat radiating under me, and I wondered if it was my imagination trying to convince me that it felt hotter than a minute ago.

"Please, sweetie." I stretched up for her once more.

Her face twisted with determination and, with a small scream, she dropped through the opening.

I caught her, the momentum knocking us both to the ground,

but I managed to keep her from hitting her head. "You're okay, you're okay." I got us both up and looked around for the door, worried that Beckett might be waiting on the other side to finish us off.

"Stay behind me," I told her, reaching for the closed door and edging it open slowly. My gaze searched the bedroom, unable to make out much beyond lumpy objects under white sheets as police lights bounced around.

I dragged in a deep breath and reached back to grab Corinne's hand as I pushed the door open and stepped into the room. A hard breath left my lungs when Beckett didn't jump out from the shadows. "Okay, let's go."

Holding her hand as tight as I could without bruising it, I pulled her to one of the windows that overlooked the front lawn.

"Holy shit." A veritable army had amassed, and I could see firefighters getting their rigs into position as people screamed orders. I looked around, but there wasn't a ledge for us to crawl onto. It was a straight shot to the ground.

Maybe I could open the window and flag someone down.

I let go of Cori and unlocked the window. My nails dug into the paint as I shoved upward.

"There's Royal!" Cori shouted, grabbing my arm.

I sucked in a deep breath to scream for him, for anyone, when an explosion from below knocked me off my feet. Cori screamed, and I rolled onto my back to see flames licking up the sides of the house outside and blocking the window.

I scrambled back, dragging Cori with me. Heat seared into my ass from the floor below.

"We're gonna die!" Cori thrashed against me.

"No, we aren't!" I framed her face with my hands and forced her to look at me. "We're not gonna die, Cor, but we need to find another way out."

"But there's *fire*, Maddie." Her big-eyed gaze darted around frantically.

I took a deep breath and felt smoke tickle my throat. "I know, baby, but we're gonna be fine. We've gotta move, though, okay? Stick with me."

Despite the hot floors, I pulled her down and crawled to the door before tentatively touching the handle to feel for heat before twisting it open.

Smoke billowed in from the hallway, but the fire didn't seem to have reached the top floor yet. That was something, at least.

We crawled forward, and I swore the floor beneath me shuddered. After what felt like an eternity, I spied the top of the stairs, but there was a strange glow coming from it that didn't look like the blue and red flashes of the cop cars out front.

I stopped, realizing this way wouldn't work. The fire was coming up the staircase.

"Maddie?" Cori asked, pressing against my side.

I sucked in a deep breath and started coughing, my head spinning. "Back up." I looked around the hallway and spotted Corinne's smashed bedroom door. "Your room." Pushing her forward, I chased her through the door Beckett had destroyed and into the space, moving her around to the far side of the bed before running into the bathroom.

From the small bathroom linen closet beside the toilet, I grabbed a stack of towels and shoved them under the bathtub faucet until they were soaked. I ran back to Cori and pressed one over her mouth. "Breathe through this, okay?"

She nodded, taking gulping breaths.

"There's another staircase, right?" I frowned, trying to remember the layout of Ryan's house, but I'd been here only a handful of times, and the smoke was starting to disorient me.

Again, Cori nodded. "On the other side of the house. It goes to the lib'ary," she told me, her voice muffled.

I pointed in the direction. "That way?"

"Yes."

"Okay, stay with me. Hold on to my ankle the whole time, got it?" I shot her a look that I hoped seemed calm but was pretty sure was terrified.

"Got it," she agreed, her head bobbing up and down so hard I worried that she'd hurt her neck.

It was awkward, but I covered my mouth with the towel and started moving forward, keeping as low to the floor as I could. The hallway was even hotter now, and when I turned to the right, flames licked through the opening of the stairwell. Black smoke writhed across the ceiling.

I turned the other way and went as fast as possible, but we'd made it only halfway when I realized the stairs that Cori told me about were also filled with flames and smoke. Ahead of us, the fire was already crawling across the ceiling, coming right for us.

We were trapped between the stairways with no way down.

Without knowing where we were, I pushed open the next door and pulled her inside. I slammed it shut and shoved my damp towel against the bottom, trying to block the smoke.

"M-Maddie?" Cori whispered, terror in her small voice.

I looked around and almost laughed.

Ryan's bedroom.

Of course.

I ran to the window that overlooked the backyard. The pool glittered beneath us. There was a small overhang, but it was a hell of a jump. I wasn't sure Cori could make it. Still, I shoved up the glass and looked around the backyard.

"Here!" I screamed, seeing a pair of firefighters.

One of them shouted something and pointed up at me, and the other took off at a dead sprint around the front of the house. The one who remained was still yelling at me, but I couldn't hear him over the sound of cracking wood and the sounds of glass exploding as windows gave under the heat of the flames.

"Maddie!" Cori's shriek made me turn. The door was glowing. I could hear the fire roaring on the other side as the towel started to smoke.

"Come on!" I pulled myself out of the window and onto the roof that hung over the back patio. It was barely five feet deep, but it ran the length of the back of the house. I turned back for Cori. "We've gotta go this way, Cor."

She came to the window. "But there's nowhere to go!"

"Be brave, remember?" I held out my hands. "The firefighters are out there."

Her face tightened with determination, and she let me help her out the window as the door to Ryan's room was engulfed in flames.

Using the overhang, I carefully guided us farther down the house, away from the flames that were now decimating Ryan's bedroom and licking out his open window.

More firefighters ran around the side of the house, and I spotted Royal with them as they started to set up an inflatable bag we could jump onto.

"I'm scared," Cori sobbed softly.

"Me, too," I admitted, my heart in my throat.

Another window shattered behind me and the roof we were standing on shuddered under my feet with a terrifying pop as the wood started to give. My gaze shot to the half-inflated bag and then to Royal. He looked terrified, having reached the same conclusion as me: the bag wouldn't be ready before the roof gave.

I turned to Cori. "Honey, we've gotta jump."

"Into the *pool*?" she screeched, eyes huge. She tried to pull her hand out of mine.

I clamped down harder. "We'll go in the deep end. I'll hold your hand the whole time, but we've got to get off here."

Behind Cori, the glass from Ryan's window exploded. She squealed and jerked around, her feet slipping and nearly sending us over the edge.

I dug in my heels and held her against me. "We've gotta jump. I need you to trust me, Cor. Can you trust me?"

She gulped down a big breath. "O-okay."

I laced my fingers with hers and squeezed. "On three, okay?"

She nodded, and I swore my heart was going to punch out of my chest.

"One," I took a deep breath, "two," I forced a smile at her, "three!"

Running forward, I hauled her with me and jumped off the roof.

We were suspended in air…and then we hit the water with enough force that Cori's hand was ripped from mine. I kicked to the surface and sucked in a deep, burning breath as I spun in the water. "Cori!"

When she didn't immediately surface, I dove back under, the darkness and water making it hard to spot her at first. But when I did, she was trying to kick for the surface, flailing her arms. I swam at her and wrapped an arm around her waist before swimming up.

As soon as we broke the surface, she took in a ragged breath.

"Are you all right?" I demanded as I kicked for the ladder at the side of the pool.

"Think so," she replied.

I crowded behind her, pushing her up the ladder before hauling myself out and turning to look back at the house.

It was a fucking disaster. The whole thing was engulfed in flames, smoke and fire pouring from the windows.

"Maddie! Cori!" Royal's roar cut through the night as he ran around the back of the house with a pair of firefighters.

"Here," I called, lifting a weak hand as I wrapped my other arm around Cori's trembling shoulders.

Royal fell to his knees in front of us, gray eyes wide. "Fucking Christ. Are you two okay?"

I took in a deep breath to tell him yes, and started coughing up a lung.

"Easy," one of the firefighters advised, kneeling behind me. "You probably have smoke inhalation. Let's get you two looked at."

"Her first," I croaked, nodding to Cori, who looked deathly pale.

"Hey, baby girl," Royal murmured, reaching for her. "Can you come with me to get checked out?"

She turned and looked at me like she was asking for permission. As soon as I nodded, she dove into Royal's big arms, and he picked her up.

"Beckett was here," I told him, wondering where the asshole had gotten away to.

Royal's expression hardened. "Oh, I know. I caught him trying to leave as I drove up. The police have him in custody."

"Seriously?"

He nodded at me. "Let's get you two checked out so I can call Ryan. He's losing his fucking mind."

"Language," Cori chided in a tiny voice from where her face was smashed against his chest.

He chuckled and rubbed a hand up and down her back. "Sorry, kiddo."

She glanced up and patted his cheek. "It's okay. I still love you."

It might have been the firelight and the smoke inhalation, but I could've sworn his eyes went a little glassy as his expression softened.

"Love you, too," he murmured. He waited for the firefighters to help me to my feet. Then we all walked away from this nightmare.

CHAPTER 65

MADDIE

Despite the hospital room having two beds, only one was occupied. Cori was curled against my side, not quite asleep but the most relaxed she'd been since…

Well, since before her father tried to barbecue us.

Royal sat in a chair on her other side, his phone in his hand as he talked to the guys and his brothers, giving them all a rundown of what had happened. Currently he was on the phone with one of his brothers that I hadn't met.

"No, man," he muttered into the phone, "we're good. You only have ten days left on your contract. Don't fuck it up by going AWOL."

"Language," Cori whispered.

Royal's lips lifted in a smirk. "Cor's already giving me sh—crap. Yeah. Hang on." He held the phone out. "Wanna talk to Rook, baby girl?"

Cori twisted in my arms, reaching for the phone and tangling up the cording of the oxygen cannula fastened to her nose. Royal patiently helped her hold the phone to her ear and move the tubing aside.

"Rook?" Cori said into the phone, hope in her voice.

I couldn't make out what he said, but it made her smile and then giggle. "A baby? What's her name?"

My gaze shot to Royal, who leaned back in the seat and folded his arms over his stomach. "Rook's been staying with the wife of a former teammate. He died in a mission gone wrong in the fall, so Rook stayed with her for a little while."

My brows raised slowly. "Wow. That's pretty big of him."

"Well, it was more complicated than that. Turned out the reason the op went south was because one of their own team betrayed them, but one of the guys got away with some pretty damning intel that Ash helped decrypt over the past few months. Anyway, the guy who fuc— screwed with them was going after the girl of another team member, and *she* was living with the widow, who just had a baby."

I blinked, trying to keep up. "It sounds like a freaking novel. Or made-for-TV movie."

"You were kidnapped and drugged by your father before being caught in an earthquake and then almost burned alive by your ex-father-in-law," he pointed out.

I winced. "That's fair."

"When will I see you?" Cori was asking Rook. Apparently he didn't give the right answer, because her face fell. Her lips turned down. "It's okay. Here's Royal, 'kay?" She paused, her small mouth twitching. "I miss you, too."

With a sigh, Cori handed Royal the phone. "He wants to talk to you."

Royal took the phone and stood but pressed a kiss to Cori's forehead before walking to the window.

Corinne snuggled her head against my chest. "When will Ryan be here?"

I glanced at the clock. "Any time now, baby." I stroked her hair, the sooty, brittle texture reminding me that we both needed a shower, but the doctor had given us strict orders to be on oxygen for at least four hours due to the smoke inhalation.

Thirty-two minutes to go before I could yank this thing off my face.

I hated the way the bitter scent of smoke clung to my nostrils. At least we'd changed into hospital gowns, so our clothes didn't reek. I didn't miss the pitying look in the nurse's eyes as she'd bagged them up before asking me if I wanted them. I told her to throw them in the trash. Cori and I didn't need a reminder of how close we'd come to dying.

Cori's thumb inched toward her lips. "I miss Ryan."

Sighing, I pressed my cheek against her head. "Me, too."

And, like he'd been summoned solely by our mutual need, the door slammed open and Ryan barged inside with the force of an army. Which, considering all the men who crowded into the room behind him, wasn't too far off the mark.

His electric blue eyes instantly found me and Cori, and his massive shoulders sagged in relief before he closed the distance. He went to Cori's side of the bed and reached down to hug us both in his strong arms. I wrapped an arm around his back and felt a tremor shudder down his frame.

"It's okay. We're okay," I whispered against his ear.

Pulling back, he gave me a curt nod. But the tightness in his jaw said everything was *far* from okay. He looked at Royal, who had ended his call with his brother and was watching.

Waiting.

Royal planted his feet and looked ready to take whatever punch Ryan was ready to throw. Thankfully, Ash intervened before Ryan could move forward. His green eyes flicked down to Cori and me before he whispered, "Not here."

Ryan gave another tight nod as the doctor appeared behind Bishop's and Linc's broad shoulders.

"Uh," he began, already frowning as he counted all the new bodies, "I'm going to have to insist some of you leave."

Linc shot him a glare that made him take a step back. "Who the fuck are you?"

"The doctor," I supplied, shaking my head. "Sorry about that, Dr. Plaskon."

"Everyone out," Ryan snapped, gesturing for the doctor to come in as he faced the now nervous man. "I'm Ryan Cain. Corinne's my sister and I have guardianship. Maddie is my girlfriend."

I smiled at each of the guys as they met my gaze before leaving. I had a feeling they weren't going far.

"No!" Cori protested as Royal went to leave. "Stay with me."

"I'll be back in a few, princess," he assured her.

She pouted but didn't argue anymore as he left. I could see it hurt Ryan, the way Cori wanted Royal, but right now he needed to suck it up. Cori had been dealt a shitty hand all around, and if she wanted Royal on a unicycle wearing pink taffeta and throwing glitter confetti, then Ryan better help him onto the damn seat.

"Corinne has responded well to the oxygen," Dr. Plaskon began, smiling in her direction before turning his attention to Ryan. "She can be released tonight, but I'd advise you to keep an eye on here and if her breathing changes, bring her back to the hospital. I would also suggest keeping her quiet for the next few days as her lungs recover."

Ryan nodded, a muscle pulsing in his jaw as he listened to the doctor.

"Miss Cabot," the doctor started, glancing at me, "I'll need your consent to share medical information with Mr. Cain."

"Consent granted," I assured him. Not that it would've mattered. Had I said no way, Ryan would've had Ash hack into the database and find my records. His obsession knew no boundaries when someone he loved was in danger, and truthfully? There was a big piece of me that secretly loved it when he got all demanding and protective.

"I got your X-rays back," Dr. Plaskon began, turning and lighting up a board on the other side of my room. He put up the scan I'd had done on my torso when they'd noticed bruising. "Thankfully it doesn't appear you've fractured or broken any ribs."

I kept my eyes glued to the scan as I felt Ryan's questioning gaze land on me.

"Your jaw is cleared, too," Dr. Plaskon added, oblivious to the way Ryan was now scanning me. I could feel the press of his gaze as it lingered on my face, noting that beneath the soot marks, the dark shadows under my ear were also bruises. "No concussion. The worst seems to be the smoke inhalation."

"Right," I murmured. My chest felt raw and hollow from all the smoke and the coughing I'd been doing, but I also felt every bruise that Beckett had dealt. Asshole.

Dr. Plaskon turned and looked from Corinne to me before clearing his throat. "Now that you've had a bit of time to recover, I suggest we clean you up and document things. Should a trial happen, I believe it will help. There's also a pair of detectives outside, waiting for a statement."

I glanced down at Cori and the way she was clinging to me. "I don't know that it's such a good idea."

"Cor," Ryan started, gently touching her hand and grabbing her attention. "The doctor needs to look at Maddie a little more."

She blinked owlishly up at him. "Because Daddy hurt Maddie?"

I sucked in a sharp breath and instantly regretted it when my side throbbed. "Cori, you were in your room. How did you—"

She ducked her head. "I heard Daddy yelling and… I got scared and stayed in my room, but I heard you, Maddie. I should've been braver—"

"No." I cupped her face with my hand. "You did *exactly* what you were supposed to do."

Dr. Plaskon coughed discreetly before moving to the foot of the bed. "Corinne, do you think you can be brave now and let me take Maddie to another room so I can check her out?"

Cori stilled beside me. "Take her where?" Panic seeped into her tone.

"Not far," I promised. "And Ryan, Royal, and all the others will stay with you while I'm gone."

Her eyes widened. "Then who will protect you?"

"I promise she'll be safe," Dr. Plaskon said with a smile.

"I'll go with her, Cor," Ryan said, looking at me over her head and daring me to push the issue. "We'll both be back soon."

Cori gave a heavy sigh. "Okay. I can be brave."

I kissed the top of her head. "I know you can, honey. You're the bravest girl I know."

"I'll get a nurse to bring in a chair to take you," Dr. Plaskon advised me before grinning at Cori. "You really are a remarkable girl, Corinne."

She beamed at him. "Thanks."

All the guys came back a few minutes later, along with a wheelchair and a nurse. She went to help me out of bed, but Ryan simply used his body to maneuver her to the side so he could scoop me up and deposit me in the seat.

I flashed him a grateful look when he managed to barely hurt my ribs at all. Neither of us spoke as the nurse wheeled me down a hallway. When we got to the end, she pushed me inside where another doctor—a woman—waited with a lot of medical equipment that looked familiar.

"I'm Dr. Coleson," she greeted, her eyes kind and her smile warm, but it tightened when she looked at Ryan. "Sir, you can wait outside."

"No," I said before Ryan could tell her to fuck off. I glanced at the table and the stirrups. "*That* exam won't be necessary. I wasn't raped."

Ryan jerked beside me, his face paling like he'd never considered that option.

Dr. Coleson frowned. "Miss Cabot—"

"Maddie," I corrected her as the nurse helped me from the chair to the exam table. Ryan seemed to remember I needed assistance at the last second, glaring at me for having the audacity to put my feet on the ground before he could pick me up.

"Maddie," she agreed. "If you were assaulted, there's only a small window where we can collect the proper forensic evidence."

"He hit me a few times before I got away," I replied, "but that was as far as it went. I swear. And I'd really prefer Ryan to stay with me."

He moved closer to my head, like a sentry who would level anyone who tried to have him removed.

"All right," she relented before nodding to the nurse, who pulled the curtain closed around us.

I lay back and tried to relax as she lifted up my gown and checked each injury as the nurse took photographs. Then they gently cleaned me up and took more pictures of the fresh marks.

With each snap of the shutter, I could feel Ryan's rage brewing like a summer storm that was about to crack the skies wide open.

"Okay, Maddie," Dr. Coleson murmured as she stepped back and pulled down my gown. "There's a shower in the other room if you'd like to finish cleaning up."

The nurse, a sweet woman named Joyce, smiled at me. "I can help you."

I glanced at Ryan. "I think we can manage on our own, if that's all right?"

Joyce nodded, understanding in her brown eyes. "Of course. I'll come by in about fifteen minutes to take you back to your room, but there's a red emergency button should you need help." She added that last part for Ryan, who gave her a simple nod.

"Take care, Maddie," Dr. Coleson told me as they left.

Once they closed the door, the silence became oppressive. I reached for Ryan when he came close, but he stepped aside before I could make contact. My heart constricted at the pain on his face.

"Ryan, look at me," I murmured.

He shook his head. "I fucked up, Maddie. I fucked up, and he almost killed you and Cori."

"But he didn't," I insisted, trying to sit up on my own. It took a little effort to smother the gasp of pain begging to be released, but I managed.

"Maddie—" He spun and stared at me.

I panted, my stomach aching and my head pounding. Right now I needed Ryan to shove aside his misplaced sense of guilt and just be with me. "If you make me stand up to hug you, I'll kick your ass," I threatened. "Or I'll have Royal do it."

He scoffed but moved between my legs before wrapping me up in his arms. "More like I'm gonna beat the shit out of Royal when I see him alone."

"Don't you dare," I retorted, leaning against his chest. "Royal did exactly what you would've done—he went out for freaking groceries,

Ry. No one knew that Beckett would show up. Hell, I bet he was already inside when we arrived. It was shitty timing."

Actually.

"Or not," I muttered.

He pulled back and shot me an incredulous look.

"What? All I'm saying is, now Beckett is in police custody," I pointed out. "He's done. Attempted murder tends to land you twenty-five to life."

He smirked at me. "It's cute that you think I'll let him live long enough to use up state resources for decades."

I rolled my eyes and pinched his side. "Look, Gary got off easy—"

"A bullet to the forehead is easy in your book?" He made a disbelieving sound in the back of his throat. "Geez, woman, what does it take to please you?"

I tipped my head back to look at him. "I want one of our parents rotting away in a jail cell, alone, while we live the rest of our lives happy."

Ryan sighed heavily. "Fine. Any other requests?"

"Just one."

He arched a brow.

"Kiss me."

The grin he shot me sent heat licking through my veins. "Hell yes."

CHAPTER 66

MADDIE

With nowhere else to stay except a hotel, Ryan and the guys all decided we should go to the beach house once Cori and I were released. Other than a lingering ache in my chest and a couple of fun bruises on my ribs and jaw, we'd made it out of the inferno unscathed.

Cori seemed to have bounced back faster than me physically, but mentally, she was struggling again with the loss of her family home. My heart broke for her all over again; going to the Cain Estate was supposed to *help* her. Instead, I was worried we'd added a whole new trauma to the ever-growing list that girl was dealing with.

When Knight and Bishop offered to stay in a hotel, Cori proved she had every Woods brother wrapped around her finger by tearfully asking why they were leaving her. Within seconds, they caved. Royal hadn't even mentioned going with them, which was clearly for the best, since Cori was clinging to him like a baby spider monkey.

On the drive to the house, she slept on Royal's lap. He carried her inside like she was made of the most delicate glass known to man.

When I reached for the handle to get out of the passenger seat, Ryan scowled at me, and I didn't even fight him. I was exhausted, so I relented and sank back against the leather while Ash climbed out of the back. Court, Linc, Bishop, and Knight had followed in a separate car.

At my door, Ryan pulled me from the cab and carried me to the house, my legs wrapped around his waist and his hands holding up my ass as I rested my head against his shoulder and let my eyes drift closed. Again, I didn't protest. If he wanted to carry me around, I wasn't going to stop him. I was freaking done with this day, and it was barely past sunrise.

Royal waited inside, looking unsure as Cori slept in his arms. "Where's her room?"

Ryan sighed. "She doesn't have one here. I guess—"

"She can have mine," Ash offered. "Top of the stairs, first door on the right. It's across from Ryan's, so if she wakes up and needs him…"

Royal met Ryan's eyes. "I'll sleep on the floor in her room, in case she needs something."

I felt Ryan relax with relief. "You sure?"

"Fuck yeah." Royal looked down at Cori with obvious concern and adoration. "I already failed her once tonight." He looked at me, regret in his usually cold eyes. "Both of you."

"Not your fault," I mumbled, shaking my head.

Ryan scoffed, clearly not in agreement, but let the comment go as Royal headed up the stairs with Cori.

Bishop yawned and rubbed a hand over his short hair. "Guess this means we're crashing on the couches?"

Knight smirked. "Beats sand fleas any fuckin' day."

"I'll grab blankets," Ash muttered.

Linc batted his eyes at Ash. "You can always sleep with me, buddy."

Ash shoved his shoulder, his green eyes sparkling. "You wish."

I giggled and pressed my face against Ryan's neck, feeling him smile at the normalcy of the moment and our friends acting like assholes.

"Okay, we're going to bed," Ryan announced, shaking his head and leaving the five of them to sort out their sleeping arrangements. "Everyone get some sleep."

"We need a bigger house," I murmured as he carried me up the stairs, barely jostling me.

He snorted. "Or our friends need to get their own."

I pulled back and looked him in the eye. "Do you really want that?"

"Do I want a house where I can fuck you in every room without worrying about my friends walking in on us?" His brows arched. "Hell yes, baby."

I rolled my eyes, but he had a point. "Fair. But I know you love them being around."

He grunted and kicked open the door to his bedroom. After depositing me on the bed, he stepped back. "I'm going to check on Cori, okay?"

I nodded. "I'll borrow some of your clothes and change."

He paused in the doorway and smirked at me. "You honestly think you need to bother with clothes?"

I dramatically laid a hand over my chest and gasped. "What kind of girl do you think I am, Ryan Cain?"

His warm chuckle was full of promise. "I think you're my girl, and that kinda says it all." He ducked out of the room before I could come up with a retort, but honestly, he was right. I was a thousand percent his girl, and right now, I needed that reminder.

My pulse pounded as I remembered how close I'd come to losing it all today. Swallowing around the panic that threatened to overtake me at the memories, I focused on the fact that I was alive.

I went to the bathroom and hurried through brushing my teeth and a few other things before stripping off my clothes.

Ryan came back as I was finishing shedding the loaned hospital scrubs. "Cori's sound asleep," he called, and I heard him moving around the room.

I stared at myself in the mirror, eyeing the new bruises with disgust. They didn't exactly scream *sex kitten who wants to play*, but Ryan had already seen them at the hospital. His touch had been featherlight and gentle as he'd helped wash away the night from my skin.

But the last thing I wanted—or needed—right now was gentle.

Taking a deep breath, I opened the bathroom door and watched him.

He'd taken off his shirt and had his back to me, the massive phoenix tattoo rolling and twisting with each movement he made. I studied the orange and red flames, appreciating the artwork and what it stood for. What he and the boys had built was nothing short of incredible, and I knew they were just getting started.

This would be their legacy. And Grandpa's.

My heart was so full my chest physically ached. "I love you." I'd never meant those words more than I did at this moment. Those three words seemed so insignificant, but there were none better in the entire world, in any language, to describe what this man meant to me.

Ryan turned, a smile on his face that turned into a grin when he saw I was naked.

"Fuck, baby," he groaned, the sound rumbling from his chest as his eyes swept the length of me.

I arched a brow, smugness spreading through me. "See something you like?"

His eyes narrowed. "I see a lot I love."

I grinned. "Right answer." I walked forward, an extra sway to my hips as I went to the edge of the bed and then crawled on all fours to the middle.

A moment of uncertainty entered his eyes as he looked at my bruises again. "You sure you're okay?"

"I'm sure I'm okay," I assured him. "And I'm sure that I really need you." Feeling brave, I ran my hands up my sides and cupped my breasts, pushing them up and squeezing before pinching and tugging at my nipples. A soft moan slipped from my lips.

He licked his lips, his eyes going hooded as he watched. "Touch yourself, Maddie. Play with that pretty little clit."

I sucked two fingers into my mouth before lowering them to my pussy and slipping between my folds. I circled my clit, my eyes drifting shut as pleasure shot through me. Fuck, I was already wet and ready for him, but I loved this power. I loved the feel of his eyes on me, watching and memorizing each movement.

Rubbing my clit with tight circles, I felt myself edging closer to what I needed. Pleasure coiled in my belly. I whimpered, spreading my legs wider and about to fall when a strong hand clamped around my wrist and pulled my fingers away from my soaked center.

My eyes shot open to see Ryan draw my hand up to his mouth and suck my fingers clean with a throaty groan of approval.

"I love the way you taste," he murmured, almost reverently.

My pussy clenched around air, desperate to be filled. "Ryan." His name escaped my lips as a needy whine. "Please."

"Turn around," he ordered, grabbing a pillow from the top of the bed. Once I did, he shoved it under my hips and pressed a hand on my back until my ass was in the air and my cheek was pressed against the mattress.

For a long moment, he didn't do anything. Didn't touch me, didn't speak. Hell, I wasn't sure he was breathing. I was about to break, to plead for him to do *something*, when I felt a finger circle my opening and then push inside.

I squeezed my eyes shut and bit my lip to keep from crying out, not wanting to confirm to the whole house what we were doing. Or worse, wake up Cori.

He added a second finger, taking his time exploring me, scissoring his fingers and massaging my walls. It was enough to make my me flutter and clench, but not enough to tip me over the edge.

I pushed back against his hand, craving more. He withdrew from between my legs, and then his hand cracked across my ass.

"Oh, fuck," I whispered, pressing my face into the bed as heat spread across my skin.

"Greedy girl," he muttered. "You take what I give you."

I glanced back over my shoulder with a challenging glare. "Then *give* me more."

He smirked, and that should've been enough of a warning, but his hand smacking my ass again still came as a shock.

"You know, Mads," he added, like this was a normal conversation as he massaged where he'd hit me, kneading the burn deeper under my skin, "I think pink is your color." Then he slapped my ass once more, and I sank into the feeling.

I lost count of how many times Ryan's hand landed on my ass, peppering slaps across the fleshy parts until everything felt warm and my eyes struggled to stay open. Seriously, why was this so relaxing? It was like I could feel the stress and tension melting out of my body as the heat spread through my limbs.

I might've even been able to doze off, until one of Ryan's slaps landed right across my pussy.

I jolted with a barely muffled screech, everything south of my hips lighting up with instant need once more. Before I had a chance to settle, his fingers were plunging inside me again, stretching and teasing as his thumb pressed firm circles around my clit.

"Oh, fuck," I whimpered into the bed, spasming around his thick fingers.

His chuckle was dark and throaty. "Who knew you were so into spankings? But I'm not nearly done with you yet. Still with me?"

I nodded, unable to form words.

His hands vanished only to be replaced with the broad head of his cock as he slowly sank into me. I felt every single delicious inch as he pushed inside me until his hips brushed the sensitized skin of my ass. His hands landed on my hips, squeezing hard, as he pulled out and thrust back in with an appreciative groan.

"So fucking perfect," he managed through clenched teeth. "Fuck, I love this pussy."

My hands fisted in the sheets as he set a hard, fast rhythm. Every time his hips snapped against mine, I felt it everywhere.

"Touch yourself, Maddie," he told me, a desperate edge to his voice. "I wanna feel you come all over my cock."

Unable to do anything but take and obey, I slipped a hand between my body and the pillow and rubbed my clit until I was convulsing around him and burying my face against the mattress as I cried out his name.

He rode me through my orgasm, never slowing until I went practically boneless beneath him with ragged pants.

A finger dragged down my spine and he kissed between my shoulders before whispering, "Can you take more?"

Feeling a little drugged, a lopsided grin pulled at my mouth. "I can take it all."

I heard the rustle of him moving, and then the click of a cap being opened before something cool dribbled into the crack of my ass. I jerked at the unfamiliar sensation and started to twist around.

Ryan splayed a hand flat against my back. "Trust me."

What had once been two words that would've sent me running, I now surrendered to. I trusted him completely and totally with my heart and my body.

When I relaxed, he started to move, his fingers slipping into my crack and massaging the lube around my asshole before he started to push against the tight ring of muscle. My already stinging ass protested, but I forced myself to relax until he was able to fit one long finger inside me.

"That's my girl," he praised, the approval in his tone making my insides flip-flop happily.

I sucked in a breath as he added a second finger, stretching me until he could add a third. Once more, my hands fisted in the sheets, desperate to anchor to something as he pushed me past any limits we'd come close to before.

And then his fingers were gone.

I braced myself for whatever plug he'd stashed in his bedside table for this moment, but what touched me next was bigger than any plug, and infinitely warmer.

"Relax, Maddie," he murmured, thrusting his cock lightly against my back hole.

"Easy for you to say," I muttered. "You're not being split in half by your monster cock."

He laughed, the sound rumbling between us. "I promise, it's worth it."

I had my doubts, but I breathed through him pushing deeper into me. It took forever as he worked his way in, until he pressed against my ass with a guttural moan. His fingers tightened on my hips, and I could barely breathe around how full I felt.

I wasn't entirely sure I liked this, but I didn't *hate* it.

"Fuck, this ass," he groaned, kissing my shoulder. "You're gonna love this."

Doubtful, I wanted to say, until he pulled out of me slowly and I felt every single nerve ending jangle to life.

"Fuck," I gasped, the unfamiliar sensations wrecking my nervous system as pleasure clawed at my insides like a rabid monster.

He laughed, the sound smug. "Told ya." Then he pushed back into me and a whole new riot of sensations rippled across my body.

"Oh, God," I choked out, squeezing my eyes shut as he started moving faster and harder until I was lifting my hips and trying to meet each of his thrusts with my own.

Bracing his weight on one arm, he reached beneath me to toy with my clit.

I cried out before I could smother the sound, and he pressed into me harder, pinching my clit. The sharp sting sent me careening into an orgasm that tore me to shreds. I sobbed against the force of it as my body bucked and jerked under him.

He pulled out of me with a deep groan and then I felt the hot splash of his release streaking across my back. Finally he dropped onto his side next to me.

I gasped, trying to catch my breath as he pushed my sweaty hair back from my forehead and leaned in to kiss me, stroking my tongue with his as his hand went to my back and traced a pattern through the mess he'd left.

I finally giggled against his mouth. "Dude, are you seriously writing your name on my back with your cum?"

He smirked at me but didn't stop. "Just marking what's mine."

I rolled my eyes and sighed. Freaking caveman.

But I wouldn't change a damn thing.

Reluctantly, he pulled back. "Let me grab something to clean you up." He rolled off the bed, and I turned my head to watch his ass as he walked into the bathroom.

I smirked as he came back out, his cock still half-hard. Unable to stop myself, I bit my lower lip. I still wanted more. I *always* wanted more of him.

"Stop objectifying me," he teased even as he flexed the muscles of his chest and abs.

I propped myself up on an elbow. "No."

He chuckled and dropped onto the bed, then wiped off my back with a damp cloth before tossing it onto the floor.

"Ryan, gross. Pick that up," I chided.

His brows shot up. "Seriously?"

"Seriously," I replied. "I'm not picking up your crusty cum-rag in the morning."

"I have a cleaning staff," he reminded me even as he got up.

"That's even *worse*," I declared, sitting up and watching to make sure he put the used towel in the hamper just inside the bathroom. I made a mental note to do a load of laundry when we got up so no one else would have to deal with that.

"New rule," I announced as he came back to bed and tugged down the sheets. "We clean up our own messes."

He laughed as he got into bed and waited for me to do the same. I tossed the used pillow from under my hips onto the floor and cringed when I saw the wet spot on it.

Fuck it.

I'd buy a new pillow.

"Not a word," I warned Ryan as he glanced from the pillow to me.

He smirked but stayed quiet as I slipped in beside him. He pulled me to his side, and I didn't hesitate to use his shoulder as my new pillow. He reached over and flicked off the lights, muting the brilliant morning sunshine.

I splayed a palm over his heart, feeling it thump beneath me before he covered my hand with his own.

"We're gonna be okay, right?" I whispered, needing to hear the words.

"Yeah," he replied, the arm wrapped around me tightening. "We're going to be more than okay, Mads. This is the start of our happily ever after, baby."

I sighed and nodded before burrowing closer into his side and letting myself fall asleep.

CHAPTER 67

MADDIE

The bedroom door flew open so hard it crashed against the wall, and then something landed on Ryan, crushing the hand I had resting low on his stomach.

"Wake up!" Corinne shouted, glee in her voice for the first time in a while.

"Cori," Ryan groaned, shifting her so she wasn't on top of us.

"Wake *up!*" she insisted, looking to me for help. "Come on, Maddie. It's *Christmas.*"

I poked Ryan's side. "Yeah, Ry. It's Christmas."

He flinched away from me, but I could see him fighting a smile. He was just as relieved as I was to see Cori happy.

After the fire, we'd sat down with Corinne and had a long talk and asked her where she wanted to live. Telling her about Beckett's arrest and explaining the house was completely unlivable had been hard, and we'd both watched her carefully as she struggled to accept her new reality before asking to go back to Brookfield.

We'd all packed up—again—and went back up north and prayed for Cori to accept this new change. Thankfully Ryan had found a terrific therapist who could meet with her daily, and that seemed to be helping,

It also didn't hurt that, by the time we got back to Brookfield, the staff had worked a miracle and converted the entire house into a winter wonderland, from the twinkle lights on the trees lining the long drive to the house, to the house itself, which was covered in lights and decorations, including a bunch of giant blowup things that Cori went nuts over.

Inside, the house was full of cheer and Christmas, and while Grandpa's absence was still felt, Cori was able to focus on the impending holiday. Another thing that seemed to help was Mrs. Beechum and Ryan agreeing that the puppy Cori had picked out—Delilah—could move into the house to keep her company. As soon as the therapist had said that a dog might be a good form of emotional support for her, Ryan had walked down to the stables and brought back the eight-week-old ball of fluff.

The last few days had been like a dream. Yeah, there had been a lot of shit to deal with since the Cain house had burned down and Beckett had tried to kill us. The fire department had officially ruled the case as arson. Apparently Beckett had splashed gasoline from the garage across both sets of stairs and throughout the downstairs to trap Corinne and I.

Beckett was arguing his innocence, but since he'd already fled the country once, he was being held without bail. Ryan told me that he had some friends looking out for his father, and I backed away, not wanting to hear any of the details when Court started laughing and Ryan smirked.

Somehow I doubted they were helping Beckett learn the ropes of the Los Angeles county prison system.

But we'd baked cookies with Ms. Flounders, decorated more of the house with Mrs. Beechum, and watched Royal try to help Cori train her puppy. Ryan had again handed me his credit card, and I'd gone a little nuts buying gifts for Cori and the guys. The best part had been when Ash gave me access to my own accounts and I was able to buy my own presents.

Ryan and I had stayed up with Ash, Royal, and Bishop to wrap presents. Linc, Court, and Knight had passed out after seeing who could drink the most eggnog.

We'd probably gotten only three hours of sleep, but no one had complained as they'd wrapped yet another gift for Cori. Still, Cori jumping on us first thing in the morning was a helluva wake up call.

At least Ryan and I'd had the forethought to put on clothes after he fucked me into oblivion last night. We'd kinda figured Cori would wake us up like a tiny blonde tornado of energy.

"There's presents *everywhere*," Cori cried, dancing around the room.

That caught Ryan's attention as he sat up. "I thought we had a deal you wouldn't go downstairs until everyone was up."

She gave him her best smile. "I'm sorry?"

He growled playfully and jumped out of bed to pick her up. Her high-pitched shrieks and giggles were the best sort of soundtrack to get out of bed to.

"Could you guys make any more noise?" Royal grumbled from the doorway.

"Here," Ryan said, practically tossing Cori at him. "Take her, and don't let her touch any presents until we're downstairs."

Royal threw Cori over his shoulder like a sack of potatoes. "On it."

"Wait!" Cori squealed, twisting to look up at her brother. "When are you coming down?"

"Couple hours," he replied, looking dead serious.

"Ryan!" she wailed.

"We'll be down as soon as we can get dressed," I assured Cori, shooting her brother a look.

She cheered as Royal carried her from the room, asking if she'd remembered to take Delilah outside for her morning potty break.

Grabbing my phone off the dresser, I grinned when I saw a message from Bex waiting for me with a selfie of her in front of her Christmas tree in Paris and wishing us all a Merry Christmas. We texted every day, and I'd been bummed when she'd decided to spend the rest of our winter break in France with her mom.

Video chats just weren't the same as spending time with her, and at this rate, I wouldn't see her until a few days before classes started toward the middle of January.

I shot her back a quick text and pulled some clothes from my dresser. I was halfway through changing when Ryan's arms wound around my waist and pulled me back against his chest.

"What are you doing?" I queried, turning my head to face him.

He grinned at me. "I figure Cori will be opening presents for at least two hours," he reasoned, a hand gliding up my rib cage to cup my breast. "We could make her wait twenty minutes while we—"

I turned in his arms and silenced him with a kiss. "No."

His face fell. "It could be your Christmas present for me."

I arched a brow. "And what was last night?"

His grin was pure devil. "A belated birthday present?"

"Nice try." I pushed him off and walked to the bathroom, then closed the door to finish getting ready as he groaned behind me.

We traded places when I was done so he could brush his teeth, and then we headed downstairs together to see Cori practically vibrating with energy in front of a pile of presents twice as tall as she was.

Okay, maybe I'd gone overboard.

The guys were all sitting on the couches, each with a mug of coffee and in varying degrees of alertness. Delilah was sniffing the floor and decided one of the bottom presents was hers as she started growling at it and trying to pull it apart with her teeth.

With a sigh, Royal scooped up the puppy and held her wriggling body in his lap. Like she knew he wasn't one to mess with, the puppy settled and was soon curled up in a ball.

"Okay, Cor," Ryan said, sitting in an armchair and pulling me onto his lap as Mrs. Flounders came in with a tray of pastries.

"Merry Christmas," she greeted. "Coffee?"

"Yes, please," I said with a smile as Ryan nodded.

With a shout of pure happiness, Cori started tearing through her presents, declaring each one was her favorite or the only thing she'd wanted her whole life.

Ryan rested his chin on my shoulder, a soft smile on his face as he watched Corinne flit from gift to gift. "Jesus, Mads, is there anything left for the other kids in the world?"

I elbowed his stomach and just smiled. Maybe I was living out my own childhood dreams via Cori, but so what? She was happy, and that was all that mattered to me.

"You're spoiling her," Royal mumbled, shaking his head.

I shot him a knowing look. "Funny, because I don't remember buying her a new bike or a fancy dog bed for her puppy." I glanced at two of the larger gifts before looking back at him.

The corner of his mouth hooked up. "No idea what you're getting at."

"Mm hmm," I murmured with a laugh.

Cori grabbed a small present and my heart stopped.

Holy shit. That wasn't supposed to be there.

I mentally recounted my evening and remembered wrapping the present… and quickly shoving it under the tree when the guys had come in to help me finish wrapping Cori's presents. I'd meant to go back and grab it, but I'd totally forgotten.

"Uh, Cor," I called, reaching forward. "That—"

"Ryan, you got a present," Cori announced, proudly wading through her gifts to hand this one to her brother.

Ryan frowned, confused, but took the small box. His eyes found mine. "Do you know what this is?"

I swallowed and nodded. "Yeah. It's from me."

Just… not exactly how I'd envisioned this moment going.

My plan had been to give him his present when we were alone, tonight. And maybe after I'd had a few shots of liquid courage.

With both arms wrapped around me, he started opening the present.

"Hold up," Linc said, raising a finger. "Is this gift child appropriate?"

I rolled my eyes. "Don't be a dumb—" I looked at Cori "—butt." With the amount of swearing the boys did, she'd started her own swear jar. After three days, she was pretty close to having enough saved up for the first year at an Ivy League school.

"Nice save," Linc scoffed.

Ryan tossed the shiny paper aside and turned over the small box before opening the lid. He stilled under me as the titanium band glinted off the light. "Uh…"

Welp, here went nothing.

I slid off his lap and grabbed the ring from the box as I dropped to my knees in front of him.

His eyes went wide and snapped to mine. "Maddie."

"Kinda had this planned differently," I admitted with a weak laugh, "but Ryan Cain, I love you. You're it for me, and I want to spend the rest of my life with you. Will you marry me? Again?"

He stared at me, and my pulse quickened as I tried to get a read on him.

"Girls don't propose to boys," Cori said from behind me.

"Some girls do," Ryan answered for me, his eyes never leaving mine. "More importantly, my girl does."

A smile pulled at my mouth.

"Hell, yes, Maddie," he told me, reaching down and hauling me into his arms. "Hell *fucking* yes."

I grinned, wrapping my arms around his neck as he kissed me.

"That's three swears, Ryan," Cori warned. "You owe me nine dollars."

I broke off our kiss with a laugh as our friends shouted and clapped their approval. I blushed at the attention.

Linc gave a breathy sigh and swooned forward. "Are you gonna put it on him, Maddie?"

"I hate you guys sometimes," I grumbled, my face on fire as I pushed the ring onto Ryan's left hand. As soon as I finished, he swooped in and kissed me until Cori squealed we were being gross.

Ryan pulled back with a grin and a promise in his eyes that we'd celebrate together tonight.

Ash cleared his throat and stood up. "So, do you want this now? Or still wanna wait until we're done here?"

Ryan laughed and held out his hand for Ash to put something in it.

When he opened his palm, a ring lay there. One diamond, surrounded by a nest of topaz and ruby gems.

The colors of Phoenix.

I glanced down at my left wrist, where my first tattoo had been inked a day earlier by Bishop. A phoenix to match all the others, since I was now a permanent part of the organization and their family.

"I planned to ask you when Cori was done," Ryan explained, slipping the ring onto my left hand. He leaned forward and kissed me before murmuring against my lips, "But you had to beat me to it."

"Can I be the flower girl?" Cori asked, excitement brimming in her voice as she twirled in place.

"You can be whatever you want," I promised, beaming at her and then admiring my ring as I leaned against his chest. It was nothing like Madelaine's ring, and not at all like the one Ryan had given me from his nana.

But this ring—these *rings*—were us, just the way Grandpa said they should be. Full of fire and promise and utterly unbreakable.

Now and forever.

EPILOGUE

MADDIE

Three weeks later

As I came in the front door, I tripped over Linc's massive shoes, which he'd left in the middle of the floor.

Again.

"Lincoln!" I shouted as I slammed the door and set my purse down on the table to the right. I scooped up the shoes before storming through the house, looking for him.

Of course he was in the large, sunken living room with a flat-screen TV the size of a Buick mounted to the wall, playing a video game.

Without waiting for a response, I hurled a shoe and hit his arm, knocking the controller from his fingertips.

"No!" He dove for the controller like it was a live grenade, but the damage was done, and his character took several bullets. The screen turned red, and the game announced that he'd died.

I smirked as he jumped up and glared at me. "Next time? Put your shoes away."

He narrowed his eyes. "You know, if I wanted to have someone busting my balls every fucking day, I'd—"

"You'd *what?*" I cut him off, hands on my hips. "Move out? Feel free."

After the holidays, we'd finally decided to do what we'd discussed weeks earlier. Ryan and I bought a house big enough for all of us near Pacific Cross. Actually, we bought two houses next door to each other. I lived in one with Ryan and the guys, along with a bedroom for Cori, while Royal, Bishop, Knight, and a newly discharged Rook lived in the other.

The second hadn't even been for sale, but when I'd offhandedly mentioned how cool it would be for us to have two houses so there was enough space for everyone, suddenly it had come on the market.

Both houses were massive and an easy drive to PC, a thing I could now do since Royal had decided me not knowing how operate a car was a problem. He taught me how to drive in a single weekend, including things like evasive maneuvering alongside parallel parking. Technically I only had my permit, but with this much testosterone around, I sometimes went out on my own anyway.

A girl needed to freaking breathe every now and then.

Especially when one of her roommates had a habit of leaving his shoes and dirty clothes all over the house like decor.

Linc hit me with a lopsided grin that I was certain had charmed off many a panty. "Aw, c'mon, Mads. You love me."

"What'd I miss?" Ash asked, coming up behind us while chomping on an apple. He glanced at the lone shoe in my hand. "Again? Fuck, dude, try to act like a grown-up."

Linc flipped him off and grabbed the controller to restart the game.

Sighing, I tossed the shoe over the extra-large sectional before turning to Ash. "Remind me why I thought all of us living together was a good plan?"

"Because breaking us up would be like ending the Beatles," Linc called. "No one likes a Yoko, Maddie."

Ash rolled his eyes. "The dumbass has a point."

"I need both hands, but I'm mentally flipping you off, pencil dick," Linc snarked.

"Hey," I called to Ash, moving closer. "Anything else on the girl I asked you to look into at Highwater?"

A shadow flickered over his face for a second, and I could've sworn he'd looked at Linc to make sure he wasn't paying attention before answering. He flashed me a grim smile. "Josslyn Grant? I'm sorry, Mads, but she was removed from Highwater after you left. No idea where she is now."

I sighed, annoyed at the lack of info. Once the dust had settled from Gary and Beckett, I'd asked Ash to help me look into the one person who'd been kind to me when I was in Highwater. Joss seemed like she'd been shoved in there the way I'd been, and I hated the idea of her out there suffering if I could help.

"Hey, micro dick," Linc said, not looking away from the screen. "Get your ass over here and help me clear this level."

Ash snorted and abandoned me in favor of offering to prove just how small his dick wasn't, which was my cue to leave. I'd learned early on that these guys had zero shame, and I wouldn't put it past them to whip out a ruler and compare lengths.

I wandered through the house, looking for my fiancé. I jogged up the stairs to check our bedroom and rounded the corner at the landing only to run smack into a barely clothed girl stepping out of the bathroom.

"Who are you?" she sneered, looking ready to bitch slap me for being in my own damn house.

"The girl who lives here," I snapped. "Who the fuck are you?"

She flipped her glossy blonde hair over a bare shoulder, not bothered at all that she was standing in *my* hallway in a bra and panties that were more sheer than plastic cling wrap. "I'm Court's girl."

My brows shot up, because was this seriously happening *again*?

"Court!" I yelled, not moving until the guy in question appeared behind the girl. He scratched a hand over his bare chest, his eyes bloodshot.

"Hey, Mads." The slight slur in his words set my teeth on edge. "Did you meet Ashley?"

She whirled. "It's *Paisley*."

"I was close," he mumbled, frowning.

"Baby," Paisley simpered, sauntering the three steps to him and running her hands across his chest as she shot me a dirty look, "who *is* this?" She lifted to her tip toes and bit his earlobe.

My disgust must've shown on my face, because Court was quick to push her back a step.

"Maddie lives here," Court told her, his tone going from sleepy to snarly in a flat second. "You don't. Get the fuck out."

Okay, now I felt a little bad for Paisley.

Her jaw dropped with a screech of disbelief. "What the fuck, Court?"

He shrugged a massive shoulder. "No, no. We already fucked, and now we're done."

"You bastard," Paisley hissed, tears in her eyes.

Court snorted. "Actually, I'm the only one who *isn't* a bastard, but whatever. Time to go, Patsy."

"*Paisley!*" Her scream echoed off the walls and ceiling.

I winced and stepped around them but shot Court a withering look. "Handle this shit," I growled as I went to my bedroom at the end of the hall and pushed open the door.

I went in and kicked the door shut with more force than necessary just as Ryan stepped out of the bathroom, a towel slung low on his hips. His brows shot up. "Everything okay out there?"

I started ticking things off with my fingers. "Let's see. Linc needs a personal maid, and Court is still coping with Bex not being here by sleeping his way through all the willing women in a ten-mile radius."

"Want me to make your day better?" he offered with a smile, coming toward me until I was in grabbing distance. He pulled me against his chest and kissed me hard.

I sighed and leaned my head back to look him in the eye. "If your way of cheering me up includes no less than *three* orgasms, then I'm all in. Otherwise, I have a perfectly good vibrator that's up for the task."

His eyes narrowed. "You're hilarious."

I lifted a shoulder with an impish grin. "You know you love me."

"Fuck yes, I do," he agreed, kissing me again and walking me toward our bed until the backs of my legs hit it. He pushed me down, and I felt my insides heat as I prepared myself for whatever he did next.

He grabbed the remote for the TV from his nightstand and turned it on.

I stared at him, because that wasn't what I'd been preparing for. "Uh, Ry—"

"Shh," he admonished, coming to sit beside me and picking a channel. "The news is coming on."

"Are you *kidding* me?" I demanded.

He turned and smiled at me, his blue eyes glittering. "Trust me, Mads." He jerked his chin at the screen and turned up the volume as the newscaster turned the program over to a field reporter.

"Thanks, Marcia," the man dressed in a blue suit that matched his eyes said, his tone solemn. The screen cut to an older man being led out of a building in handcuffs as FBI agents swarmed the area. "Earlier today Peter Lansing was arrested on charges of disseminating and creating child pornography. The Fortune 500 CEO's assets, along with his company, have all been seized by the federal government after an anonymous tip. Sources tell us that recordings of Lansing engaging in lewd and unlawful acts with a teenage girl were sent in by what they're calling 'a concerned citizen.'"

I gasped softly, my hand flying to my mouth as I turned to Ryan. "The drives?"

He turned off the TV and nodded, his expression smug.

With a joyful laugh, I climbed over and straddled him so I could wrap my arms around his neck, part of the weight on my heart lifting.

Peter Lansing would be the first of many to fall, thanks to the recordings my sister had collected. Tyler and Ash had spent nearly a month organizing them, and last week, Phoenix had made the decision to start releasing the dirty secrets to the world and holding people accountable for their crimes.

"We're really doing this," I whispered, pulling back to look at Ryan.

His hands settled on my hips. "We really are," he vowed, his eyes bright.

"We should celebrate!" I cried, practically bouncing on his lap. "I heard from Mrs. Delancey today—she said to tell you thanks for helping her and her son."

Ryan let out an amused sort of scoff. "She needs to know that was all you, baby. If it'd been up to me, I'd have left her to rot in the sewer with the rest of Gary's staff. They knew what he was doing and didn't lift a fucking finger to help you or Madelaine."

I tipped my head to the side. "They weren't all bad." Mrs. Delancey had been in an impossible spot as Gary held her son's health issues over her head. She'd done what she could to protect him, and I'd also convinced Ryan to hire the gardener that had been kind to me when I'd first come to stay in Los Angeles.

Another loud scream that sounded like Paisley echoed down the hall, and moments later the front door slammed.

I sighed heavily. "What are we going to do about Court?"

Ryan's brow furrowed. "He's a grown man, baby. He has to figure his shit out."

"We both know he's only acting like this because he's given up on Bex," I argued. My shoulders slumped. "I should've known he'd hear me say she was going on a date with the guy in Paris."

"Maddie," he told me, looking in my eyes, "we can't control what our friends do. Court and Bex have to figure their shit out for themselves."

I nibbled on my lower lip. "It's just so stupid. They're both acting like they don't care when it's obvious to anyone with eyes that they do."

He inclined his head. "But *they've* gotta realize it. We can't lock them in a room until they work their issues out."

"We can't?" I grinned at him.

"Are you asking me to kidnap two of our best friends and lock them in a room without their consent?" He stared at me.

"Maybe?"

Sighing, he rested his forehead against mine. "I mean, I'm sure Bishop and Knight would help."

"And Linc," I chimed in. "So, whatcha think?"

"I think I'd do anything you asked me to," he admitted. "What's a little kidnapping among friends, if it makes my girl happy?"

I leaned in and kissed him, moaning when his tongue touched mine. Breaking away for air, I teased, "You know what else would make me happy?"

"Hmm?" He slipped a hand up the back of my shirt, his cock thickening beneath me.

"Those three orgasms," I murmured against his ear.

With a growl, Ryan stood up with me in his arms and spun us until my back was against the mattress. He loomed over me, his gaze raking down my body as he licked his lips. "I think we can do better than three."

I arched a brow. "Prove it."

"I plan to," he rumbled, reaching for the waistband of my pants. "Now, tomorrow, and for the rest of our lives."

ACKNOWLEDGMENTS

My favorite part has arrived! Time to shout out (or type out) all the people I owe a massive thank you to!

All the thanks to the people that made this book possible: my editor, Natashya Wilson (thank you for making this series all it could be and never letting me cheat Ryan & Maddie's story); my incredible PA, Tracy Kirby; the cover queen, Quirah Casey (Temptation Creations); and Kathy Williams.

To my favorite humans on planet earth (outside those related to me): Krista Davis, Nicole Sanchez, Katie Mingolla, Bella Matthews, Elle Christensen, and Jenn Wolfel.

Endless love and hugs to my Inner Sanctum peeps. I have the best readers EVER. Thanks for being so supportive and excited; your comments give me *life* and keep me going.

If you didn't know, I also have the most incredible, supportive family. Mom, Dad, Micah, Sherry, and Lauren: I love you all so much more than you'll ever know.

Finally to my two littlest cheerleaders with the biggest hearts: Aria & Nora. The words haven't been invented to describe my love for you both.

And if you're reading this, thank YOU for letting me tell you a story.

ABOUT THE AUTHOR

Hannah McBride has been many things in her life: a restaurant manager, a clinical research coordinator, a dreamer, a makeup brand ambassador, an event coordinator, a blogger, and more. But at heart, she's always been a writer, and in 2020 she decided to make it official. Good luck stopping her now.

ALSO BY HANNAH MCBRIDE

Blackwater Pack Series:

SANCTUM

BROKEN

PREY

LEGACY

SCARS

REQUIEM (coming Winter 2023)

Mad World Series:

MAD WORLD

MAD AS HELL

MAD LOVE

Anthologies:

A Bridal Party To Remember

Hell Hath No Fury (coming Fall 2022)

Devour (coming Fall 2022)

Made in the USA
Middletown, DE
28 September 2023